BLO

I am forbidden by Oath sworn on pain of death by mutilation, a mutilation that would leave my intestines arranged delicately over my left shoulder, to say too much about the details of my Initiation. Once we had all unmasked, since I was hardly the only master of disguise, it suffices to say that I relished that Sabbat of the Adepti, when the wine of the Red Jar of Avallanius boiled and bubbled in my veins and I soared beyond the pylons of space and time to embrace a being of splendour and corruption that was, in a deeper sense, my inmost self . . .

Also by Gerald Suster in New English Library paperback

The God Game

About the author

Gerald Suster was born and raised in London and educated at the University of Cambridge. His first published novel was the cult classic *The Devil's Maze* and he has several other notable novels of supernatural terror to his credit. He has also written nonfiction books on such varied subjects as the Tarot, boxing, military history, the occult roots of Nazism, the Hell-Fire Club and Aleister Crowley. He lives in North London with his wife.

The Labyrinth of Satan

Gerald Suster

NEW ENGLISH LIBRARY
Hodder and Stoughton

Copyright © 1997 by Gerald Suster

First published in 1997 by Hodder and Stoughton
A division of Hodder Headline PLC

A New English Library paperback

The right of Gerald Suster to be identified as the Author of
the Work has been asserted by him in accordance with the
Copyright, Designs and Patents Act 1988.

10 9 8 7 6 5 4 3 2 1

ISBN 0 340 66649 8

British Library Cataloguing in Publication Data
A CIP catalogue record for this title
is available from the British Library.

Typeset by Hewer Text Composition Services, Edinburgh
Printed and bound in Great Britain by
Mackays of Chatham plc, Chatham, Kent

Hodder and Stoughton
A Division of Hodder Headline PLC
338 Euston Road
London NW1 3BH

To James

CONTENTS

AUTHOR'S NOTE

The following documents came into my hands following the grisly murder of Ms Rosa Scarlett, allegedly by her employer, the celebrated private detective Adam Stride. These were sent to me without a contact address by Mr George Scarman, a literary gentleman of private means with whom I enjoyed friendly acquaintanceship.

Mr Scarman has since vanished and I have reported him to the Metropolitan Police as a Missing Person.

As Mr Scarman rightly asserts, Adam Stride was a friend of mine, and I was greatly distressed both by the atrocious manner of Rosa Scarlett's death and the mysterious manner of Adam Stride's disappearance.

Presently, I have nothing further to add.

Gerald Suster
London

FOREWORD

by

George Scarman

*Editor's Note: George Scarman is
the author of* The Victim (*London, 1982*)

An excruciatingly ghastly murder shook the nation on 30 April 1996. This was the date of Walpurgis Night, a principal celebration of Satanism and Witchcraft. The head of Ms Rosa Scarlett, personal assistant to the private detective Adam Stride, was found by a cleaner in the latter's office, placed upon a pole in a plant pot. The body was missing and has still not been recovered.

In common with most, I was hideously shocked by this atrocity, especially since I knew both Rosa Scarlett and Adam Stride. Rosa Scarlett was a strong, intelligent, capable woman of East African origin who had helped Stride faithfully for over ten years. Whenever he made extra money, he always gave her a bonus, and throughout their professional association, I always saw him treat her well.

Adam Stride was at this time a man in his forties, earning roughly £25,000 a year as an astute private detective. He was also the author of this ensuing novel, *The Labyrinth of Satan*. We had become friends during our days at Cambridge University and I have the fondest memories of his caressing charm and careless wit. Senior officials of the Metropolitan Police had a very high opinion of his skills at detection. Knowing him as I did, although over the previous year I had only seen him infrequently, one would have expected him to devote his formidable intelligence to tracking down the vile brute who murdered his assistant.

It is a matter of personal grief to me, unfortunately, that

on the night of this repulsive murder, my friend Adam
Stride seems to have vanished from the face of the Earth.
I find it virtually impossible to believe that he could have
committed this grisly crime: but the police have a warrant
for his arrest.

I feel that I owe it to his memory that a bizarre chain
of incidents be explained insofar as is possible.

In 1894, an unjustly neglected author called Arthur
Machen set about writing a novel called *The Three
Impostors: or, The Transformations* which was published
in London in 1895. Although Machen had made some
impression with his previous novels *The Great God Pan*
and *The Inmost Light* that had been published together
in one volume (London, 1894), *The Three Impostors* was
excoriated by reviewers and condemned as decadent,
largely on account of the disgrace of Machen's friendly
acquaintance and great contemporary Oscar Wilde who
had been sentenced to imprisonment with hard labour in
that same year.

The Three Impostors derives from 'the New Arabian
Nights' manner of Robert Louis Stevenson in *The Dyna-
miter* (London, 1885), containing tales within tales and
fantastic adventures as in the original *The One Thousand
Nights and a Night of Sheherezade* as translated by Sir
Richard Burton (London, 1885), also known in previous
translations simply as *The Arabian Nights*.

Two tales from *The Three Impostors*, 'The Novel of the
Black Seal' and 'The Novel of the White Powder', were
republished in Machen's *The House of Souls* (London, 1906)
and in his *Tales of Horror and the Supernatural* (London,
1949), after his death in 1947. A slightly abbreviated version
of *The Three Impostors* was published in London in 1966 and
a definitive edition emerged in London in 1995, whereupon it
won a nomination for the retrospective 1895 Booker Prize.

Adam Stride was obsessed with this novel and by the work of Machen generally, so much so that he spent his leisure hours penning a sequel, the book you hold in your hand, *The Labyrinth of Satan* (London, 1990). He was not the only author to become intrigued by Machen's fiction. Publishers had often asked Machen to write a sequel to *The Three Impostors* but he had always declined, stating: 'I shall never give anyone a white powder ever again.' Indeed, in Machen's second autobiographical volume, *Things Near and Far* (London, 1923), he states that the characters of *The Three Impostors* came to life all about him in the streets of London, though he subsequently refused to discuss the matter in any detail.

A sequel was essayed by Gerald Suster in *The Devil's Maze* (London, 1979 and 1994; New York, 1983). Here, Suster introduced a new character, Septimus Keen. Adam Stride used this character in his *The Labyrinth of Satan*, and this led to correspondence and a series of meetings between these two authors who had so many interests in common.

The sensational, grisly death of Rosa Scarlett and the incredible disappearance of Adam Stride provoked Mr Suster to write *The God Game* (London, 1997), in which he gives a fictionalized account of what might have happened to Adam Stride. Whilst I cannot give full credence to Mr Suster's account, since it would strike the rationalist as being too fanciful to believe, conversations and correspondence with this author have led me to think that he may not be so far from the truth. Nevertheless, I still find it hard to believe that Adam Stride has had his memory erased by a surgeon posing as the Dr Lipsius of fiction written by Machen, Suster and Stride; and that his sex has been changed, leading him to wander the streets as a demented woman, owing to the surgeon's knife wielded by Dr Lipsius or someone claiming his identity. Suster admits that the conclusion to *The God Game* is pure speculation concerning the fate of his friend.

However, there must be a summary of the present position for the reader:

1 – Arthur Machen wrote *The Three Impostors* in which the villains, playing an infernal game of human chess upon the streets of London, are: Dr Lipsius, mastermind of satanic and criminal evil, and his three shadowy accomplices who fake all sorts of false identities.

2 – These 'three impostors' have distinguishing physical characteristics.

3 – Arthur Machen thought that they had erupted into his life during the year 1899–1900.

4 – Adam Stride thought that they had erupted into *his* life in 1996, six years after the original publication of his *The Labyrinth of Satan*.

5 – I had conversations with Adam Stride in which he seemed to be quite panic-stricken, which was also Mr Suster's impression. Both of us, on separate occasions, met Stride's mistress/girl-friend Antonina; both of us found her charming. As I said, I do not know if I believe Gerald Suster's work of admitted fiction; but certainly it has been impossible to trace the whereabouts of Antonina.

6 – Suster's *The God Game* suggests either that the three impostors and Lipsius and 'Septimus Keen' are aliens from another planet or else that there is some sort of 'Black Lodge' with certain parts to play, which parts are renewed over the generations. One thinks of the three assassins of Hiram Abiff in the rituals of Freemasonry. One also thinks of a play in which new actors come to play the same parts.

Certainly the behaviour of Adam Stride was becoming increasingly eccentric during the year before the ghastly murder of Ms Rosa Scarlett. Mr Suster's novel may indeed be unduly speculative yet I concur with him in believing that Adam Stride, this man we both knew, could not have committed so gruesome and macabre a crime.

For my own part, I remain unhappy regarding Stride's obsession with Jack the Ripper, which matter is so prominent in *The Labyrinth of Satan*, and I urge him, if he is still alive and reading this, to give himself up to the authorities for a fair trial which, one trusts, will clear his name.

I also wish to record my appreciation of Gerald Suster's assistance in ensuring the republication of Adam Stride's novel.

George Scarman
London

PREFACE

by

Adam Stride

Whatever you do, don't call me mad. Eccentric, yes, a little, perhaps, but not mad. I shall be telling you the truth calmly and clearly; where to begin?

In common with Gerald Suster, author of *The Devil's Maze*, 'I have always been a fervent admirer of the work of Arthur Machen and his *The Three Impostors* has always held an especial appeal for me.' Suster then relates how, in a Kentish Town pub, he fell into company with an elderly gentleman who professed a similar admiration and who invited him to a bedsit in Highbury to study the papers of Septimus Keen, upon which papers Suster avowedly based his own novel.

In my conversations with Mr Suster, who was consistently courteous and helpful to me, he always insisted that Septimus Keen was his own invention. I have reason to believe otherwise.

Truth is often stranger than fiction and one night, in a pub in St John's Wood, I met an elderly gentleman straight out of Suster's book, and indeed he shared my passion for the works of Arthur Machen. I think that the pub was the Rosetti, just by the barracks, and we sat in a space framed by two mirrors, one on each side, reflecting our presence into all Infinity. If I looked to the right or looked to the left, the pair of us just went on and on and on.

This old man, who insisted that he be nameless in any book I wrote, invited me back to a bedsit in Highbury, just as he had invited Suster. There I spent many hours, days even, in poring over the papers of Septimus Keen, who knew Arthur Machen and so many other artistic, literary and criminal figures of his era.

Faced with this documentary evidence, I could no longer believe that Suster had invented this character. With all respect to him, it is obvious that he missed or chose to miss or preferred to omit certain bundles of documents, including the *Diaries* of Septimus Keen, from which Suster only quotes scraps; and which *Diaries* may well contain the final solution to the mystery of the murders committed by Jack the Ripper.

When I mentioned this latter matter in a letter to Mr Suster, he did not reply. I subsequently learned from a mutual friend, Mr George Scarman, that he had gone abroad for a time. Even after a century has passed, the ramifications of matters which disturbed minds in the 1880s and 1890s shock us now in our recrudescent *fin de siècle*.

Why is it that those who know disappear so fast? I have naturally sought out the old man of Highbury but he has disappeared too, taking with him, one guesses, the papers of Septimus Keen. There is a new landlord of his house and my every endeavour to trace him has proved fruitless.

I can only give the reader the private papers of Septimus Keen which I copied and, based upon these, my own fictional interpretation of events which actually occurred.

Adam Stride
London

CHAPTER ONE

FROM THE DIARY
OF SEPTIMUS KEEN

(ARE YOU HAPPY NOW?)

1st May 1894

Twenty-one today! Twenty-one today! Is that my age or the number of people I have murdered? In fact, I was twenty-one years of age today *last* year. It was then that I was finally released from hateful tyranny and oppression and came into my majority. It was then that I realized that, at last, I could do whatever the hell I liked.

When I obtained control of the money left to me by the munificence of deceased relatives, I was an orphan who had been cared for by my grandparents, for whose love and care I thank them though both of them died during the past year. There was the delight of knowing that I was not responsible at all to anybody whatsoever. I have erased all traces of my past. One year ago to this day, I resolved to live only for the present and the future. It is appropriate, however, that I open this Diary to record what I have done since I essayed this resolution.

My money has enabled me to translate all my fantasies into reality. I admit that I have been influenced by *Doctor Jekyll and Mr Hyde* by Robert Louis Stevenson, only he did not go far enough. The chemical process that transforms Jekyll into Hyde reads like an experiment out of *The Lancet*. Although I take drugs, I do not need any potion to enable me to lead a double life. Why lead a double life when you can lead a treble one?

I have sufficient funds to maintain three establishments and three identities. Mr Richard Knight is a scholar and a gentleman who enjoys modest comfort at a house in Great Russell Street, just opposite the British Museum where he spends much of his time either gazing at antiquities or else studying books in the Reading Room. Locally he is noted for the moderation of his habits, the strict excellence of his dress and the courtesy of his manner. Anyone who had occasion to follow the trail of Richard Knight Esq. on certain evenings might observe him visiting a woman who has a rather more ostentatious house just off Cheyne Walk: Mrs Venetia Fielding, a wealthy young widow.

She has long flaming red hair, a magnificent figure accentuated by her bustle and many wealthy admirers and suitors for her hand. It is said by her acquaintances that she is a bitch to men but extremely kind to women. She has been called 'a fast lady'. So she is and only one person knows her secret: Hortense, her exquisitely pretty French maid who is both deaf and dumb and whom she treats with exquisite kindness. Yes, I have always had a fascination for everything female and I adore the sensation when Hortense laces me tightly into my corset and I step into ladies' drawers, stockings, stays, petticoats and skirts. No one has ever identified this frivolous sexy bitch I am as being a man.

There is also a bedsit in Fitzrovia, in Cleveland Street on the border with Bloomsbury, where Bill Smith lives. He is an absolute slob who leaves his clothes lying all over the floor. He is usually unshaven, badly dressed, scruffy and all too eager to discuss pugilism, though he is popular in the pubs. What a bastard he is! Whereas Richard Knight seduces a lady with gentlemanly charm, Bill Smith just fucks her senseless and kicks her out in the morning. Although he is slender of build, he has taken lessons from

Chinese masters of martial arts and his name is feared by denizens of the foulest dens. The locals have on occasion been astonished by the visits of Mrs Venetia Fielding in her carriage. Although Richard Knight Esq. is a known and frequent visitor to the area, they are surprised to see him entering the humble home of Bill Smith and wonder what these two men could possibly have in common: dark rumours are spread about rough trade. Well, there *is* much in common between Bill Smith and myself: we are the same person.

I have a fourth identity: Septimus Keen. He writes stories that are strange. He does this for the satisfaction of no one other than himself. I was quite pleased with this one:

ARE YOU HAPPY NOW?

by

Septimus Keen

It is impossible to see things strictly in terms of black and white, I think, though some, unfortunately, do just that.

When I was around eleven, I was living with my parents in a comfortable Kensington mansion. Next door there was an elderly eccentric retired from the Colonial Service – he had served in both West Africa and Jamaica – who always used to declare to my father over the port that he deplored racial prejudice and liked black people. In consequence, and living in his basement, he had a Jamaican manservant whose wife had died and who had three sons living with him.

One day, through our garden railings, I started talking to the three boys, who were playing in the neighbour's garden: I invited them to come and play with me in mine. My parents agreed to invite them to tea since they, my parents, were gentry, not snobs, and the manners of the Jamaicans were impeccable. Afterwards I went into our garden to play games with them.

Jamie was twelve, Chas was eleven and Ike was ten. We played many of the games that boys do with bats and balls but at that time, my favourite game was wrestling Graeco-Roman style as used to be done at the original Olympic Games and as taught to me by my father. You won the match if you could obtain two 'falls' – pinning your opponent's shoulders to the ground for three seconds – two 'submissions' – having your opponent in a grip so

9

painful that he said 'Submit' – or a combination of the two. Jamie, Chas and Ike eagerly agreed to essaying the sport.

I beat Ike easily: he was younger, smaller and weaker. It was a grim struggle with Chas, who was my own age, weight and height, but finally he beat me. Jamie, a year older, was bigger and stronger and beat me with relative ease.

I returned to a term at boarding school where I studied and practised wrestling quite obsessively, beating everyone in my year and even in the year above and learning grips such as 'the claw', acutely painful to the cheeks or the temples, and the 'flying body check' in addition to the trips one can use. Upon returning for the holidays, I again challenged the sons of my father's neighbour's manservant to wrestling. Once again, I beat Ike easily. This time I also beat Chas easily. Unfortunately, Jamie still beat me easily. Throughout the holidays, this pattern continued. Try as I might, there was nothing I could do to counter Jamie's superior size, strength and skill. However, I continued to enjoy the three brothers' company

After another term of endeavour at school, in which I was acknowledged as the champion of wrestling, I returned home boasting of my victories. Ike and Chas came to see me and I handled them as if they were babies. Unfortunately, Jamie wasn't there.

'He can't come today,' Chas told me.

'Well, tell him to come tomorrow,' I said, 'because I challenge him to a wrestling match. He has beaten me in the past but I shall beat him in the future.'

A few days later, Ike and Chas came again and once more I beat them with ease.

'Where is your brother Jamie?' I demanded.

'He couldn't come today.'

'Tell Jamie,' I declared, 'that if he does not come tomorrow, I say that he is a coward.'

I spent the evening practising grips and moves, everything to counter the fact that Jamie was bigger and stronger than I was and also swift and skilful. In all our contests, I had never gained a single fall from him, let alone a submission.

The three brothers came to see me in the garden on the ensuing afternoon.

'Oh, well, jolly good, may the best man win and all that,' my father had said.

'Now,' I said to Jamie, 'for the moment of truth.' Although I had never gained the slightest victory over him before, I sprang at him with total confidence. To my amazement, he crumpled like wet tissue paper and fell over. I pinned him.

On the next round, he slowly extended a strong arm. I grabbed it and twisted his wrist.

'Submit,' he said in a tone of total indifference. Barely able to believe that I could possibly have won over him in less than thirty seconds, I stared into his eyes to see hatred, ridicule and contempt.

'Are you happy now?' he asked me. Then he turned to his younger brothers and said: 'Let's go.' I felt defiled in a way I could not explain.

2.

I had felt sick to the stomach at my ludicrous wrestling defeat of Jamie and there were further consequences. At the time, my childlike mind failed to understand precisely what had happened. I boasted of my victory whilst knowing that it was hollow yet without comprehending precisely what had transpired. The three brothers subsequently refused all invitations and shortly afterwards Sir Edward Granby, the neighbour of my father, died. My father told me that his Will had made a generous bequest to Bob, his manservant, and

Bob's three sons Jamie, Chas and Ike. They all eventually went to live somewhere else. But prior to this, there were three events that I remember.

Once, I was leaning out of my bedroom window and watching the street. Bob, Sir Edward Granby's manservant, was marching his sons along that street. All of them were wearing immaculate white shirts with grey flannel trousers and it was as though the crinkles in their jet-black hair had been smoothed out with a hot, steaming iron. It was painful when the brothers ignored me but the father beamed up at my window and proudly declared:

'We are going to Church.'

Without having full comprehension of the matter, I felt sick once again. It took a time before it dawned on me that Bob the father had sternly instructed his son Jamie to throw the match because 'You just don't beat the white folks'.

The second incident occurred when I was again leaning out of my bedroom window and staring at the garden of Sir Edward next door, one which was festooned with roses, forget-me-nots, pansies, tulips and daffodils, a veritable riot of colour. Jamie was seated in the centre of the garden and he had his back to me. He had a knife in his hand and he appeared to be whittling something out of wood. As though he were committing an act of complete contempt, he threw the object into our garden.

I rushed out to fetch it. A black doll with a grinning face had landed behind a rose bush. I picked it up. Jamie was still staring at me. Casually, he lit a match and threw it at me. Yes, he threw the match. His dark eyes blazed with hatred.

I kept the black doll as a souvenir.

The third incident occurred just as Bob and his three sons were leaving the residence of the late Sir Edward to depart in a black carriage which resembled a hearse. In one final attempt to effect reconciliation, I walked out into the street to bid them a pleasant farewell. The father smiled and waved. The brothers ignored me. The carriage clip-clopped away and I saw an envelope being tossed out of the window and into the gutter. I picked it up and saw my name, all splashed with mud. Returning within my home, I opened it to see the following words scrawled in purple crayon:

'Ever heard of Voudon? Maybe you call it Voodoo, voodoo-hoodoo-mumbo-jumbo. My father rejects it and wants to be a white nigger. My mother and my grandmother taught it to me. The Voudon curse is upon you, whitey, and though it may take years, you are dead meat as from this moment. Are you happy now?'

No, I was not; and I took both the note and the doll to my father. He merely laughed and dismissed it all as childish nonsense. Even so, as Wordsworth says: 'The Child is father of the Man.'

3.

It was shortly after I obtained my financial independence that I came to live in Hampstead for a period, where I had rented a pleasant flat. One of the pleasures of life in Hampstead is the close proximity of Hampstead Heath. I adore its variety: the woods of West Heath, the fields of East Heath and the views from Parliament Hill. I frequently used to walk within the Vale of Health. It is said that an oak tree exists on a hillock there and that if you embrace it, you will learn the truth about your life. Unfortunately, no book gives you the exact whereabouts of this tree: I fancied that perhaps it might be in alignment with the clump of thin trees that is called the tumulus. I saw one that might be *the* oak and approached it.

A young black man who had long, crinkled black hair

was sitting at the base of the tree and was calmly whittling wood. His knife was carving a doll identical to the one he had fashioned and thrown into my garden so many years ago.

'Hello,' I said. He stared into my eyes and carried on with his work. 'I think I know you from before, Jamie.'

He carried on whittling.

'Aren't you even going to talk to me?' I demanded.

'Not now.' At last he spoke. 'But if you want to talk to me, I shall be ready for you here at midnight in precisely two days' time, the twenty-first of June, the Summer Solstice.'

'Jamie, can't we just sit down and talk about it?'

'No.' His eyes were smouldering. 'Not until the time I've said.'

'All right, I'll see you here and then. Bye.' I turned my back and walked away. The whittling of his knife whistled in my ears.

'Are you happy now?' he called out after me.

4.

On the following morning, still highly disturbed by the encounter but resolved to keep the appointment on the following midnight, I had my usual breakfast of tea, hot buttered toast and marmalade and opened my morning post. To my stupefaction, there was a rent demand, claiming arrears, from a Mr Obeah. I was not in arrears with my rent and my landlord was a Mr Lewis of Willesden Green yet the address was the same. I decided to send a telegram from the nearby post office demanding what the hell was going on. As I left the house, slamming the front door behind me, I encountered a fat black man blocking my path out of the front garden.

'Sorry to spoil your morning, sir,' he said politely, 'but it is my solemn duty to serve you with this.' I was too astonished to do anything other than take the document as he vanished swiftly. It was a creditor's summons for debt from my tailor in Hampstead, Goldstein & Isaacs, the sum being two hundred pounds. This was utterly astonishing. Yes, I had indeed owed Goldstein & Isaacs sums of money in the past and I did owe the firm two hundred pounds at present but I had always paid in the end. I would have to go and see them, demanding an explanation for this outrage.

Yet there was something very different about Hampstead on this particular sunny morning. Just about everyone walking on the street was black. There had always been a few black people living in Hampstead, a bohemian area noted for its tolerance, but now there was only one white person to every hundred blacks. I have never had any kind of stupid prejudice on account of colour but the sight disturbed me for it was hardly the Hampstead I knew. I went to the post office to send my telegram. On the previous day when I had gone there to buy stamps, the counter staff had all been white clerks. Now they were all black, and two of them were women. I retained my composure and sent my telegram.

'Seems to have been a bit of a management change,' I remarked.

'You could say that, sir,' the black woman clerk replied with a smile, 'but your telegram has been sent. Are you happy now?'

I was all puzzled perturbation as I approached Goldstein & Isaacs. Of course, the tailor for my finest suits is in Savile Row but Goldstein & Isaacs has always been excellent not only for repairs but also for cavalry twills and grey flannel trousers tailored to Savile Row quality but at a much more reasonable price. It was somewhat surprising to find a smiling black face behind the counter.

'Good day,' I said. 'Is Mr Goldstein available?'

'No, I'm afraid he's not, sir. And nor is Mr Isaacs. We continue to trade under the same name and we endeavour to maintain their high standards. Mr Goldstein and Mr Isaacs have retired, heaven bless them. Now what can I do for you, sir?' I produced the summons. 'Ah, yes, indeed, sir. Naturally we value your custom but,' his face hardened, 'when do you propose to settle the sum? Obviously we cannot give indefinite credit.'

'In two days,' I sighed.

'Thank you, sir.' He smiled. I left. 'Dying for a drink' was hardly the phrase for it as I crossed the road to a pub I had always liked. I entered to see that everyone was black, apart from two whites sitting together shyly in a far corner table. I was served my beer with courtesy yet I was feeling increasingly one of a minority. I drank my beer swiftly and returned home.

On my walk home there were many gleaming black broughams and Victorias upon the High Street and Heath Street, drawn by glossy black stallions, and within them there were stylishly dressed black men sitting with exquisitely dressed white women. The pedestrians I passed were all black, besuited, walking with stylish hats and canes and shining shoes. I saw only two white men. One was shining black men's shoes for pennies just outside Hampstead Underground Station. The other was lying in the gutter and vomiting into the road.

I wondered if perhaps there might be some sort of rational explanation. Perhaps there was some sort of carnival . . . though that could hardly explain what had happened to Goldstein & Isaacs. It would be a relief, I thought, to go home and think it over. Unfortunately, my key did not work. In sheer frustration, I started trying to break the door down. Suddenly it was opened by a handsome black woman who had a willowy figure and a tight clinging dress.

'Hello,' she said. 'Why are you assaulting our door?'

'What are you talking about?!' I yelled. 'This is *my* house. What the devil are you doing here?'

'What are *you* talking about?' she answered me with a maddening calm. 'This is not your house. It is *my* house. Please go away and disturb us no longer.' Then she slammed the door in my face.

My brain was reeling as I pondered the options. Obviously one is dazed by having one's own home taken over by complete strangers who shut one out. They had to be burglars bluffing and I needed help so I ran straight to the local police station where several polite faces greeted me, all of whom where black.

'Burglars,' I said, 'and they've taken over my house! For the love of God, do something!'

'Of course, sir,' said the thin female Duty Sergeant. 'I shall make a call-out for an investigation immediately. Meanwhile, if you would care to step into that room, just through the door and to your right, Detective Constable Dixon will be with you very shortly.'

There was no alternative so I complied with her instructions. About five minutes later, a big, burly black man in Metropolitan Police uniform entered the room.

'Detective Constable Dixon,' he said. The thin policewoman had followed him into the room. 'Evening, all.' He balanced on his toes. 'Now, now, what's going on here, then? Don't you know it's against the law, sah!?'

'Yes, I do,' I answered. 'It is against the law to take over and burgle my home.'

'Your home?' He sneered at me. 'Where is *your* home?' He stared at me contemptuously and disbelievingly as I told him my address. '*You*!?' he exclaimed. 'A whitey living *there*? Don't make me laugh. You're a liar.'

'I am not,' I insisted vehemently as I endeavoured to keep my composure. 'It is *my* home.'

'WPC Wilson, the papers, please,' DC Dixon demanded and she willingly complied. 'The house at the address you have given belongs to Mrs Obeah and has done so for many years. She has registered a complaint against you and I can see why. You are under arrest and will be charged for being drunk and disorderly and for threatening behaviour.'

'I want my lawyer!' I shrieked as I sprang to my feet to protest. 'You can't do this to me!'

'Of course I can,' said DC Dixon as he kicked me in the testicles. As I doubled over in agony, WPC Wilson smashed my jaw with an elegant kick from a police boot. Dixon then trod on my stomach so hard that I shat myself as WPC Wilson broke my nose with a well-aimed kick. I was vomiting as they hauled me to my feet.

'Get out,' said Dixon, 'and never come back. We don't like whitey scum like you.'

They threw me out into the gutter and I started to lose consciousness, though not before hearing a voice saying: 'Are you happy now?'

Then I blacked out.

5.

I recovered some form of consciousness to realize with surprise that I was standing atop a hillock on Hampstead Heath, and that the sun was setting in a manner that sent a dull red glow all over London, as though the very sky itself was drenched with blood and fire.

Turning my dazed head, I saw an oak tree, its branches waving softly, shimmering as the leaves breathed. Jamie was sitting beneath the tree. In his right hand he held a black doll identical to the one he had thrown at me all those years before. In his left hand he held a Colt .45 revolver.

'Are you happy now?' he asked.

'No,' I replied. 'What have you done to me?'

'Just shown you some things.' He smiled painfully. 'Do you realize that two days have passed and all you have been doing is wandering around Hampstead Heath?' I stared at him incredulously. 'Voudon can give a man sweet dreams. It can also give a man nightmares. Maybe now is the time to talk. Would you like to come and sit here?' I nodded my assent and went to sit by him.

'Jamie,' I said, 'what did you do to me?'

'Sent you into dreamland for you to learn a lesson. Voudon is good for that.'

'Oh, for heaven's sake,' I burst out exasperatedly, 'you're not still angry with me over that wrestling match your father told you to throw?'

'Yes, I am,' he replied, waving his doll and his gun lazily in the air. 'My father was made unemployed and he killed himself. He shot himself with the revolver I am holding here because he tried to adapt to a white society and they wouldn't have him. Ike? Remember him? He was clubbed to death one night in the East End with cricket bats on account of the colour of his skin. I went and found every bastard who had done that. First I shot them in the balls. Then I watched them dying before my clean shots killed them. Remember Chas?' I nodded. 'He died in a police cell for something he did not do. I found the policemen, I shot them in the balls and then I killed them. Right now, the entire Metropolitan Police force is looking for me and I don't regret a thing – you understand me?'

'Well, sort of . . .' I answered as my body grew icy, yet my palms exuded sweat. 'But what have I ever done to you other than win one wrestling contest which was fixed, unbeknown to me, by your father's command?'

'You showed me how terrible life is if you're black.'

'And you're going to kill me for being a naive child?'

'Possibly, yeah.' I wanted to shiver but I did not. Instead I stared him in the eyes, recalling how warm and strong they had been. Now they were neither. They were like the cold brown stones that have formed the massive buildings of New York City, the same stones that were also used to build the more gentrified blocks of Harlem.

'To what end?' I asked.

'Because I have hated you for all these years.'

'That's ridiculous!' I shouted. '*I* never did any of this shit to you.'

'Didn't you?'

'Not with intention. Look, if it means so much to you, why don't we repeat the wrestling match under the same rules, okay?'

'No,' he said, brandishing his revolver, 'this time we play for keeps.' His smile was quite agonizing to witness. It was like the grin on a skull.

'You have a gun and I don't. What you propose is hardly fair.'

'Was our wrestling match fair?'

'No; but *I* didn't fix it.'

'All right,' he said with an air of decisive finality. 'You and I will play Russian Roulette. It is just that the odds will be loaded against you. I will have one bullet in the chamber when I spin it. You will have two.' He passed me the gun, keeping his right hand in his pocket. I wondered momentarily whether or not to shoot this madman so as to save my skin yet I could not bring myself to do so. Jamie must somehow have discerned my thoughts. 'Don't bother trying to pull the trigger on me. I have another gun in my pocket here. Of course, you would not dream of doing that, would you? You are, or claim to be, an honourable white man. I am an honourable black man. As long as you play the game, I will not shoot you.'

I reflected that my chances of survival were a mere three to one as I put the revolver to my temple, having spun the chamber.

'Let Baron Samedi decide!' he declared as I pressed the trigger. There was a hollow click. I have to admit that it was difficult to pass the revolver back to Jamie without my hand shaking.

'Jamie,' I said, 'with all respect to Baron Samedi, surely honour is satisfied? Please put down your gun.'

'How can it be' he replied indignantly, 'when you have been sufficiently courageous to face the matter? *I* shall do what you have done and play the game with two bullets!'

'Jamie . . .' I was sweating, 'please don't.'

'I am as honourable as you are,' he responded, raised the revolver, spun the chamber, squeezed the trigger and promptly proceeded to blow his brains out. Was it my imagination that made me hear the dying words:

'Are you happy now?'

'That is rather fine, my dear Septimus,' Dr Lipsius said to me when he first read it. Ah! I must write of my relationship with Dr Lipsius.

I have always sought after the perverse and decadent in life. This desire has led me to join every society that might promise these delights to me. For example, I thought that the Seventeen Nineties Society might give me glimpses of the Neo-Gothic, of the tales of horror that were told at that time, mention of the Marquis de Sade, perhaps; but I found a grouping of elderly gentlemen sipping sweet sherry and discussing scansion in the early work of Wordsworth. I fancied that the Byron Society might be better and there I learned that he was much nicer than he has been portrayed from a grouping of over-eager old ladies. I joined the Hermetic Order of the Golden Dawn, which celebrated Ceremonial Magic. Here I have to admit that I was impressed, even though I eventually let my membership lapse. The problem was that they were genuinely involved in a quest for the Light and *I* was genuinely involved in a quest for Darkness.

I tried the Brotherhood of Satanism. This was really rather childish since all they accomplished was a boring parody of the Roman Catholic Mass. The Devil's Foot Society sounded more promising, and I admit that I enjoyed the orgies. But the rituals were too long and tedious: though the members spoke of doing wicked things, they did not do

22

much other than fuck. I would that they had done so without all that boring ritualistic preamble. In short, after exploring every so-called secret society in London, I was still looking for one able to cater to my own depraved tastes.

One cannot be depraved all the time, unfortunately, and so I sometimes passed my mornings and afternoons by reading esoteric literature within the glorious dome of the British Museum Reading Room in my guise as Richard Knight Esq. Occasionally I noticed a man I came to know as Dr Lipsius. He radiated benevolence and serenity from the crown of his bald domed head to the soles of his handmade shoes. Two features, however, detracted from this pleasing initial impression. One was the tight, compressed mouth, the lips of which were moist. As he pored over the works (which I could not help noticing) of Dr John Dee, Paracelsus, Cornelius Agrippa, Robert Fludd and other books related to witchcraft, his tongue used to flick greedily in and out of his thin lips, reminding one of a serpent. I also noticed his eyes, which were small, yellow, beady and hooded by fleshy eyelids. I became increasingly intrigued by this short, stout man with plump legs who always wore such immaculate dark suits. I was therefore very pleased to fall into conversation one night with this gentleman who had so aroused my curiosity.

There is a tavern a stone's throw from the British Museum where I used to repair for refreshment after reading in my guise as Richard Knight. On this particular night, Dr Lipsius went there too. I was drinking a pint of port: so was he. I introduced myself as a fellow reader in the British Museum and it soon developed that we had many interests in common. I found him, on the whole, to be absolutely charming, apart from his irritating habit of the middle-aged in assuming ignorance on the part of the young. He would say things such as:

'Probably, my dear young sir, you are not acquainted with *A Rebours* and *Là Bas* – allow me to translate this as *Against Nature* and *Down There* – by J-K Huysmans and find witchcraft, black magic and satanism to be something of a puzzle.'

I had to explain to him that I was familiar with the work of Huysmans, had French of a reasonable reading standard and had participated in rituals of witchcraft, black magic and satanism.

'But it's all very disappointing, Dr Lipsius,' I told him. 'All these people *say* they want decadence and evil, but none of them actually *do* it.'

His tongue flicked out greedily to moisten his thin lips. 'And that is what you want?'

'Yes,' I said, 'that is what I want.'

'It is a pity,' he pulled a golden pocket watch from his waistcoat and glanced at it briefly, 'that I have an urgent appointment. Eh? Hm?' His smile was wicked. 'Yet you do strike me as being quite an interesting young man. Allow me to invite you to dinner at The Savoy at precisely this time, one week from today.'

It was very tempting a prospect to attend at the Savoy in the guise of Venetia Fielding so as to say to Dr Lipsius: 'Good evening, doctor. Richard could not come so I came instead,' just to observe his reaction. However, I decided to play matters straight for the time being; or at least insofar as I am capable of doing. I even brought my story 'Are You Happy Now?' and told him that I used the pen-name of 'Septimus Keen'. He was impressed and regarded me with greater and growing attention.

'What would you say, Mr Knight,' he asked me over the Armagnac, for he had feasted me royally, 'if I were to tell you that some call me the most evil man in London?'

'I'd say that I have heard that story before, that it is never true and almost always disappointing.'

He smiled. 'What do *you* know about evil?'

'Not nearly enough. I was hoping that you might teach me more.'

'Oh, I can, my dear Richard, I can. Eh? Hm? But only if you will let me.'

'Of course.'

'How would you define "evil"?'

'Doing harm to other people for the pleasure of it.'

'Quite so. Would you not agree that the pleasure is augmented if these matters are accomplished with artistry?'

'Certainly.'

'Would you agree that there are sacraments of evil that elevate one to a state of ecstasy?'

'Definitely,' I said. 'I am just trying to find people who think the same way as I do.'

'I have met too many people who talk much and say little, meaning less and doing nothing,' Lipsius said.

'So have I.' I stared into his eyes. I have not encountered any others quite like them. The closest analogy would be to the eyes of a crocodile on the Old Nile.

'Very well,' said Dr Lipsius, 'let us see if you are serious or merely a dilettante. I am offering you a part in a play. Do you see that man there?' The little finger of his left hand flickered to indicate a florid-faced man who was shouting at a waiter.

'Do you know who I am?' he was yelling, quite upsetting the other diners. I was tempted to inform him that I didn't, but I could find out for him if he wanted to know.

'That is Arthur Bullock,' said Dr Lipsius, 'Conservative M.P. for a Tory seat so safe that they could put up a pig and he would still be elected. He is also quite something in the City. I find him to be obnoxious and offensive. Tell me,

25

Richard, have you ever read Thomas de Quincey's essay "On Murder Considered as One of the Fine Arts"?'

'Yes.'

'And did you like it, eh? Hm?'

'Yes.'

'Are you interested in any form of emulation?'

'Yes.'

'I,' said Dr Lipsius, 'can initiate you into the ecstatic rites of satanic deities and introduce you to like-minded spirits.'

'Good. When?'

'As soon as you bring me the head of Arthur Bullock.'

CHAPTER TWO

FROM THE DIARY
OF SEPTIMUS KEEN

3rd May 1894

S trewth! I feel rather like the lord who left a note to his valet stating: 'Tuesday, wind and weather permitting, I propose to be drunk. Place a crate of sherry by my bedside and call me the day after tomorrow'. Hell's teeth! It hasn't only been drink. I felt a compulsion to go and be Bill Smith so I found some tart and shagged her brains out. Then, as Venetia Fielding, I seduced some delectable debutante. She was somewhat surprised by my tool when I lifted my petticoats but thereupon appeared to relish the matter even more.

It is time that I returned to recording my relationship with Dr Lipsius. He had asked me to bring him the head of the ghastly Arthur Bullock.

'I have nothing personal against him,' I had informed Lipsius.

'Neither have I.'

'Then what is the point?'

'The point is that there is no point.' Dr Lipsius shrugged.

'Oh, very well, if you insist: he has bad manners and he dresses abominably.'

Unknown to Lipsius, I was no virgin when it came to a kill. It took me two days to discover the mechanical habits of Arthur Bullock. His town house was just off Baker Street and his wife, whom he visited at weekends, lived in Herefordshire. He was attended by one manservant.

He was a man who led a life as mechanical as a Swiss cuckoo clock.

Every morning he emerged from his house at 9:30 a.m. and went for a walk in Regent's Park, where he stared at the swans and cormorants. From there, he walked back home whence his brown brougham took him to the City. Between 10:30 and midday, he visited various bankers and stockbrokers, after which he repaired with some to a tavern for refreshment. Emerging slightly groggy around 3:30 p.m. he stumbled into his carriage that took him to the House of Commons. Normally he slept there for a couple of hours, though on the day I sat in the public gallery he actually arose unsteadily to put a Parliamentary Question to the Prime Minister, Lord Salisbury, and had quietly to be reminded that Salisbury could not answer his question since the Prime Minister was sitting in the House of Lords.

'Very well, Mr Speaker,' Arthur Bullock came back, 'but I presume there is one amongst us here who speaks for the Prime Minister.' There was, though I forget his name. 'I would like to ask the Right Honourable gentleman: Is not the solution to the Irish Question twenty years of strong, resolute Government?'

'The honourable gentleman is absolutely right,' came the firm reply, 'and I applaud his sterling defence of the Prime Minister's policies.' Bullock sat down to Tory cheers: hardly surprising, since he had quoted the Prime Minister. Having done his bit for the Party, Bullock then vanished from the chamber for a while, presumably to refresh himself. I went to a nearby public house and spoke with some of the journalists. Apparently Bullock was of paltry political significance and always left the House at 6:00 p.m. returning only if there were a three-line whip. Then he always voted exactly as his Party instructed him to do. If that was not required, he returned home to change for dinner.

At 7:30 precisely every evening, Arthur Bullock emerged from his home, proceeded to Regent's Park once more and there watched the swans and the cormorants. At 8:00 in the evening, he returned to his carriage that took him to his entertainments of the evening. These might be a play, a restaurant, a brothel or all three and unless some lady could tempt him into staying all night, he usually returned home around 2:00 in the morning.

Now, there are various methods of murdering a man and one of the principal problems is the disposal of the body. Moreover, one does not wish to be noticed by a witness.

A gun is very noisy and knives and clubs are bloody and messy. A rope around the neck can do the job effectively; but this would not solve the problem of securing the head. Fortunately, I have paid much attention to the study of poisons, and some of the deadliest have been brought back by our intrepid explorers from the Amazon Basin. I forget the name of the one whereby, after one scratch, death follows painlessly within fifteen minutes. Curare, possibly. All I needed was a poisoned needle.

I was sitting and sewing on a bench as Venetia Fielding when Arthur Bullock MP came as usual to regard the swans and cormorants at 7:30 p.m. precisely. Well, I wasn't quite Venetia Fielding, who often wears a wig of flaming red hair. I was wearing a wig of curly blonde hair, surmounted by a hat of black. This is a good disguise since, if a woman does that, all witnesses will remember is her curly blonde hair and black hat. I carried on sewing as Arthur Bullock regarded the birds of the water. I was wearing a dress of shimmering purple. Everyone would notice that, especially and including Arthur Bullock.

In no time at all he was sitting on the bench beside me and talking to me. His words were exceptionally boring and I had no regrets or difficulty in substituting the poisoned needle for my sewing needle and then scratching him as if by accident, an action for which I apologized profusely. He waved my apologies aside and said that it didn't matter. After two minutes, he started to become somewhat groggy. I had two rubber masks in my sewing bag and I slipped them over our faces. We walked out of the park looking as though we were slightly drunk and going to some sort of macabre carnival.

There was a cab as expected just where we emerged from the park. I had previously paid for that. The cabman was in fact my servant, the dear deaf and dumb Hortense, now disguised as a man. Arthur Bullock twitched violently and then expired on the journey. As per my instructions, Hortense had left a very large canvas bag upon the floor. It took me some minutes to stuff the body within it.

Any casual observer in Cleveland Street, Fitzrovia, would have seen a cab draw up outside a rooming house and from it step a young lady with flaming red hair and dressed all in black. It was well known that she sometimes came to visit Bill Smith and he had even given her a key to the place. This time the cabman appeared to be humping a very heavy bag on her behalf. The lady let herself in and the cabman helped her again with her baggage, emerging a few minutes later and driving away.

Naturally Hortense changed the licence plate on the cab at some point between Soho and Chelsea, then proceeded to abandon it.

I changed into my Bill Smith clothes, stuck on my false moustache and beard, then spread a rubber sheet across the floor of the bedsit. Soon I had the body spreadeagled on that sheet. I took an axe from the tool cupboard and, with one swift stroke, severed the head from the body. The amount of blood that gushed from the stump of the neck really did surprise me as did the deluge of gore from the head as I held it up by the hair and let it drain.

Any casual observer in Fitzrovia would have seen Bill Smith departing from his home carrying two luggage cases and hailing a cab. This cab took him to King's Cross Station whereupon he vanished through the door marked 'Gentlemen'. So far as is known, he vanished off the face of the earth at that point, though two suitcases were found in a cubicle. One of them was soaked in blood.

No one noticed Richard Knight Esq. stepping out of the door marked 'Gentlemen' and carrying a Gladstone bag in his hand.

Of course, the matter was splashed all over the papers. Arthur Bullock MP had mysteriously disappeared. He had last been seen sitting on a bench in Regent's Park with a young lady in a shimmering purple evening gown, who had blonde curls and a black hat. The cab in which they had left could not be traced.

There was also the mysterious though as yet unconnected matter of Bill Smith. His neighbours became concerned about the foul stench emanating from his bedsit. Eventually, when he refused to respond to their knocking and shouts of protest, they broke down the door to find a headless, putrefying corpse upon a blood-soaked rubber sheet. Obviously I had removed the wallet from the clothing and all other marks of identification, including and especially the head.

'One of the difficulties in these matters, Dr Lipsius,' I said as I handed the head within Richard Knight's Gladstone bag to him, 'is the disposal of the body. I have left the body for others. It is there for anyone to examine. There was no need to dispose of it. No, I have disposed of the *murderer*.' This was true since Bill Smith no longer exists. He has outlived his usefulness. I flushed him down the lavatory at King's Cross Station.

'How so?' Lipsius asked.

'That is my secret,' I replied.

'Oh, fair enough,' Lipsius said. Within three months he would have the head shrunken so he could place it in his grotesque and macabre museum. 'Well done, Septimus. I can't resist calling you that, eh? Hm? This bodes well for the future. Just remember that for every secret you can give me, there are a thousand and one that I can give you.'

CHAPTER THREE

FROM THE LETTERS
OF AMELIA STANHOPE
TO BARBARA CROCKFORD

Dear Barbara,
I thank you for your most delightful letter. I'm glad that things are going so well for you up in Yorkshire, since I have found Harrogate to be a most delightful town on my previous visits. I am pleased to learn also that your husband Thomas is in good health and that his steel business is flourishing. You recommend the delights of married life so well and advise me to have a husband. Should I really? As far as I can see, husbands are never there when you need them and always there when you don't want them.

Now, there *is* one man who does genuinely interest me and I fancy that you have met him. Do you recall Sir Percy Sulgrave? I think you may have met him at one of the London soirées of Lady Dorothy Neville. If you had, you could not have missed him. He is a big, beefy young man and heir to a fortune. Sir Percy seems to have led a somewhat adventurous life, having worked for the Foreign Office out in India and China but he was wounded in the leg due to some native uprising and presently works only for himself.

He has excellent taste in clothes, wines and food and I find him to be utterly charming company. His major fault is that he cannot stop talking about his obsessions, but most men are like that, aren't they? However, in this particular instance, I find his obsessions to be quite interesting. Do you recall the 'Jack the Ripper' murders in the East End of London back in 1888? No one knows who Jack the Ripper was but Sir Percy is obsessed with solving these horrendous crimes. He is convinced that the trail leads to the highest in the land, so much so that he has given me the enclosed document. Only show it to those who can exercise discretion:

SOME NOTES TOWARDS
THE SOLUTION OF THE
JACK THE RIPPER MURDERS

by

Sir Percy Sulgrave

In an endeavour to solve the murders attributed to 'Jack the Ripper', it is essential to begin with the facts of 1888.

August 31: Mary Nichols murdered.

September 8: Annie Chapman murdered.

September 30: Elizabeth Stride and Catherine Eddowes murdered.

November 9: Mary Jane Kelly murdered.

All these women were at that time working as prostitutes. Their bodies were quite hideously mutilated. Panic spread throughout the East End; yet subsequently there were no more murders of this nature. It is very clear that whoever committed these 'murders most foul' had a profound knowledge of anatomy, implying sound medical training.

There is the letter enclosed within a parcel that also contained a kidney – subsequently identified as human – and which was addressed to Mr George Lusk, president of a Vigilance Committee formed to help police suppress crime in the East End. This reads:

Mr Lusk
   Sir,
   I send you half the kidne I took it from one woman prasarved it for you tother piece I fried and it was very nise. I may send you the bloody knif that took it out if you what a whil longer.

41

signed Catch me when you can,
Mishter Lusk. Jack the Ripper.

This has led some to conclude that Jack the Ripper was an illiterate Jewish butcher; but that is nonsense. No butcher could have worked so swiftly and with the skill of a surgeon. The above letter is either the macabre jape of a medical student; or else it was done deliberately to throw the police off the trail of the true criminal.

I have heard it alleged by policemen that Jack the Ripper was one Montague Druitt, a failed doctor turned failed barrister, a man who had a taste for low-life prostitutes whom he then murdered most hideously. Druitt subsequently threw himself into the Thames and drowned. The police closed the file on the Jack the Ripper case.

I do not believe that Jack the Ripper was either Kosminski, the Polish Jew, nor Druitt the doctor turned barrister turned suicide, nor Michael Ostrog (whose very existence remains a matter for conjecture) nor the violent Thomas Cutbush, who was lacking all skills of surgery. No, he was a highly literate man.

My reasoning is based on the fact that on the 8th June 1888 I was present at a dinner at Cambridge. My fellow guests were the Duke of Clarence, Prince Albert Victor, also known as 'Eddie'; Lord Salisbury, the Prime Minister; and Lord Randolph Churchill who, it was then thought, would succeed Salisbury. The Sulgraves have served the Royal Family for many generations and I was only too keen to do my bit. The problem before us was that although it was clear that the Prince of Wales would eventually succeed Queen Victoria as King Edward VII and that Prince Albert would then succeed his father as King Albert I, there was the possibility of yet another scandal.

I did not dislike Prince Albert, Duke of Clarence: I

THE LABYRINTH OF SATAN

merely found him to be something of a drooling simpleton. After all, the Hanoverians have never been noted for their intelligence. One reason I was present consisted in the fact that both of us were friends with Walter Sickert, the artist, who lived in Cleveland Street, Fitzrovia, London. I had met Walter Sickert because I admired his paintings and he was such a cantankerous yet flamboyant individual. The Duke of Clarence had met him because his mother, Princess Alexandra, wife of the Prince of Wales, had asked Sickert to introduce her son to the artistic and literary society of London.

Unfortunately, perhaps, while mixing in these circles, the Duke of Clarence was introduced to Annie Elizabeth Crook, an occasional model for Sickert, who worked at the tobacconist and confectioner across the road. Curiously enough, Annie was distantly related to J.K. Stephen, the Duke's tutor at Trinity College. The Duke fell in love with Annie, made her pregnant and married her in a secret ceremony, causing an impending constitutional crisis.

Annie was both a commoner and a Roman Catholic. The latter fact barred the Duke's way to the throne; the former fact was merely scandalous. What was to be done? To make matters worse, Annie had told all to Mary Jane Kelly, also a model for Sickert, a shop girl in the tobacconist's store where Annie worked and later the governess employed by Walter Sickert to nurse the illegitimate royal child, Alice. Mary Jane Kelly had now quarrelled with Walter Sickert and left for the East End. There she spoke with three whores as she drifted into prostitution: Mary Nichols, Annie Chapman, and Elizabeth Stride (Catherine Eddowes was a different case). Their plan was blackmail of the Royal Family using Sickert as their contact.

'Well, I think it's really quite simple,' I said that night over the port. 'First, we deny everything. Second, these tarts won't want *that* much money. We simply pay them to keep their mouths shut. As for Sickert, he'll keep quiet as long as we buy his paintings and do our bit to make him highly fashionable.' In common with all present at the table, I was a Freemason, Royal Alpha Lodge, into which the Duke of Clarence had been initiated in 1885.

'It is not *quite* as simple as you suppose, Sir Percy,' Lord Salisbury growled. 'What about Annie Crook?'

'Pay her, too.'

'Too many people might know,' said Lord Randolph Churchill. 'That's the difficulty.'

I excused myself to visit the lavatory and heard a name mentioned just after I left the room. When I returned, the subject had been closed and changed. The name I had heard, though, was 'Doctor Lipsius'. At the time I had no idea what on earth this name boded or might mean.

Events followed fast after that occasion. Four East End prostitutes were murdered between 31st August and 30th September. On 8th November, Sir Charles Warren, the Chief Commissioner of the Metropolitan Police, resigned. This did no good to Mary Jane Kelly, former friend of Walter Sickert, since she was carved up hideously within her own home on the following day.

In July 1889, police raided a male brothel on Cleveland Street. I gather that there was evidence of the Duke of Clarence being a frequent patron. On 1st November 1891, there was a fire at the royal residence of Sandringham. On 14th January 1892, the death of the Duke of Clarence was announced – though there are rumours that he is still alive and hidden away in some asylum for the insane. I have heard some say that he was Jack the Ripper but this can hardly be so. On the night of the double murder of Elizabeth Stride and Catherine Eddowes, he was seeing his mother, Her Majesty the Queen, at Balmoral. I know: I was there.

Equally curious is the fate of Clarence's tutor, J.K. Stephen of Trinity College, Cambridge. He ended up in a lunatic asylum in Northampton, having first talked to Inspector Abberline, a detective working on the Jack the Ripper case. Upon being told of the death of the Duke of Clarence, J.K. Stephen refused food and died three weeks later on 3rd February, 1892.

On 6th February 1892, Alice Margaret Crook (b.1885, 15th April), daughter of Annie Elizabeth Crook and the Duke of Clarence, was the victim of attempted murder. A coach endeavoured to run her down two months before her seventh birthday. Walter Sickert was convinced that this coach was driven by J.C. Netley, driver for the Ripper murders, though fortunately the attempt did not succeed. On 6th February 1892, a man answering to the description of Netley attempted suicide by flinging himself into the River Thames: when he was rescued, he gave his name as 'Nickley' but declined to give his address. On the following day, Inspector Abberline, who had taken such a close interest in the Ripper case, unexpectedly retired from the police force.

It is also difficult to know what to make of events that took place in 1885. Walter Sickert informed me that Annie Crook was kidnapped one bright day in Cleveland Street and driven by the evil coachman Netley to Guy's Hospital where she was confined for 156 days and certified insane by Sir William Gull, Royal Physician and Lecturer and Professor at Guy's Hospital Medical School. Apparently no one really knows the nature of the operation which was performed upon her but Gull was certainly an expert on paraplegia and diseases of the nervous system, the spine and the brain. Annie Crook emerged from that hospital with a severe case of amnesia.

I got drunk with Sickert one night and he let it slip that, in his opinion, the motive for the Ripper murders was to silence the whores given to blackmail and that these horrendous crimes were executed by Sir William Gull, with Netley as his coachman. I protested:

'Sickert, I have met Sir William Gull. He is an elderly gentleman who has had two heart attacks. How could he possibly overpower strong East End prostitutes well used to dealing with drunken sailors?'

'The grapes,' said Sickert.

'Sorry?'

'Sir William Gull was always eating grapes.' Sickert leaned back against his easel and smiled like a weasel just about to kill a rabbit. I was finding the stench of linseed oil and turpentine to be virtually overpowering. 'He put poison on the grapes. Look at it this way, Sir Percy. Most of the East End girls will turn a trick for a bob. If they see a carriage, that means more money, so they will gladly turn a trick in there. Gull gave them some grapes that drugged them. Then he went to work on them, easy as chloroform. Then he dumped them.'

'That leaves certain matters ill explained. Mary Jane Kelly was hideously carved up in her own home. A fire was still glowing.'

'He was one of her regular clients. That's why she let him in.'

'But why the hideous mutilations? Wouldn't it be enough merely to silence them?'

'Masonic significance. Don't understand it. Same reason as where the bodies were left. Positioned with significance.'

'Significant of *what?*'

'I don't know . . .' he swayed as he poured us both another brandy. 'Look, I'm tired, must go to bed soon.'

'Have you ever heard,' I asked, 'of a Doctor Lipsius?'

Sickert staggered, crashed into his easel and both painter and painting went sprawling. Eventually he recovered his composure and arose, gulping brandy and looking somewhat wild-eyed.

'No,' he said, 'I haven't.'

It has since proved impossible to see Walter Sickert. My letters go unanswered and every time I arrive at his door and knock, a woman with a pleasant face answers and informs me that Mr Sickert is not at home in that supercilious tone of voice that lets you know that actually he is.

I am intrigued now and am going to pursue this matter further.

Now you have met Sir Percy, Barbara, and you possibly know how obsessive he can be. For my own part, I can barely begin to believe his hideous accusations against Doctor Lipsius, even though I think that, underneath it all, Percy is really rather super. Lack of acute intelligence in a man is really not a problem to a woman as long as he will listen to her, which Percy does on the whole, and as long as he has a good heart, which latter matter is undeniable. Unfortunately, we had a bit of a row the other night. Allow me to describe it to you. We were sitting in Percy's drawing room in Maida Vale, which overlooks the Canal. I know it is not an especially fashionable area except for expensive whores, but Percy insists that he likes it there.

He has furnished his drawing room unusually. The ceiling has been painted with the fights of demons and angels. The floor is festooned with Persian rugs, embroidered with exquisite Islamic tapestry. The western wall looks out onto the Canal. The eastern wall is furnished entirely with books, including works of erotica and of curious esotericism: one finds *The Greater Key of Solomon* nestling against *The Romance of Chastisement*. There is a sofa, well-cushioned, and embroidered with skilful copies of scenes from the Bayeux Tapestry, since sir Percy is proud of his Norman ancestry and so of the Battle of Hastings. There is a carved oaken chest that must be medieval. There are also chairs of stout old English oak.

Percy served me a dry fino sherry while taking manzanilla for himself.

'Percy,' I said, 'whilst I can understand your desire to identify the horrible individual who committed the hideous "Jack the Ripper" murders, I cannot at all connect it to the man you suspect, Doctor Elias Lipsius.'

'That is where you are wrong, Madam, with all respect,' he replied coolly as he placed a black Russian cigarette with a gold tip in his ivory holder. 'My enquiries have assured me that Doctor Lipsius is perhaps the most poisonous individual in London.'

'Oh, don't be ridiculous, Percy,' I said. 'I have met Doctor Lipsius at quite a number of charitable functions, and he is a benevolent and most charming man.'

'Rubbish!' Percy shouted angrily. 'I know that he does all this charitable work and that he is an individual of considerable charm but you have not investigated the matter as I have done. Some hashish?' I nodded. I find that it is very good for one's health. 'The City tells me, via my informants, that he is not to be trusted.'

'Nor is anyone in the City,' I retorted.

'He has made a great deal of money through the flotation of spurious companies.'

'So have so many and so what?'

'All right,' said Percy, 'so far he is just another City swindler. What would you say if I told you that he controls the importation of drugs into England?'

'Not much, actually,' I replied. 'After all, that's perfectly legal and we are smoking hashish now: Her Majesty the Queen herself takes it dissolved in alcohol for her lumbago.'

'He has people killed in order to preserve his monopoly.'

'Have you any proof of this?'

'I am working on it.'

'Oh, Sir Percy!' I burst out laughing. 'Next you'll be telling me that he is "the Napoleon of Crime"!'

'He *is*!' Percy burst out vehemently. 'Have *you* pursued investigations down the East End? One just mentions the name of Lipsius and people, hardened thugs and prostitutes, freeze with terror. He has a very lucrative trade in human flesh: female and male prostitution and also children for the paedophile market.'

'And you have proof of this?'

'That is my problem. I do not.'

'Then what are you talking about?'

'I shall *find* the proof. I am sure that he was behind the Jack the Ripper murders.'

'Oh, don't be so ridiculous, Percy,' I chortled. The very idea of the serene and benevolent and charitable Doctor Lipsius being behind these hideous murders of East End prostitutes quite beggars belief.

Still, I suppose that an unemployed and wealthy man requires some sort of hobby.

That is all for now. Do stay in touch. Heaven bless.

Love,

Amelia.

PS: I forgot to mention one thing, Babs, something that makes me feel that Percy is perhaps a little bit strange. Upon his north and his south walls, he has mirrors facing one another, so that I see Percy and me going on to all eternity. I find it all a little unnerving.

EDITOR'S NOTE

Lord Blandford, the Duke of Marlborough, died suddenly on 9th November 1892. His close relative, Lord Randolph Churchill, died shortly afterwards on 24th January 1895.

On 20th September 1903, a man identified as John Netley, previously thought to be a failed suicide (1892), was run down and killed by horses close to Clarence Gate. It was alleged that he was the coachman for the Ripper murders.

On 3rd February 1920, the amnesiac Annie Elizabeth Crook (mother of the Alice Margaret Crook born on 15th April 1885 as bastard daughter of the Prince of Wales's son, the Duke of Clarence died.

On 22nd October 1922, there was the birth of Joseph Sickert, the son of Walter Sickert and Alice Margaret Crook; the mother died in 1950.

Joseph Sickert is still in being, to my knowledge, and telling the tales which his father Walter (d. Jan. 22nd 1942) told to him.

(A.S.)

CHAPTER FOUR

FROM THE DIARY
OF SEPTIMUS KEEN

2nd June 1894

O! Glorious First of June! What a wonderful time I had! I sometimes become so depressed that I contemplate suicide but I think that having a good time is better.

I woke up thinking of Thomas De Quincey's 'On Murder Considered as One of the Fine Arts'. Then I thought of Dr Lipsius and the murder with which I had got away.

Taking breakfast, which consisted of softly scrambled eggs upon toast accompanied by Assam tea, strongly made and accompanied by milk and two sugars, in my guise as Richard Knight, I looked forward to the dinner I had been invited to by Dr Lipsius at his house in Sheen Street, since I have always enjoyed the area of Marylebone. Obviously I would go there as Richard Knight who wrote tales under the pen-name of Septimus Keen. But who would I be during the day? I could be Miss Venetia Fielding. I could hardly be Bill Smith, murderer, yet I wanted to rebuild that identity. Yes, that was how I spent my morning.

South London is like a foreign country to men from North London and that is why I chose to base my new identity there. Wearing a false moustache and a battered bowler hat, I purchased some suitably awful clothes and soon enough secured a bad furnished room just off the Old Kent Road, about a mile from the Elephant & Castle, under the name of Bob Brown. As Bob Brown, I wanted to turn back into

Richard Knight but by the time I reached Holborn, I was virtually dying of thirst and had to visit a tavern. I sat there and drank beer for a while. After a time I noticed there was a smooth, smiling, clean-shaven gentleman sitting opposite me. He was drinking black-and-tan – dark stout with light ale – and appeared to be scribbling furiously. After a time, he looked up abruptly and his bright blue eyes stared at me. They were very clear and very cold.

Suddenly he spoke.

'Excuse me for troubling you, my dear sir, but I am a writer and I am suffering from a problem. What would *you* call a young swan?' Had I been Richard Knight or Venetia Fielding, I would have replied 'A *cygnet*'. But I was Bob Brown so I said:

'Why don't you call 'im Alfred?'

'Ha! ha! Most amusing, my dear sir. I do appreciate your wit. Goodness me, I see that I must have another pint. Would you care to join me?' I nodded acquiescence and he smiled as he returned to the table. 'It is always a pleasure to speak with a man of wit,' he said, 'for that's far too rare these days. Professional man, are you, sir?'

'You could say that. I lay bricks.'

'Ah! Splendid! And where would we be without that? Without housing, one imagines, and without buildings too. Allow me to introduce myself. My name is Harding, Clive Harding, and pleased to make your acquaintanceship.'

'Brown. Bob Brown.' We shook hands. 'You said you were a writer, Mr Harding. Have you had anything published?'

'Yes, it sold badly,' said Mr Harding, 'but my day will come. You see, what I try to convey in my work is *ecstasy* but the publishers do not want that. They prefer the stodge of *Robert Elsmere* served up by Mrs Humphrey Ward and selling in tens of thousands; possibly hundreds of thousands. And what is it about? A Clergyman Has Doubts. He had Doubts for three volumes and it is badly written and monumentally boring. Excuse my vehemence, but truly it is abominable, atrocious, awful and appalling, not to mention abhorrent. Even so, the public buy it and the critics praise it. Is it a wonder that our culture is presently held so low in European esteem?'

'Well, I haven't read the book you mention, Mr Harding, and given your description, I hope I never will. What is *your* book about?'

'Mr Brown, allow me to show you the review of my first novel, as reviewed by the *Morning Star*.' He passed me a yellowed clipping.

From the *Morning Star,* London, 23.6.1892.

Review of *Life and Lives* by Clive Harding.

Quentin Tayleur

M r Clive Harding is clearly of the opinion that the German notion of the novel, the *Bildungsroman*, the tale of personal development via experience, is the way forward. To my mind, this has always implied a certain amount of self-indulgence and Mr Harding is clearly in alliance with the Decadent Movement of Oscar Wilde, Aubrey Beardsley and Arthur Machen. One smells also the scents of foreign orchids wafting from France, of Baudelaire, Huysmans, Verlaine and Rimbaud. *Life and Lives*? Let us look.

The first part consists of a manuscript written by a boy of sixteen. He has extraordinary visions and perceives the possibilities of life unfolding before him so that he may realize them.

The second part is taken from his journals of ten years later. The past which he had formerly romanticized is now described with a cynical and destructive air. He has destroyed everything in his past, including his relationship with his parents and with the girl he loved as a youth. He is isolated, lives in a sordid Hammersmith bedsit, survives via involuntary contributions from his friends and is utterly arrogant.

In the third part, his novel is finally published and achieves wide sales and astonishing acclaim. He is called 'the most promising young writer in England today' and is lionized by High Society. During this social whirl, he encounters

Carol, an ordinary shop-girl, and falls in love with her, even though she is utterly unsuited to the world he has entered. She is beautiful and he does not care, spending as he does an idyllic summer with her. He is torn between his love for her and his love of fame and society functions. Unable to write the second novel of which Carol declares him to be capable, he repeats all the tricks of his previous work and is rewarded and further acclaimed. Carol is deeply disappointed. She truly admired his first novel but she tells him that he has betrayed the noblest elements in his own soul by writing the second one. Insulted by her remarks, he leaves her. Carol is hit by a cab and is believed to be dead.

He continues to enjoy High Society and for a time changes his political views, abusing his own original convictions, and in this he is aided and abetted by Arabella, a *femme fatale* with whom he has a tempestuous relationship in this third part of the novel. Her corrosive cynicism leads him now to despise those who made him rich and famous. He lacerates all pretension in every society encounter, makes enemies and laughs in their faces, openly and insolently.

His third novel is brilliantly written and brutally honest. The novel is panned by every single critic and sells poorly. His enemies pounce, he is no longer in High Society and Arabella insults him and leaves him.

In the fourth part, without much money or reputation left, he joins the Decadents and enjoys in their company every kind of sensual and drug-induced experience. Spending more money than he can afford, he withdraws to a single room and severs his connection with outside reality, living only for his dreams and visions. Gradually he drifts into the sordid life of an educated derelict.

Carol re-enters the narrative in the fifth part, for it seems that she was not killed after all. She has finally tracked him down and she hands him a revolver, asking him to choose between life and death. He demands her reasons why he should not shoot himself. She gives him answers from every school of religious and philosophical thought and he demolishes all of them. Carol challenges him to put his views to the test. Placing five bullets in the cylinder of his revolver, he prepares to blow his brains out.

As he thumbs back the hammer, he recovers the glorious vision he had at sixteen. There is a total affirmation of Life as he pulls the trigger. The hammer clicks down on the empty chamber. Having lived to tell the tale, he marries Carol, writes an excellent, best-selling book and they both live happily ever after; and what would you like to hear next?

Although *Life and Lives* is written well, it suffers from two serious defects. It is not realistic that a man such as our 'hero' should finish in domestic bliss writing excellent books for plenty of money. Life is rarely like that. Also, I deplore the self-indulgence of Decadents such as Mr Harding.

Mr Harding appears to despise our way of life. He appears to think that a man can exist only for himself, that he can rebel against society or else be an outsider from society. This is the creed of the Decadents and it is surely abhorrent to any right-thinking Christian Englishman.

Buy *Life and Lives* by Clive Harding, read it and then burn it. It is good for nothing else. The author should be forcefully reminded of John Donne's words: 'No man is an Island . . . and therefore never send to know for whom the bell tolls; it tolls for thee.'

'This is the sort of thing I am up against, you see, Mr Brown,' Mr Harding informed me.

'Well, I don't know, really,' I returned in my guise as Bob Brown. 'Can't say that I read that much – oh, yes, now and again – but if I had read that review, I would want to go on and read your book. Where can I get hold of a copy?'

'Nowhere.' Mr Harding smiled sadly. 'The limited first edition sold out and presently I cannot persuade the publishers to print a second. Well, it has been a pleasure meeting you, Mr Brown. I wish you all the best in the laying of bricks. A craft, isn't it? Ha! ha! My dear sir, *everything* done well is a craft.' I noticed that he had finished his drink swiftly and had glanced at his fob watch. 'I hope to see you again here at some future date.' He took his leave and I remained quiet and thoughtful as I drank up my beer.

It is a short walk from The Princess Louise to the home of Richard Knight in Great Russell Street. Bob Brown, I decided, would be Richard Knight's handyman: he would even mind the place if Richard Knight went on holiday. I was reflecting on the question of multiple identities when I suddenly realized that I had forgotten the tobacco. I had to buy some slim Cuban panatellas for Richard Knight. Bob Brown smoked a pipe and loudly declared that the finest tobacco was shag and nothing went better with it than a pint of four ale. There was a

THE LABYRINTH OF SATAN

tobacconist on my way and I stepped inside there to be astonished.

'Mr Davies!' the shopkeeper was crying out. He was a fat, bald, bespectacled Cockney whom one would not normally expect to be frightened of anything. 'Please, Mr Davies, I'm truly sorry that I may have slipped up there but I'll set it right for you, honest to God, I swear I will.'

'You had better,' said the sinister Mr Davies. He turned to go – and I saw Mr Harding.

'We meet again,' I said. 'Good day, Mr Harding. Problems?'

'None that can't be solved without a little application, Mr Brown,' he replied with a smile as charming as the bared teeth of a shark. 'Good day to you, sir.'

As Bob Brown, I returned to the Cheyne Walk home of Venetia Fielding. It was a pleasure to abandon one personality and to turn into another. I have found it to be such a relaxing relief to change into women's clothing. *Whoosh!* I exult as I switch my skirts and petticoats: I feel oh so utterly feminine. Clearly I was not the only man in London who was leading a multiple life: I was leading a quadruple life; Richard Knight, Venetia Fielding, Bob Brown and Septimus Keen. I wondered whether Mr Clive Harding alias the apparently fearsome Mr Davies might be leading a quintuple life.

I felt ever so relaxed as I walked, my skirts swishing, to a bench overlooking the river, Father Thames. My contemplation of its flow was abruptly interrupted by a sneeze.

'Bless you!' I said automatically, then turned to see a young lady whose face was quaint and piquant rather than beautiful and whose hazel eyes shone piteously as though she had just been crying. 'You seem somewhat unhappy, my dear.'

'I am.' She broke down into a fit of sobbing. I noticed that her blue dress with its bell-shaped skirt had clearly been quite expensive. 'I am so sorry,' she cried.

'That is all right. Would you care to take a little tea with me and unburden yourself of the troubles with which I see you are afflicted? Madam, I can promise you a most sympathetic ear.'

'Tea, alas, is quite powerless to console me,' she returned. 'I have lost my brother!'

'How is that possible?'

'Oh, Madam, you are too kind. Yet I fear that your patience would only be exhausted by my sad narrative.'

'Not at all,' I replied, producing a silver flask of cognac from my bag. 'Please. Take some.' I poured a generous measure into the cup of the flask and she drank it greedily. 'Allow me to introduce myself. Venetia Fielding.'

'Sarah Chingford.' We touched gloves. Hers were of red satin and mine were of green silk. 'Oh, is it possible that you may have seen my brother? I was meant to meet him here today. He is a tall man, well-dressed, who usually wears a high silk hat and he is smooth, smiling and clean-shaven. I was so eager to know what had transpired regarding his novel, *Life and Lives*. You have not read it, by any chance?'

'This is all most extraordinary, Miss Chingford . . .'

'Mrs , actually . . .'

'Sorry, Mrs Chingford. Shortly before I came out here to sit by the river, I saw an old friend of mine. By sheer coincidence, he told me of his interesting encounter with the author of *Life and Lives*. Clive Harding is his name, is it not?'

'You are quite correct, Mrs Fielding . . .'

'Miss, actually . . .'

'Sorry, Miss Fielding. Clive Harding is indeed my brother

and he has written what is, in my opinion, an excellent book. Clive is, I believe, a very good novelist but unfortunately he has not hitherto made much money. Even so, I am his sister and I feel obliged to support him until he obtains the recognition that he undeniably deserves. My husband, Mr Harold Chingford, a most talented man of business, is quite fond of his brother-in-law and recognizes the reality of the situation. He has also financed my own school which,' Mrs Chingford smiled, 'has fulfilled a dream of mine.'

'How so, Mrs Chingford?'

'I have always wanted to run a school for ill-disciplined boys and girls. Certain local authorities pay me to take pupils into care. A number of parents pay me to take their recalcitrant sons and daughters. Our educational record is excellent and there is strict discipline. Any infringement of the rules is visited by a sound birching, sometimes in front of the whole school. If a boy misbehaves, he is put into skirts. These methods work, believe me, Madam.'

'Does putting a boy into skirts *really* work well, Mrs Chingford?' I demanded as I swirled mine. 'They might get a taste for it later.'

'So much the better,' she replied. 'It certainly makes them more respectful to ladies. But changing the subject, you have not seen my brother?' I shook my head. 'Oh, well, I suppose that he is late again. Perhaps *he* should be put into skirts. But I see that I have taken up too much of your time and I thank you for your kindness.' Suddenly Mrs Sarah Chingford arose and hailed a passing cab. 'Farewell.'

It was hard to make sense of all that had transpired as Miss Venetia Fielding became Richard Knight, emerging from Cheyne Walk to hail a cab for transportation to a Bloomsbury tavern, prior to his meeting with Dr Lipsius. I needed a double whisky. I was enjoying that when my train of thought was interrupted by a harsh, stentorian voice.

"Scuse me. Is this seat taken?' I looked up to see a most insalubrious personage. He had a ginger moustache that merged into a pair of bulbous chin whiskers and his grey suit was far too tight for his bulky body. His blue tie was screaming blue murder as it threatened to strangle his thick, sweaty neck; and droplets of sweat had stained his cream-coloured shirt. I nodded tired acquiescence as he sat down opposite me.

'Excuse me,' he said again, 'I don't wish to trouble you but I wonder if you can help me.' I grunted and nodded. 'I am a Reader at the British Museum!' he announced proudly. 'I have often seen you there.' I could hardly deny that as Richard Knight though, in that identity, I wondered about the sort of chaps they were letting in these days. 'There is a book for which I am looking,' he continued calmly, 'and it appears to have disappeared.'

'With all respect, how can a book "appear to have disappeared", Mr . . .?'

'Chingford. Harry Chingford.' I froze momentarily.

'Richard Knight. A pint, Mr Chingford?'

'Yeah, make it a dark one, Dick.'

'What an astonishing day I've had!' I declared heartily as I returned to the table with our pints, his glass containing good stout. 'I have just come from having tea with a good friend of mine who lives by Cheyne Walk and she told me that she had met Mrs Sarah Chingford whilst contemplating the beauties of the River Thames upon a park bench.'

'Probably my wife,' said Harry Chingford. 'Did your friend say anything more?'

'I gather from my friend that she was in some distress concerning the mysterious disappearance of her brother, Clive Harding, author of the novel *Life* and *Lives*.'

'Well,' Mr Chingford drained his pint in several voracious gulps. 'Well, well, well.' His throat appeared to be indeed a bottomless well. 'This is all extremely strange, sir. First a book by Clive Harding is lost by the British Museum and next my wife tells your friend that she has lost her brother. Well, he's my brother-in-law! Whatever next?'

'God knows,' I said; and Mr Chingford promptly bought another round, even though I was only half way through my pint.

'God knows possibly,' he replied, 'or maybe the Devil knows better. Tell me, Mr Knight, can you drink a pint of beer in five seconds?'

'No. Nor would I understand why anyone else would wish to do so.' Bob Brown, of course, would had to have leaped at that challenge.

'Ah, it sorts out the men from the boys.' He drained his pint within five seconds, pouring it down his throat as one might pour a bucket of cleansing mixture down a drain. 'God! I had a good time last night, I can tell you. Made a nice change from the wife and we didn't play chess either, I swear.'

'Gosh,' I said. I was not quite sure what else to add: *Did you really?* did not seem to be an entirely appropriate response. 'Forgive me. I am a little naive in these matters and I could be wrong, but I gather from some that when a man and a woman are together and they find one another attractive, certain things – um – well, just happen, so to speak. Perhaps you could correct me if you think that I could conceivably be mistaken.'

'I don't like your attitude,' said Mr Chingford. 'Have a good evening.'

I pondered the events of the day as I strolled towards my dinner invitation at the house of Dr Lipsius. Some might call it peculiar for me to be three separate individuals on the same day. For my own part, *I* was finding it highly perplexing, during the course of assuming my various identities, to meet a man, his sister and his brother-in-law all on the same day and as if by chance.

The walk to the house of Dr Lipsius as the evening sun blazed with a warmth devoid of ferocity in a sky of clear cobalt blue was a pure pleasure. I was wearing evening dress, though I had a cloak rather than a coat, and my silken topper was somewhat taller than the present fashion, rather resembling the stove-pipe hats of the late 1840s. I liked striking my ivory-tipped ebony walking cane upon the paving stones and was reassured by the knowledge that within it lurked a long blade of sharpened steel.

Dr Lipsius had an elegant and discreet Queen Anne house tucked away in a Marylebone terrace facing onto a quiet street. I strode up the marble steps to the maroon front door, seized the chunky brass knocker fashioned in the form of a sphinx, and knocked loudly three times. The door was opened promptly by a butler whom I judged to be of foreign extraction, from the Pacific possibly, and who welcomed me with a smile but without words. Moments later, after my hat, stick and cloak had been taken, Dr Lipsius approached me and shook my hand warmly.

'My dear Richard!' he exclaimed. 'Or should I say Septimus? No matter, it is a pleasure to see you again, eh? Hm? I have some guests here and I hope that you will enjoy their company, ha! ha! my dear Richard, for I know that you always enjoy good company.' He ushered me into the drawing room that I had visited before, the one with large oak presses, two bookcases of extreme elegance, and a carved wooden chest that must have been medieval. Two men and a young woman, all dressed at the height of fashion, occupied a sofa in the far corner. 'Good evening, lady and gentlemen,' Dr Lipsius declared with a theatrical flourish of his pudgy white hand. 'Allow me to introduce our guest of honour for this evening's dinner, Richard Knight. Mr Knight, allow me to introduce you to my equally honoured guests, Mr Henry Richmond, Mr James Davies and Miss Helen Sutherland.'

'Good evening, Mr Knight,' said Mr Harry Chingford.

'Good evening, Mr Brown,' said Mr Clive Harding.

'Good evening, Miss Fielding,' said Mrs Sarah Chingford.

'Good evening, Septimus Keen,' said Dr Lipsius. 'Should I call you Mr, Mrs, or Miss?'

CHAPTER FIVE

FROM THE DIARY
OF SEPTIMUS KEEN

I am forbidden by Oath sworn on pain of death by mutila-tion, a mutilation that would leave my intestines arranged delicately over my left shoulder, to say too much about the details of my Initiation. Once we had all unmasked, since I was hardly the only master of disguise, it suffices to say that I relished that Sabbat of the Adepti, when the wine of the Red Jar of Avallanius boiled and bubbled in my veins and I soared beyond the pylons of space and time to embrace a being of splendour and corruption that was, in a deeper sense, my inmost self.

After I had given of my own blood, we all sat down to dinner. The first course consisted of shellfish: lobster, crawfish, crab, scampi, prawns, shrimps, oysters, mussels, cockles, winkles and even things that tasted like hard-rubber teething rings and that, Richmond informed me as he ate them with evident joy, were called whelks. There were also dishes of octopus, cuttlefish, squid and jellyfish, which last was surprisingly tasty.

'This dinner,' Dr Lipsius declared, 'is dedicated to celebrating human and planetary evolution. What we are eating now are the first forms of life. We shall proceed, my friends, to eat a dish that I myself have created: Cosmic Soup. Be warned that it contains eminently edible insects. That will be followed by bony fish: I prefer it raw myself, a custom I learned in Japan. A dish of frogs' legs is to commemorate the amphibians. For the reptiles, there will be a bowl of turtle soup and slivers of roasted crocodile.' He smiled. 'Sliced trunk of elephant will honour the mamma's, roasted ostrich the birds and, of course, after the Cosmic Soup, vegetables and fruit will be served throughout the meal. Now, for the primates: I do hope that you are not too squeamish, since I learned of this delicious speciality during my travels in South-East Asia. Look.' I looked and saw a wooden table with a circle in its centre. 'A monkey will be placed there. I shall personally slice away its scalp and we shall sup on the delicious delicacy of lightly braised live brains. Eh? Hm. For pudding, there is a surprise.'

Whatever my doubts concerning the eventual dishes chosen by Doctor Lipsius, I could not fault the initial course, which was accompanied by copious quantities of iced Gewürtztraminer. For condiments, there were plates of brown bread spread with unsalted Dutch butter, tartare sauce, mayonnaise, chilli sauce and chilli vinegar, also generous helpings of thin, dry toast. Doctor Lipsius suddenly surprised the company once again when a servant brought a barrel into the room and ripped away its lid. I had fancied that it would contain beer but it proved to hold the finest Beluga caviar which Doctor Lipsius ladled out with a huge soup spoon. Pepper vodka was served and this goes very well with caviar: then there was a popping of champagne corks and Krug '88 was served.

'It is customary at this table,' Doctor Lipsius informed me, 'for tales to be told.' I nodded acquiescence. 'I suppose, really, that I should set an example, eh? Hm. Tell me, my dear Septimus, or should I call you by another of your very many names, do you know much about Jack the Ripper?'

'Not much,' I replied. 'Five women were slain quite hideously and no one knows who was responsible. Queen Victoria publicly expressed her displeasure regarding the inefficiency of the police. Then – suddenly – the murders stopped as abruptly as they had begun.'

'You know the outline of the matter as anyone might, sir,' Lipsius responded silkily, adding: 'Or should I call you madam? Would you like to know the truth, pure and simple?'

'As my acquaintance Oscar Wilde has said,' I responded, 'the truth is never pure and rarely simple.'

'Quite so, quite so, my dear Septimus.' And then he commenced:

THE TALE
OF DOCTOR LIPSIUS

There is no point in explaining at tedious length the details of my early life. Do you not find that these are the most insufferably boring chapters in any biography or autobiography you might read? It is sufficient to say that by the age of twenty-five, I had inherited riches beyond the dreams of avarice and proceeded to use them in my pursuit of knowledge, to which end I essayed travel all over the World. I learned from every culture, finding, of course, that an action regarded as being evil in some is regarded as being good in others. Naturally, I discovered contradictions. Buddhism which, when strictly interpreted, forbids one in theory to swat a fly does not prevent in practice a man from slitting his brother's throat in order to gain five rupees, the price of getting blind drunk.

Knowledge alone is not enough to give satisfaction. I wanted power, power over the lives and destinies of people, the perfume of which mastery is perfectly intoxicating. When one has wealth, it is easy enough to have power, especially if one of the weapons is knowledge. May heaven and hell bless the hypocrisy of our age! It did not take me long to gather information regarding the most influential in the land. Excuse my taste for the clichés, since I soon had them under my thumb, around my little finger and toeing the line. 'Doctor Octopus', some have called me, and certainly my tentacles reach out everywhere. Some enjoy the visible trappings of power; I thrive merely on its substance.

I made a Pact with the Devil in Paris many years ago. I do not accept the Christian position at all: it is childish to believe in a fixed fight that God is predestined to win. If God really wanted a world of truth and justice, He would have snuffed out the Devil billions of years ago. No, no; I accepted the view expressed by Zoroaster of Persia that the World is the scene of a battle between Light (*Ahura Mazda*) and Darkness (*Ahriman*). The outcome is indeterminate. I do not believe in the myth of Mithras the Redeemer of Light. I am a Lord of Darkness in the service of Ahriman. I have learned all the secrets of Black Magic. The only trouble with Black Magic – as its incompetent practioners find out soon enough – is that it works.

What is a captain without a team? I have various teams working for me: but my favourite team is the lot I call 'The Three Impostors'. These masters of disguise are ruthless, efficient and determined. I felt that they were the only possible team for the job on the occasion when I met with some of the highest in the land.

There really was a serious problem back in 1888. 'Eddy', Duke of Clarence, son of Prince Edward, the heir to the throne, was addicted to debauchery in low company and gave his favours to either sex. Walter Sickert, one of England's finest painters and already favoured at Court, was asked by Princess Alexandra to tutor her wayward son. Sickert did what he could, but he could not prevent Eddy from going to a male brothel in Cleveland Street and it was probably there that he caught the syphilis that rendered him insane and accounted for his premature death. There was on the same street a tobacconist where one might find two shop girls: Mary Jane Kelly and Annie Elizabeth Crook. The latter was seduced by the Duke of Clarence and bore him a child, Alice Margaret Crook. Walter Sickert endeavoured to help by having this child brought up in his own home for a time, employing Mary Jane Kelly as nurse and governess. Unfortunately, Mary Jane Kelly became dissatisfied with the low wages and poor treatment she alleged that she received from Sickert, left his employment and drifted into an East End world rife with drink, crime and prostitution. There she opened her mouth after too much cheap gin and blabbed her story to three fellow prostitutes: Mary 'Polly' Nichols, Annie Chapman, and Catherine Eddowes. All of them were in debt, barely able to pay the rent without a continuous turning of tricks, and so they sent a blackmail demand to Walter Sickert, asking him to pass it on to the highest in the land. And this is where I came in.

On 8th June 1888, 'Eddy', bisexual Duke of Clarence, dined with the Prime Minister, Lord Salisbury, and Lord Randolph Churchill at Cambridge, with Eddy's clever tutor, the homosexual J.K. Stephen, subsequently being informed of the details of the discussion.

As I understand the matter, Salisbury argued in favour of bribing the four girls, adding that, given the wretched nature of their incomes, this policy would be cheap. However, there were counter-arguments. There was no telling what four drunken prostitutes might do once they had spent the money. Eventually, and this was hardly surprising since I control a number of seats in both the Commons and the Lords, I was contacted so as to arrange the elimination of the four girls involved. For a certain sum, I agreed that it could be very easily done. My demand was simply that the matter be left to me.

I have never seen the point of crude butchery and I can count myself to be an expert upon the aesthetics of Murder. Moreover, fortunately I am assisted by three masters of disguise who appreciate these matters as much as I do. We are all very thorough in our work although we do like to relax during our hours of leisure. The names used in my favourite team are Richmond, Davies and Helen. I enjoy watching Richmond playing billiards with human skulls; it is a pleasure witnessing Davies playing the Ancient Roman game of 'jacks' or 'knucklebones' with the remains of the hands hacked away from the foolish; and my museum has a fine collection, thanks to Helen, who calls the 'pricks preserved'. 'Alas, poor Yorick!' as Shakespeare might put it concerning the predilections of Richmond. 'Alas, poor Dick!' I myself might well exclaim regarding those of Helen.

Now, when we come to the goodly Mr Davies, we are speaking of the Director of this auspicious company that takes to the streets of London to become what it is not, performing a ballet before the unseeing eyes of the public.

Is not the study of London the most fascinating study in the whole wide World? There will always be something there that you do not know and that will forever elude your closest endeavours at research. There will always be places into which you may casually stumble and which you will never be able to find again. London is a labyrinth and no one has ever written a book that might successfully guide you through its more obscure quarters. Take this street in Marylebone, for example, and who knows Marylebone in any proper manner? Of course, everyone is familiar with the Courts of Justice, the Public Library, the close proximity of Regent's Park and the delights of its High Street. It is close also to Harley Street and Wimpole Street and Devonshire Street, where the wealthy go to meet their doctors and dentists. But who really knows the Marylebone beneath these superficialities? Beneath the roof of one house, such as this, outwardly so respectable, the most awful rites and ceremonies may be performed and just across the road from us there may be a respectable couple compelled by circumstances to take in a lodger in their attic, where this wounded poet is dying by inches. For all we know, just across the street from us a failed lawyer may have poisoned his wife. My next door neighbour might be a High Court Judge, yet I might know that he has somewhat *unholy* passions for the birch and the rope.

There are occasions when I walk in nearby Regent's Park to contemplate the sight of the squirrels, who are merely pleasant tree-rats, and of the herons and the cormorants by the pond, so astute in the catching of fish.

I distinguish very strongly between Fantasy and Imagination, as Coleridge did. Fantasy is merely dreaming on air. I*magi*nation is the Science and Art of the *magi* whereby dreams may be made real. Being somewhat expert in this matter, I demanded of Davies whether or not he was equal to the demand of aestheticism in the task provided. He replied in no uncertain terms that he was. I was pleased with his proposals and commissioned him for four months in order to have them executed. We met again on 15th November 1888 and my Memorandum here declares exactly what he told me:

THE TALE OF MR DAVIES

*AS RELATED IN THE
MEMORANDUM OF DOCTOR LIPSIUS*

Very well, my dear Doctor, I shall do precisely that which I am asked, which is to relate to you how the murders ascribed to 'Jack the Ripper' were accomplished. Excuse me if I do not give you any details of my past, present or future, for these are hardly germane to the matters at hand.

The fact of the matter is that four women had to be killed. Since they were East End prostitutes, this could be done very easily and cheaply, though this would negate the doctrine of style that you have always expounded and with which my colleagues and I are in full concurrence. The murders, therefore, had to be done in a way that would baffle both the police and the nation, spreading terror all across the East End. Rumours of gross behaviour in that area normally terrified the West End, too.

As Director, what I wanted to commit was a work of art, creating a mythology of 'Jack the Ripper' that would resonate for at least an hundred years. I thought that the best way to do so would be to make the killings dramatic but in an arcane style that could be called that of Freemasonry. Those of us who are Freemasons are familiar with the myth that Hiram Abiff built the Temple of Solomon at Jerusalem, as is recorded in the Bible, but, as Masonic lore informs us, Hiram Abiff had three apprentice masons who murdered him because he would not divulge his masonic secrets to them. Jubela, Jubelo and Jubelum were then hunted down and put to death 'by the breast being torn open and the heart

and vitals taken out and thrown over the left shoulder'. This
gave me a very good idea.

A second idea came from Black Magic, which of course
we love to practise. Is it not declared in the *grimoires* that
evocation of demons may be easily achieved with candles
made from human fat and various parts of a whore's body?
This method is most efficacious, so the medieval *grimoires*
relate – I speak especially of *The Red Dragon* more than of
The Grimoire of Pope Honorius – and so I could anticipate
pleasant side effects for our Black Lodge later, when all
had been duly accomplished.

The initial stages were really rather simple. My dear
colleague Helen became the gin-sodden prostitute 'Edna',
enabling her to fraternize with and gain information on
the habits and movements of all our victims. My dear
colleague Richmond shaved off his ginger moustache and
chin-whiskers, which some have found to be insalubrious,
and became a boozer in the East End. For the first time
in my life, I grew a moustache and beard and became a
known visitor of East End prostitutes, a gentleman who
enjoyed 'going slumming'.

Now, the East End is, of course, one of the most depraved
areas of London, which is probably why I like it so much.
It is a shocking place, an evil plexus of slums that hide
human, creeping things, where filthy men and women
live on penn'orths of gin. Whitechapel is the East End
of the East End. The Flower and Dean Street rookery
contains perhaps the foulest and most dangerous streets
in the whole of the metropolis. This suited my purposes
perfectly, especially since there were lodging houses. Annie
Chapman often stayed at No. 35, Flower and Dean Street,
Catherine Eddowes at No. 55. Mary Anne Nichols, also
known as 'Polly', was using Nos. 56-57, known as the
'White House'.

Life is cheap within the East End and the fog and the maze of streets and interconnecting alleyways make it rather easy literally to get away with murder. Any drunken sailor with a penny to spend can pick up a girl for something fast by a wall. Moreover, carriages cruise the area and the girls stand on street corners. Mary Anne Nichols had her patch and was only too willing and eager to step inside my carriage, driven by Netley, coachman to Sir William Gull, Her Majesty's Royal Physician. I chatted pleasantly as I fed her with some drugged grapes. She had fallen asleep by the time I placed the rubber sheet upon the floor of the carriage and took out my knife. She had either been drinking too hard or working too hard for the drug to have taken effect so quickly.

For a moment, I felt slightly sorry for her. She was aged around forty-five yet she was still not unattractive. She would have been about five feet three in height with a dark complexion, her eyes brown, her brown hair turning grey. I noticed bruises on her lower right jaw and left cheek, indicating that some brute of a man had hit her. Really! Where is gentlemanly conduct these days? She wore a brown frock and I shall not forget that it was fastened by seven large brass buttons, each one of which portrayed the figure of a female riding a horse with a man at her side. Yes, I felt a little bit sorry for her but I have never allowed considerations of sentiment to interfere with my passion for murder, whether it be of a man or of a woman. Doctor Lipsius has added high attunement to my already formidable surgical skills.

I opened her abdomen from the ribs down, then slashed the stomach lining and stabbed the genitals before cutting her throat back to the spine and depositing the body. After all, the Director of the play has to set a good example.

I shan't forget, however, those looming high warehouses

which cast such a malevolent shadow over Buck's Row, which was where I dumped the body, about sixty yards from the nearest gas lamp. Nor shall I forget the date: 31st August.

Having established a position on Buck's Row, it was now vital that we play by it. What a pleasure it was to see the police so baffled by an apparently motiveless murder! I started to prepare semi-literate letters signed 'Jack the Ripper' so as to perplex them further in the process. The police would receive these, written by various hands, in due course and soon enough. I saw no harm in having the matter blamed upon the Jews.

What was much more important, however, was where the bodies were to be deposited. The first pattern that occurred to me was that of a trapezoid, a quadrilateral shape in which no two sides run parallel: a shape sacred to Black Magic. The second idea was that all the corners should be joined in the form of a misaligned cross, which might lead some to blame the Freemasons. Some graffiti left on walls could leave many thinking that 'Jack the Ripper', for such was the identity I invented for our collective capers, was merely an illiterate brute.

Very well: there remained Annie Chapman, Catherine Eddowes and Mary Kelly to be murdered with sublime artistry and their bodies placed in appropriate geographical locations, making up the geometric design. There was also the matter of adding to those inner bodily organs already collected. Murder gives off a powerful stench that is useful for the augmentation of the rites of Black Magic.

As a Director, I consider the matter of casting to be vital. Helen had only killed men before, in a manner which I would blush to repeat before ladies, were any present, and was now eager to essay another part by slaughtering a woman. I therefore gave her Annie Chapman. I would attend to the matter of Catherine Eddowes and Richmond would dispose of Mary Kelly in his usual plain way, I supposed. As I have said to the man:

'It is no use my telling you to improve your style. I might as well give you more opium and hashish. You are just the same on them as you are off them.'

'"The best laid schemes o' mice an' men gang aft a-gley"', as Burns has it. I knew that something had gone badly wrong that night of 30th September. But the best account of the Operation and its eventual success is surely that of Helen, which reads:

THE TALE OF HELEN

AS RELATED IN THE MEMORANDUM OF MR DAVIES AND RECORDED IN THAT OF DOCTOR LIPSIUS

I have always loved Evil for its own sake. There is such a spiteful joy in being quite excruciatingly nasty. Myself, I concur with Hassan-al-Sabbah, the Old Man of the Mountains and Grand Master of the Sect of Assassins: *Nothing is true; Everything is permitted*. I take pride in being a member of the team that Doctor Lipsius has termed 'The Three Impostors', though I sometimes think of us as being 'The Three Imps'.

It was my task to kill Annie Chapman, whose acquaintanceship I had already made in the guise of 'Edna', a fellow gin-sodden prostitute. Annie was very drunk again on the night of 8th September when the carriage clattered into Spitalfields and dropped me at the corner of Brick Lane and Fournier Street. A thick fog hid me from any viewers in the squalid slums and hellish havens. Having listened to Davies, I had determined to leave the body in a certain private place and I'd be hanged if I didn't. Pardon my gallows humour.

As 'Edna', I had a few glasses of gin with Annie Chapman, who was swaying and drunk as usual, though otherwise quite pleasant. She too was around forty-five, roughly five feet tall, with a large, thick nose; glazed blue eyes; hair that was a wavy dark brown; and she had a pale complexion. She mentioned that she sometimes stayed at 29 Hanbury Street, a lodging house run by a Mrs Amelia Richardson, who manufactured packing-cases in her ground-floor shop. Seventeen people lived in this dingy dwelling, a place of peeling paint, and it was easy to discern her hollow-eyed hunger. Depressed, I stared at her black jacket, black skirt and laced boots, all of which were old and dirty, as she informed me that the front door was usually unlocked.

'That's quite useful,' she told me. 'The Dicks can go from the street to the back yard without anybody noticing them. I sometimes give them a fourpenny knee-trembler up against the back wall.'

'Well, I have good news for you, Annie,' I said.

'Where d'you get that accent from?' she demanded as she swigged her gin and I bought her another large glass of it.

'In common with our friend Mary Kelly,' I replied, 'I've been down on my luck, though recently I've had a piece of good fortune. There's this man in the House of Lords who has a taste for rough trade, shagging up against the wall and doing it like dogs, you know. Each time he gave me a guinea.'

'A guinea!?' Annie's blue eyes were suddenly illuminated by a blaze of comprehension flaring from her inebriated brain. She had a vision of paying the rent for her own apartment over the next three months, with as much gin as she could drink as well.

'Unfortunately,' I said, 'he has tired of me but I have recommended you.'

'Oh, thanks, Edna, thanks a lot. Cheers! When?'

'Later tonight. Be in the back yard at four o'clock this coming morning.' She nodded eagerly, thinking of her guinea. 'And don't breathe a word about this to a single living soul. Must go now. More tricks to turn.'

'God bless you, Edna!' she called out after me.

Once back in the carriage and amidst the fog, it was very easy to disguise myself as a nondescript man of indifferent appearance having, as Oscar Wilde states: 'The sort of English face that is often seen and never remembered.' I had two worries: one was that 29 Hanbury Street might not be as easy of access and egress as Annie had described and the other was that she might have become too drunk to keep the appointment, though I trusted in the promise of a guinea.

Fortunately she was there and her directions had proved accurate as I entered the bare, drab courtyard. She was waiting for me, rather as though she were coming to meet her maker.

I embraced her up against the wall and was glad that I had received such expert tuition in surgery from Doctor Lipsius. In fact I have no argument with the subsequent account of Inspector Joseph Chandler:

'I at once proceeded to No. 29 Hanbury Street and in the back yard found a woman lying on her back, left arm resting on left breast, legs drawn up, abducted, small intestines and flap of the abdomen lying on right side above right shoulder, attached by a cord with the rest of the intestines inside the body; two flaps of skin from the lower part of the abdomen lying in a large quantity of blood above the left shoulder; throat cut deeply from left and back in a jagged manner right around the throat.'

The worthy Inspector omitted to mention that I had removed the woman's uterus and two-thirds of her bladder for magical purposes and that also, in the tradition of the Freemasons, I had laid the intestines *over* her shoulder.

I wrenched three brass rings from her fingers. Future investigators will ponder in agony over the motive when all I wanted was a souvenir for the Doctor's museum. One's first murder usually makes one sick. The second can make one cry. The third, as in my case, simply makes you laugh.

After a few days of well-earned rest and recuperation from hard physical labour, it was necessary for there to be action once again. Davies studied the map.

'Life,' he informed me in his airy manner, 'begins with a *point*. Then somehow there is another point, Helen, and there is a *line* between them. We are then going from one dimension to two dimensions.' He scrutinized the map of the Whitechapel area and decided exactly where the bodies of Catherine Eddowes and Mary Kelly would be placed. 'This will take us on to three dimensions,' he added.

I was rather looking forward to the cross within the trapezoid, that quadrilateral shape with no sides parallel that means so much to us. However, my job that night was not especially exciting. I had to give the men food and drink after they had done their jobs, since it was rightly adjudged best to essay the slaughter in one night. I thought that raw fish followed by steak tartare and accompanied by baked potatoes and green salad with sticky toffee pudding with custard for dessert might be good for hungry men after a hard night's work. There would, of course, be copious quantities of champagne, whisky, brandy and rum; the serving of gin, though would surely have been somewhat tasteless. Merging my identity into that of an ageing spinster, Miss Maud Merton, I had rented a flat in Belsize Park.

Richmond stormed in soon enough, as he always does, and demanded a very strong whisky.

'It's done,' he told me, taking large gulps of his drink and then asking for another. 'Mary Kelly is no more. But it did not go according to plan.'

'Why not?' I demanded.

'I can't wait to grow back my moustache and chin-whiskers,' Richmond replied. 'Posing as a client, I was hoping to lure her into Dutfield's Yard, off Berner Street, as Davies had directed. It's just inside the borders of the City. I find it incredible that the poverty and squalor of the East End nestle so close to the wealthiest square mile in the World and I suppose that's all a part of Davies's humour.

Well, I was trying to get the girl into position by buying her a few glasses of gin at some pub when I became nervous. It's not only those letters that you and Davies sent to the police about Jack the Ripper, it's not only the rumours that his code-name is 'Leather Apron', it's the very *fact* of the *murders* that makes people so alert. There was nothing but talk about that in the pub and so,' Richmond held up his large hands helplessly, 'I judged it best to leave. The words heard were clearly making her tremulous too, despite all the drink. I urged her to give me a quick shag up against the wall. She told me: "No, not tonight, darling, some other night, all right?" I held my arm against the wall, hemming her in as I said quietly: "For you, Mary, I'll double the price." Unfortunately, a man was passing by just then and he may have overheard us.

'To make matters worse,' Richmond continued, 'she kept shouting "Let me go!" and I threw her to the ground as though I were a typical drunken sot. But the matter was witnessed by two men, who looked Jewish. I yelled "Lipski!" at them, you know, common East End insult to a Jew, and they ran away. Thinking that they might come back, I pushed Mary into the yard, placed my left hand over her mouth and with my right took a butcher's cleaver and slashed through her throat, taking care to step aside from the fountain of blood that thereupon spurted from her jugular.'

'Did anyone see you get away?' I asked.

'I don't think so. No one can follow you through that maze of alleys in a fog like we had tonight. It's easy to change a jacket and a hat, a voice and an accent. Anyway, who can detect a murder without any apparent motive?'

'So all you did was slit her throat?'

'That was all I had time to do.'

'No souvenir for the doctor's museum?'

'Give over, Helen. You know I can't abide that barbarian custom of yours.'

'I deplore,' I told Richmond, 'murder without artistry.'

'I deplore getting caught,' he replied.

Our deliberations were interrupted by the entry of Davies, as smooth, smiling and clean-shaven as ever, having had his moustache and beard removed. He took off his high silk hat and put down his Gladstone bag. I thought of the celebrated Prime Minister after whom the bag was named and who used to spend much of his leisure time visiting prostitutes in order to 'redeem' them. Davies asked for a stiff whisky too.

'It is done,' he told us coolly and calmly. 'Mitre Square was the obvious place, since it is in almost total darkness. In any event, the poor woman was completely drunk so I don't suppose she felt a thing. I know what they will find, though, since tonight I have excelled myself in artistry.'

How true! I quote from the medical report given at the post-mortem by Dr Frederick Gordon Brown:

The face was very much mutilated. There was a cut about a quarter of an inch through the lower left eyelid, dividing the structures completely through. The upper lid on that side, there was a scratch through the skin on the upper eyelid, near to the angle of the nose. The right eyelid was cut through to about half an inch. There was a deep cut over the bridge of the nose, extending from the left border of the nasal bone down near to the angle of the jaw on the right side of the cheek. This cut went into the bone and divided all the structures of the cheek except the mucous membrane of the mouth. The tip of the nose was quite detached from the nose by an oblique cut from the bottom of the nasal bone to where the wings of the nose join on to the face. A cut from this divided the upper lip and extended through the substance of the gum over the right upper lateral incisor tooth. About half an inch from the top of the nose was another oblique cut. There was a cut on the right angle of the mouth as if the cut of a point of a knife. The cut extended an inch and a half, parallel with lower lip. There was on each side of the cheek, a cut which peeled up the skin forming a triangular flap about an inch and a half. On the left cheek there were two abrasions of the epithelium under the left ear.

The throat was cut across to the extent of about six or seven inches. A superficial cut commenced about an inch below (and about two and a half inches below and behind the left ear) and extended across the throat to about three inches below the lobe of the right ear. The big muscle across the throat was divided through on the left side. The large vessels on the left side were severed. The larynx was severed and below the vocal cord all the deep structures were severed to the bone, the knife marking intervertebral cartilages. The carotid artery had a fine hole opening. The internal jugular vein was opening an inch and a half; not divided. The blood vessels contained clot. All these injuries were performed by a sharp instrument like a knife, and pointed.

The cause of death was haemorrhage from the left common carotid artery. The death was immediate and the mutilations were inflicted after death.

We examined the abdomen. The front walls were open from the breast bone to the pubes. The cut commenced opposite the enciform cartilage. The incision went upwards, not penetrating the skin that was over the sternum. It then divided the enciform cartilage. The knife must have cut obliquely at the expense of the front surface of that cartilage.

Behind this the liver was stabbed as if by the point of a sharp instrument. Below this was another incision into the liver about two and a half inches, and below this the left lobe of the liver was slit through by a vertical cut. Two cuts were shewn by a jagging of the skin on the left side.

The abdominal walls were divided in the middle line to within a quarter of an inch of the navel. The cut then took a horizontal course for two inches and a half and made a parallel incision to the former incision, leaving the navel on a tongue of skin. Attached to the navel was two and a half inches of the lower part of the rectus muscle on the left side of the abdomen. The incision then took an oblique direction to the right and was shelving. The incision went down the right side of the vagina and rectum for half an inch behind the rectum. There was a stab of about an inch on the left groin; this was done by a pointed instrument. Below this was a cut of three inches going through the peritoneum about the same extent.

An inch below the crease of the thigh was a cut extending from the anterior spine of the illium obliquely down the inner side of the left thigh and separating the left labium, forming a flap of skin up to the groin. The left rectus muscle was not detached. There was a flap of skin formed from the right thigh, attaching the right labium and extending up to the spine of the illium. The muscles on the right side inserted into the frontal ligaments were cut through. The skin was retracted through the whole of the cut of the abdomen, but the vessels were not clotted. Nor had there been any appreciable bleeding from the vessels. I draw the conclusion that the cut was made after death and there would not be much blood on the murderer. The cut was made by someone on the right side of the body, kneeling below the middle of the body.

I removed the contents of the stomach and placed it in a jar for further examination. There seemed very little in it in the way of food or fluid, but from the cut end partly digested farinaceous food escaped.

The intestines had been detached to a large extent

from the mesentery; about two feet of the colon was cut away. The sigmoid flexure was invaginated into the rectum very tightly.

Right kidney pale, bloodless, with slight congestion of the base of the pyramids.

There was a cut from the upper part of the slit on the under surface of the liver to the left side, and another cut at right angles to this which were about an inch and a half deep and two and a half inches long. Liver itself was healthy.

The gall bladder contained bile. The pancreas was cut, but not through, on the left side of the spinal column. Three and a half inches of the lower border of the spleen by half an inch was attached only to the peritoneum. The peritoneal lining was cut through on the left side and the kidney carefully taken out and removed. The left renal artery was cut through. I should say that someone who knew the position of the kidney must have done it.

The lining membrane over the uterus was cut through. The womb was cut through horizontally leaving a stump of three quarters of an inch. The rest of the womb had been taken away with some of the ligaments. The vagina and cervix of the womb was uninjured.

The bladder was healthy and uninjured and contained three or four ounces of water. There was a tongue-like cut through the anterior wall of the abdominal aorta. The other organs were healthy.

There was no evidence of recent connexion.

I believe the wound in the throat was first inflicted. I believe she must have been lying on the ground.

The wounds on the face and abdomen prove that they were inflicted by a sharp pointed knife, and that in the abdomen by one six inches long.

I believe the perpetrator of the act must have had considerable knowledge of the position of the organs in the abdominal

cavity and the way of removing them. The parts removed
would be of no use for any professional purpose. It required
a great deal of knowledge to have removed the kidney and
to know where it was placed. Such a knowledge might be
possessed by one in the habit of cutting up animals. I think the
perpetrator of this act had sufficient time, or he would not have
nicked the lower eyelids. It would take at least five minutes.

I cannot assign any reason for the parts being taken away.
I feel sure there was no struggle. I believe it was the act of
one person.

'The goodly medical officer was somewhat sloppy,' Davies
observed. 'He omitted to mention that I carved a triangle
on each cheek, one upward, one downward so as to make
the six-pointed star of the Hexagram. So the Cross within
the trapezoid has been performed impeccably,' he sipped
champagne, 'and we can congratulate one another. The
Royal Throne is saved from scandal and so we have
contributed to the national health. Doesn't it make you
feel proud, Richmond?'

'Oh, I'll always do my bit for the Royal Family,'
Richmond replied.

We feasted royally that night.

Men! They can be so smug and are so prone to these
orgies of self-congratulation. For a woman, this can be
quite enjoyable to witness, providing that they have actually
succeeded in accomplishing something worthwhile. That
was why I was pleased to feast them and applaud their
violent boasting. On the following day, though, I became
'Edna' once again and slipped into the East End just to
make sure that everything had gone according to plan.

My opinion of the matter is best expressed by the following social occasion when I saw Davies and Richmond

as Helen in one of my homes in St John's Wood. They were somewhat surprised to be welcomed with tumblers of hot tap-water accompanied by rich-tea biscuits, which I have always found to be exceptionally horrid. Davies, of course, raised an eyebrow in query and Richmond asked if I was upset about something.

'Upset?!' I burst out. 'Of *course* I'm upset. You apes, barbarians, cretins, dullards, epileptics, fart-faces, gormless, horrible, idiotic . . . and I can't be bothered with the rest of the alphabet because you're not worthy of it. You are both fools, imbeciles and morons, the pair of you! Your night's work of 30th September is abominable, atrocious, appalling and awful.'

'Helen, do I detect a slight trace of annoyance in your attitude?' Davies asked quietly.

'Yes! *Don't you realize that you have murdered the wrong women*?' I shrieked.

''Ow's that possible?' Richmond demanded.

'There have been two ghastly errors,' I responded. 'Richmond, you say that you killed Mary Kelly. You did not. You killed "Tall" Lizzie Stride. Davies, you killed Catherine Eddowes, believing her to be an intimate of Mary Kelly and privy to the blackmail demand via Sickert to the Royal Family. Timid, shy, little Catherine Eddowes wasn't privy to the blackmail plot at all. The names became confused. Mary Kelly is the classiest whore in the East End. She has a reputation for her skills with her mouth that has spread far and wide so that she can charge five times the normal prices. This is why both Lizzie Stride and Catherine Eddowes claimed to be Mary Kelly, to up their prices. Congratulations, gentlemen: Davies has murdered an innocent; Richmond has murdered a guilty one thinking that she was Mary Kelly; and Mary Kelly is still alive and well and walking the streets.'

'Looks like we'll have to get rid of her,' said Richmond, 'and looks like we made a couple of mistakes. But you have to understand that the East End is like a bloody rabbit warren . . .'

'. . . and, yes, whores all look the same,' I completed his sentence. 'Davies, you're looking uncharacteristically quiet and thoughtful. What is the matter, pray? You can't have possibly made a mistake, surely? I had always thought that you were so perfect and you have always agreed with me.'

'Oh, do shut up, Helen,' Davies exclaimed wearily, rather like an older brother talking to a younger sister. 'I *have* made a mistake. *Shimitah!* as Doctor Lipsius would say, which means the same thing and is the only swear-word in the Japanese language. It is dreadful! If Catherine Eddowes was nothing to do with this and so I sliced her for nothing, then my whole aesthetic schema of a misaligned cross placed upon a trapezoid does not work. Give me a map of London, Helen!' he snapped. 'Ah . . .' he mused after a few moments, without exhibiting the slightest sign of contrition, 'yes, if the cross within the trapezoid is to be fulfilled . . . where did you say the *real* Mary Kelly lives, Helen . . .?'

'I haven't set it yet,' I answered, 'nor have I said it yet. But here it is: Room 13, Millers Court, Dorset Street.'

'Let me trace it . . .' Davies always looks so keen and alert at these moments. 'I have it . . .' he murmured. 'If we kill her there, in her own home, we *still* have the cross within the trapezoid. Look!'

'And feeling that there's been, Helen, a slight upon my honour,' Richmond added, 'I shall perform the execution *and* bring you a souvenir from Mary Kelly for the doctor's museum.'

I did not see Richmond until the morning of 10th November and this is what he told me:

THE TALE OF RICHMOND

*AS RELATED IN THE TALE OF
HELEN IN THE MEMORANDUM OF
DAVIES RECORDED BY DOCTOR LIPSIUS*

I have on occasion been asked how it feels to kill someone. The first time, you throw up and you never forget the eyes. Number two makes you go quiet and thoughtful. After that, the third one makes you laugh. Then it comes easily if you have a taste for it and, after a while, you feel nothing at all. Nothing at all.

Unless you are a psychopath, there is a tendency after a time to lose your enthusiasm. Murder becomes a rather routine matter. You wake up in the morning thinking 'Who am I going to kill today?' and 'How much am I getting paid for it?'.

Naturally, the first thing that you do is to stake out the territory of your victim. The next matter you establish is how to get away. Also, you have to make sure that you get paid. I usually charge half of my fee up front which, having my honour, I return if the kill is not possible. But that has only ever happened once.

Now, in the matter of Mary Kelly I knew all about her habits from you, Helen, in your guise as Edna. I felt that my honour had been highly insulted by my error in killing the wrong 'Mary Kelly' and also by the slights that have been made upon my style. I admit that it is very straight and to the point but I have always felt that its economy and ease have been insufficiently appreciated by connoisseurs of this noble art.

Mary Kelly was living at Room 13, Millers Court, Dorset

111

Street, an area I know well, for, yes, I know every twist and turning in this most squalid and sordid quarter. I began by visiting her as an ordinary client: Slam! Bam! Thank you, ma'am! That was me. I paid and always left a generous tip. This was why she was so pleased to welcome me on the night of 9th November 1888. Curiously enough, Sir Charles Warren, Commissioner of the Metropolitan Police, had resigned on the previous day, probably because this honest copper objected to the impending cover-up.

I can't help admitting that I felt a little bit sorry for her. She was an attractive woman, charming, vivacious and surprisingly well-educated. It was obvious that she had actually been for a time the governess to Alice Margaret Crook, bastard daughter of the Duke of Clarence in the home of Walter Sickert. She was known in the East End as 'Ginger', since she sometimes wore a wig, 'Fair Emma' and 'Black Mary'. I would judge her as being around twenty-five years of age. She wore a black velvet dress, tight-fitting, with a scarlet shawl wrapped around her shoulders. Her eyes widened as I drew the knife with my right hand while my left enveloped her face and choked off all screams.

By the time I had finished with Mary Jane Kelly, all that remained was a butchered animal, for her face no longer existed, since her nose, eyebrows, ears and cheeks lay in a small pile next to her head. I could not bring myself to damage those beautiful, terrified eyes. In fact, the matter is best described by the *Illustrated Police News*.

The throat had been cut right across with a knife, nearly severing the head from the body. The abdomen had been partially ripped open, and both of the breasts had been cut from the body, the left arm, like the head, hung to the body by the skin only. The nose had been cut off, the forehead skinned, and the thighs down to the feet, stripped of the flesh. The abdomen had been slashed with a knife right across downwards, and the liver and entrails wrenched away. The entrails and other portions of the frame were missing, but the liver etc., it is said were found placed between the feet of this poor victim. The flesh from the thighs and legs, together with the breasts and nose, had been placed by the murderer on the table, and one of the hands of the dead woman had been pushed into her stomach.

Myself, I didn't feel that I had done too badly, especially when one reporter praised my style by calling it 'the worst sight this side of hell'.

Well, well: haven't I got a way with women?

ALL TALES RESUMED
AND SUMMARY GIVEN IN
THE TALE OF DOCTOR LIPSIUS

'Stop!' Doctor Lipsius commanded. 'Otherwise Richmond will relate a tale he heard from someone else and this process of tales within tales will go on forever. Is there anything further to be added?'

'Helen has heard my story, as have you now,' said Richmond.

'Davies has heard mine, as have you now,' said Helen.

'I have told my tale,' said Davies. 'The trapezoid and the cross.'

'And I haven't finished yet,' Lipsius declared. During this intriguing process, wines of the finest vintage had been served along with the food, and these wines had been so exquisite that they made the food seem to be merely an accompaniment to the wine. 'I masterminded the cover-up and, yes, I did enforce the resignation of Sir Charles Warren. He was simply too honest and efficient to exist in public life. It is unfortunate that in July 1889 the police raided the Cleveland Street male brothel and found evidence that declared the Duke of Clarence to be a visitor. However, the Duke was going mad by that time. I think it was on the 1st November 1891 that he set fire to Sandringham and was subsequently confined to an asylum. Let us face it, madness runs in the Hanoverian line. In any event, "Eddy", Duke of Clarence, died on 14th January 1892. By this time, his erstwhile tutor J.K. Stephen, fully aware of the murderous plot, had also been confined in a madhouse. He refused food the instant that he heard that his beloved "Eddy" had died, and followed him to his grave on 3rd February 1892.

'There were still a few mopping-up operations. We had no need to worry about Annie Crook since the skilful surgeon's knife of Dr Gull had ensured her amnesia. There was still the problem of her daughter by the Duke of Clarence, Alice Margaret Crook. I wasn't quite sure what to do here since, despite some errors, the "Jack the Ripper" murders had been executed with such superlative skill, the bodies and entrails rightly placed, so as to leave behind an enduring myth of terror.

'I do wish that people would not run into rash actions without previously consulting me. That wretched fool, Netley the coachman, decided to act upon his own initiative in order to please me. On the 6th February 1892 he tried to run down that little girl, Alice Crook, and although he injured her he failed to kill her. Netley knew that I hate gross inefficiency, utter incompetence, blundering stupidity and useless bungling so he flung himself into the river and, as I believe, fabricated his own death. This event must have affected the goodly Inspector Abberline, who had been probing too close for comfort into the matter of Jack the Ripper, since the following day saw his retirement from the police force. Now, I know that Netley is hiding somewhere. We shall track him down and remove him in an artistic manner in the fullness of time.'

(Editor's Note: John Netley was run down by a horse-drawn carriage close to Clarence Gate on 20th September 1903.)

'Pass the cheese, please, Louise . . .' Lipsius was grinning at Helen as though he were the Cheshire Cat of Lewis Carroll's *Alice in Wonderland*. 'Oh, and the Madeira, m'dear. Thank you. Hm, eh? What shall I have? English or French or both? Who's playing for England? Ah! Cheddar,

Cheshire, Wensleydale, Lancashire, Double Gloucester, Red Leicester, cottage cheese, cream cheese, curd cheese, Caerphilly from Wales and ah! – the glory of Stilton! Who's playing for France? Eh? Hm? Brie, Camembert, Port Salut, Pont Yveque, Roquefort, and . . .' he lifted his eyebrows as his servant placed yet another board before him, 'fifty more cheeses with which we are not yet sufficiently well acquainted. Italy: ah! Gorgonzola, mozzarella, Parmesan, Bel Paese, Provolone . . . distinguished players all but not much more to back them up, eh? Hm. The Swiss can field Gruyère and Ementhal, the Dutch have Edam and Gouda, Norway has Jarlsberg; and America has Limburger, courtesy of the Jews. Why not eat them all? Oh, and don't omit the feta from Greece. Last but not least, shall we say. Now, my dear Septimus, it is the custom once every three months at our dinners here for every member of the company present to tell a joke wherein there is wisdom. Perhaps I should start the ball rolling.'

Lipsius sipped some Madeira. So did I, since it was absolutely excellent. 'One day, a scorpion who cannot swim asks a frog to take him across the river. The frog agrees, provided that the scorpion solemnly swears that he will not sting him. The oath sworn, the scorpion mounts the back of the frog and halfway across the river, the scorpion stings him fatally. "How can you do that?!" the frog protests as they sink. "You broke your oath and now we shall both die." The scorpion replies: "It's just my nature."' Dr Lipsius beamed as all of us laughed and then it was the turn of Richmond.

'A lion,' he said, 'goes out one day in the jungle to show all the animals that he's the king. He approaches the python and roars: "Who's the king of the jungle?" "You are," the python says and slithers away. The lion approaches the crocodile and roars: "Who is king of the jungle?" "You are," the crocodile says and slides back into the water. Then the lion approaches the elephant and roars: "Who is king of the jungle?" The elephant takes him in his trunk, smashes him upon the ground and stomps him. "All right, all right," the lion says, "no need to get so sore just because you don't know the answer.'"

'My turn,' said Helen. 'A very poor man in the desert finds a bottle and opens it to reveal a Genii. He is awestruck as the Genii informs him that he may have three wishes, including those for women, riches, power and wisdom . . . "Hey, slow down," the peasant says. "Certainly," the Genii replies, "you have two wishes left." "No!" the peasant shouts, "I would to God you'd see how you're wrong there." "Yes, I am mistaken, sir," the Genii replies; "you have one wish left." "No!!" the peasant shouts. "You don't see, I'm just a peasant. I wish to God that you would listen to me." "I just have," the Genii tells him, "and now you have no wishes left."'

'My joke,' said Davies, 'is based upon my visit to Japan with Doctor Lipsius where we were studying Zen mysticism. Zen Masters often ask: "What is the sound of one hand clapping?" The question is as easy as the answer is obvious. It is the flat of the Master's palm striking the head of an insufferably dull student. That is the sound of one hand clapping, but you never know, though that blow might cause instant Enlightenment.'

'Very good.' Doctor Lipsius continued to smile with all the charm of a great white shark. 'And do you have a story for us, a joke perhaps, my dear Septimus?'

'Certainly,' I replied. 'Once upon a time there was a writer called Septimus Keen who lived under a number of identities. One evening he was invited to dine with Doctor Lipsius and three of his associates, all of whom possessed multiple identities. During the course of this elegant occasion, Doctor Lipsius told a tale. Within it, like Chinese boxes, there was a tale by Davies, within that there was a tale by Helen, within that there was a tale by Richmond, and when we came out of that, there was a tale by Septimus Keen that included all that had gone before and which begins with Keen saying: "Once upon a time there was a writer called Septimus Keen who lived under a number of identities. One evening he was invited to dine with Doctor Lipsius and . . .'"

'STOP!' Lipsius cried out. 'You are giving us eternal recurrence.'

'I thought that was what you wanted,' I answered. 'After all, doesn't Nietzsche say that this is an inevitable process?' Davies offered me a cigarette from his silver case and Helen struck a match for me as Richmond passed me a golden ashtray. 'It's funny, isn't it?' The tight lips of Doctor Lipsius smiled thinly.

'Hm. Ingenious,' he murmured. 'We shall discuss this further over pudding, with a vintage Chateau d'Yquem. There's nothing like a tale of "Once upon a time, they lived happily ever after". And there's nothing like roasted baby fat to put into the suet for a nice fruit pudding!'

CHAPTER SIX

FROM THE DIARY
OF SEPTIMUS KEEN

(THE SPITTING IMAGE)

I am absolutely enchanted by Doctor Lipsius and my colleagues. At last I have met my peers and equals, three men and one woman who welcome me with sympathy, understanding and style. Up until the Initiation, I had fancied myself to be the only one on this planet who thought that even the most trivial acts, such as the opening of a door or correct conduct with a walking cane, were matters of the utmost importance.

As Doctor Lipsius has since explained to me after that fateful night, there is the Law, which is style and honour within the Black Lodge; there are the Rituals, which must be correctly performed with beauty and with joy; also, there are the Ordeals. My next Ordeal was simple enough: I had to have a tattoo. This consisted of the inverted Pentagram being etched upon my belly, just above my pubic hair, with the ears, horns and bearded chin of the Devil engraved within it. I had been told that it would hurt but it did not. The first cut, done by Helen, indeed caused me to bleed but as the needle did its work I became increasingly drowsy and grew to enjoy the sensation. Afterwards I felt as high as a kite and I wandered the streets of London in a state of rapture, wondering why I had never noticed before just how beautiful they are, how every house tells a story and how every leaf that trembles in the wind tells one a truth.

I felt god-like, pressed by the need to take my trousers down and show my tattoo, yes, show it off. On the following day, as Sir Richard Knight, I was invited to a *soirée* in Knightsbridge given by Lady Dorothy Minford. There I met Mrs Barbara Crockford, a blonde and curvaceous young lady in possession of a fortune owing to the death of her parents in a railway accident. She was staying at the Cadogan and, being the gentleman that Sir Richard Knight undeniably is, I insisted upon escorting her to her rooms. One thing led to another, as the poet has it, and she gasped as I drew down my trousers. I am not sure as to whether this was caused by the sight of my erect member or of my tattoo.

I could go on for pages about the sensual, erotic delights I received at the hands of Barbara Crockford. Were a publisher to commission pornography from my pen, I probably would provide it gladly. Here it is sufficient to state that I enjoyed a flying fuck and so did she. I went to one of my homes to become Venetia Fielding and she went back to her husband in Harrogate.

There was one matter, other than the obvious, that I noticed, though. She mentioned her dear friend, Amelia Stanhope, and the latter's obsession with a Sir Percy Sulgrave, a man apparently determined to solve the Jack the Ripper murders whilst utterly convinced that he has seized the tentacle of an octopus and that its head consists of Doctor Lipsius.

I mentioned this to Lipsius who smacked his thin lips with pleasure when I saw him in my Septimus Keen mode a few days later. Here I thought that a narrow black frock coat, black drainpipe trousers, black high-heeled boots, seamed black stockings, a pale blue shirt of satin and a yellow chiffon scarf might be appropriate. He had invited me for after-dinner port.

'What can I give you, my dear Septimus, eh? Hm?' he chortled. 'Nuts? I have plenty of nuts. Walnuts, hazelnuts, peanuts, cashew nuts, coconuts, pecan nuts, pistachio nuts, almond nuts, oh, indeed, sir, there are plenty of nuts around. Port wine enables one to savour the matter, I find. Would you prefer ruby, tawny, crusted or vintage? Ah! I see! You want a vintage tawny if possible. You are in luck since I have a perfect Quinto here for you. I shall have some myself. Always best to start on a light note, eh? hm? Let us discuss your second ordeal. I refer, of course, to the matter of Sir Percy Sulgrave.'

'Tell me more.'

'We have set up an enduring mystique of Jack the Ripper. Sir Percy Sulgrave wishes to expose it. Naturally we shall have to get rid of him. That is your job. I want you to prove yourself fit to be among our company. I want you to be each and every one of the team, my team, the excellent and exquisite Three Impostors. Play with him, my dear Septimus, play with him as an angler would with a fish – and then just reel him in.'

'Very well. But how do I go about it?'

'That is your ordeal, my dear fellow. Still, we will help you. Here are the details of Sir Percy that we have at present.' Lipsius passed me a bulky file. 'Set it all up from the information there but do remember that it must all contain *artistry*.'

Some time later and after I had left the house of Doctor Lipsius, I decided to have a drink in a Marylebone pub that was in a side street and looked rather cosy and enticing. As I bought my gin-and-tonic and took my seat, I overheard much talk about Oscar Wilde. Some voices were saying that he was the most brilliant dramatist since the days of Sheridan and, before him, Congreve. Others whispered loudly of foul rumours involving debauchery. As I listened to the discussion, a man with a pleasant face who was wearing a bottle-green velvet suit and a black cape asked quietly if the seat opposite was taken. I nodded my assent to his joining me and he sat down with his pint of beer and began to scribble notes on the backs of old envelopes with a well-worn pencil.

'Writer, sir?' I enquired.

'Yes, indeed, sir,' He smiled and nodded.

'Contemplating another creation?'

'Yes, as it happens.' He turned out to be Arthur Machen, one of whose books I had read: *The Great God Pan and The Inmost Light*, with a frontispiece by Aubrey Beardsley.

'Very fine work,' I said sincerely.

'Thank you, sir, you are too kind.' He smiled and that smile was pained.

'You must be enjoying your literary success.'

'Success?' Machen's smile froze. 'I have received modest critical acclaim, along with vicious critical condemnation, and my reward has been a paltry few hundred pounds. I never thought that it would happen to me but for many years in the Eighties, I was literally starving in a garret, subsisting on a diet of bread, green tea and tobacco. I had come from Wales and I knew virtually nobody in London so I was isolated, like a Robinson Crusoe of the soul, I suppose. I used to envy the coal brazier and companionship of workmen digging the road; their joys were much beyond mine. Some of my tastes of that time actually still abide with me.' He produced a briar pipe and proceeded to pack it with shag tobacco. 'Cut'n'spun Virginia that is very strong,' he said, 'but I enjoy it. I also enjoy Four Ale; a pint used to be such a treat for me.'

I always start my judgement on people by a sensing of their energies and those of this man were good. Unlike so many, he seemed to be entirely genuine. I myself am not, for I lead four lives. This requires not only efficiency and mastery of disguise but strict mental discipline: the thoughts appropriate to Sir Richard Knight are not appropriate to Bob Brown or to Septimus Keen. All my personae have differing views on everything. In the unlikely event of a meeting, Septimus Keen and Sir Richard Knight would quarrel furiously about politics, with Keen calling Knight a Tory swine and Knight calling Keen a rabid lunatic of an anarchist. Bob Brown would have little patience with Arthur Machen, Venetia Fielding would find him 'sweet', Knight would find him to be a slightly dubious character: but as Keen I could warm to an author I much admired. Seeing that his glass was empty, I offered him another drink.

'Thank you, how kind,' he answered quietly. 'I see that you are drinking gin. I'm rather fond of gin on occasion, as it happens. May I join you for that?'

'Of course.' I bought Machen a large one though, in Keen style, I could not resist buying myself a pint of Four Ale. I knew that Bob Brown loved the brew; as Septimus Keen I was trying it for the first time on Machen's recommendation and of course I found it to be a most pleasant surprise. 'So what are you working on now, Mr Machen?'

'My publisher wants another novel from me,' he replied in a tone of mild surprise. 'Oh, publishers! Have you ever had any dealings with them?' I pulled out a snakeskin cigarette case containing a mixture of Russian and Egyptian cigarettes, placing one of the latter in a long ivory holder. I do hope that one day I do not make a ghastly error and produce the silver case of Virginia cigarettes from Jermyn Street belonging to Sir Richard Knight.

'I try to write,' I said, adding, 'sometimes. Tell me about publishers.'

'I'll tell you merely one short anecdote; other cries of author's indignation would fill a three-volume novel,' he replied. 'I finished *The Great God Pan* at white heat after years of neglect, during which I earned a small jobbing living as a private tutor, one who catalogues esoteric literature, the translator of the *Memoirs of Casanova* and so on. The misguided generosity of a few deceased relatives enabled me to persist in my endeavours to create Literature.' He spoke that word with reverence. 'Well, to my delight, the publisher asked me to come and see him. He informed me that he thought my work to be fine Literature indeed. He mentioned a sum that was to me a small fortune and declared that he would be deeply gratified if I might possibly write a book a year for his company in the future, for an advance as against future royalties, of course. I was virtually walking on air when I left his office. O fortunate author! Enter into the Glory of thy Publisher! Two weeks later, the manuscript of *The Great God Pan* was returned to me with a standard form rejection slip. I am not customarily a man of aggression but, as Blake has it, "The voice of honest indignation is the voice of God." I wrote a letter to this publisher and after a time received a pained reply to the effect that if I had only wit to realize "the cares of a publisher's life" then he was sure that I would not have written "so caustically".'

'I hope this frightful creature shot himself.'

'No.' Machen looked regretful. 'He is flourishing. Fortunately, I managed to sell *The Great God Pan* to John Lane for the Bodley Head *Keynotes* list and, since it has done moderately well, here I am being asked to execute another.'

'Are you not pleased?'

'It is difficult.' Machen frowned, puffed at his pipe and drank some gin. 'One dreams in fire and one works in clay.' I nodded agreement. 'The job of the novelist is to tell a wonderful story and to tell it in a wonderful manner. That is easier said than done. Ohh . . .' he sighed heavily, 'a shadow falls between the conception and the execution. You see, sir, I have taken the Queen's Shilling, so to speak, and what I must deliver to the publisher is a novel of sixty thousand words.'

'What is the problem, sir?' I demanded. 'Isn't this something that you have always wanted? Although I think that Oscar Wilde has said: "There are two tragedies in life: one is not getting what you want and the other is getting it". Surely, though, sixty thousand words can hardly be a problem when you have translated the *Memoirs of Casanova* in twelve – or is it ten? – volumes?'

'Translating the work of another man is easier than translating one's own vision,' Machen answered sombrely. 'You see, sir, take this great city all around us. No man can ever get to the bottom of London. It is the study of a lifetime and still one cannot know it in full. Outside this public house, in homes across the street, modest cups are being filled and emptied as the citizens continue with their dull and sober lives. Yet next door, in the attic, a poet may be dying by inches and next door to that, amidst the chink of the teacups, a man may have butchered a woman in a most horrific and grisly manner. I walk and explore the hidden areas of London, I see visions . . . yet my difficulty lies in communication. How I want to shake your heart with the vision of a young man burning for the adventure of Literature as he struggles in poverty and obscurity in a Notting Hill bedsit! How I want to shake your very being with spiritual atrocities that are committed within our very midst in the heart of our metropolis!' His eyes blazed with burning conviction for an instant, then: 'Sorry, I didn't mean to bore you. Just got a little carried away then.' He smiled uneasily. 'May I offer you another drink?' I nodded but asked for gin this time whilst he returned to Four Ale.

'I'm very interested in what you are saying, Mr Machen, and incidentally, my name is Septimus Keen. Now, I have much admiration for your writing. *Why* are you finding it so difficult to write this novel of which you speak?'

'I thought I'd already told you of some difficulties.' Machen relit his pipe and puffed out clouds of somewhat acrid smoke. 'But the main one is that my stories are too short. I take much pride in my craft and to make a tale longer than it should be is like cracking the bones of a man stretched on a rack. I have made three attempts hitherto for the writing of this book. I have written "The Novel of the Dark Valley", "The Novel of the Black Seal" and "The Novel of the White Powder". None of them are long enough and I cannot stretch them further. I think that I have not wrought them too badly, yet I have tried to bring about awe and have made it awful. I wanted to create a sense of horror and it becomes horrible. I still do not have a sixty-thousand-word novel as demanded and the deadline is approaching. Dear old Doctor Johnson said: "Sir: when a man is about to be hanged, it concentrates his mind wonderfully." I would that this were true in my case.'

'Mr Machen, you are too modest and despondent. Didn't Doctor Johnson also state: "Any man can write were he to set his mind doggedly to it"? Didn't he also state: "No man but a blockhead ever wrote but for money"?'

'Then I suppose I am a blockhead. I have never been much good with money, though I like it as much as the next man. *Lack* of money I abhor even more than the next man, to be candid. Yet I do not write primarily for money. Writing is a puzzling activity and hard to explain. It is unique to human beings. For instance, we have much in common with pigs, do we not? Both human beings and pigs wish to be kept moderately warm in the summer and moderately cool in the winter and demand at least a stye and a daily trough of swill, which in some circles they call consommé. Yet a pig will not labour to write a book that expresses all that is within him. One can suppose that there might be a very clever pig who writes a book in expectation of more swill but not, I think, a clever pig who writes something that is truthful or beautiful or both, simply for its own sake. What insanity is it that leads human beings to pursue this path and still write the wisest things yet known to mankind despite all despair and torment?'

'Yes, what does make a human being true and good?' I mused; 'since one might equally well ask: what makes a human being evil? What is evil, anyway?'

'Would you care to dine with me, sir?' Machen enquired gently. 'Or do you have another pressing engagement, Mr Keen?'

'What a charming idea. Where would you propose?'

'Do you enjoy experimentation in cuisine?' I nodded. 'Have you ever essayed Jewish cuisine?'

'No.'

'Neither had I until I came to London and found it one day by accident. To my surprise, I found it to be quite delicious. If you don't mind a walk of around a mile, I know a little place in Soho that might gratify the urge of your palate for a little culinary exploration. Don't be like my dear grandfather, who always used to say: "I don't want to try it because I might like it".'

Some moments later, we were walking through the smoky air of London and relishing the sights of the streets through which we sauntered. Machen proved to be an excellent guide, pointing out so many small items of interest underneath the shining stars. It amused me to think how this kindly, decent and creative man, who nevertheless wrote of horror and evil, knew nothing of my own involvement, already quite intimate, with these affairs.

'Evil . . .' Machen mused aloud. 'Are you familiar at all with the concept of *ecstasy*? Rapture, awe, wonder . . . call it what you will . . .?'

133

'Yes,' I responded truthfully as I thought of the Rites of Doctor Lipsius and his disciples.

'Sorcery and sanctity,' said Machen, 'these are the only true ecstasies.'

'What are they, in your opinion?'

'The saint accepts Nature and the sinner goes against it.'

'Can you give me an example of Sin?'

'Yes, and it is not vulgar crime. What would you think if your dog started talking to you in human accents? What would you think if the roses in your garden suddenly began to sing?'

'I'd be delighted,' I replied, 'if somewhat startled. I'm afraid I don't quite see where "Sin" comes into the matter. Show me something better – or, better still, something worse.'

'Well, you might find this three times worse for all I know,' Machen murmured as we entered a dingy side street and he pointed out a Star of David, which I had seen in the ritual of Lipsius as the magical Hexagram. As we came closer, I noticed that there was a light shining from within shuttered windows and a sign proclaiming 'Silver & Goldman'.

'The majority of Jews,' Machen explained to me, 'like to go home and go to bed early. However, a minority don't, which explains the existence of this establishment. Oh, one thing. Don't have their wine. It is *awful*.' We entered and I saw plain tables and benches and chairs and heard a positive *furore* of argumentation from some of the tables, since the place was packed. There were also silent men playing chess or solitary and reading books or newspapers while making notes. The only decorations on the bare white walls consisted of prints of Jewish prizefighters in the bare-knuckle ring, such as Daniel Mendoza, 'Dutch' Sam, 'Young Dutch' Sam and Barney Aaron; also, behind the counter, two sepia photographs of two fat women who were, Machen informed me, the mothers of Mr Silver and Mr Goldman.

'Good evening, Mr Machen, what a pleasure it is to see you again.' A large, fat, bald man with a huge hooked nose greeted Machen warmly. 'I think we have still your usual table for you.'

'Thank you, Mr Silver. And how is Mr Goldman?'

'He is cooking, as always. You know how he loves to cook. Ah, now, your table, sir.' As we sat down, it was impossible not to overhear conversation.

'No, no, Isaac, you're totally wrong. The Liberalism of Lord Rosebury is Liberalism only for the aristocracy. All right, his horses win the Derby. What else does he do?'

'If only Gladstone weren't so senile . . .'

'Bring back Disraeli!'

'What? From his grave?'

'Lord Randolph Churchill, that's the man!'

'Don't be ridiculous, Abie. Haven't you heard he has gone mad from the syphilis?'

'With Salisbury, at least it is safe.'

'What would you like, gentlemen?' I looked up from a menu I found virtually incomprehensible to see a slim and exquisitely handsome young man.

'Ah, good evening, Mr Goldman,' Machen greeted him pleasantly.

'And how are you, Mr Machen? It's a pleasure to see you here again.'

'Oh, I know good food,' Machen responded. 'Mr Keen, since you have confessed that you are not familiar with this style of cuisine, would you perhaps allow me to select the dishes?' I nodded immediate acquiescence. Machen rattled off some orders.

'Very good, sir,' said the dainty and pretty Mr Goldman.

'And will you be wanting your usual gin before and brandy after?'

'Thank you,' said Machen, 'and with our meal, we shall have beer. *Anything* but their wine,' he muttered as Mr Goldman departed for the kitchen. 'It is quite astonishing,' Machen said to me. 'I knew nothing of the Jews at all before I came to London save that I had always been told never to trust one. Instead, on the whole, I have found a very fine people. It amazes me that people still blame the Jack the Ripper murders of some years past upon the Jews.'

'It wasn't the Jews,' I said. 'Though it would be quite a clever idea to blame it on them.'

'You sound very certain about that.'

'I have taken quite an interest in the case.'

'There you go, Mr Machen!' Mr Silver declared heartily as his burly arms plonked down two gins with tonic in front of us. 'Enjoy it!' He walked over to a table where a pale man with a beard appeared to be unhappy about something. 'What's that? Yer salt beef sandwich? What's wrong with it? What?! You say the beef's no good?' To my stupefaction, Mr Silver peeled away the top slice of bread, seized the salt beef that was minus one bite, picked it up in his enormous hand to take an enormous bite, chewed thoughtfully and then said: 'What're you talking about? It's lovely beef!' He slapped it back on the bread and replaced its covering. 'Lovely! Go on! Eat it!'

'I am going,' said the customer. He put the money on the table. 'Here, I pay for everything I have eaten, Mr Silver. But not your salt beef sandwich. This I would not give to my dog. Give me my hat and my coat.'

'Get 'em yourself, Mr Finkelstein!' Mr Silver bellowed. 'Some people don't know good food when they see it. Or taste it.'

The pale Mr Finkelstein took his broad-brimmed hat and long, dark coat, slipping a book stamped with Hebrew letters into one of his pockets.

'I am not coming here again, Mr Silver,' he stated gravely.

'Too bloody right!' Mr Silver retorted as Mr Finkelstein left stiffly, though I overheard him muttering in an undertone: "'E'll be back. Where else 'as 'e got to go?'

'I can't help feeling, Keen,' Machen said to me very quietly, 'that the Jews do things just a little bit differently from the way we do.'

'Your soup, sir,' said the smiling Mr Goldman, suddenly appearing from nowhere.

'Ah, thank you.' Machen looked pleased. 'Now do try this. It is essentially chicken soup with dumplings made from unleavened bread which they call *matzo*.' I did try some and it was absolutely delicious. There was also a curious sensation of immediate nourishment. 'But you said that you had been studying the case of Jack the Ripper . . .?'

'Indeed.' Now the imp of the perverse, as Edgar Allan Poe has it, was dancing within my soul and I could not resist teasing Machen. 'Don't you find it strange how fact and fiction intermingle?'

'Yes . . .'

'I'm glad that you do. For you see, I really liked your story "The Inmost Light", published with *The Great God Pan*. In there, as I recall, there is a sudden appearance by a sinister character who is called Mr Davies and who is hunting for the jewel of the Inmost Light, which contains a human soul, and his appearance, mild enough in itself, strikes terror into a shopkeeper.'

'Not quite,' Machen answered. 'Mr Dyson, hero of my story, comes into possession of a mysterious package thrown at some man by a drunken prostitute. This contains verses:

> *Once around the glass*
> *And twice around the grass*
> *And thrice around the maple tree.*

'Below that, there is an address. Dyson goes there and finds it to be an ordinary London shop. However, as soon as he chants the above verses, the proprietor thinks that Dyson is the deadly Davies and hands over the package that contains the manuscript of the truth and the gem of the Inmost Light. I am not entirely happy with how I executed that story.'

'I have met Mr Davies.'

'Sorry . . .?'

'Well, Machen,' I said, 'I have at least met a man who *claims* to be a Mr Davies and I have seen him frighten a shopkeeper. Moreover, it is from him that I have learned the identity of Jack the Ripper.'

'Finished with your soup, gentlemen?' Mr Silver asked as Machen gasped and then nodded. The bowls were taken away and then new dishes were placed before us with equal lack of ceremony. 'Oh, and 'ere's yer beer. Glasses, mustn't forget those. Enjoy your meal!'

'I'm glad these knives are blunt,' said Machen, 'given the subject that we are discussing. Here is their rye bread, which goes well with it all. Here is what they call gefillte fish, a selection of minced white fish with onion and herbs, boiled and fried into balls. This pickled beetroot mixed with horseradish goes rather well with it, I find. And here is chopped liver. Take it, as they do, with chopped egg and chopped onion. The Jews say it is very good for the heart, and that may be so, but certainly I hope you share

138

my view that it tastes jolly nice.' I tried the dishes. 'What do you think!'

'Lovely!' a stentorian voice shouted out from behind us.

'Mr Silver, this is every bit as good as what my own mother makes! My compliments to Mr Goldman.'

'I'm sure he'll be pleased to hear them, Mr Cohen, glad you're enjoying it all. Mr Goldman learned it all from his muvver.'

'Actually, it's excellent,' I told Machen.

'Glad you're enjoying it as much as I am. But to return to Mr Davies and Jack the Ripper . . .'

'Of course.'

'I had always thought that Jack the Ripper was some deluded maniac.'

'He wasn't,' I said. 'Have you not noticed that these murders were not committed without a certain redeeming grace, a saving wit, a mitigating sophistication and savoir faire?'

'No,' said Machen. 'I just find them to be utterly revolting. A human being at his most bestial.' His face puckered with sincerely held disgust.

'These murders were done for the purposes of Black Magic,' I informed Machen, who promptly fastened upon me his entire attention. 'Look at the pattern. Look at where the bodies were laid out. Look at the Masonic nature of the mutilations: don't they all conform to a pattern of a penalty for breaking the Oaths of the Freemasons?'

'I am not one of the Widow's Sons, nor am I on the square.'

'Possibly not.'

'*Certainly* not.'

'But don't the *grimoires* of Black Magic state that certain human entrails must be obtained for certain spells?'

'Some . . . a barbaric superstition, surely?'

'A barbaric practice also.' I was enjoying myself at the expense of his growing perplexity. We had eaten all the food and Mr Silver whipped away our plates. Mr Goldman presented us with new ones and then proudly placed a large dish upon the centre of the table and whisked away its cover.

'Ah!' Machen beamed. 'Cold plaice that has been fried and soaked in the oil of the olive. The waiters won't be helping you here, so allow me, sir. I think you will find it quite exquisite. Oh, thank you, Mr Goldman, sliced, pickled cucumbers, quite essential, ah, and potato salad. *Bon appetit*! Now, Keen, are you seriously expecting me to believe that the Jack the Ripper murders were committed by a black magician?'

'Yes. Mmmm, this plaice is quite delectable. But it's more than that. We are talking about a *grouping* of black magicians.'

'Bah! That's ridiculous. Things like that simply don't happen in this day and age.'

'Yes, they do; and why do you write about them as if they did?' I chewed thoughtfully. 'Perhaps you want your horrors to come true? I'm telling you that some of them already have come to pass. Isn't "Helen" the name of the woman in *The Great God Pan*, possessed by Pan as the result of an experiment, who corrupts, perverts and destroys all men who come into contact with her? Well, I have met a woman calling herself Helen who claims to have had a part in the Jack the Ripper murders. I heard the story from Davies and Helen only recently, some days ago.'

'Days . . .' Machen looked dazed.

'Certainly. I am a member of a circle dedicated to Black Magic, though I had no part in the Ripper murders. I suppose it's all a rather extraordinary coincidence but Davies and Helen, along with a man called Richmond, are members of a highly sinister Black Magic circle committed to evil for its own sake and for the power which it can bring them. The head of this circle is Doctor Lipsius, an extremely learned man and a supreme master of evil. His disciples are encouraged to commit hideous crimes and to lead multiple lives, being most adept in disguise. One could almost call them The Three Impostors.'

Machen was silent for a time as he finished his meal and drained the last of his beer. Then he extracted an envelope and a pencil stub from his pocket.

'You have just given me a very interesting idea, Keen,' he said. 'Do you object if I make a few notes?'

'Not at all.'

'Thank you.'

'Hope you enjoyed that, Mr Machen,' Mr Silver barged in to seize our plates. 'Now, Mr Machen, with the brandy, will it be your usual lokschen pudding?'

'Yes,' he replied. 'Try some too, Keen. It's a bit like a cross between our suet pudding and our bread-and-butter pudding and, personally, I find it to be delightful.' I agreed. 'I think we shall enjoy that without any difficulty. Where I do have a difficulty is in endeavouring to believe your story. It was told to you, on your own admission, by people claiming to be "Davies" and "Helen". Am I seriously expected to believe that you are a member of a Black Magic circle consisting of people who commit hideous crimes under multiple identities?'

'I didn't think that you would believe me,' I replied, 'and I can hardly imagine you going to the police with so preposterous a tale. That is why I told it to you. Take it or leave it. I thought it might assist you in resolving the problems with your latest novel about which you were complaining earlier. Simply put your tales *within* tales: and have them told, in the Arabian Nights manner, by three people who pretend to be what they are not.'

'What an intriguing idea!' Machen exclaimed as the pudding and the brandy arrived. 'I must think about that further.'

Sometimes there is a sadistic glee to be had in telling the truth and *not* being believed, but I like to think that I did this man some good.

(*Editor's Note*: The Three Impostors *by Arthur Machen was published in 1895 and condemned by critics as 'decadent' in the wake of the Oscar Wilde scandal. In 1905, the publisher, Grant Richards, renewed his request to Machen for a sequel to* The Three Impostors. *In 1906, he published Machen's* The House of Souls, *which contained two tales from* The Three Impostors, 'The Novel of the Black Seal' *and* 'The Novel of the White Powder'. The Three Impostors *was republished as* Black Crusade *by Corgi, London 1966, omitting* 'The Novel of the Iron Maid': *and in 1995, J.M. Dent under the Everyman imprint published the full text of* The Three Impostors, *which was shortlisted for the retrospective 1895 Booker Prize. The sequel that Machen did not write,* The Devil's Maze *by Gerald Suster (Sphere, London 1979; Dell/Emerald, New York 1983: Penguin/Roc, London 1994), was shortlisted for the David Higham Literary Award, 1979.*)

'Are you really keen?' Arthur Machen asked me over the brandy.

'How do you mean?' I coughed. 'I'll pardon the pun.'

'With all respect,' Machen said politely, 'you have been telling me somewhat tall stories. Do you write at all yourself? Do you actually go out and murder people?'

'Well, I can tell you a story about killing, Machen,' I replied, grinning quite easily. 'Just give me another brandy.'

'Of course.'

I thereupon commenced to relate:

THE SPITTING IMAGE

by

Septimus Keen

L ife can be very boring. What more to it is there other than birth, copulation and death? This is why, having savoured the alleged joys of life, from an early age I resolved to become an assassin.

I think that I was swayed in that direction by reading thrilling accounts of the Old Man of the Mountains, Hassan-al-Sabbah, who preserved the balance of power in the Middle East by ordering the killing of anyone who threatened it. His disciples were initiated with the imbibing of the strongest hashish. After they had passed out, they were taken to a garden constructed so as to represent the Paradise of the Holy Qu'ran, an oasis of flowers, fountains and flowing streams, and for their attendants they had the legendary *houris*, beautiful whores sworn to attend to and satisfy every conceivable sensual craving. Following on from this bliss, they would be given drugged wine and would recover consciousness in the presence of the Old Man of the Mountains.

He would then explain to them that by his Magick, they had indeed visited Paradise and they could do so again in their lifetime as well as in their afterlives as long as they swore a life of obedience to his every word and proceeded to kill anyone at his command. Successful assassins were celebrated and given the temporary Paradise the Old Man had promised prior to being sent forth upon their next mission. Failures were killed, of course, but it was a quick death. Torture was only for traitors.

The Old Man of the Mountains once showed off his powers of command to a visiting ambassador. With a snap of his fingers, he ordered a sentry to hurl himself away to his death from the summit of a mountain. Thinking of eternal Paradise, the sentry obeyed the order.

I would have been happy under the regime of the Old Man of the Mountains but that is long gone. Back in 1892, I reached the conclusion that Life is absurd and that, in consequence, the taking of life is equally absurd, that there is no difference between one action and another. As the Old Man of the Mountains had said: *Nothing is true: everything is permitted.*

I trained with a gun, a knife, a rope, even a length of lead piping. My aim was straight and simple. I wanted to kill people quickly and cleanly in exchange for plenty of money that I would then spend on women, food, drink, clothes and entertainment. This seemed to be a very easy way of earning a living and enjoying life via death. I had no interest whatsoever in the infliction of unnecessary pain. One could say that my desire was to put people out of their misery.

I had no desire to murder at random unless some kind person would *pay* me to do so. I approached a cousin who worked at the War Office. He obtained an interview for me with one Major Short.

'I believe in Queen and Country,' I began. 'There are secret enemies of Queen and Country. I would like to kill them.'

'That's all you have to say?' Major Short. Short by name, short by nature, he had a wispy moustache and pale china-blue eyes.

'Yes.'

'Have you ever killed a man before?'

'No.'

'So you just dream about it, do you?'

'For the present, yes. In the future, I hope not.'

'Do you enjoy the idea?'

'Yes, but not excessively so.'

'Would you feel guilt if you killed a man?'

'I don't think so.'

'No guilt.' Short's fingers tapped irritably upon the top of his teak desk. 'I'm sorry, I don't think we have a place for you.'

'Why not?' I gasped. 'Queen and Country have enemies and surely you want them killed . . .?'

'No, it's not quite like that, old chap,' said Major Short. 'Allow me to explain something to you. Have you ever heard of *fair play?*'

'Yes.'

'Well, we couldn't possibly turn a loose cannon such as you upon the enemy,' Major Short said. 'Wouldn't be cricket. Good day.'

I left in disgust, wondering whether I should hire my services to an American industrial corporation bent upon expansion into Europe. Curiously enough, though, agents of British Intelligence did track me down and at a strictly unofficial meeting, where cricket was not discussed, I agreed to work for them.

I executed a series of kills, preferring methods that were straight and to the point. I felt no personal animosity towards any of my victims. The first time I shot a French spy; I watched the expression and anxiety in his face, the structure of it. You cannot kill a human being and forget his face. You never forget a man you kill. The first time, I cried and my guts came out of me. On the second occasion, there was no feeling. It was all a question of expediency.

I experienced satisfaction from staking out the kill. The first problem, of course, is how to get away. Too many amateurs lack a grasp of that basic truth. Frankly, I enjoyed my work and took a professional pride in the matter. There is a cold satisfaction in being paid for squeezing the trigger on a man who means nothing to you, nothing at all. One has the joy of a job done well. Yes, there is the smell of death about one and you can never shake it off, yet it seems to make one quite irresistibly fascinating to women even if they have no idea about one's occupation. No doubt this why women look so beautiful at funerals.

I was contented with my life, or at least as contented as any man can be, when I received the next briefing. Oddly enough, and of all people, it was Major Short who wanted to see me, especially since I had never been given any official rank.

'I'm told that you aren't doing a bad job for us,' he said. Oh, what an endearing piece of faint praise! 'There's a chap who is working for the French. Being rather a nuisance. Peter Evebury.' Superficially I remained calm though it was very difficult to stop my hands from trembling. Peter Evebury was an alias I had used two years before when I was building a cover for myself as an eccentric artist in Holloway. 'From all descriptions, he looks rather like you,' Major Short observed. 'Not your brother or anything, is he?'

'I don't have a brother.'

'Oh, well, there shouldn't be any problem, then. Have a look at the details.' He passed over a slender file and I read it with growing consternation, which I trust was not visibly reflected in my features. This Peter Evebury lived in exactly the same address as my alias, a bedsit on the Holloway Road just past the railway bridge as one goes north towards Archway, and he apparently pursued the occupation of artist. The physical description was virtually identical to mine, save that he had a beard. 'He's done for a number of our chaps.' Major Short lit his pipe, a calabash fashioned out of meerschaum and blew clouds of sweet pipe smoke into the air, latakia and perique, probably, on a base of cavendish. 'Any problems?' Outside, there was a thick, damp fog.

'Yes, sir,' I replied. 'I used to be Peter Evebury, living at this very address and pursuing the career of an artist.'

'Hm, curious. Well, you must be feeling rather indignant about this flagrant imposture.'

'Indignant, certainly. And also taken aback by the sheer audacity.'

'Well, I'll leave it to you,' said Major Short. 'Four weeks should be sufficient time, shouldn't it?'

As I stalked my prey, I really *was* flabbergasted *into a state of shocked silence* by the sheer audacity of the man who claimed to be Peter Evebury since, in my guise as a man looking for labouring work who smoked a clay pipe on street corners, I observed that he followed minutely the routine I had established for 'Peter Evebury'. Were it not for the brown and bristly moustache and beard, he could easily have passed for me. He never arose before midday. Then he went to a nearby café to have bacon and eggs with toast and tea. He purchased a cheap newspaper to read in the pub afterwards over a pint of porter. He then shopped to purchase the necessary provisions and, on occasion, artist's materials before returning to his home, 'my' former home, and, for all I knew, in the afternoons he did as I had done and actually worked at the art of painting. On the first day, he emerged at around six o'clock and I do not know where he went since he took a hansom and I was hardly in a suitable disguise to do likewise.

On the second day, I disguised myself as a clergyman

and hailed a cab to follow him. His cab took him to a brothel I had occasionally visited in the past so I could hardly follow him within its portals. Observation of his habits added to my growing perplexity. In the evenings he either dined in reasonably priced Soho restaurants with attractive women who sometimes returned to his lodgings, there being no landlady on the premises, or else he drank with men in local pubs, some of whom I had drunk with myself; he appeared to be on friendly terms with them.

Really, I had absolutely no idea who he actually was or why he should wish to adopt the identity and habits of my former alias. The essence of the matter was that he had to be killed and my method for so doing might give me a clue or two.

It is relatively easy to slay a man who has regular habits. I simply provided myself with a false beard and moustache, a faded frock coat and a battered topper, all of which had seen better days, so that any casual observer might mistake me for him. I have always found it a useful rule, when leaving a place where one has lived, to have copies of the keys cut, since one never knows when one might need them. When Peter Evebury went for his lunchtime pint and perused his deplorable newspaper, I entered the lodging house as though I had forgotten something and fortunately passed no one on the stairs. Still more fortunately, he had not changed the lock and so it was easy to obtain entry. For the most part, everything appeared to be exactly as I had left it. The bed and the table had not changed at all, nor had the chairs. The easel stood in the same place as before and the materials for painting were scattered around the floor. However, there was something really rather different about the oil paintings, watercolours and pastels that I saw. I had always painted, albeit not frightfully well, in a figurative style derived from Classicism. This man slashed broad strokes on canvas and paper in a manner I had never seen before. Some of his paintings consisted simply of *shapes* of things, though there was dazzling colour and a perplexing use of geometry, distorting all customary notions of perspective. I also noticed a series of townscapes, painted, in a seemingly haphazard manner, that were all upon the same theme: a man with a beard was chasing a clean-shaven man who resembled him through various streets of London in order to murder.

Although my nerves were troubled, there was a job to be done. An ill-placed wardrobe gave me a space to hide and wait. After a couple of hours, the man purporting to be Peter Evebury returned to the room, softly humming tunes to himself. It was easy to leap out and cosh him so as to render him unconscious. I happen to be quite skilful with a rope so it was all a matter of doubling up the body like a jack-knife, tying a noose around his neck and connecting it to his ankles while ensuring that his arms were rendered immobile. It took a time to put the unconscious body into a sack and to stuff old newspaper into his mouth, but eventually the matter was accomplished and the sack was placed within the wardrobe.

When he recovered consciousness, assuming that I had not hit him too hard, his first reaction would be to straighten out his legs. Of course, this would tighten the noose around his throat, causing him to become all out of breath. When the corpse would finally be found, one could argue that he had committed suicide, since he would have had every chance of living longer had he not chosen to straighten out his legs.

I informed Major Short that it was a case of 'Mission Accomplished' though I was somewhat surprised not to see anything in the newspapers. That was when my nightmare really began.

Major Short summoned me.

'You happen to have made an absolute pig's ear of the matter,' he told me angrily. 'You were just being too clever by half and Peter Evebury seems to be some sort of escapologist. He's also since done for another of our agents. Well done!' he sneered with biting sarcasm. 'Peter Evebury is now living in Vauxhall as the *Reverend* Peter Evebury. Here's the address. Kindly finish the bloody thing this time.'

I took no chances as I tracked the movements of 'the Reverend Peter Evebury'. A pea-souper of a London fog assisted my tracking of him through Vauxhall, an area notable for absolutely nothing whatsoever other than its own dismal mediocrity. Nobody saw me shoot him through the back of the neck in a dark alley he had chosen for his route home and, just to make sure of matters, I shot him four more times in the head. It was easy to escape into the mist.

'It's not possible,' I said when Major Short curtly informed me that I had bungled the job again and that Peter Evebury was, according to all reports, alive and well and living in Clapham, now disguised apparently as a building labourer. This information proved to be true in that there was a man identical to the description doing precisely that.

I was utterly bewildered by what had transpired but this time I was determined to kill the man once and for all. His habit of walking on Clapham Common after he had enjoyed a few pints following his work made the matter relatively easy. This time I used a butcher's cleaver to slash his throat and cut off his head. Since the reports had informed me that he wore a silver ring on his right index finger, and there it was, I chopped it off and gave it as proof to Major Short, though he said that I was 'going just a little bit too far'. The event, thank heavens, *was* finally reported in the newspapers and I assumed that, eventually, I had seen the last of the man who had assumed the identity of 'Peter Evebury'.

As Oscar Wilde says: 'The truth is never pure and rarely simple.' Over the succeeding year, I was employed to kill five people, matters accomplished with my customary efficiency. Unfortunately, every single victim, though he did not have the name, had the face, as he died, of Peter Evebury.

Some element of truth came home to me on the night I entered my house in Chelsea, near the river and just off the King's Road. A lightning attack put me on my back with a razor held against my throat and I looked up with horror into the features of Peter Evebury.

'It would give me great pleasure,' he said in a voice curiously like mine, 'to slit your throat. After all, haven't you tried to kill me? Don't you claim to have killed me?'

'Who are you?' I gasped.

'Peter Evebury,' he replied, 'otherwise known as Death. Have you not sworn yourself to be an assassin? I am your deity. You have not made a Pact with the Devil: but you *have* made a Pact with Death. Every human being is a condemned criminal, only he or she does not know the date of the execution. You, as an assassin, are subject to the rule of Death. I can kill you now. I can kill you any time I desire. The question is simply whether I kill you now or later. Do you want to live longer?'

'Yes.'

'Most people do,' Death said, 'though I sometimes fail to see why. Still, I suppose it is not a bad life as an assassin. Looking around your home, I see that you live well.'

'Could you please take that razor away from my throat?'

'Makes you nervous, does it?' Death chuckled. 'On one condition.'

'Yes . . .?'

'I will give you five more years of a prosperous life providing that you kill Major Short. His hypocrisy annoys me and his manner bores me. You have four weeks to do so or I shall come and see you again for the last time, if you understand me correctly.'

'Yes . . .' I said, then I coughed and choked: and when I finally recovered my senses, there was no evidence to show that I had had any visitor at all.

Killing Major Short proved to be a relatively easy matter. I invited him to dinner and for pudding gave him apple crumble, apparently his favourite dish, with plenty of whipped cream. There was sodium morphate in the pie: this tastes exactly like apples and brings on a fatal heart attack, accompanied by profuse vomiting. The poison comes out in the vomit, which is not usually analysed. The whole matter was really rather socially embarrassing, though I found it quite amusing when Short's florid face turned purple and then became a sickly green. I had never really liked him, anyway.

Inevitably, suspicion fell upon me but, since nothing could be proved, I was soon cleared for further work. Two years have passed since my fatal night with Major Short and I enjoy my life more than ever before. I simply have to live with the fact that Death will come for me three years from my writing of this account. Death has been a gentleman in my case and I am making the best of the time that I have left. However, I do wish that the finishing touch of Death had not been to transform the bloated features of Major Short into those of Peter Evebury, which features are my own.

'A most absorbing and provoking tale,' Arthur Machen commented. 'Not autobiographical, surely, by any chance?'

'Yes.'

'Forgive me, sir, I find that very hard to believe. A man who kills other men for his living does not relate the details of the matter to strangers whom he meets in public houses.'

'You don't believe me at all, do you?'

'Frankly, no.'

'That is why I told it to you. I am in no danger on account of it. I told it to you *precisely* because you would not believe me.'

It was then that an event occurred that later led Machen to exclaim in a review written for the *Pall Mall Gazette*: 'The world is a much stranger place than is commonly supposed.' Although I was as astonished by the matter as he was, I maintained my composure. There are, I am convinced, random events within the Universe that are, in rational terms, inexplicable.

A man walked into the Jewish restaurant and asked for chicken soup. In appearance, he was the spitting image of me save that he had a moustache and beard.

'Must be Death,' I laughed, casually tossing enough money to pay for our dinner onto the table. 'A pleasure dining with you, sir, and thank you.'

Pleasant Mr Machen looked somewhat more pale than usual as I left.

So did I.

CHAPTER SEVEN

FROM THE LETTERS
OF SIR PERCY SULGRAVE

Dear Amelia,
   I do hope that you are enjoying your time in Harrogate with Barbara Crockford – to whom, incidentally, do send my best regards. For my own part, I have been hot on the scent of Jack the Ripper.

I am sure that there is rather more to all this than meets the eye. I have spent many an hour studying the various newspaper accounts and also such information as the police are prepared to release. As you know, I am convinced that these atrocious murders could not have been done by some crude brute.

I awoke this morning determined to go and make my own personal investigations. It's a hearty breakfast that sets me up and running and so Martin, who is a frightfully good chap, made me my customary porridge with cream and demerara sugar followed by bloaters on toast and then eggs and bacon with tomato, sausage and kidneys, baked beans and mushrooms, all fried well. There was plenty of toast with lashings of deep-yellow Jersey butter and orange marmalade from Seville to follow that, of course, a perfect accompaniment to the perusal of my morning newspaper. I don't know why I demand that Martin irons it. Tradition of the manservant, I suppose. Then, as you know, I like a couple of stiff whiskies with seltzer after breakfast to put me in the mood for things in general.

I thought that a private carriage might conceivably be

too conspicuous in the East End, though I was to be proven wrong, and resolved that my strategy would be based around the taking of hansom cabs. The East End is, of course, a somewhat dangerous and desperate area, so I packed my Webley revolver just in case. But what to wear? I tell you, Amelia, I now know the feeling of the debutante who says: 'But mother, I don't have a *thing* to wear!' when she happens to have two wardrobes.

Eventually I decided upon an old and worn bowler hat of good quality and an ageing grey suit, immaculately tailored, so as to give the impression of fading gentility. I also took my swordstick.

It is very easy to hail a cab if you live just off Maida Vale but as I clambered within, having given directions to Whitechapel, it suddenly occurred to me that the East End might be easy to enter but difficult to leave. This turned out to be a needless worry. As I saw soon enough, there were plenty of elegant carriages in the East End, some belonging to men who enjoyed sexual experiences with 'rough trade' and others owned by those who organized and controlled it. The dens of gambling, opium and prostitution, sucking in the wealthy with a taste for dissipation, ensured that there would be a roaring trade in the hiring of cabs.

In the cab I read *Tales of Mean Streets* by Arthur Morrison, noting the passage:

'The East End is a vast city, as famous in its way as any the hand of man has made. But who knows the East End? It is down through Cornhill and out beyond Leadenhall Street and Aldgate Pump, one will say: a shocking place, where he once went with a curate; an evil plexus of slums that hide human creeping things; where filthy men and women live on penn'orths of gin, where collars and clean ties are decencies unknown, where every citizen wears a black eye . . .' I was going to what one journalist has described as being 'perhaps the foulest and most dangerous street in the whole of the metropolis.'

It was midday when I left the cab, dreading importuning custom. Fortunately, this did not occur: I imagine that the gin-sozzled were still sleeping off the effects of the previous night's excess. I walked along the Flower and Dean Street rookery, which consisted almost entirely of dubious lodging houses. I was struck by the intensely unpleasant smell of boiling cabbages; and some women were frying the remains of these boiling cabbages in cheap oil. It was all most insalubrious. I noted that this was the haunt of the Jack the Ripper victims. Annie Chapman and Elizabeth Stride had stayed at No. 35, and Catherine Eddowes at No. 55. Next door, at Nos. 56–57, known as the White House, there had been the lodger Mary Anne Nichols, first victim of the Ripper. I noticed that any criminal could enter the street at one end with the police, criminal enemies or vigilantes on his tail and easily flee into other streets by means of connecting passages and doors.

There was a rough public house further up the street where, even at this early hour, men and women were becoming quite disgracefully drunk on cheap gin. I took a beer and perused the official report, since the local police could make no sense of the matter, of Inspector Abberline of Scotland Yard, formerly in charge of the Whitechapel Criminal Investigation Department.

About 3.40 a.m. ult. as Charles Cross, carman of 22 Doveton Street, Cambridge Road, Bethnal Green, was passing through Bucks Row, Whitechapel (on his way to work) he noticed a woman on her back on the footway (against some gates leading into a stable yard). He stopped to look at the woman when another carman, also on his way to work, named Robert Paul of 30 Fosters Street, Bethnal Green, came up and Cross called his attention to the woman, but being dark he did not notice any blood, and passed on with the intention of informing the first constable they met. On arriving at the corner of Hanbury Street and old Montague Street they met P.C.55H Mizen and acquainted him of what they had seen and on the constable proceeding towards the spot he found that P.C.97J Neil had found the woman, and was calling for assistance.

P.C. Neil turned on his light and discovered that the woman's throat was severely cut. P.C.96J Thain was also called and sent at once for Dr Llewellyn of 152, Whitechapel Road, who quickly arrived on the scene and pronounced life extinct and ordered the removal of the body to the mortuary. In the meantime P.C. Mizen had been sent for the ambulance and assistance from Bethnal Green station, and on Inspector Spratling and other officers arriving, the body was removed to the Mortuary. On arriving there the inspector made a further examination and found that the abdomen had also been severely cut in several places, exposing the intestines. The Inspector acquainted Dr Llewellyn who afterwards made a more minute examination and found that the wounds to the abdomen were in themselves sufficient to cause death, and he expressed an opinion that they were inflicted before the throat was cut.

The body was not then identified. On the clothing being carefully examined by Inspector Heston he found some of the underclothing bore the mark of Lambeth Workhouse which led to the body being identified as that of a former inmate named Mary Anne Nichols, and by that means we were able to trace the relatives and complete the identity. It was found she was the wife of William Nichols of 37, Coberg Street, Old Kent Road, a printer in the employ of Messrs. Perkins Baker and Co., Whitefriars Street, City, from whom she was separated about nine years through her drunken and immoral habits, and that for several years past she had from time to time been an inmate of various Workhouses and entered the service of Mr Cowdry, Ingleside, Rose Hill Road, Wandsworth. She remained there until the 12th July when she absconded stealing various articles of apparel. A day or two after she became a lodger at 18, Thrawl Street, Spitalfields, a common lodging house, and at another common lodging house at 56, Flower and Dean Street up to the night of the murder.

About 1.40 p.m. that morning she was seen in the kitchen at 18, Thrawl Street when she informed the deputy of the lodging house that she had no money to pay for her lodging. She requested that her bed should be kept for her and left stating that she would soon get the money. At that time she was drunk. She was next seen at 2.30 a.m. at the corner of Osborne Street. Whitechapel Road by Ellen Holland, a lodger in the same house, who seeing she was very drunk requested her to return with her to the lodging house. She however refused, remarking that she would soon be back and walked away down the Whitechapel Road in the direction of where her body was found. There can be no doubt with regard to the time because the Whitechapel clock chimed 2.30 and Holland called attention of the deceased to the time.

We have been unable to find any person who saw her alive after Holland left her. The distance from Osborne Street to Bucks Row would be about half a mile. Inquiries were made in every conceivable quarter with a view to trace the murderer but not the slightest clue can at present be obtained.

Not the slightest clue, eh? Through my various connections with the police I had managed to obtain a special report by Inspector J. Spratling of J Division.

P.C. J. Neil reports at 3.45 a.m., 31 inst. August, he found the dead body of a woman lying on her back with her clothes a little above her knees, lying with her throat cut from ear to ear on a yard crossing at Buck's Row. Whitechapel. P.C. [Neil] obtained assistance of P.C.s 55H Mizen and 96J Thain. The latter called Dr Llewellyn. No. 152, Whitechapel Road. He arrived quickly and pronounced life to be extinct, apparently but a few minutes. He directed her removal to the mortuary, stating that he would make a further examination there, which was done on the ambulance [a sort of handcart].

Upon my arrival there and taking a description I found that she had been disembowelled, and at once sent to inform the doctor of it. He arrived quickly and on further examination stated that her throat had been cut from left to right, two distinct cuts being on the left side. The windpipe, gullet and spinal cord being cut through, a bruise apparently of a thumb being on the lower left jaw, also one on left cheek. The abdomen had been cut open from centre of bottom of ribs on right side, under pelvis to the left of the stomach, there the wound was jagged. The omentum or coating of the stomach was also cut in several places, with a strong bladed knife, supposed to have been done by some left handed person, death being almost instantaneous.

Description: age about 45, length 5ft 2 or 3; complexion dark; hair dark brown turning grey, eyes brown, bruise on lower right jaw and left cheek, slight laceration of tongue, one tooth deficient front of upper jaw, two on left of lower.

Dress: brown ulster, 7 large brass buttons (figure of a female riding horse and a man at side thereon), brown linsey frock, grey woollen pettycoat, flannel drawers, white chest flannel, brown stays, black ribbed woollen stockings, men's spring sided boots, cut on uppers, tips on heels, black straw bonnet, trimmed black velvet.

I made enquiries and was informed by Mrs Emma Breen, a widow, New Cottage adjoining, and Mr Walter Purkis, Eagle Wharf opposite, also of William Louis, nightwatchman to Messrs. Brown and Eagle at wharf near, none of whom heard

any screams during the night, or anything to lead them to
believe that murder had been committed there.

P.C. states he passed through the Row at 3.15 a.m. and
P.C.10 Kirley about the same time, but the woman was not
there then and is not known to them.

Buck's Row is an ugly place. Even in daylight, Essex
Wharf is high, dark and sinister, casting a malignant
shadow over a street that reeks of abominable deeds done
by dark. Drunken beggars lay sprawled in the doorways
and even more drunken prostitutes implored my custom as
I followed in the footsteps of the Ripper. I felt disgusted by
the abominable slaughter he had committed and resolved
that I would solve the case. Here I could already discern
the scabrous hand of Dr Lipsius. I know you think that
this is an unhealthy obsession of mine but consider the
following facts.

PC Mizen and PC Neil, who patrolled Buck's Row every
half-hour, had seen no one acting suspiciously. The same
is true of Carman Cross, who saw the body and informed
the police. Two nightwatchmen, one from a nearby tar
factory and the other from a wool depot in Buck's Row,
declared that it had been an unusually uneventful night.
Mr Walter Purkis, the manager of Essex Wharf, was in
bed with his wife. His house overlooked the spot where
Mary Anne 'Polly' Nichols was found, roughly fifty yards
from the nearest gaslamp. Neither Mr nor Mrs Purkis heard
anything untoward, even though Mrs Purkis was suffering
from insomnia. At New Cottage, further down the street,
a Mrs Emma Green was also suffering from insomnia, yet
although her first-floor bedroom window was just roughly
fifteen feet from where the body was found, she alleged
that there had been nothing to alert her attention.

Well, I ask you, Amelia, how in heaven or on earth (or

in hell) did Jack the Ripper manage to seize Mary Anne 'Polly' Nichols, smash her to the ground, tear her abdomen from the ribs down and under the stomach, slit the lining of the stomach itself, stab the genitals and slit the throat all the way back to the spine, then depart without anybody intimately connected with this street noticing anything?

Obviously, the woman wasn't murdered in Buck's Row: the body was dumped there; and nobody paid much attention to the dumping of what could have been a sack of rubbish.

I proceeded to Spitalfields, just half a mile north west of Buck's Row, and No. 29 Hanbury Street, in the courtyard of which what remained of Annie Chapman had been left. What a set of squalid slums populated by demented derelicts! Inspector Abberline has told me that there was no doubt that the same person committed both murders though I might add the possibility that a team directed by Lipsius was operating all the while in a similar style.

The keynote is this: at 6:20 a.m., police doctor Phillips examined Annie Chapman's body, discovered at 5:55 a.m. by John Davis, a market porter, and concluded that the victim had been foully murdered around 4:20 a.m. The problem here is that John Richardson, son of Amelia Richardson, the landlady of No. 29, went into the courtyard at 5:00 a.m., sitting on the steps leading from the back door of his mother's house to trim a loose piece of leather from his boot. This took him quite a few minutes until he decided that his knife was too blunt for the job and went off to the nearby market so as to borrow another from a workmate. It is quite impossible that he could have sat there at 5:00 a.m. without noticing a body quite hideously mutilated and dumped just forty minutes previously in front of where he was now sitting.

The deduction is inexorable. The murder was done at

4:20 a.m. and the corpse was dumped in the backyard some minutes after 5:00 a.m. As John Richardson said at the inquest:

'I was there about a minute and a half or two minutes at the outside. It was beginning to get light but not thoroughly. I could see all over the place. I couldn't have failed to notice a dead woman if she had been lying there.'

The Lancet observed that the murders were 'obviously the work of an expert – of one, *at least*, who had such knowledge of anatomical or pathological examinations as to be enabled to secure the pelvic organs with one sweep of the knife.' The emphasis is mine.

At the inquest, Dr Phillips broadly concurred.

'There were indications of anatomical knowledge. The whole of the body was not present, the absent portions are from the abdomen. The way in which these portions were extracted showed anatomical knowledge.'

It was now off to Berner Street in the City, a place described rather well by *The Times*.

The scene of the . . . crime is a narrow court in Berners [sic] Street, a quiet thoroughfare running from Commercial Street down to the London, Tilbury and Southend Railway. At the entrance to the court are a pair of large wooden gates, in one of which is a small wicket for use when the gates are closed. At the hour when the murderer accomplished his purpose these gates were open, indeed, according to the testimony of those living near, the entrance to the court is seldom closed. For a distance of 18ft or 20ft from the street there is a dead wall on each side of the court, the effect of which is to enshroud the intervening space in absolute darkness after sunset. Further back some light is thrown into the court from the window of a workmen's club, which occupies the whole length of the court on the right, and from a number of cottages occupied

mainly by tailors and cigarette makers on the left. At the time
when the murder was committed, however, the lights in all
the dwelling-houses in question had been extinguished, while
such illumination as came from the club, being from the upper
story, would fall on the cottages opposite and would serve to
intensify the gloom of the rest of the court.

The victim was Elizabeth Stride, a prostitute known in the
trade as 'Long Liz'. This time there was no mutilation; it
was a simple slash of the throat. Blood was still running
over the cobbles when it was discovered at 1:00 a.m. by
a Mr Louis Diemschutz, steward of the International
Working Mens' Club at 40 Berner Street, where he had
been enjoying a debate on 'The Necessity for Socialism
among Jews' followed by a communal sing-song. He was
going home in his pony and trap when he first sighted
the body and prodded it with his whip. Subsequent details
are contained in the official Home Office report by Chief
Inspector Donald Swanson.

I beg to report that the following are the particulars respecting
the murder of Elizabeth Stride on the morning of 30th
September.

1 a.m. 30th Sept. A body of a woman was found with the
throat cut, but not otherwise mutilated, by Louis Diemschutz
(secretary to the socialist club) inside the gates of Dutfields
Yard in Berner Street, Commercial road east, who gave
information to the police. P.C. Lamb proceeded with him
to the spot and sent for Drs Blackwell and Phillips.

1.10 a.m. Body examined by the doctors mentioned who
pronounced life extinct, the position of the body was as
follows: – lying on left side, left arm extended from elbow,
cachous lying in the hand, right arm over stomach, back
of hand and inner surface of wrist dotted with blood, legs

drawn up, knees fixed, feet close to wall, body still warm, silk handkerchief round throat, slightly torn corresponding to the angle of right jaw, throat deeply gashed and below the right angle apparent abrasion of skin about an inch and a quarter in diameter.

Search was made of yard but no instrument found.

Given the curious positioning of the body, I began to contemplate the signs, pains and penalties of oath-breaking in Freemasonry, or Black Magic.

Certainly the police reacted with alacrity. Seventy-six butchers and slaughterers were investigated, eighty people were detained for questioning at various police stations and no less than eighty thousand pamphlets were distributed. At the end of the day, still nobody had a clue. It is a macabre thought that working Jewish socialists were singing cheerful and inspiring songs just by the gate entrance to Dutfield's Yard where the body of Elizabeth Stride was found.

There was another murder most horrible on the very same morning of 30th September, that of Catherine Eddowes in Mitre Square, which is where I next went. She had collapsed drunkenly on the pavement of Aldgate High Street, apparently imitating the noises of a fire-engine. The police had taken her into custody, then released her at 1:00 a.m., the very moment that the body of Elizabeth Stride was found. She had given her name to the police as 'Mary Kelly.'

PC Watkins found her lying in a pool of blood in Mitre Square roughly forty-five minutes later, describing the sight as being 'like a pig in the market'. The one feeble lamp in Mitre Square stood sixty-five feet away from the body. I quote from the medical report given at the inquest by Dr Frederick Gordon Brown:

The body was on its back, the head turned to left shoulder, the arms by the side of the body as if they had fallen there. Both palms upwards, the fingers slightly bent. A thimble was lying off the finger on the right side.

The clothes drawn up above the abdomen, the thighs were naked. Left leg extended in a line with the body. The abdomen was exposed, right leg bent at the thigh and knee.

The bonnet was at the back of the head – great disfigurement of the face. The throat cut. Across, below the throat, was a neckerchief. The upper part of the dress was pulled open a little way. The abdomen was all exposed. The intestines were drawn out to a large extent and placed over the right shoulder; they were smeared over with some feculent matter. A piece of about two feet was quite detached from the body and placed between the body and the left arm, apparently by design. The lobe and auricle of the right ear was cut obliquely through.

There was a quantity of clotted blood on the pavement on the left of the neck round the shoulder and upper part of the arm, and the blood coloured serum which had flowed under the neck to the right shoulder; the pavement sloping in that direction.

Body was quite warm, no death stiffening had taken place. She must have been dead most likely within half an hour. We looked for superficial bruises and saw none. No blood on the skin of the abdomen or secretion of any kind on the thighs. No spurting of blood on the bricks or pavement around. No marks of blood below the middle of the body. Several buttons were found in the clotted blood after the body was removed. There was no blood on the front of the clothes. There were no traces of recent connection.

Now there are some curious facts about this particular grisly murder that I hope you will find as peculiar as I do. They concern the testimony of two police constables,

Harvey and Watkins, which latter discovered the savagely mutilated corpse. PC Watkins testified that having passed through Mitre Square as a church clock struck 1:30 a.m., he returned 'about twelve or fourteen minutes later' to discover the body.

That is 1:42 to 1:44 a.m.

PC Harvey stated that on his beat along Church Passage, he looked into Mitre Square at 'about 18 or 19 minutes to 2'.

That is 1:41 to 1:42 a.m.

It is possible that owing to the gloom, PC Harvey failed to see anything unlawful in Mitre Square. That would give the murderer twelve to fourteen minutes during Watkins's patrol. During this time, however, both constables were going around all three entrances and every street around Mitre Square.

If the murder actually took place in Mitre Square, it was done in at least three minutes and at most fourteen minutes with PC Watkins thirty-five yards' walking distance from the corpse and nineteen yards' hearing distance.

I think of the testimony of Dr Brown at the inquest:

'. . . it would take a great deal of skill and knowledge as to the position of the kidney to remove it. The kidney could easily be overlooked, for it is covered by a membrane.'

I think of the testimony of Divisional Police Surgeon George William Sequeira as stated at the inquest:

'I know this locality. This is the darkest portion of the square. There would have been insufficient light to enable the perpetrator of the deed to have committed the deed without the addition of any light.'

It is obvious, Amelia, to any thinking person, that even one expert with a knife could not have disembowelled Catherine Eddowes, taken a kidney and slashed intricate signs upon her face in virtual darkness within, at maximum, fourteen minutes. One can only conclude that she was murdered elsewhere and her body dumped in Mitre Square with its historic freemasonic associations in the cause of Black Magic of the deepest dye.

It was now time to look at the site where Mary Kelly, former nanny to the illegitimate daughter of the Prince of Wales and in the employment of the artist Walter Sickert was horribly butchered. This had taken place at Millers Court, Dorset Street, known locally as 'Dosset Street' on account of its brightly lit doss-houses. As I wandered through this street that stank of urine and dead fish, I saw a bundle of rags, though this turned out to be a drunken old woman with raggedy hair who was singing hoarsely:

> 'I wish I was
> A pretty little whore . . .
> I'd always be rich
> I'd never be poor.
> In my pretty little house
> With my little red light
> I'd sleep all day
> And I'd dance all night.'

I consulted my notebook where I had copied out statements made to the police:

Statement of Thomas Bowyer, 37, Dorset Street, Spitalfields, in the employ of John McCarthy, Lodging house keeper, Dorset Street.

Says that at 10.45 a.m. 9th instant, he was sent by his employer to number 13 room, Millers Court, Dorset Street for the rent. He knocked at the door, but not getting any answer he threw the blinds back and looked through the window, which was broken, and saw the body of the deceased woman whom he knew as Mary Jane. Seeing that there was a quantity of blood on her person and that she had been apparently murdered, he immediately went and informed his employer Mr McCarthy, who also looked into the room and at once dispatched Bowyer to the police station, Commercial Road, and informed the inspector on duty (Insp. Beck) who returned with him and his employer who had also followed to the station. He knew the deceased and also a man named Joe, who had occupied the room for some months past.

Statement of John McCarthy, Lodging House Keeper, 27 Dorset Street, Spitalfields.

I sent my man Thomas Bowyer to No. 13 room, Millers Court, Dorset Street owned by me for the rent. Bowyer came back and called me, telling me what he had seen. I went with him back and looked through the broken window, where I saw the mutilated remains of deceased whom I knew as Mary Jane Kelly. I then despatched Bowyer to the Police Station, Commercial Street (following myself) to acquaint the police. The Inspector on duty returned with us to the scene at Millers Court. I let the room about ten months ago to the deceased and a man named Joe, who I believed to be her husband. It was a furnished room at 4/6 per week. I sent for the rent because for some time past they had not kept their payments regularly. I have since heard the man named Joe was not her husband and that he had recently left her.

Statement of Joe Barnett, now residing at 24 and 25 New Street, Bishopsgate (a common lodging house).

I am a porter in Billingsgate Market, but have been out of employment for the past 3 or 4 months. I have been living with Marie Jeanette Kelly who occupied No. 13 room, Millers Court. I have lived with her altogether about 18 months, for the last eight months in Millers Court, until last Tuesday week (Ulto) when in consequence of not earning sufficient money to give her and her resorting to prostitution, I resolved on leaving her, but I was friendly with her and called to see her between seven and eight p.m. Thursday (8th) and told her I was very sorry I had no work and that I could not give her any money. I left her about 8 o'clock same evening and that was the last time I saw her alive.

Elizabeth Prater, wife of William Prater of No. 20 room, 27 Dorset Street, states as follows:

I went out about 9 p.m. on the 8th and returned about 1.30. I was speaking for a short time to a Mr McCarthy who keeps a chandler's shop at the corner of the court. I then went up to bed. About 3.30 or 4 a.m. I was awakened by kitten walking across my neck, and just then I heard screams of murder about two or three times in a female voice. I did not take much notice of the cries as I frequently hear such cries from the back of the lodging-house where the windows look into Millers Court. From 1 a.m. to 1.30 a.m. no one passed up the court, if they did I should have seen them. I was up again and downstairs in the court at 5.30 a.m. but saw no one except two or three carmen harnessing their horses in Dorset Street. I went to the 'Ten Bells' P.H. at the corner of Church Street and had some rum. I then returned and went to bed again without undressing and slept until about 11 a.m.

Statement of Sarah Lewis, No. 24 Great Pearl Street, Spitalfields, a laundress.

Between 2 and 3 o'clock this morning I came to stop with the Keylers at No. 2 Millers Court as I had had a few words with my husband. When I came up the court there was a man standing over against the lodging house on the opposite side in Dorset Street but I cannot describe him. Shortly before 4 o'clock I heard a scream like that of a young woman, and seemed to be not far away. She screamed out murder. I only heard it once. I did not look out of the window. I did not know the deceased.

Sarah Lewis further said that when in company with

another female on Wednesday evening last at Bethnal Green, a suspicious man accosted her. He carried a black bag.

Statement of Mary Ann Cox, No. 5 Room, Millers Court, Dorset Street, Spitalfields.

I am a widow and an unfortunate. I have known the female occupying No. 13 room, Millers Court about 8 months. I knew her by the name of Mary Jane. About a quarter to twelve last night I came into Dorset Street from Commercial Street, and saw walking in front of me Mary Jane with a man. They turned into the court and as I entered the court they went indoors. As they were going into her room, I said good night Mary Jane. She was very drunk and could scarcely answer to me, but said good night. The man was carrying a quart can of beer. I shortly afterwards heard her singing. I went out shortly after twelve and returned about one o'clock and she was still singing in her room. I went out again shortly after one o'clock and returned at 3 o'clock. There was no light in her room then and all was quiet, and I heard no noise all night.

The man whom I saw was about 36 years old, about 5 ft 5 in. high, complexion fresh and I believe he had blotches on his face, small side whiskers and a thick carroty moustache, dressed in shabby dark clothes, dark overcoat and black felt hat.

Mary Jane was dressed I think, last night when I saw her, in a linsey frock, red knitted cross-over around shoulders, had no hat or bonnet on.

Statement of Julia Venturney.

I occupy No. 1 room, Millers Court. I am a widow but now living with a man named Harry Owen. I was awake all night and could not sleep. I have known the person occupying No. 13 room opposite mine for about 4 months. I knew the man who I saw down stairs (Joe Barnett) he is called Joe, he lived with her until quite recently. I have heard him say that he did not like her going out on the streets. He frequently gave her money. He was very kind to her. He said he would not live with her while she led that course of life. She used to get tipsy occasionally. She broke the windows a few weeks ago whilst she was drunk. She told me she was very fond of another man named Joe, and he had often ill used her because she cohabited with Joe (Barnett). I saw her last yesterday, Thursday about 10 a.m.

Statement of Maria Harvey of 3, New Court, Dorset Street.

I slept two nights with Mary Jane Kelly, Monday and Tuesday last. I then took a room at the above house. I saw her last about five minutes to seven last night in her own room, when Barnett called. I then left. They seemed to be on the best of terms, I left an overcoat, two dirty cotton shirts, a boy's shirt and a girl's white petticoat and black crape bonnet in the room. The overcoat shown me by police is the one I left there.

Statement of Caroline Maxwell, 14 Dorset Street, Spitalfields, the wife of Henry Maxwell, a lodging house deputy.

I have known deceased woman during the past 4 months, she was known as Mary Jane, and that since Joe Barnett left her she has obtained her living as an unfortunate. I was on speaking terms with her although I had not seen her for 3 weeks until Friday morning 9th instant about half past 8 o'clock. She was then standing at the corner of Millers Court in Dorset Street. I said to her, what brings you up so early. She said, I have the horrors of drink upon me as I have been drinking for some days past. I said why don't you go to Mrs Ringer's* and have ½ pint of beer. She said, I have been there and had it, but I brought it all up again. At the same time she pointed to some vomit in the roadway. I then passed on, and went to Bishopsgate on an errand, and returned to Dorset Street about 9 a.m. I then noticed deceased standing outside Ringers public house. She was talking to a man, age I think about 30, height about 5 ft 5 in, stout, dressed as a

Market Porter. I was some distance away and am doubtful whether I could identify him. The deceased wore a dark dress, black velvet body, and coloured wrapper round her neck.

These dry details disguise what could be called the worst sight this side of hell. Tom Bowyer, the rent collector, failed to obtain entrance to Mary Kelly's room at 10:45 a.m. Then, deciding that the door was locked against him, he tried the window. Pushing aside a coat hung over the broken window pane, he pulled back the curtain and saw a slaughtered animal, what was left of Mary Jane Kelly, lying on the bed. The murderer had slashed off her nose, ears, eyebrows and cheeks, all of which lay in a little heap next to her head. The lips had been torn away and the cheeks sliced into ribbons.

The throat had been cut through to the spinal column. As for her breasts, one was placed by her right foot, the other under her head along with her uterus and both kidneys. Her liver lay between her feet. Her intestines lay on the right side of her body and her spleen on the left. The Ripper had hacked through her right lung and also removed her heart in its entirety. A small amount of flesh, congealing in its own blood, lay on the bedside table next to the body. The right buttock had been mutilated, the right thigh torn open to the bone and the left skinned down to the knee, with the calf slashed open also.

I felt a deep and abiding sense of horror and disgust. It was barely possible to accept that any human being could conceivably have committed so vile an atrocity. These women, whatever their faults, were human beings as you and I are. Then and there, I swore that I would bring the murderer or murderers to justice so that he or they would be hanged by the neck until they were dead, dead, dead.

One thing was certain. Given the fact that the slaughter was unquestionably committed in Mary Kelly's room, she must have known the killer in order to admit him.

Well, my dear Amelia, I am sorry to have burdened you with matters so morbid and macabre but as you know, I am determined to get to the bottom of the matter even if the police have so far proved to be quite lamentably hopeless. Despatches from the front, eh? so to speak. But I know where to point Percy if you'll pardon the pun.

I am writing this in the Red Lion, a pub halfway down the Commercial Road. The trade is somewhat rough but the oysters and prawn sandwiches are absolutely excellent. Fortunately, I have stamps with me and intend to post this directly since, as I have not mentioned earlier, I have had all day the uniquely unpleasant sensation that I have been followed, yet whenever I have looked, there appeared to be nobody doing so. In fact, I rather welcome the idea of being followed as I pursue my enquiries since it might just give me the chance to discover more and perhaps turn the tables.

With all respect and affection to my dearest Amelia,

Percy

PS: A young man has just entered this pub and I do not care for the way in which he regarded me. I would describe him as being about five feet, ten inches in height, slim in build, with a pale complexion and thick brown hair, brushed back. He also sports a waxed handlebar moustache. He is wearing a loud check suit in pepper-and-salt laced with a green chessboard pattern to compound his sartorial crimes, a grey bowler hat, a bright blue shirt and a scarlet cravat.

Having bought a pint of beer, he is looking at me again now with a cold and curious eye of dazzling blue. I shall post this immediately and return to the pub. Perhaps I can engage him in conversation.

CHAPTER EIGHT

FROM THE LETTERS
OF SIR PERCY SULGRAVE

(WHODUNNIT?)

Dear Amelia,

By now, I trust you will have read my previous letter. It is now midnight and I have had a quite extraordinary day. I write this now in the comfort of my book-lined study with a decanter of port to hand.

As soon as I had posted my letter to you, I returned to the Red Lion and ordered another beer, since I find that I am developing quite a taste for four ale. The excellence of the shellfish obviously draws the populace to this pub and it was difficult to find a seat. Suddenly I spotted one opposite the young man with the waxed handlebar moustache, the young slim man who may or may not have been following me but who had certainly been regarding me curiously five minutes earlier. He was tucking into a large plate of eels, pie, mash and liquor with evident enthusiasm and drinking frequently from his pint of stout. Since I'm a great believer in taking the bull by the horns, so to speak, I approached him and asked if the seat opposite were taken. He shrugged and indicated that I was free to sit there.

Now, as he ate, he showed precious little interest in me. I drank my ale with every appearance of beaming contentment and listened to the raucous conversation all about me, peppered by oaths unfit for the ears of the gentler sex, although, to be candid not unfit for a gentleman's club dinner after the port has been passed. Some were loudly debating the relative merits of the prizefighters Jem Smith and Charley Mitchell. I take quite an interest in pugilism but they obviously knew the facts in far greater detail. Others either praised or railed against prominent political figures.

'Say what you like about Lord Salisbury!' roared one huge, hirsute bear of a man. 'But you can't deny he's the only one with a proper solution to the Irish troubles. As he said: "'Twenty years of strong, resolute government!'''

'That's been tried, Mike, and it's still as bad as ever. Nah, Gladstone's got the right idea! Just give it to the bloody bog-trotters!' bellowed his companion, a bald man with the physique of a gorilla. A heated argument developed and I observed that both men had hands that looked capable of breaking bricks. 'We don't want Ireland!' the bald one shouted.

Opposite me, the young man with the demented blue eyes continued to eat and drink impassively. When he had finished, he took his plate and jug back to the bar and ordered another pint of stout and two enormous crabs, which he carried back to the table. The man called Mike and his companion suddenly stopped their argument and approached the young man opposite me with surprising respect. One whispered in his ear and he nodded. The other whispered in his ear and he shook his head. The little finger of his left hand flicked out to indicate the crabs and each man took one.

'Thanks, guv'nor,' said the bear. 'Much appreciated!'

''Ere's to you, guv'nor.' As the gorilla drank the young man's health in one voracious gulp, one could barely discern the pint jug within his massive fist. These men did not bother with the niceties of eating a crab. They simply cracked the shell open with their fingers and their teeth and scoffed the flesh greedily, using their fingers to scoop up the brown meat and throwing everything they didn't want upon the floor. The young man with the waxed moustache now surprised me further by producing a slim Havana cigar, slicing off the end with a silver cigar cutter and, having lit it, smoking it with evident enjoyment as his shining blue eyes regarded me.

'Come 'ere often?' he enquired with insolent Cockney sarcasm.

'Not on the whole.'

'Not on the whole,' he repeated. 'Not on the square either, I suppose?'

'Sorry?'

'Not even Mitre Square . . .?' The tone was sneering. 'After all, that's quite an historic place for Freemasons, ennit?'

'I don't know what you mean,' I replied, somewhat indignant. Who *was* this Cockney coxcomb? I thought longingly of my horsewhip.

'That's what they all say,' he retorted. 'Funny, that.'

'Just what the devil is this all about?'

'The Devil,' he answered with an ugly smirk. 'I hope you don't mind my asking, though it is part of my work to mind things – and people – but what brings a gent like you to these parts?'

'How's that your business? Are you with the police?'

'The police?' He virtually choked on his beer. 'Don't make me laugh. No, I'm a businessman. It's part of my business to help people, you know, protect them, like. And that's why you worry me. Are *you* with the police, by any chance? 'Down on yer luck? Working for them?'

'Certainly not!' I expostulated. The sheer impertinence of the fellow to think I could be associated with such lowlife! 'Of course, I do have acquaintances in the higher ranks,' I said truthfully to avert any possibility of violence. I was glad of my swordstick and revolver for at that moment the bear and the gorilla were looking at me with stares that were distinctly unfriendly.

'Didn't think so,' he sniffed. 'Too much of an amateur.'

'Look, what's this all about? I'm simply having a drink here.'

'Yeah, nice to have a drink, isn't it?' I saw the grin of a shark. 'Come here for a pleasant stroll? Or are you going slumming?' The last word was spat at me with contempt. 'What is it? Cheap girls?'

'No!' I've never been so insulted.

'Then, since you strike me as being a gent, would you kindly tell me why a gent should choose to pay a social call here?'

'Oh, for heaven's sake!' I burst out irritably. 'I like London. I like walking around London and exploring areas of historical interest. And it was a pleasant stroll until you began this preposterous interrogation.'

'I see.' He blew a cloud of cigar smoke into my face as though it were a careless accident. 'Sorry about that, mate.' Mate! The sheer presumption. 'So a gent goes walking around all the sites of the Jack the Ripper murders, all for 'a pleasant stroll', does he? And he takes his swordstick with him? Don't bother pulling it, *old chap*, it's too bleeding crowded in here to swing the fucking thing effectively. Oh, and you must do something about that shooter in yer faded suit; anyone here finds it about as subtle as a steam engine. It can be seen a mile away.'

(No apologies for the language, Amelia. That is how they speak and I know that despite your refined tastes, you are no prude.)

'If you're wondering,' this uniquely arrogant and unpleasant man continued, 'whether I was following you, you're partly right and partly wrong. Information travels fast in these parts. It reaches the *right* people. Tried and tested people. I saw you staring hard at Millers Court off Dorset Street where Mary Kelly was ripped to ribbons. See, we're very sensitive about that sort of thing in this area. If Jack the Ripper were exposed here, why, the women would give him what he gave the girls and worse. He'd be strung up by his balls from the nearest lamp-post and no one would say a thing. He'd hang there with his guts spilling out of him. Alive.'

There followed on my part a slow and hideous awakening to the ghastly fact that he suspected *me* of being Jack the Ripper.

'He's still alive, you see. I have very good reason to believe that. *Very* good reason. And let's face it, criminals often do feel – um – *compelled* to revisit the scene or scenes of their crime or crimes . . .' His voice was curt and insinuating.

My guts turned to water at his insinuation. My stomach essayed a double somersault. My heart dropped into the soles of my boots. It was impossible to flee since that would identify me as being Jack the Ripper. It seemed possible that, at a word from my frightful inquisitor, I might be seized by the mob and torn to pieces with hideous tortures. Fortunately, I have attained to some degree of self-control. I knew that my swordstick was useless in the circumstances and that any endeavour to pull out my revolver, now that it had been spotted, would be perfectly futile. I might just have time to shoot myself.

'Well, I'm jolly glad to hear you say that,' I heard myself say. '*I* am sure that he is alive too. I am a gentleman of independent means who is devoting much of my time to discovering the identity of Jack the Ripper so that he can be brought to justice and I want to have him – ah – strung up just as much as you do. It is simply that I wish this to be accomplished by due process of Law. Here,' I reached for my wallet and he did not react since it was in another pocket from the embarrassingly obvious bulge of my Webley, 'my card.'

'Sir Percy Sulgrave of St James's, eh? Then why're you wearing such an old, faded suit?'

'It's comfortable.'

'Well, let me give you a word of advice, *Sir* Percy. Next time you come down the East End, for Christ's sake dress better; *if* you come again. We don't mind a gent coming down these parts as long as he shows us a bit of respect.'

At that instant, I wanted to show him his bit of respect by shoving the barrel of my revolver through his gleaming white teeth and watching him smile after *that*. But I was completely outnumbered.

'I'm new here,' I said instead. 'Given the way in which you spotted me so easily, I could hardly be the invisible killer Jack the Ripper.'

'Only in a bad light, Sir Percy. I'll keep this card if I may. Here.' Now it was his turn to extract his wallet and present me with a card. 'Have this. Another beer?' Under the circumstances, I could hardly refuse and in any case I was feeling horribly thirsty. I studied the card as he slid towards the bar with a gracious ease and the bear and the gorilla studied me. The card read:

BOB BROWN
SECURITY & REMOVALS
55 Marcia Road
London SE1

'Thank you, Mr Brown,' I said when he returned with the beers. 'One trusts that you no longer suspect that I am Jack the Ripper. The very suggestion is utterly ridiculous. Since you are obviously interested in the case, possibly as interested as I am, indeed, we may at least have *something* in common and we might be able to assist one another. May I just ask you what a South Londoner from across the river such as yourself is doing taking so great an interest in matters of the East End?'

'Simple. I like Sarf London but I have friends here. Some family here. Muvver's side. Business here, if you want to know the truth about it. Also there's something about it that's personal. Long Lizzie Stride was a friend of my cousin's. Lovely girl. I'm good at finding out about fings in general. Ah! nuffink like it!' He took a deep pull at his pint of four ale. 'Stout's the best to go with fish, but afterwards, give me ale any time!'

He stubbed out his cigar and pulled from his pocket an ageing briar pipe which he filled with shag tobacco. 'Hardly ever smoke cigars. Much prefer a pipe on the whole. It's just that business went quite well today.' Having lit his pipe he puffed out clouds of acrid smoke.

'So, Sir Percy,' he resumed his discourse – and he really did pronounce the first word as 'sow'. 'Have your interesting enquiries resulted in there being any particular suspect? Mine have. You tell me yours and I'll tell you mine.'

'Have you ever heard,' I asked coolly and calmly, 'of Montague Druitt?'

'Ah, yes, that peculiar barrister bloke whom the police suspected. Drowned hisself in the Thames, as I recall. Nah, nah, it weren't 'im.' Again his bizarre blue eyes stared into mine. 'You're on a wild goose chase that way. Whatever gave you that idea? He's dead. Lorst and gone. Pushing up the ruddy daisies.'

'Oh, I know that. It's just a theory I heard from a very interesting man I occasionally meet at my club. A Dr Lipsius. Keen criminologist. He was absolutely convinced that it was Druitt.'

'Never heard of the gentleman you mentioned just then.'

189

The face of Bob Brown was impassive though with alarm I
realized that mention of the name had abruptly interrupted
the fierce argument of the bear and the gorilla who were
now subjecting me to acute scrutiny. I wondered if I had
gone too far since the tentacles of Lipsius, poisonous and
slimy, do reach very deep into the East End: protection,
prostitution, opium dens and even the child slave trade.
'Well, you get all sorts of bizarre theories. Friend of yours,
is he, this Doctor . . . er . . .?'

'We're members of the same club.' Instantly I saw respect
and even fear in the eyes of the bear and the gorilla and I
knew that for at least a couple of hours I would be absolutely
safe in the East End. After that, providing I could get away,
I would require the finest bodyguards in London were I to
return and if Lipsius realized that I was hunting for him.

'Well, he sounds like an armchair theorist,' said Bob
Brown. 'And anyway, in your view, he can't be right,
since you told me that you fancied that Jack the Ripper
is alive, right?'

'Yes,' I said. Then I lied, relying on my knowledge of
police files. 'I refer to Vassily Konavalov, who killed a
whore in Paris in 1886, then fled to London where he
assumed the alias Alexei Pedachenko. Can you help me
find him?'

'I could,' Bob Brown answered, 'for a price. Only he's
not Jack the Ripper, whatever else he may have done.'

'Who is? Me?'

'It seems unlikely,' he replied, 'but then, you haven't met
Septimus Keen.'

'Who? Never heard of him.'

'For all I know,' Bob Brown stated casually, '*you* might
be Septimus Keen.'

'Why would I wish to be somebody whom I don't know
from Adam?'

'*He* might wish to be *you*.'

'Whatever for?'

'Disguise. I've never met such a master of disguise. For all I know, he might be your a Konavalov alias Alexei Pedachenko since he's more than capable of it. That's your man, believe me. That's my man, too. For all I know, you may have encountered him without knowing it at your club, since he sometimes moves in the highest social circles. Interested in hearing more?'

'Yes.'

Here is what followed:

Bob Brown's tale of Septimus Keen

It is impossible to establish the true origins of the man I know as Septimus Keen. To many he claimed that he was Robert Donston Stephenson, born in 1841 and the son of a Yorkshire mill owner, though in early life he sometimes called himself Roslyn D'Onston. When I first met him in 1887, courtesy of a woman friend of mine, he was only too eager to tell me of the formidable achievements of his youth, though by that time he was earning some sort of living as a freelance journalist.

And what a sensational and stormy life he had led! That's if you trusted a single word he said. He had mined for gold in California, was connected with the African slave trade, had witnessed devil worship in Cameroun, studied the art of the Indian rope trick, studied medicine in Munich, practised Magic in Paris and taken part in forty-two battles as a Surgeon Major under Garibaldi – and all this was done by the age of twenty-two!

The Italian War of Independence opened in 1859 when he was eighteen and closed in 1861 when he was twenty. Quite a lad. The next campaign of Garibaldi was in 1862 but he told me on the same evening that he spent the year in Paris learning how to conjure *Doppelgangers*, the doubles of any human being. A further Garibaldi campaign took place in 1867 but an elderly acquaintance of mine swore blind that if we were talking about the same Robert Donston Stephenson, and my description tallied with his, then at that time Stephenson was a Customs official in Hull. What a liar!

He had seduced my friend Julie with a really classic story of tragedy: a previous love, a prostitute he had endeavoured to rescue from a life of woe and sin, had left him only to commit suicide on Westminster Bridge, and whenever he walked there, he still heard her ghostly footsteps.

He claimed to be an expert on the occult. On 1st December 1888, he proceeded to advertise his disgusting crimes in the *Pall Mall Gazette*: 'Who is the Whitechapel Demon? (By one who thinks he knows)'. It was his intention boldly and deliberately to confuse all investigations by telling *part* of the truth. There he stated that Jack the Ripper was a black magician seeking to evoke demons who would give him power to rule the realms of the natural, the unnatural and the supernatural. To this end, the Ripper had to obtain the skin of a suicide, nails from a murderer's gallows, candles made from human fat and secretions from a prostitute's vagina. After that, there had to be four human sacrifices placed in the form of a cross.

This, of course, confuses matters further in that it omits Mary Kelly as a victim. But it was *intended* to mislead. As I soon realized, if you take a map, pinpoint the positions of the *five* murders and join up the dots, you have, roughly speaking, an inverted five-pointed star: the Inverse Pentagram, the Star of Satan.

The next move of Keen/Stephenson/Dr Roslyn D'Onston was even more ingenious. He informed a halfwit, a George Marsh of Pratt Street, Camden, that possibly he was the Ripper. Marsh went to Scotland Yard on 24th December and in his mumbling, slobbering, utterly unconvincing way, informed an Inspector Roots that Stephenson was the murderer. Stephenson, having wanted Marsh to do precisely that, entered Scotland Yard two days later and denounced a Dr Davies at the London Hospital. A friend of mine in the police showed me a document that accompanied the testimony that Dr Davies had given patients a minute description, accentuated by perplexing enthusiasm, relating precisely how the Ripper killed his victims. This peculiar document reads:

'24th December 88 – I hereby agree to pay to Dr R D'O. Stephenson (also known as *Sudden Death*) one half of any or all rewards or monies received by me on account of the conviction of Dr Davies for wilful murder (signed) Roslyn D'O. Stephenson MD, 29 Castle Street, WC, St Martin's Lane.'

The man, if he can be called that, had thus promised to pay half of his reward money to himself. Mad, one might think, as mad as claiming to have been present at the California Gold Rush when he was only eight years of age. But there is method in this madness. Although Inspector Roots duly sent the Statements of Marsh and 'Stephenson' to his superiors, they took absolutely no notice of the matter, regarding it as being mere nonsense on the part of two imbeciles. By this stratagem, Septimus Keen, black magician, was in the clear and left free to pursue his revolting, necromantic activities whilst being regarded by the police as a harmless eccentric, or at worst a nuisance and a crank.

Now you may well ask how come I am so sure that Jack the Ripper was Septimus Keen.

About a year ago, in the course of my business dealings, I had occasion to undertake a transaction involving one Baroness Vittoria Cremers, one of the hardest bitches that I have ever met. I don't think that I will ever forget her hawk-like nose and her beady brown eyes. The undertaking of the transaction was accomplished successfully and Cremers was pleased with my execution of the matter. Subsequently she contracted with me to further her interests in a variety of ways and I found her to be a cold but useful partner in

certain areas of business. Although she was a lesbian and
therefore you wouldn't expect her to take to a man like
me, it turned out that we had quite a lot in common. We
used to drink together sometimes and although she had the
strongest head for drink I have ever known in a woman, it
is fortunate that my head for it is stronger, or else I would
never have heard her story.

Vittoria Cremers had joined Madame Blavatsky's Theosophical Society on account of her obsession with the occult.
I used to listen to Cremers, as she preferred to be called,
expounding on Theosophy over the brandy and I found
her notions to be amazing.

Suppose you have an immortal spirit within you that has
been on earth so very many times before in one body or
another and that will go, not to heaven or to hell, but on
to a hundred, a thousand or even many million more lives.
Suppose that the law of the Universe is that everything
you do will inevitably come back to you sooner or later.
Suppose that there are indeed Hidden Masters, beings
of extra-human intelligence, who are concerned with the
evolution of life on this planet and who may get in touch
with you if they think you have potential and may be
useful. Suppose that there are practices by which you
can expand your awareness, enhance your every faculty,
come into contact with non-physical beings of various
kinds, transform your life and lift yourself into states of
consciousness whereby, if you yourself are not a Hidden
Master, you are at least in their class . . . Now, you might
totally disagree with these notions, so trenchantly advanced
by Madame Blavatsky. I did when Cremers put them to me.
But you cannot deny that even a momentary acceptance of
these ideas will vastly expand the horizons of the mind.

It was at the Theosophical Society that Cremers had met
a young woman and aspiring author, Mabel Collins, and in

1889 they became lovers. Cremers then had occasion to visit
America and after some months returned to find that Mabel,
a rather soft, elfin, feminine lady was now involved with
Stephenson/Keen. Once again he was telling outrageous
tales. He was a great Magician possessed of fabulous
magical secrets who had once vanquished an African
female witch doctor in a contest of magical powers, since
he had been initiated into the secrets of sorcery by the
original of Ayesha, 'She who must be obeyed' in the novel
She by Rider Haggard. He had also been a cavalry captain
in the Liberation Army of Garibaldi.

Initially, Keen-as-Stephenson managed to charm Cremers,
an exceptionally difficult feat. With Mabel, they established
a cosmetics business. At first, all went well. But both women
became increasingly wary of the man, particularly since he
drank too much and, whenever he had passed a certain
limit, spoke obsessively about Jack the Ripper.

Once again he insisted that the murderer was the innocuous Dr Davies, just as he had told the police. Once again he
asserted that the sites of the murders had been deliberately
chosen with a cold and deliberate geometric design, the
purpose being Black Magic of the deepest dye. He swore
that Dr Davies had actually confessed his crimes to him.
Cremers and Mabel were informed that Dr Davies as Jack
the Ripper had tucked the missing organs of the victims in
between his shirt and tie.

One day, when Stephenson was out, Cremers searched
his room. There she found a number of black ties, all
knotted and stiff with clotted blood . . .

Obviously the Ripper was Stephenson, who still stalks
the streets. How do I know that he was an alias of Septimus
Keen? Why, in the tin box he had hidden the following tale
– which was copied out by Cremers.'

WHODUNNIT?

by

Septimus Keen

I think it was Oscar Wilde who said to me the other day: 'He who leads more lives than one, more deaths than one must die.' How true. And the maxim applies to women as well. No doubt Oscar will at some point put his words to me in his plays or his poetry for he often plagiarizes from himself.

My intent is to tell the tale of the most astonishing railway journey I have ever experienced. It occurred in the days when I was working as an assassin connected to the British Secret Service and occasionally reporting to Major Short, whose untimely demise I deeply regret. (I have described this acutely distressing experience in another story.)

The fact of the matter is that I had to travel to Edinburgh to kill a woman. She was a spy working for the French in endeavours to cement 'the auld alliance' with Scotland and to encourage the extreme terrorist activities of Scottish Nationalism. There is no point served by my entering into the details. It suffices to state that the kill was accomplished swiftly and with maximum efficiency. I doubt if she felt any pain. All that remained was for me to travel by night express to London and make my report. I think that the express was called the *Flying Scotsman*, though I could not swear to the matter.

In the dining car I espied a delightfully voluptuous brunette, dressed at the height of fashion. Her breasts threatened to split her white blouse and her bottom was so tightly swathed within its purple, shimmering bell-shaped skirt that I found myself to be longing for her intimate charms. The only perplexing factor was that she bore a disturbing resemblance to the lady I had killed. Obviously this could not be the case, so I put the possibility out of my mind and bent my attention towards her seduction.

Her name, she told me, was Jean MacDonald, daughter of a Highland chieftain. As we drank champagne, she talked with a charm I found quite enchanting. She appeared only too happy and willing to invite me into her sleeping compartment after we had finished our coffee and brandy. I do not intend to retrace, moment by moment, all our delicious passages. I will limit myself to a description of the most striking facts of this adorable *liaison*, which I wished could last all eternity. My lover knew how to vary our pleasures without ever reaching satiety: she felt a singular joy in the arts of passion and she found in me a willing and eager student. Sometimes a woman in her mid-forties can be the ripest fruit of all.

Jean MacDonald taught me all the obscene Scottish names for genitalia, sometimes making me say them, but only in the whirl of passion. She used them herself too in supreme moments of bliss, rightly stating that such a high spice 'should never be too much hackneyed, else 'twould lose its flavour. As I write on, I forget myself in these sweet recollections . . .

What cunning caresses! What lecherous postures did she *not* teach me! What innocent play and prolonging of pleasure there was on both sides! And what *refinements* of pleasure did we not realize as soon as thought of as the train rattled onwards through the night! At one instant she exclaimed in French: '*Moi! Je suis fou!*'

Was she mad? I have only a dim and hazy memory of the last hour before the train steamed into King's Cross station; and that is unfortunate in view of the ensuing consequences. I tell my friends and acquaintances that I have led, on the whole, a quiet and retiring life, remote from the fields of front-line adventure, and they do not believe me. '*Always tell the truth but lead a life so improbable that no one will believe you*' is virtually my motto and may well be my epitaph. Even so, I remain unused to the unusual and have to tell now of one of the strangest things that has ever happened to me.

One supposes that, in my customary fashion, I would have escorted Jean MacDonald onto the station platform, though I cannot recall the fact. After all, we had been drinking vintage champagne and the finest cognac all night in between the bouts of our frenzied *amours*. Naturally I would have ordered porters for the lady's luggage at the station but I have no memory of the fact, if fact it be. All I know for certain is that I have a visiting card before me as I write this now that informs me that Jean MacDonald lives at 56 Knightsbridge Terrace whenever she is in London. I have another card informing me that whenever she lives in Scotland, it is at Castle Mortimer, Kirkcaldy, Fife. On the back of the first visiting card, a spidery feminine hand had written in hard yet delicate pencil an invitation to dinner in Knightsbridge upon this very night. I imagine that I escorted my fair lady to a cab and bade her a sweet goodbye until the evening.

As the sun set in a blazing glow of bright orange that illuminated the housetops of London, I was resolved to be punctual. I hailed a cab in good time only to be told that there was no such place in London as 56 Knightsbridge Terrace. Cursing the driver for an imbecile, I tried another cab, with no better result. Finally I simply took a cab to Knightsbridge and explored this highly stylish area on foot. No, there was no Knightsbridge Terrace, let alone a number 56.

I might add that subsequently I discovered that there was no 'Castle Mortimer' in or near Kirkcaldy, Fife, either.

Major Short was pleased with my efficient dispatch of the Franco-Scottish spy, the accidental death of whom had been reported in the Press, but less happy with the tale I told him in my quest for further information. To my mild astonishment, he even became visibly agitated and poured a stiff whisky for both of us.

'According to the police,' he told me, ''you have been duped by an international confidence trickster known to them as Myrtle Smith.'

'Just a moment, Major. She did not take my money.'

'That's because she didn't have à chance to do so. Do you realize that the corpse of Myrtle Smith, alias Jean MacDonald, was found by railway officials at the precise spot reached by the Edinburgh-London night express one hour before it gets into King's Cross?' I could scarcely believe that I was hearing this. 'I have it here.' Major Short tapped the newspaper before him with a questioning index finger. 'The lady you intended to see tonight at a non-existent London address ... this confidence trickster and female impostor died at 7:00 a.m.'

'Oh . . .' I said very slowly as my face paled.

'So far . . .' it appeared to be an effort for Major Short to stay calm, 'so far, it appears that her death was suicide. All the evidence points to her flinging herself from the opened door of a moving train. Prob'ly couldn't endure her duplicitous life any longer, poor bitch.' I froze with horror, to deny furiously within myself the possibility that I might have had anything to do with the death of this wondrously enchanting woman. 'But don't worry about this one, old chap, you did the right thing and nobody will ever be able to pin it on you.' He continued blithely, 'You're in the clear. Every document, including relevant newspapers, concurs with the fact that Myrtle Smith died at 7:00 a.m. *twenty-four hours* ago. So the woman you were with was probably pretending to be Myrtle Smith, who was herself pretending to be Jean MacDonald.' His fingers flicked to a photograph upon his desk and he held it up before me. 'Recognize her?'

'Yes,' I said. 'That was the woman I was with last night and this morning on the Edinburgh-London night express.' I dug my railway ticket out of my pocket for impartial verification.

'Can't be, old boy,' the Major responded. 'As I've told you, *she* died twenty-four hours ago.'

'*And you're asking me to believe that I slept with a ghost of the impersonator of an impostor?*' A kill has always made me lascivious but this was too bizarre.

'Possibly . . .' Major Short murmured thoughtfully. 'Although we old London hands do have a curious legend among ourselves. It's that there *is* a ghostly lover on the Edinburgh-London night express after every – ah – termination in Edinburgh; and that she gives the man a quite incredible fuck and that she is compounded of all the ghosts of adventurous women, disillusioned and despoiled in love, who have committed suicide on that particular journey. Oh, that one you looked after in Edinburgh . . . you didn't make love to her beforehand, did you.' I nodded, frozen otherwise to my seat. Major Short coughed hoarsely. 'More whisky?'

'A ghost could not give me visiting cards.'

'They were false ones, though, weren't they?' Major Short said. 'Be a good chap and have another whisky.' He would die soon, too.

GERALD SUSTER

As Christopher Marlowe has it:

Thou hast committed—
  Fornication? But that was in another country:
  And besides, the wench is dead.

'And there you have it!' Mr Bob Brown exclaimed triumphantly.

'Mr Brown,' I replied, 'I am not at all sure what I do have.'

'Who is?' He shrugged. 'But the important thing is to find Septimus Keen. I know, some might say I am bad. Maybe I *am* bad. Who knows? But Septimus Keen is *evil!*'

'Well – um – how does one find Septimus Keen? I mean, who is he?'

'Could be anyone.'

'Where is he?'

'Everywhere and anywhere.'

'This seems to me, Mr Brown,' I said, 'rather like some wit's definition of philosophy: a route of many roads leading from nowhere to nothing.'

'I appreciate your wit, Sir Percy,' he answered, studying my face carefully. I was glad that someone did. My own wits were spinning dizzily. 'But let's be practical. I happen to know that the vile Septimus Keen has many contacts in the East End; on occasion, he even poses as an East Ender himself. Now, what I'm proposing is that we pool our resources. Cooperation! That's the name of the game, ennit? See, he knows I'm looking for him, so he'll be after me. He'll find out that you're looking for Jack the Ripper so he'll be after you. He might be a man you see snoozing in his armchair at one of your clubs in St James's. He might be some nondescript mediocrity sitting opposite you in the Underground Railway, assuming you ever take so low a mode of transportation. But one thing is for certain. Both you and me have attracted the attention of Jack the Ripper. I have your card. You have mine. My proposition is that we contact one another if anything *unusual* occurs.'

'Your proposition, Mr Brown, has my unqualified assent. And now I fear I must take my leave though it has certainly been a most fascinating encounter.' Out of the corner of my eye, I had noticed that the bear and the gorilla appeared to have departed. I rose and extended my hand. 'A pleasure meeting you, Mr Brown . . .' He rose and shook my hand. I noticed that although his wrist was as delicate as that of a fashionable woman of society, his grip had the strength of a professional wrestler.

'A pleasure meeting you, Sir Percy. 'Ope you didn't mind the nature of my earlier enquiries and sorry if I may have offended you. No hard feelings, I trust, and I hope that we may meet again shortly to discuss a matter that concerns us all.' I thought that his farewell pleasantries would never end since, in my dazed condition, I was aching to leave and was at the point of prayer for no further impediment. 'Now mind 'ow you go and do bear in mind wot I've said. Any time you're down this way, Bob Brown is the man you ask for!' As I left, he strode to the bar and ordered another pint of ale, still puffing furiously at his pipe of shag.

Outside in the courtyard – the keen blast of cold fresh air was so welcoming – I saw that the bear and the gorilla were involved in a dispute and punching one another. Both were bruised and bleeding as the bear landed a blow to the jaw that enraged the gorilla. Seizing an empty bottle from an outdoor table he smashed it down hard upon the skull of the bear.

'Ye fucking bastard!' the bear yelled as he staggered

backwards and then forwards once more. 'Take that, ye swine!' And he slogged the gorilla with a blow to the belly that made him gasp and grab the bear within his arms. I could see that these two men were going to be at it for quite a while and would probably be the best of friends on the following day, prior to another fight.

I was relieved to find a cab and leave, though the ease of finding one in this area, after my peculiar meeting with Bob Brown, gave me a sensation of prickly cold comfort.

The morning sun is rising and as I look out over the rooftops, I wonder how many insoluble mysteries are contained therein. One can never get to the bottom of London, no matter how well one may think one knows that dear, dirty old whore. Every mystery one discovers reveals a hundred more.

And here is another. I do not know what to make of Mr Bob Brown save to state that I neither like him nor trust him. I have no intention of seeing him again; yet upon my return to my home, I was possessed suddenly by the uneasy sensation that, in some form or another, I must have seen him before. A flick through my files disclosed an artist's impression, sketched from a police description at their request, of a Bill Smith, a suspect in the horrendous murder of Arthur Bullock MP some while ago. I took a tracing from this drawing, omitting the hair, moustache and beard. I then added the hair and waxed handlebar moustache that I had seen on Bob Brown.

The faces were identical, given those superficial amendments.

I shall inform the police.

My darling Amelia, I am about to drop from perturbation of the brain and utter exhaustion. I look forward so much to seeing you again soon. Kindly give my best regards to Barbara.

Love and best wishes,

Percy

EDITOR'S NOTE

Whatever lies Bob Brown may have been telling to Sir Percy Sulgrave, he was nevertheless advancing some truths about theories held over the past forty years concerning the identity of Jack the Ripper. Nor were the endeavours of Sir Percy Sulgrave to mislead Bob Brown entirely without foundation.

Montague Druitt, son of a surgeon and born in 1857, *was* one of the prime suspects on police files, hence Sir Percy's mention of his name to Brown. Druitt won a scholarship to Winchester and then a place at Oxford, in both places excelling at Fives and cricket. Unfortunately, he appears to have left his golden future behind him. Although he had aristocratic connections, obtained partly by education and partly by homosexuality, he earned a modest living as a tutor at a crammer in Blackheath and, although he was called to the Bar in 1885, he made little impression. In July 1888, his mother attempted suicide, was certified insane and confined in the Brooke Asylum, Clapton. The Ripper murders took place August-November 1888. At the end of November, Druitt was dismissed from his teaching job. On 1st December at Chiswick, he flung himself into the River Thames and drowned. The body was discovered some weeks later and the inquest was conducted on 2nd January, 1889, where his elder brother William a solicitor, produced a suicide note, printed in the *Acton, Chiswick and Turnham Green Gazette* as follows:

'Since Friday I felt I was going to be like Mother, and the best thing for me was to die.'

The finest case against Druitt is made by Daniel Farson in his *Jack the Ripper* (Michael Joseph, London 1972).

When Sir Percy Sulgrave endeavoured to confuse Mr Bob Brown by naming Vassily Konavalov alias Alexei Pedachenko as his suspect, again this is a plausible theory advanced in *The Identity of Jack the Ripper* (Jarrolds, London, 1959) by Donald McCormick alias Richard Deacon. Here it is argued that, after the Ripper murders, Konavalov/Pedachenko changed his identity to Andrey Luiskovo and fled to St Petersburg where he murdered another woman and was caught and confined in a lunatic asylum. The only problem, as William Beadle has pointed out in his excellent *Jack the Ripper: Anatomy of a Myth* (Wat Tyler, Essex, 1995) is that 'there is no accessible documentary evidence that Konavalov ever existed!. The only "proofs" come from two missing documents.' Mr Beadle then proceeds with a devastating demolition of the veracity of these cited yet missing documents.

There is some telling support for the theory of Bob Brown that Jack the Ripper was Robert Donston Stephenson, though none to support Brown's viewpoint that he was an alias of the mysterious Septimus Keen. Here, the most persuasive case has been presented by Melvin Harris in *Jack the Ripper: the Bloody Truth* (Columbus, London, 1987). The theory of Harris is supported by earlier writings by Aleister Crowley, the magus, yogi, poet, mountaineer, chess master and heretic denounced in the tabloids as 'the wickedest man in the world' in his own time and our own. Crowley knew both Vittoria Cremers, who was for a time his business manager and a participant in his magical rituals, and Mabel Collins, whose books *The Light on the Path* and *The Blossom and the Fruit* are today regarded as being New Age classics. Crowley was sure that Stephenson was the Ripper, that the bodies had been placed deliberately in geometric form and that the purpose was to acquire the powers of Black Magic.

Crowley was of the opinion that, by these bizarre methods, Stephenson, Black Magician, had acquired the power of invisibility that Crowley as a White Magician had already acquired for himself by somewhat more salubrious means. There are references to the Ripper in his privately published set of journals, *The Equinox* (London, 1908–14) and *The Confessions of Aleister Crowley* (Cape, London 1969). Here the fog grows thicker, though: enter a journalist called Bernard O'Donnell who interviewed Crowley, Cremers and Betty May, an artist's model, wife of Crowley disciple Raoul Loveday, a brilliant Cambridge graduate, and author of the autobiography *Tiger Woman*. Betty May claimed that during her stay at the Abbey of Thelema, Crowley's commune in Cefalu, Sicily, she had found the stained ties of Stephenson, concerning which Cremers had spoken, and that Crowley proceeded to tell her the story he had heard from Cremers. Given the fact that Crowley and Cremers had quarrelled viciously in 1912–13, it is hard to discern how these macabre, coagulated ties could have passed from the one to the other. In any event, Cremers, Crowley, Mabel Collins and Bernard O'Donnell believed that Stephenson was Jack the Ripper and, according to Richard Whittington-Egan in *A Casebook on Jack the Ripper* (Wildy, London, 1976), O'Donnell placed all his revelations in a book that remains unpublished. Crowley's concurring theory may be studied by access to the Yorke Collection in the Warburg Institute of the University of London.

If Stephenson was Jack the Ripper, it is curious that he abandoned his addiction to serial killing, since his book about the Christian Gospels, *The Patristic Gospels*, was published in 1904. It is even more curious that nothing of his later life appears to be known.

(A.S.)

CHAPTER NINE

FROM THE LETTERS
OF AMELIA STANHOPE

(THE LOST LOVE)

D ear Percy,
Thank you so much for your utterly fascinating letter.
It is all too utterly utter. But do be careful, won't you? This
Bob Brown sounds to me like a highly sinister character and
I think that you are quite right to alert the police regarding
your suspicions. I always found Arthur Bullock MP to be
a rather dull man and boorish to boot, but the poor chap
certainly did not deserve to be murdered for that.

First of all, allow me to apologize for my unduly tardy
reply. I have only recently returned from visiting Barbara
Crockford in Harrogate, where I had a delightful time. The
flower gardens are so exquisitely beautiful at this time of
year. Her husband Thomas is not a particularly enlivening
man in conversation and I can fully understand why Barbara
welcomes some light relief; though, after all, the matter is
summarized adequately in her following words, spoken
on the railway on one occasion when we were travelling
together. I was admiring the diamond on her finger and
remarked that it was one of the biggest diamonds that I
have ever seen.

'Oh, yes,' she replied. 'It is the Crockford diamond and
it is among the largest in the World. Unfortunately, there
is a curse upon it.'

'What is the curse? Do tell me!'

'Mr Crockford.'

Upon my return to London, I found myself once more

flung into the giddy social whirl and this rendered me unable to scrutinize your missive with the care and attention it so obviously deserves. When I was finally able to do so, such brains as I have were sent into a spin.

This has been so accentuated by recent events that presently I feel as though I were a whipping top. Given your own experiences regarding your laudable investigations concerning the Jack the Ripper crimes, I think you may find my account to be of some interest.

Yesterday I decided to ignore the pleasures of socializing in favour of the enjoyments of solitude. After a light luncheon of caviar from the Caspian Sea accompanied by plenty of thin dry toast (which latter I find to be an essential accompaniment), then *paté de foie gras* with thicker, more moist toast and then a cracked crawfish with thick mayonnaise sauce, followed by *tarte tatin* and accompanied by an acceptable bottle of Pouilly Fumée, I ordered my coachman to drive me to the British Museum. There I spent a most enjoyable hour or so gazing at the masterpieces of antiquity and I was especially struck by the sight of a statue in the Egyptian Gallery on the Ground Floor. It was a statue of Horus, the Ancient Egyptian God of War, also associated with the hawk-headed Sun God Ra.

It was not only the fact that the sculpture was done quite exquisitely that made me marvel, though I did wonder at how so primitive a people could have attained to such a mastery of craft. There was *something* about that statue itself that seemed *alive*, although I know that sounds rather silly. I stared into the orbs of the eyes, as blank and pitiless as the sun, and fancied myself transfixed by this merciless, stony gaze. And as I gazed back and trembled, I heard a voice say clearly:

'God is he with the head of a hawk, having a spiral force.'

I turned around in shock to see Sir Richard Knight.

Have you met him at all? You might well have done so. If not, I strongly recommend that you do make endeavours to meet him for reasons I am about to describe.

You may have encountered him on social occasions; he is a frequent guest at the *soirées* and dinners of Lady Dorothy Neville and quite a dandy. Keep this well under your hat, Percy, but Barbara Crockford knew him rather well, shall we say, prior to her marriage, and pronounced him to be charming and delightful. This appears to be the opinion of all women who encounter him. He is a young, slim, clean-shaven man with luscious, brushed-back blond hair, and his blazing blue eyes are quite unforgettable. On this particular day, he was wearing a severe black frock coat, tight black trousers of velvet, a silken shirt of pale blue and a butterfly bow tie of royal blue, held fast with a stick-pin surmounted by a sapphire. He wore what were obviously hand-made black boots, though it seemed that he had forgotten to polish them. That did not trouble me since I never trust a man who appears to be too much of a gentleman. He was regarding me with a gentle and amused smile.

'Lady Amelia,' he said. 'What an unexpected pleasure it is to meet you here, and before this wondrous statue of Horus.'

'Sir Richard!' I greeted him, all pleasantries, and he kissed my hand. 'It is certainly a pleasure to see you. What brings you to the British Museum?'

'Knowledge, Madam, or rather, the pursuit of knowledge.' I was pleased to hear this, since I had always thought of him as being no more than a charming social butterfly, an idler of the pavements of Piccadilly, a stylish *flaneur* who looked upon life without essaying much of its experience. 'I have come from the Reading Room where I often spend my mornings deriving great profit and enjoyment from my hours of study.'

'Then can you tell me more about this extraordinary object we have before us?'

'Certainly, and with the utmost of pleasure.' Sir Richard proceeded to launch into a learned but mercifully short discourse on all myths and legends relating to Horus, rather as though he had all the facts at his fingertips. As you are aware, Percy, I happen to know E. Wallis Budge, the Curator of Egyptian Antiquities; and Sir Richard's account tallied with everything that Dr Budge had told me.

'What was it that you said before?' I asked. 'I mean, the words you spoke when I was staring at Horus . . .'

'God is he with the head of a hawk, having a spiral force. It comes from the *Chaldean Oracles* of Zoroaster, an Ancient Mesopotamian work of great wisdom. I am convinced that scientists will eventually find in this saying a key to human evolution.'

(Editor's Note: Sir Richard had a point. Modern scientists declare that DNA is the genetic code of Evolution and that it has a spiral force.)

'How so?' I enquired.

'Madam, I give you the three most honest words in the English language for my response: "I don't know". But our scientists are working upon the matter, and I am following their experiments with the utmost interest.'

'I had no idea that you were so absorbed by scientific enquiry, Sir Richard.'

'Oh, indeed, Lady Amelia, it is a passion of mine. In fact, I have only just concluded a scientific experiment of my own, which has had perplexing results. I live just across the road from here, in Great Russell Street. Why don't you join me there for tea and I can demonstrate the matter to you?'

'It's nothing to do with frogs nailed on boards, is it?' I queried, wrinkling my nose.

'Not at all. It is all to do with Light.'

'Do we really *want* tea?' Sir Richard asked as we entered the downstairs drawing room of his house. 'Do we *have* to have tea? Why is it that at this time of day one *has* to have tea, one is *forced* to have tea? You may have tea, of course, if that is what you wish, but for my own part, I shall have champagne.'

'What a delightful idea!' I usually do take afternoon tea but this activity can be wearisome and champagne was a rather more enticing prospect. As Sir Richard left the room, I sat and admired his taste. There was no extraneous clutter in his blending of the interiors of centuries. The fireplace was Robert Adam. The furniture harmonized Hepplewhite, Chippendale and Sheraton. The curtains and wallpaper had been designed by William Morris. There were etchings by Whistler depicting the Thames upon the walls and also what I assumed to be ancestral portraits by Reynolds and Gainsborough. Sir Richard returned with silver tankards and a bottle of Krug which he opened expertly. 'No servants?'

'No, none at all, though I do have quite a useful man who comes and cleans the place occasionally, you know, tidies up, that sort of thing. To be candid, Lady Amelia . . .'

'Amelia . . .'

'Richard . . . yes, to be candid,' he spoke in that clear, mellow tone of his, 'I was brought up with servants and I don't want them. I find them to be an intrusion upon my privacy. One is always bumping into them at inconvenient moments. Now, I hope you enjoy my champagne. It is an 1888 vintage, light and pleasant for this sparkling afternoon. I shall fetch you a flute glass if that is what you would prefer but myself, I always find that it tastes better out of a tankard. After all, champagne is a wine to be drunk, not to be sipped.'

'My father was always of the same opinion and so am I.' I quaffed the sparkling vintage from my tankard and found it to be excellent. 'So where is your laboratory?'

'Here,' he replied simply. 'You may also be wondering where I keep my tools of experiment. Here.' He opened an oaken chest to produce a shoebox and an electric lantern. 'That is all I require to demonstrate the Mystery of the Universe. That and my little Faraday dynamo downstairs which is connected, as you can see, by wires to my electric lamp here. Ah, and I have also used scissors to make vertical slits and sticky tape to make flaps on my shoebox here so as to show you something quite beyond belief.' I was starting to wonder whether Sir Richard had gone mad and was glad that my coachman was waiting outside his house, especially when my host drew the thick drapes together. 'Now we must have darkness for this.' If this were some ploy for making a pass at me, I resolved firmly that I would not respond; though at that instant, he was arranging the shoebox upon the table and removing its lid. I stared bemusedly at two flaps of cardboard held by sticky tape at the front of the box. He held up his electric lamp. 'Would you care to assist me?'

'Very well.' I really needed to quaff some champagne. 'What would you like me to do?'

'Amelia, could you please point this lamp at the front of the shoebox here?'

'Yes.' He passed me the lamp.

'The lamp gives off beams of light, does it not?'

'Lamps usually do, I find.'

'Good. When you point it here, what do you see?'

'The front of a shoebox that has two flaps held by sticky tape.'

'Precisely.' He opened one of the flaps to reveal a vertical incision made with the blades of a pair of scissors. 'Please shine the light through that vertical slit, Amelia: thank you. Now, what would you expect to see at the end of the shoebox?'

'A vertical slit of reflected light, presumably . . .'

'Quite so, Come and look. Open up your eyes now. Tell me what you see.'

'A vertical slit of reflected light . . . is that the experiment, Richard?'

'Hardly. I shall open up the second flap.' He did so to reveal a second vertical slit made by an incision of scissors. 'If you shine the beam of light on the front of the shoebox, what would you expect to see at the back?'

'*Two* vertical slits of light.'

'One would expect that, wouldn't one? So shine the light, yes, that's it; and open up your eyes now and tell me what you see.'

A bore and a shoebox and an electric lamp, is what I thought, but on further inspection, I was puzzled. In place of the two separate slits of light I had logically expected to see, there was a wide pattern of dark and light strips shading into one another.

'This is irrational,' I said. 'Is it a conjuring trick?'

'No.'

'When one slit is open you get a thin strip of light at the back of the shoebox but when both are open, one sees this complex pattern. Why? Is it a trick of the light?'

'No. It goes deeper than that. Would you not agree that when only one slit was open, the light was behaving as though it was made up of particles, like a succession of tiny bullets going through the slit?' I nodded. 'We open the second slit and the light behaves like waves. So tell me, my dear Amelia, does light behave as a wave or as a particle?'

GERALD SUSTER

'Um . . .' At the time I feared I was the victim of a clever illusion though subsequently I have repeated this experiment in my home, as any fool can do, and there is no trick involved at all. That is how light behaves. 'Um . . . could it be both?' I faltered helplessly.

'How can it be both? Either it is a particle or it is a wave, at least according to our every notion of Science. And Logic.'

'Then could it be that our present notions of Science and Logic presently cannot explain how light behaves?'

'Well *done*, Amelia!' Sir Richard beamed at me. 'More champagne?'

(Editor's Note: Sir Richard has crudely pioneered in explaining one of the foremost notions of the succeeding century's Quantum Physics, which confirmed all he demonstrated under the strictest laboratory conditions. Amelia is also right in her statement that anyone can essay the experiment with no more than a shoebox, scissors, sticky tape and a torch.)

'"And God said, Let there be light:"!' Sir Richard exclaimed, striding towards the drawn curtains. '"And there was light."' Summer sunshine came flooding through the windows. 'You see, Amelia, we presently haven't the remotest notion concerning how or why Light *behaves*, let alone what it *is*. It is a far more difficult matter than Electricity. At least we have some idea as to how Electricity *behaves* and can harness it for our usage. But as to what it *is* . . . I am reminded of my Cambridge days and old Professor Bloemstein who challenged any student in his lecture to tell him what Electricity *is*. '"Professor!" some bright spark at the back piped up. "Stand up, young man," Bloemstein growled, "and tell us what Electricity is." "Um . . ." said the young man; "I am sorry, Professor, I thought I knew what Electricity is, but I fear I have forgotten." "Just my luck!" the Professor growled, "for there was only one man

226

on the planet who could tell me what Electricity *is* – and he has forgotten.""

'Oh, Richard,' I said, 'you're so clever.'

'I wish I were.' He smiled modestly and looked at his shoes. 'What I am trying to explain, Amelia,' he threw himself into a Hepplewhite chair, 'is that when it comes to the subject of Light, we are still totally in the Dark. The Universe is a far stranger place than is commonly supposed. Nothing is ever as it seems. Science is not my only interest. Archaeology, antiquarianism, the Arts and, above all, Literature are among my passions. Also I adore the Theatre, taking an especial pleasure in the writing of Drama and its enactment. Another great interest of mine is Criminology and all subjects connected with it such as Psychology and the Science of Society, which we may call Sociology. And I have been finding that the curious effects of Light, which I showed you, appear to have been to some degree replicated in the course of my investigation of the Jack the Ripper murders of 1888.'

'Sir Richard!' I cried out. 'This is all most extraordinary! Why, a very dear friend of mine is presently engaged upon solving the Jack the Ripper murders. Perhaps you have met Sir Percy Sulgrave?'

'It is perfectly possible that I have and the name does ring a bell, though I cannot say that I have ever enjoyed anything more than a glancing acquaintanceship with him hitherto. Possibly you might be kind enough to arrange at your convenience a meeting where we might conceivably discuss these matters?'

'I would be only too pleased to do so,' I responded, 'and over a bottle of bubbly! Percy is always telling me about his hunt for Jack the Ripper and I'm sure that you two men would have *so* many things in common. Tell me, Richard, what is *your* theory?'

'I know who Jack the Ripper was and is,' he replied solemnly. 'I am encountering some difficulty in finding him.'

'And who was he? Don't keep me in suspense or else I shall be tempted to take off my gloves and bite my fingernails.'

'No need to do that, Madam. Have you ever heard of Septimus Keen?'

'Possibly . . .' I muttered as I recalled the letter that you, Percy, had written to me. 'The name does ring a very dim and distant bell.'

'Let us smoke cigarettes,' he responded, picking up a box carved of ebony wood and flipping open the lid with his thumb. 'Turkish on the left side, Virginia on the other. Ah! Turkish? I shall join you. It is a pleasure to smoke tobacco with a lady of discernment.' He lit my oval cigarette with a long, thick match that continued to burn as he picked an ivory holder from the walnut table before us and, having inserted the cigarette, proceeded to light it with the same flame, after which he blew out a perfect smoke-ring. 'You see, Amelia, I have been finding this matter of darkness every bit as difficult as my investigations of light.' I could not help but notice that his blue eyes were fixed in a steady gaze upon me, though I retained my composure. 'Kindly allow me to tell you about Septimus Keen.'

SIR RICHARD KNIGHT'S
TALE OF SEPTIMUS KEEN

I doubt if it would be possible to meet a more fiendish individual than Septimus Keen, whom I knew as my Tutor at Trinity College, Cambridge, where he was for a time a Don under the name of J.K. Stephen, not to be confused with Robert Donston Stephenson, who in my considered opinion was little more than a man who fantasized about the murders.

Septimus Keen did not fantasize about anything since he understood the distinction of Coleridge between Fantasy and Imagination. He would imagine something that could be real and then he would make it so. He could forge any document quite immaculately and disguise himself in many ways. And at the time I knew him, I was reading for the Tripos in Moral Sciences.

As James Kenneth Stephen, a Cambridge Don at twenty-six, a barrister and a poet with two published books to his name, he became something of a cult figure among the undergraduates, many of whom admired rather than repudiated his taste for debauchery, tastes in which he indulged during the Vacations. In this guise, he was a notorious homosexualist, seducing among others the Duke of Clarence, heir to the Throne after his father Prince Edward, and a peculiar fellow, Montague Druitt, a rather sad sort of chap who was a frequent visitor from Oxford. I resisted all his blandishments but I have to admit that in his capacity as a Tutor, he did have the knack of making the mind expand, accompanied by a tickling wit.

For instance, there was a pleasant, stolid but rather dull fellow called Isaacs whose father had made a fortune in finance. Actually I once met the father of Joseph Isaacs and really, there is no one as self-righteous and self-centred as a genuinely self-made man. This type tends to have no sympathy for anyone who has not done as well as he has: though I have to admit my admiration for self-motivated achievement. However, Stephen/Keen was always teasing young Joseph Isaacs about his obsession with money.

'You will make plenty of money in your later life, Mr Isaacs,' he used to say. 'Oh, yes. Now, listen to me, Mr Isaacs. The first way is to buy cheap and sell expensive. The second way is to pile it high and sell it cheap. A third way is to be like the man who put an advertisement in the paper stating: *A Guaranteed Way to Make Money!!! Send Five Pounds to Box* . . . and every imbecile who sent him five pounds received a postcard saying: *Do What I Do*. Then there is the story of the man who sold the Secret of Infinite Riches in the form of a key to a safety deposit box for one hundred thousand pounds. The chap who bought it went to that safety deposit box and opened it to see a scrap of paper upon which were written the words: *A Mug is Born Every Minute*.'

'Mr Stephen,' Joseph Isaacs replied, 'I thank you for your advice and I mean no disrespect, but may I please ask you, if you are so clever, why you are not rich?'

'But I *am* rich,' Stephen responded. Joseph Isaacs glanced around the shabby and untidy rooms of John Stephen.

'Really?' he enquired gently.

'Oh,' said Stephen with his withering scorn, 'I didn't realize that you were talking about *money*.'

Actually, the tutoring of Stephen seems to have done Joseph Isaacs some good in financial matters, since I gather that he has since made a million by establishing a mail-order business in Chicago selling goods to housewives in remote rural areas. I think that he is the junior partner of a Mr Sears.

In spite of his wit and learning, James Kenneth Stephen did possess some infuriating habits. He used to invite his undergraduates to breakfast and then he had the sheer impudence to be *brilliant at breakfast*! Can you imagine? Myself, I cannot bear anyone who is brilliant at breakfast and would like him shot.

Even more infuriating was his habit of *must be going*. There would be a tutorial session and, just as one was about to leave, he would insist that one stayed on the grounds that he *must be going* and would like to walk with one to, let us say, another College where he had an appointment. Few things infuriate me more. I mean, it must be your misfortune too to be acquainted with visitors who say: 'Well, must be going . . .' and then they don't go. Thirty minutes later, they are still looking for their hats and sticks and after an hour, they are still talking in the doorway. I knew a chap like that at Corpus Christi called Charlie Grace. In his first year, he earned the name Charlie 'Must be Going' Grace. In his second year it was Charlie 'Hurry up and go' Grace. In his third year, he was ostracied as Charlie *Dis*grace. I wish that people would either stay or go, since one can't settle down to anything until the issue is resolved. The habit is quite *maddening*. It is also, of course, a particularly boring and odious method of personal control.

A more serious issue, however, is that of his poetry. Whilst it is technically competent, the hostility displayed towards women is deeply disturbing:

'I do not want to see that girl again:
I did not like her: and I should not mind
If she were done away with, killed or ploughed.
She did not serve a useful end.'

And:

'If all the harm that women have done
Were put in a bundle and rolled into one,
Earth would not hold it,
The sky could not enfold it . . .'

However, he could be every bit as vitriolic about men, as here:

'Oh mayst thou suffer tortures without end:
May fiends with glowing pincers rent thy brain,
And beetles batten on thy blackened face!'

What had the poor man done to him? You may well ask. He had trod accidentally on Stephen's toe as he left a railway carriage. The venom within Stephen is revealed by the following lines, which I believe are applicable to Jack the Ripper.

'But if all the harm that's been done by men
Were doubled and doubled and doubled again,
And melted and fused into vapour and then
Were squared and raised to the power of ten,
There wouldn't be nearly enough, not near,
To keep a small girl for the tenth of a year.'

This obviously refers to Alice Crook, daughter of Annie Crook, a distant cousin of Stephen's, incidentally.

Stephen was handsome and usually his charismatic personality matched his looks. His wit could be scintillating and one cannot doubt the excellence of his classical scholarship. It is a pity that, at the age of twenty-seven, his skull was struck by a windmill vane, since this blow to his brain would drastically alter his life.

Stephen had already fallen in love with Prince Eddy, the Duke of Clarence, becoming insanely jealous whenever the former enjoyed sexual or emotional relations with anyone else. It was too much for him when the Duke of Clarence became involved with Annie Crook, and this was mainly because Annie so reminded the Duke of his mother, Princess Alexandra.

The murders took place during half-term holidays or University vacations. On account of Stephen's relationship with the Duke and the fact that the murders were convenient for the ruling Establishment, everything was smoothed over and Stephen was treated by Sir William Gull, the Royal Physician. When the Duke was betrothed to Princess Mary of Tech, it was feared that there might be another outburst of murderous rage and Stephen was incarcerated in a lunatic asylum. So was the Duke of Clarence, who died on 14th January 1892. It is said that, on hearing the news, J.K. Stephen refused food in a deliberate endeavour to starve himself to death and died on 3rd February. Sad.

This last allegation is not the true case at all. Stephen escaped – and Septimus Keen was reborn to pursue his path of evil.

'**P**ray more champagne, Sir Richard,' I said, fanning myself furiously. 'I find all of this rather hard to believe. If J.K. Stephen did escape, who died in his stead?'

'No one.' Sir Richard smiled wickedly as he now placed a Virginia cigarette in his holder. 'No one. A body already dead was buried.'

'But surely the resources at the disposal of the Establishment would be directed towards the recapture of Stephen?'

'They were. And hitherto they have failed. No one knows *who* Septimus Keen is, let alone *where* he is. It is all too embarrassing to be publicly admitted. After all, the general public is under the impression that Prince Eddy, Duke of Clarence, died two years ago but has no idea that he died while incarcerated in a lunatic asylum.'

'This is not the same account as I heard from my friend Sir Percy Sulgrave.' I informed Sir Richard briefly of the contents of the letter and the meeting with Bob Brown. 'Here, Septimus Keen was alleged to be one Robert Stephenson.'

'I fear that the estimable Sir Percy has fallen victim to a brazen deception,' Sir Richard answered gravely as he sipped more champagne. 'It is so easy to confuse the reality and the fake article, though I am fascinated by the distinctions. For instance, let us suppose that I have a painting signed by Botticelli and five internationally accredited experts on the matter have sworn on their honour and their knowledge and their reputation that it is indeed an authentic work by Botticelli. How much money do you think that painting might be worth?'

'I don't honestly know. Half a million pounds, perhaps? Possibly more?'

'Around that, Amelia. Now suppose it is something that Botticelli painted on a bad day after a row with his wife and a drunken night. Let us say that it is not in fact terribly good, that if anyone other than a celebrated artist such as Botticelli had painted it, no one would give it more than a cursory glance. Would it not still fetch the sum you mentioned?' I nodded. 'Why?'

'Because it was painted by Botticelli.'

'Quite. On account of that factor, even if it were a painting he had executed badly out of spite towards a patron who had upset him, it would be worth a substantial sum. Now, suppose that in fact my Botticelli is an exquisite painting, arguably even finer than his *Venus Arising from the Waves* but unfortunately, a couple of experts come along and prove beyond all measure of reasonable doubt that this painting is a fake produced ten years ago. How much would it be worth then?'

'Not very much.'

'Quite. And this is despite the fact that the artist of ten years ago painted so astonishingly well that experts thought that he was Botticelli. Why is there far more money for a bad painting done by Botticelli than for a brilliant painting done by Bill Snooks? Are people paying for a painting or paying for a signature as a sign of social and economic prestige?'

'I don't know,' I heard myself say, 'I must think about it further.'

'Oh, indeed, Amelia, you should.'

'Richard, you are confusing me.'

'That is not my intention, my dear Amelia.' It obviously was. 'Some years ago, an ingenious thief stole a Rembrandt from a renowned gallery and proceeded to offer it to five American multimillionaires, charging each one a quarter of a million pounds. He then employed an excellent artist to make five perfect copies of this Rembrandt. All of them paid gladly for these treasures, whereupon the painting was returned to the gallery ... To take another example of the fake and the real, what about the art of Acting? You probably think of an actor as one who assumes a role, steps on stage and receives his money. Have you ever thought about what the assumption of so many identities might do to his *own* identity? Having subsumed his identity in that of King Lear, Falstaff, the Noble Hero in a melodrama and perhaps the Wicked Villain on the following week, after which it's *Trousers Down Fast* at the Palace Pier, Brighton, could there not be some confusion of identities? What *is* identity, in any case? I find this problem to be particularly perplexing when I consider the peculiar position of Septimus Keen.'

'Yes . . .' I returned, looking quiet and thoughtful, though the words of Sir Richard were enough to make anyone feel quiet and thoughtful. Even so, I was glad to be away from metaphysics and back to the possibility of grasping hold of some fact that might be solid. 'Richard, I am in no position to say whether or not I think that J.K. Stephen was Jack the Ripper. For all I know, it could have been R. Stephenson, or heaven knows who else. What I would like to know is why you believe J.K. Stephen and this Septimus Keen to be the same person.'

'A good question, Madam, a very good question. And I am glad that you have asked it. Would you like something to eat? A little smoked salmon, perhaps?' I shook my head. Normally the idea would have tempted me but I had quite lost my appetite. 'My reasoning is based on two facts: the rest is circumstantial evidence. James Kenneth Stephen, in addition to his poetry, used to write strange tales under the pseudonym of Septimus Keen that he would then read to his undergraduates. I liked one of his short stories so much that I asked if I could make a copy and he gladly acceded to my request.

'I thought no more of the matter,' Sir Richard continued, 'though I did subsequently pursue my investigations of the Jack the Ripper murders. About a year ago, I came to know a charming and delightful young lady by the name of Venetia Fielding. Perhaps you may have come across her? No? Of course. She is, shall we say, more a part of the *demi-monde* rather than the *beau-monde*, as the French, our Continental neighbours, have it. She informed me that she had known a man called Septimus Keen, a handsome and accomplished young rogue who nursed aspirations to become a writer. For various reasons, he had abandoned her and "gone to the Continent to find himself, whatever that may mean," though I think that Septimus Keen might search all over the globe without ever finding himself. *I* simply want to find *him*. Her description of Septimus Keen, given to me last year, 1893, matched all my memories of J.K. Stephen. More to the point, she had so enjoyed one of his short tales that she had employed a servant to copy it out. It was the same tale that had so impressed me. Here it is:'

THE LOST LOVE

by

Septimus Keen

You may think that I am mad if I tell you this tale, which is of so strange a nature that I have never told it to anyone before. I am sufficiently sane to have worked for the British Government, if that be any kind of qualification, and at one period in my life, when I was working to uncover a foreign spy network based in London, I found myself the victim of several murderous assaults.

I fought off these assaults successfully, though on occasion I was saved more by luck than by design. Indeed, whilst I knocked one of my assailants clear into the Regent's Canal with a smashed skull, on another occasion I was saved only by the fact that the revolver placed in my face refused to fire. I took the blackguard's gun away from him, gave the man a good, hard pistol-whipping and handed him over to the appropriate authorities. On another occasion, a man attacked me with a knife and his wrist had that slinky movement one associates with a man who is accustomed to killing for money. His intention was to make a good, neat slit to the body but I had his wrist by the time that his knife had passed through my thick Harris tweed jacket, done up on all three buttons, my Guernsey sweater, oh, and the leather vest beneath it. Sad fellow. I think he's no longer with us. But the whole operation, I admit, did make me feel a trifle nervous at the time.

I had a rascally acquaintance of the name of, let's say, Bill Smith. He was quite a character.

'Always tell the truth but lead a life so improbable that no one will believe you': that was one of his favourite sayings. How true! How very, very true! To my knowledge, most of his money came from illicit erotic literature, some rather seedy gambling dives in Soho and a few opium dens in the East End, which is not to deny that he was, nevertheless, superbly genial company. Oh, how Bill loved to laugh!

On one occasion, there was a bet. The terms were that within three months, I had to walk a route between the Underground stations of Kilburn and St John's Wood that did not pass a single pub. I explored this matter meticulously in my leisure hours.

'Well, you won that bet, Bill,' I said when I paid up. '"One cannot go from Kilburn Underground station to St John's Wood Underground station on foot without passing a pub."'

'You don't *pass* the pubs, you fool!' he roared with laughter. 'You go *into* them!'

I was a little disturbed when I did not see Bill for some weeks. On making a few enquiries at various public houses he was known to frequent, I discovered merely that he was 'away', which is the slang of his class to denote that the villain is in prison. However, the Metropolitan Police cooperated fully with my enquiries and according to their intelligence, he was not, in fact, 'away'. It was around this curious time of my life that certain peculiar aspects of it increased in intensity.

Unknown to me, during that period there was a war going on between various low-life gangs of thugs for control of the streets and a number of regrettable places of dubious business. I had been seen imbibing beer with Bill Smith in many of these locations and no one was aware of my own position. Not did it help that I was ignorant of many expressions of slang. I would walk into a Kilburn High

Road public house with a cheerful smile upon my face, blithely oblivious to the tension between three rival gangs, the members of which would be murdering one another later that evening. The local people would greet me in friendly fashion, making earnest enquiries after my health. 'Oh, jolly good!' I'd say, 'oh yes, in a good mood. Just bought myself one of those new typewriter things.' Then I would be surprised at the suddenness at which the place became silent. I simply didn't know that to them it meant a Colt repeating revolver.

One night I went out for an evening stroll along the Kilburn High Road and was possessed by the horrible sensation that I was being followed. When I crossed the road, so did two burly, hairy thugs behind me. I noticed that as I increased my pace, so did they. Fortunately I knew, or thought I knew, the area quite well. I marched proudly along the old Roman road of Watling Street, recalling that the area had grown up in the Middle Ages because it was one day's travel by horse and cart from the London Docks to the inn and the blacksmith, were one transporting goods to the North of England. Just as my strolling pursuers and I were approaching Maida Vale, I sprinted down an alleyway and whirled through a series of left and right turnings, all the while conscious of a hard pounding of footsteps in the distance. I nipped into what I had anticipated to be a short cut – but it turned out to be a dead end.

There I was in a small square of Queen Anne houses. In the distance I could hear the heavy tread of boots. I looked around to discern that a blue door, with a number 56 wrought upon it in gold, was ajar. I stepped within and closed it, only to be confronted by the sight of a strikingly beautiful young woman with bright blue eyes and masses of flaming hair, wearing a tightly belted black ball-gown of silk. There was both fire and light in her blazing gaze.

I apologized profusely for disturbing her and endeavoured to explain my predicament. She listened sympathetically and invited me to partake of some refreshment, being obviously a cultured and wealthy woman. As she served me with a glass of vintage Krug, I noticed the diamond, sapphire, emerald and ruby rings, set in platinum, that graced her left hand and sparkled in the candlelight. The room in which we sat was simply but charmingly furnished. There was a table of oak and two stout chairs of the same wood. It puzzled me to notice that two places had been set and I wondered who else she may have been expecting. Along the walls, there were delicately framed prints by Doré, Moreau, Whistler and Beardsley.

The strange lady, who asked me to call her by the curious name of Nuit Babalon, served me Persian gold caviar with thin, dry toast, chopped egg and chopped onion, accompanied by ice-cold Russian vodka. To follow, there was goose liver paté, studded with Italian truffles. Moist white, lightly grilled toast accompanied that, along with a bottle of chilled Gewürtztraminer.We then tackled a cold lobster each, with a dozen oysters as a side-dish. There was mayonnaise and tartare sauce with exquisite capers, also brown buttered bread and a bottle of chilled Pouilly Fumé to refresh our palates for the next course. This consisted of Steak Tartare accompanied by a small portion of buttered spinach and with it a bottle of vintage Château La Tour. It was hard to find room for the subsequent board that groaned with a delectable selection of ripe cheeses, raspberry tart with cream, a bottle of vintage Château d'Yquem, crystallized grapes, Blue Mountain coffee and Hine cognac.

I find it very hard to recall the precise nature of the conversation vouchsafed to me by this extraordinary woman. All I can state for certain is that she had wit, she had intelligence, she had beauty – and that we went to bed together that night. Never have I known such sensual ecstasy. Moreover, every erotic thought that passed through my mind and my nervous system somehow seemed to be transmitted to her. Every spoken obscenity evoked another orgasm. No woman has ever satisfied me so completely.

When I awoke in the morning, she had gone, leaving me a note that stated that it had been a delightful night but pressing matters required her attendance. It also invited me to sup with her at eight o'clock that coming evening. I wrote that I would and departed.

'There was no menace at all on the Kilburn High Road as I walked along it that evening to see a woman with whom I had fallen in love. But I was to receive another kind of shock altogether. Her house was in darkness and outside it there was a sign stating: 'TO LET'.

The following morning saw me call upon the estate agent in question. I purported to be a potential tenant and he showed me around the house. It was empty. Everything had gone. The agent assured me that the house had not been occupied for three months. The freeholder, he informed me, was an elderly gentleman of private means who led a quiet and reclusive life. Considerations of health had led him to move to another property he possessed in the South of France but he was interested in either selling a leasehold or else letting a tenancy, though the agent had never actually met him.

I returned to the house about a month later to find that builders were wrecking the place. They had no idea why they were doing that, informing me that they were simply obeying the agent's instructions. I returned to the estate agent and made enquiries after previous tenants but he had no information at all about any ladies and when I insisted that I had enjoyed a splendid dinner in the house as the guest of a beautiful woman, he looked at me as though I was mad.

Meanwhile I was learning from the newspapers and from local gossip that a number of people vaguely acquainted with me in the district had been killed. Their bodies were customarily found in the Thames with bricks in their coats. As I endeavoured to make sense of this, I received an unsigned letter in feminine, spidery handwriting. The writer was sorry but it could not be helped. There was no hope for the future but the memory would never fade.

No, it never would and I still nurse an aching grief. I was bursting to tell at least *someone* of my bizarre experience but I feared that no one would believe me. Eventually, I encountered Bill Smith on the Kilburn High Road. He was wearing a high silk hat, probably from Lincoln Bennett, and wore morning dress that could well have been tailored by Pope & Bradley. His highly-polished boots were probably hand-made by Wildsmith and his golden fob had to be either Garrard's or Carrington's. He informed me that he was extremely pleased over the way in which his business was expanding. Hailing a hansom, he took me to luncheon at the Savoy, which seems to be letting in all sorts of flash coves these days. Over our port, I told him the story and he burst out laughing.

'No,' he said, 'I don't think you're mad at all. The people who attacked you – or me – the people who the papers say ended up brick-drowned in the river, them's the ones who're mad. Now, your story, squire, I can't make any sense of it any more than you can. I don't know the explanation and I don't pretend to know it. It's a funny old world, guv'nor, and don't believe nobody who tells you different. For all you know, I might've met this lady too. But would you believe me if I were to tell you the story you've just told me? I doubt it.

'But I've survived by a bloody miracle, me old chum, and that's why I accept your story. What do I always say? Always tell the truth but lead a life so improbable that no one will believe you.'

'**R**ichard,' I said, and my temples were throbbing with the ache of unreality, 'this has been absorbing and provoking but I fear that I must take my leave for I have an engagement to which I must attend.'

'Oh . . .' he replied with mild surprise, 'I was hoping that you might join me for a spot of supper.'

'On another occasion, perhaps,' I replied, desperate to be gone. 'I would be grateful if you would kindly escort me to my carriage.'

'Certainly, Amelia, if that is your wish.' And then he escorted me to my carriage with the utmost probity. The curious matter is that he escorted me out of a different door to that by which we had entered and in the hallway I saw again what I had seen at your own flat, Sir Percy: two mirrors placed opposite one another, reflecting us to all Infinity.

Loads of love,

Amelia

EDITOR'S NOTE

The Duke of Clarence has been the suspect in more than one book concerning Jack the Ripper. In his essay *Jack the Ripper – a Solution?* published in *The Oriminologist* (London, 1970), Thomas E.A. Stowell declared that the murders were committed by 'S', 'the heir to power and wealth'; subsequent reports suggested that 'S' was the Duke of Clarence but Stowell denied this in a letter to *The Times* of 5th November 1970 but repeated that 'he was a scion of a noble family'. Curiously enough, according to *The Times* of 14th November, Stowell had died on the day he wrote the letter, 4th November, and his son had destroyed all papers pertaining to Jack the Ripper.

In *Prince Jack: the True Story of Jack the Ripper* (Doubleday, New York, 1978) Frank Spiering maintained that the Ripper was the Duke of Clarence but that the letters to the police were written by J.K. Stephen.

The case for J.K. Stephen having been the Ripper was made by Michael Harrison in his *Clarence: the Life of H.R.H., the Duke of Clarence and Avondale 1864–1892* (W.H. Allen, London, 1972).

The matter is further confused by the claim made in *The Ripper and the Royals* by Melvyn Fairclough (Duckworth, London, 1991) that the Duke of Clarence was alive and well and living contentedly and painting at Glamis Castle in 1910: there is a photograph within the book apparently taken in that year by his mother, Queen Alexandra. According to Fairclough, quoting Joseph Sickert, the self-alleged illegitimate son of the artist Walter Sickert and Alice Margaret Crook, illegitimate daughter of the Duke of Clarence, the Duke did not die until 1933.

(A.S.)

CHAPTER TEN

FROM THE LETTERS
OF BARBARA CROCKFORD

(MORE AND MORE)

Dear Amelia,
What a pleasure it was to entertain you in Harrogate:
It was all really frightfully super! Thank you so much for
your letters! *Do* tell sir Percy to be careful. I am rather
disturbed by what you have written to me.

Insofar as I understand the somewhat sordid matter of
the Jack the Ripper slayings of 1888, it seems that the
gallant Sir Percy is in hot pursuit of a solution. In the
course of his quest, he has encountered the insalubrious
Mr Bob Brown in some awful dive in the East End and this
Mr Brown has informed him that the Ripper is a Septimus
Keen, who assumes a bewildering variety of identities and
who on this occasion posed as R. Stephenson, a pervert
addicted to Black Magic.

Sir Percy is also of the opinion that Bob Brown may be
the man who murdered Arthur Bullock MP.

Sir Percy also appears to think that these sordid matters
have something to do with Doctor Lipsius of London, with
whom I am acquainted. I have always found Lipsius to be a
gentleman of considerable charm and weighty integrity and
have enjoyed the display of his most formidable learning
whenever I have had occasion to visit London.

You inform me that Sir Percy sent the police to investigate
Bob Brown as the suspected murderer of Arthur Bullock
MP. You also tell me that when the police raided the house in
Marcia Road, they found, not Bob Brown but a semi-senile

and gibbering fool called Mick Jones, who had taken over the flat from Bob Brown. With all possible respect, Amelia, I am starting to question the validity of the judgement of Sir Percy.

Then you have informed me about your interesting afternoon with Sir Richard Knight: and is he not *such* a delightful man!? Even if that gentleman endeavoured to be boring, I doubt if he would succeed in his endeavour. Even so, Sir Richard – and please give him my very best regards – appears to have been bitten too by the bug for the solving of the Ripper murders and he has informed you that these were committed by J.K. Stephen, an eccentric Cambridge don.

Both Sir Percy, via Bob Brown, and you, via Sir Richard, have been informed that both R. Stephenson and J.K. Stephen, was actually a master of disguise by the name of Septimus Keen. It is not impossible, I suppose, that this Septimus Keen could have been one or the other or neither; but certainly he could not have been both. The two theories are mutually exclusive.

Now an event has happened that impels my writing to you and which bears upon these matters. I received what I enclose, a telegram:

IF YOU WISH TO LEARN THE TRUTH ABOUT JACK THE RIPPER COMMA SIR PERCY SULGRAVE COMMA LADY AMELIA STANHOPE COMMA AND SEPTIMUS KEEN BE FOR TEA AT THE ATHENA CLUB FIVE TOMORROW COMMA BEST WISHES COMMA VENETIA FIELDING STOP

I have, in fact, met Venetia Fielding at a number of social occasions in London and I have always found her to be perfectly charming. She lives in Cheyne Walk, I believe, and is possessed of a magnificent head of flaming red hair. I think that she is of independent means and on the previous occasion that I had met her, I think at a *soirée* given by Dr Lipsius, she told me all about her plans for setting up a women's club to be perfectly exclusive. Men were perfectly entitled to do this, this engaging woman argued, and so women should be entitled to do the same. I could not help but agree.

In no time at all, The Athena Club, in premises just off Pall Mall, had been founded and Venetia Fielding had sent me a card of the Three Graces, informing me of its address. I suppose I should have made endeavours to join there and then but what with the problems Thomas is having in his business affairs and so on, the matter simply slipped my mind. Nevertheless, I did rather like the idea of a club which men could not enter.

There was no problem concerning the making of the date. Thomas was away and so I ordered the cabriolet and the appropriate railway bookings.

The Athena Club has a dainty and discrete Queen Anne exterior and interior. Two features, however, detract from this initially delicate impression. They consist of two absolutely enormous women at the desk of Reception, who look capable of tearing the arms away from the strongest men in the World. Even so, their manner was polite and I was escorted into a drawing room where many ladies were taking tea before a statue of Athena. Venetia rose to greet me and pointed out many other beauties of the interior. Female conversation trilled as I was shown exquisite paintings of the Goddess in her various guises, as Athena, Minerva, Aphrodite, Venus, Hera, Juno, Isis and Nuit, She of the stars. What extraordinary blue eyes Venetia has!

'Oh, Barbara!' she exclaimed. '*What* a pleasure to see you

here! I'm *so* glad that you could come after all. Good to get away from the men for a time and be just girls together, isn't it?' she giggled. 'Would you care for the Club Tea?' I acquiesced. 'And for your tea, would you prefer Assam, Darjeeling, Ceylon, Orange Pekoe, Lapsang Souchong or Jasmine?' I decided upon Assam, which was brought by a young and slim French maid who was all black satin and lace and who presented us with the finest Chinese porcelain upon a tray of shining silver. 'Milk?' I nodded. 'There's a reason for putting the milk in first, you know. If you put the milk in first, it will keep the tea leaves down.' Accompanying the tea, which proved to be excellent, there was a silver platter of cucumber sandwiches that looked as though they had been sliced with a razor. Utterly exquisite pastries followed that: tarts of apple and cherry and also the very velvety seduction of rich chocolate éclairs. I noticed that the pretty young maids dropped a curtsy after each action intended to lead to our greater satisfaction.

We chatted and chattered about matters inconsequential for a while and Venetia confirmed what I had always suspected, which is that fortune had contrived to give her a large income independent from the necessity of having a husband.

'Husbands, Barbara . . .' she smiled as she nibbled delicately at a cucumber sandwich. 'Always there when you don't want them and never there when you need them.' How true, I reflected; how very, very true. 'Men can be such fools,' she continued. 'Men think and ask *why*? Women dream and say *why not*? But enough of this. The pastries and sandwiches were simply to encourage your appetite. Let us enjoy hot crumpets soaking in deep yellow Jersey butter, and honey, if that is what you would like as well, along with thickly buttered toasted teacake in which raisins have been embedded, and scones with strawberry jam and

Devonshire clotted cream.' Suddenly she burst into verse, announcing the brief poem as The Petty Bourgeois:

'In my nicest, sweetest, most dulcet tone
I asked the young lady to bring me a *scone*.
Damn! The bloody bitch has gone
Back to the kitchen and brought me a *scone*!'

As I laughed, I was not expecting her to beckon me, after our tea, into another and rather different sort of room where women were smoking cigars and drinking brandy, the air being full of the sounds of champagne corks being popped and raucous female laughter. We both took a mixture of champagne and brandy, which went down a treat, and I admired the Ancient Egyptian paintings of Bastet, the Cat Goddess, and of Sekhmet, the Lioness and Goddess of War.

From there we passed into a rather quiet room where women lay in languid attitudes, enjoying opium or hashish from water-pipes or *hookahs*: it was a pleasure to recline upon a divan myself. Although some set of imbeciles will no doubt make these pleasures illegal in the future, for my own part I have always relished them, as I believe is also the case with Her Majesty the Queen. Here there were Hindoo paintings of Durga, consort of Shiva, Lord and God of Sex and Death, and herself a Goddess of Destruction: and of Kali, Goddess of Annihilation.

From there we passed on to a plain, private room where there were just the two of us. We reclined upon couches. There was a clear pool in the centre of this room and goldfish swam within it. At the centre, there was a fountain fashioned in stone in the form of the poetess Sappho and the water sprang from her every orifice, including the nipples of her breasts. As I rested, Venetia vanished momentarily, then returned with a maid who bore a silver tray with a set of glasses, a bottle of champagne and a bottle of cognac.

'Thank you,' Venetia said to the maid, 'oh, and do put up the "Do Not Disturb" sign outside, won't you? There's a good girl.' She now extracted a silver cigarette case from her bag and offered a cigarette to me. These were Russian and wrapped in black paper with gold tips. 'What do you think of this club?' she enquired.

'It is very fine,' I replied with sincerity. 'I only wish that there were more clubs such as this one for women.'

'It is a start.'

'And a good one.'

'About time too, Barbara,' she smiled. 'One of the matters that will emerge from this is that women will eventually have the vote.'

'Are you serious?' I gasped.

'Oh, certainly. There may even be a day in the next century, though hardly within your lifetime, when we may have a woman Prime Minister.'

'Impossible!'

'Anything is possible, Barbara.' She was expert in opening the bottle of Krug and pouring its contents into our crystal flute glasses without spilling a drop. 'But let us take up the thread which led us to a moment here and now. I am acquainted with both Sir Percy Sulgrave and, albeit only on the basis of chance meetings at musical evenings, with Lady Amelia Stanhope. I lead the life of a lady of leisure, though I sometimes take employment in order to give my hours further interest. This is what has led me to take an interest in the case of Jack the Ripper. I would like the swine who committed these horrendous crimes to be brought to justice and hanged upon the gallows.'

'Venetia, I entirely agree. But where does one start? There seem to be ever so many suspects.'

'Indeed, Barbara. Tell me,' she sipped champagne, 'have you ever come across an Inspector Abberline?'

'No, I have never enjoyed that particular privilege.'

'I enjoyed our acquaintanceship and thought him to be one of the finest detectives I have ever met. Unfortunately, he retired from the police force on the 7th February 1892, though fortunately he is still very much alive and he is still pursuing his somewhat obsessive interest in the case. I volunteered for the position of being his unpaid research assistant. Abberline was at Miller's Court, Dorset Street after the report of the hideous death of Mary Kelly, the woman who apparently knew the secret about the bastard daughter of the Duke of Clarence. He gave orders for Miller's Court to be sealed off: no one was to enter or to leave. He fired off a telegram to Commissioner Sir Charles Warren demanding bloodhounds without knowing that the man had resigned the day before.

'I have respect for Abberline. He had joined the Metropolitan Police in 1863, becoming a Sergeant in 1865 and an Inspector in 1873. I used to go and see him at his home in 41 Mayflower Road, Clapham. I happen to have a skill possessed by few men: I can use a typewriter and, to be candid the man was a heavy drinker and he doubted if women had brains except for the most mechanical of tasks. Even though he could be perfectly infuriating at times, he nevertheless had his own skills and integrity which led me to take him seriously. He had been head of Whitechapel CID for thirteen years, which gave him an intimate knowledge of the East End.

'His heavy drinking caused carelessness on his part. I noticed that he kept writing in a diary that he sometimes locked and sometimes did not, and on these occasions, he simply shoved it into an unlocked drawer. On one occasion, he went away for a day, asking me to copy up his notes. I took away his diaries, had them photographed and returned them to the drawer. On one double-page spread of the journal concerned, he had listed – in sprawling handwriting – the names of J.K. Stephen, H.R.H. the Duke of Clarence, Sir William Gull, Lord Randolph Spencer Churchill, along with a cryptic reference to that old rhyme about a butcher, a baker and a candlestick maker. There were also notes of various dates ranging from 1890 to 1895.'

'Venetia!' I expostulated. 'You are not seriously suggesting that there is some sort of link to the Royal Family here, surely?'

'I deeply regret that I am,' she replied gravely as she poured more champagne for both of us. 'Here, do take this copy to Sir Percy. And I have further documents for you, photographed from the diaries of Inspector Abberline. Here.

Catherine EDDOWES
4th April 1842 – Sept 29th 1888

Catherine Eddowes was born to George and Catherine Eddowes on the 4th April 1842 at Gaisley Green, Wolverhampton. Her father was a tin-plate worker. The family moved to London living at 4, Baden Place, Bermondsey, where her brother was born. Over the next 10 or 11 years the family lived in Long Lane, Bermondsey, and the children went to the St John's Charity School at Potters Field, Tooley Street. In 1851, they lived at 35 West Street, Bermondsey. On Nov 7th, 1855, Mrs Eddowes died of phthisis (TB of the lungs). She was 42 when she died. Catherine was only 13 years of age. Her brothers and sisters were sent to the workhouse for the best part of 12 years. At the age of 19 Catherine met an army man, Thomas Conway. She bore him 3 children although she never married him, and they parted in 1880. Conway took the two boys and she took the girl, Annie. In 1880 she took up with another man, an Irish porter named John Kelly. They lived in Flower & Dean Street, Whitechapel. Last record of Catherine was when she was admitted to Whitechapel Infirmary, 14th June 1887, suffering with foot burns. She was known as Kate Conway, and put her religion as R.C: she died age 46, on 29th Sept 1888.

No connection with any of the others.

Pawn ticket in the name of M.J. Kelly

Mary Jane KELLY
Ref. to Marie Jeanette Kelly. August 1865 – Nov 1888.

Through a letter sent to me in Jan 1889, from Miss Nora O'Brien of Roofer Castle, Limerick, Ireland, when she stated that Marie Jeanette Kelly was her niece, daughter of her brother who was in the army. Officer of the Inniskilling Dragoon Guards. Her real name was Mary Jane O'Brien. Kelly was a name of a distant relative. She had been receiving letters from her in the name of Mary Jane Kelly. But after her letters stopped coming she had found out about the Whitechapel murders. I now know she was never an unfortunate. No record of Workhouse or Infirmary or any other help or assistance. Bellord Domestic Agency helped her to acquire service to a West-end family as a nanny in Cleveland Street. Had made friends with a house parlour-maid – Winifred May Collis, 20, of 27 Cleveland Street off Great Portland Street, who went to stay with Mary Jane Kelly in Dorset Street in Nov 1888, due to an unwanted pregnancy. Never heard of again.

I discovered—

(1) She was not an unfortunate, and she never lacked money.

(2) She mysteriously appeared from nowhere, then disappeared. I believe she was a P.A.

The aunt received a christmas card from Kelly, sent from Canada after Kelly's murder.

I was advised not to pursue any more to this investigation.

'Note,' said Venetia, 'how Abberline states that "*I was advised not to pursue any more to this investigation*".'

'You are really making me feel quite giddy, Venetia. Are you still working with the former Inspector Abberline?'

'Not any more,' she replied. 'He has his qualities but I am afraid that his attitude to an unpaid typist and research assistant is not all that a woman could desire. There was an unfortunate misunderstanding and I left his employment. I do not think that he will ever crack the case, as a cold matter of fact. The Establishment is simply too powerful. In any event, Jack the Ripper could not possibly have been Sir William Gull, however ghastly a man he might have been under other circumstances. For heaven's sake, Barbara, he was seventy-five and had suffered two heart attacks in the previous year.'

'Surely you are not alleging that it could have been Lord Randolph Churchill, who died a couple of days ago? I know that his behaviour has been perfectly lunatic for the past couple of years or so, since I gather that he has been very ill, but that is really beyond the bounds of belief.'

'Quite so. No, Inspector Abberline was convinced, however, that a cabal at the very centre of Government had conspired to silence five blackmailing prostitutes. In consequence, I know that an assassin was hired to perform the job. I can recall Abberline complaining: "*Theories: We were almost lost in theories; there were so many of them.*" Have you heard, by any chance, of William Henry Bury?'

'No.'

'Some people have all the luck!' she chortled. 'He was

a sordid and vicious drunkard. He arrived in Dundee on the steamer *Cambria*, taken from London on 19th January 1889. There he and his wife Ellen took a basement flat at 113 Princes Street. On 5th February, he strangled his wife with a rope, slumped into a drunken stupor and awoke to stab her, after which he ripped open with a knife her abdomen: when the police found her body, the intestines were protruding. He then stuffed her into a large wooden trunk. On the 10th February, Bury confessed at Dundee Police Station. Detective Lieutenant James Parr went to investigate the matter and found a chalked message: '*Jack Ripper is at the back of this door*'. '*Jack Ripper is in this sellar*' (sic) was the message chalked on the stairway wall leading to the basement flat. William Henry Bury was executed for the murder of his wife Ellen a mere eleven weeks later.

'From April to December 1888, William Henry Bury was living in the East End as a self-employed merchant of sawdust at 3 Spanby Road, Bow, where he stabled his pony and cart. He was a drunken misfit who hated women. Case closed.'

'Venetia!' I burst out, 'you're not saying it's as simple as that, are you?'

'It should have been,' she answered coolly, 'and it would have been if Inspector Abberline had not played some part in the case. For the murderer, it could not have been more convenient if the entire matter had been blamed on the atrocious William Henry Bury and had finished with him dangling on the end of a rope on a Scottish gallows. Unfortunately for Jack the Ripper, Inspector Abberline spotted that this was merely a copycat murder. The Ripper had tried to set up the wretched Bury in order to have the case closed.'

'Then who *was* Jack the Ripper?'

'Have you ever heard,' Venetia enquired, 'of Septimus Keen?'

'Oh . . .' I said, very slowly.

'Clearly you have,' she responded in her clear, crisp voice.

'You know I have. You know that I know Sir Percy Sulgrave and Lady Amelia Stanhope. You know that I have heard of Septimus Keen, though I have never met him. All *I* know here is that two individuals, encountered separately by my friend and by my acquaintance, have insisted that Jack the Ripper *is* Septimus Keen, though they ascribe to him two entirely separate identities.'

'Have a brandy, my dear,' Venetia poured out generous measures, 'and allow me to tell you the truth about Septimus Keen.'

MISS VENETIA FIELDING'S
TALE OF SEPTIMUS KEEN

'I am sure,' said Venetia Fielding, 'that the Decadent Movement in the Arts and Literature of France has moved into England and that Septimus Keen embodies it. He is a very slim and handsome young man whose behaviour is often utterly outrageous, though frequently amusing. I think we may have met at some *soirée* or other. I found his company to be enchanting and came to know him as well as, I suppose, anyone can.

'Keen does not believe in the notion of identity and with the philosopher David Hume points out that if we look into the notions of "I" and "Self", there is no "I" and there is no "Self": there is merely a succession of ideas and impressions. He adds that Hume's conclusion was reached centuries ago in India by Gautama Buddha. He ridicules the notion of Descartes stating that our ultimate certainty is *"I think, therefore I am,"* since, he argues, it begs the question of what is the "I" that does the thinking: Keen states that the only certainty is *"There is a thought now."* To this end, he often spends weeks resolving to be a different person every day. He perceives no contradiction between being the Reverend Cyril Prendergast, a mild-mannered clergyman of liberal views from South Devon, on Tuesday and being Jack the Ripper on Wednesday. On Thursday he may well be Mr Frank Kirkwood, a married man with a suburban villa in Wimbledon and who is something in the City. He might even metamorphose into a professional impersonator who gives music-hall turns on Friday evenings.

'I have to confess that a wild and dangerous young man is highly attractive to the female of the species, and so I came to know him further. He was living, he told me, in a bedsit in Canonbury, North London, an area as unknown to the majority of Londoners as is the North Pole. I used to welcome him to my house at Cheyne Walk where he on occasion alarmed me, not by his behaviour, for he was always graceful in terms of his manners, but on account of the thoughts he expressed. He informed me that he was a Satanist: you can imagine how perturbed and alarmed I was.

'"Kindly don't be so agitated, Venetia," he responded, his voice playing as softly as a cello in a Brahms Symphony. '"The Devil' is, historically, the God of any people that one personally dislikes. The serpent Satan, as named in *Revelations* and first described in *Genesis*, is not the enemy of Mankind, but He who made the Gods of our race, knowing Good and Evil; He bade us 'Know Thyself,' and taught Initiation. Confusion came about in Ancient Egypt when the Cult of Osiris, the god who died and rose again, supplanted the cult of Set, god of the Mysteries of Sex and Death. Etymologically, the Middle Eastern 'Saitan' of the Yezidi in Mesopotamia is derived from 'Set' and the Christian 'Satan' is derived from 'Saitan'. The Christians, when they had political power, simply co-opted all deities of the pagans into their pantheon as Mother of God and as Saints and what-not; and they demonized whatever didn't fit."

'This was all very well, as far as I am concerned, since I concur with Gibbon in his magnificent *The Decline and Fall of the Roman Empire* that the cause was Christianity, a disease of mind and body more contagious and deadly to civilization and evolution than syphilis, and twice as disgusting, to state the least. In fact, I found the discourse of Septimus to be stimulating and refreshing until we began to discuss the matter of Jack the Ripper.

"'There is a proverb, Venetia," he told me. "'*Always tell the truth, but lead a life so improbable that no one will believe you.*' Who would ever believe that, sitting here in your home, sipping your excellent manzanilla sherry, I would calmly tell you that I am Jack the Ripper? Why don't you inform Inspector Abberline? Oh, sorry, I forgot, he has retired. Then inform Commissioner Sir Charles Warren: oh, I *am* sorry, he has taken early retirement too. What a pity! Oh, and the day before Abberline retired from the police force, John Netley, coachman to Sir William Gull, Royal Physician, ran down Alice Crook, illegitimate daughter of the Duke of Clarence, and then drowned himself in the Thames. It is unfortunate for the conspirators, I think, that the young lady managed to survive.

"'Allow me to tell you the truth, Venetia. *I* was Jack the Ripper. I am an assassin who often works for the Government. I murdered all five prostitutes on a contract coming from the highest in the land, do you understand? Now I don't simply kill. I like the matter to be done with wit and style. It was vital to me, if you will pardon the pun, that certain things were done with the *vitals* of the victims so as to mislead some into suspecting the Freemasons. In fact, this gentle and charitable organization had nothing to do with the matter whatsoever. I used my worship of Satan. I thought that the Devil might be relishing my series of human sacrifices if the bodies were placed in the form of an Inverse Pentagram. I also wanted to create a new mythological figure, Jack the Ripper, the memory of whom would haunt London for longer than a hundred years and so might even become an obsessive study for future historians and criminologists and even a fitting subject for future museums. Worthless women died for blackmailing the Establishment and for my creation of a future mythology.' I think that Satan was satisfied."

"'You horrify me!" I shouted.

"'Why?" he smiled gently, showing dainty white teeth. "Satan is merely the Lord of Sex and Death and we do Him honour with these Sacred Rites. The same Holiness has been perpetrated in India by the Thugs. In India, Shiva, Lord God of Death and Destruction and one of the Eternal Trinity of Brahma the Creator, Vishnu the Preserver and Shiva the Destroyer, is rightly venerated: and if, in India, you were to denounce Shiva as being Satan, you would be stoned to death by Hindoos outraged by your blasphemy and otherwise leading lives of the utmost piety."

"'Septimus," I said, after taking a deep breath, "your shocking words would convince me more if somehow you seemed to care whether I believed you or not."

"'Quite right, Madam. I *don't* care whether you believe me or not."

"'So you expect me to believe that I am sitting here with the vile butcher of five prostitutes?"

"'Yes." He smiled. "Or no. What can I expect you to believe? Maybe so." Abruptly he produced a white clay pipe from his pocket and packed it from a cheap pouch of shag tobacco. From his bag he produced a cloth cap of the sort that only costermongers wear. He took off his his stylish blue frock coat, whipped away his golden cuff links and rolled up his sleeves. Then he lit his pipe, puffing foul fumes into the room. "Sorry about that, lady," he said in a completely different accent.

"'Septimus, what are you doing?"

"'Dunno why yer calling me Septimus," he replied in the authentic accents of the East End, insofar as I have heard them. "Bury's the name. William 'enry Bury. Wouldn't want to be buying any sawdust, would yer? Useful fer loads of fings an' vat." For an instant, he really *was* William Henry Bury, then:

"'No good, Septimus," I said. "'William 'Enry Bury' would not wear trousers of the quality you have."

""Course I would," he pleaded hoarsely and blew his nose on his fingers. "Don't mean no offence to you, Miss Fielding, but a man can pick up fings of quality in this business. Dahn the parts where I come from, people respect you if you *dress well*. I'm always telling that to me boy: 'Dress well, son,' I say, "cos you are wot people see you as being.' See vese trousers, Miss Fielding? Beautiful cloth! Bought 'em the day after the funeral. Jack Naylor, the tailor. Now, 'e was a good man. Sad that he had to go the way he did. Still, that's life, ennit? One minute you've got it all and the next minute . . . nah, reckon I'm teaching my grandma to suck eggs, the way I'm talkin'."

"'Oh, for heaven's sake, shut up!" I snapped. "And do take off that horrible cap." He did so as he gave me a wicked grin. "What was the point of that demonstration, Septimus?"

"'I was being the ineffably boring and utterly banal William Henry Bury," Septimus replied as he removed his awful cap and resumed his former persona. "You see, my strategy was to have all my murders blamed upon him. That was why he suddenly fled to Dundee, since he knew that he was under suspicion. Had it not been for the acute and alert Inspector Abberline, everything could have been dumped upon this useless and unpleasant fool and the matter would have ended with his hanging. Damn Abberline! Ha! But I laugh for a good reason. The authorities already have done so."

"'Septimus," I said, "are you mad?"

273

GERALD SUSTER

"'Definitely,' he replied. "Absolutely no question about it at all. Yet there is a method in my madness. Allow me to ask *you* a question, Miss Fielding. Are you sane?"

"'Of course I am!' I responded indignantly. "Really! What a ridiculous question!"

"'How do you know that you are sane?'"

"'As assuredly as I know that two and two make four. I know what reality is and I act accordingly. In consequence, there is no danger of my being carted off by men in white coats because I believe that I am Cleopatra nor will I be run over by a bus because I suffer from the delusion that my body is invulnerable.'"

"'How do you know that I exist?'"

"'I think,' I retorted with crisp asperity, "that if I were to punch you on the nose, which presently I feel like doing since you are being *so* exasperating, there would be no doubt at all about the matter. *I* would know that you exist and *you* would know that *I* exist in no uncertain manner.'"

"'Rather commonsensical, aren't you?' he taunted me.

"'Yes. It is a pity that this seems to trouble you.'"

"'Do you have the pleasure of being acquainted with Inspector Cutforth of Scotland Yard?'"

"'Cutforth of the Yard? The celebrated detective? Why, yes, I have enjoyed the good fortune of meeting him on a few occasions. He is a brilliant and fascinating man.'"

"'Do you allow that he is sane?'"

"'Of course he is!' I burst out. "How else could he have solved so many crimes?"

"'Not this one,' he smiled, "not this one. For I knew him quite well. Here,' he produced a manuscript, "read it for yourself.'"

MORE AND MORE

by

Septimus Keen

R obert Cutforth was unquestionably one of the most interesting men that I have ever met. He was a friend of my father's, which is how I came to know him after his retirement as one of the most celebrated detectives in the Yard's illustrious history. He had solved the matter of the Sloane Square burglaries, the Kentish Town rapist, the serial killer of Willesden, the robberies of banks in Knightsbridge, the murder of Lady Sarah Harrington and the theft of the Countess of Westmoreland's tiara, among many others. I thought that it was a pity that he had retired just prior to the Jack the Ripper murders, since if any man could have solved that complex case and apprehended the true culprit, it would have been Cutforth.

He was a very tall, thin man whose forehead was twice the size of that of an average man and untidy grey hair sprouted behind it in wings. He always wore horn-rimmed glasses and, if a caricaturist were to draw Cutforth, he would leave out the eyes to show stern blank panes. Never an ostentatious man, he usually wore a plain black suit with a black bowler hat, immaculately shined black boots, a crisp white shirt and a pale blue cravat, fastened with a very small diamond stick-pin.

'There is nothing harder than a diamond for cutting through surfaces,' he used to say, 'though let us not forget that diamonds come from compressed coal.' His father had been a coal miner. It was very kind of him, after my own father died, to invite me to his house in Highgate. He lived alone, his wife having died some years earlier, and his material life was one of modest comfort. He had little interest in material possessions and although the exterior of his house was in the discreet and graceful style of the Queen Anne period, the interior was strikingly spartan. He hated fussy ornamentation and excluded any object that was not useful. One did not dine like a gourmet when one went to see Robert Cutforth but one certainly ate well. A typical meal would consist of fresh prawns with brown bread and lemon, then bangers and mash with onion gravy followed by treacle pudding with custard. To drink, there was always a barrel of best ale served in pewter tankards and he served enough to satisfy any man, though there was always a bottle of sweet sherry if (infrequently) there were ladies present. Tobacco was his only other vice and he used to smoke huge quantities of Virginia flavoured with Perique soaked in rum in his gnarled black briar pipe which, like the man himself, was as straight as a die.

'The popular Press is so preposterous,' he told me one evening. 'They have made me out to be some sort of hero with virtually supernatural powers of detection. I am nothing of the sort. Here are *my* rules of detection: Reason. Observation. Logic. And Documentary Evidence. Nothing else. It is all patient, plodding work. This,' he sighed regretfully, 'is why the More case, one of the few I failed to solve, baffled me so much and still tortures me here and now and in retirement. *Life is not like that*, I keep saying to myself.' I knew nothing of the More case and asked him to tell me about it. 'How is it possible?' he sighed heavily, 'how is it possible for a man to be murdered in a room he has locked from the inside, and there are no broken windows nor signs of a struggle? Suicide? Possible, of course, but how the hell do you shoot yourself without a gun? The only clues I had were these documents.' He extracted them from a neatly arranged box file and passed them to me.

THE JOURNAL OF PETER MORE

1

Three days ago, I woke up in a hospital for the poor in one of the gloomiest parts of South London, not knowing how I had come to be there or even who I was. There was a woman whom I did not recognize sitting by my bedside whose face wore an expression of concern. I am keeping this journal in an endeavour to retain my sanity.

This rather blowzy, buxom woman informed me that she was my wife Martha and was visibly distressed by my inability to recall the fact. She told me that some ruffian had coshed me and that I had been in a coma for seven days.

'But you're all right now, aren't you, darlin'?' she said anxiously. A doctor came to ensure that there was nothing wrong with me organically.

'Just a case of concussion and shock, Mrs Johnson,' I heard him inform Martha. 'He'll recover soon enough.' Since more of the hospitalized and impoverished required beds than there were beds to spare, I was discharged from the hospital and went home with this woman by clanging tram. Home turned out to be a two-room basement flat with kitchen and bathroom in a faded Clapham terrace of the 1840s.

'Would you like a drink, ducks?' the woman who was allegedly my wife asked me. When I nodded, she brought me a thimble of sweet sherry in a crude glass tumbler. It tasted like syrup of figs. "Ow are you, then? You was found lying in the street. Coshed. London just isn't safe these days.'

'Martha,' I said, 'can you help me?' She nodded. 'I am obviously suffering from amnesia.'

'Am . . . what?'

'Loss of memory.'

'Yeah, well, you'd better get it back before Monday, which you should, it being only Friday today. That's plenty of time, ducks.' She smiled and the fact that many of her teeth were missing made her look like a whore from Hell. 'Mr Gorringe has been ever so understanding about it all. Obviously yer lose yer week's pay but at least yer have yer job back on Monday.'

'*What* job?'

"'Cor, 'e must've 'it yer 'ard, ducks. Don't worry. It'll come back to you.'

'Possibly,' I murmured. 'But it's all really rather confusing. I think I need some brandy to pull myself together. Where's the nearest place where I can obtain some fine *cognac*?'

'Eh? Wot?'

'You know. Good brandy.'

'Are you mad, Derek? 'Ow're folks like us goin' to be able to afford vat?'

'Then give me another sherry.'

'No. You know as well as I do is that one a day is all we can afford.'

'Damnit, I'll buy another.'

'What *wiv*?' She snorted disgustedly. 'You and your fancy ideas. It's not for the likes of us. Always talking posh, you was.'

I stared blankly at the hideous design of the room. The only pictures on the stained, pale yellow wallpaper were of the Virgin Mary, Jesus Christ and the Virgin Mary cradling the Infant Jesus. There were also little wooden placards nailed to the walls. One read: 'Jesus Loves All Sinners'. Another read: 'Home, Sweet Home'.

'Martha,' I said, 'I know it sounds stupid but I *was* coshed. Help me to bring back my memory by telling me everything you know about me.'

'I was 'opin' you might ask that,' she replied, wiping her dripping nose on the back of her hand. Then she sniffed loudly and proceeded to talk. It seemed that I was Derek Johnson, I had been married to her for seven years, and we had lived in this wretched basement for five. She did not go out to work because the neighbours would frown upon the fact. For the past eight years I had earned a small but steady wage as a book-keeping clerk at Gorringe's of Streatham, a store that sold carpets, linoleum and paint to people such as myself. I was expected there for work at 7:00 a.m. on Monday. We had to save every penny in order to survive and we had no friends apart from Bob and Myrtle. Bob was a bank clerk and he and his wife would be coming over for supper on Saturday.

That night, I lay in bed with this bloated lump of lard beside me and wondered what I could do for the time being other than survive. It was fortunate that she did not expect me to make love to her. On the following morning, she made me a horrible, greasy breakfast and the tea tasted like liquid sawdust. There were no books in the house other than a few that apparently belonged to me but that aroused no sense of recognition. Fortunately, however, they were all to do with book-keeping. I proceeded to study them and had mastered the general principles by the time that our visitors arrived. They were both ugly and monumentally boring though I pretended that I had known the ghastly Bob for years. The meal was unfit to be served to a dog but everyone present praised it. There was that frightful sweet sherry before the meal and, as a special treat for us and our honoured guests, there was a jug of ale.

On Sunday, I endeavoured to master the intricacies of book-keeping and clerical work, since one needs money in order to survive, obviously, and I had discovered that my savings amounted to the princely sum of two pounds, six shillings and seven pence. At no time was there any flash of recognition. Martha spent the day ironing my shirt and ensuring that the trousers of my dreary grey suit had sharp creases. As I put on my cheap bowler hat on Monday and departed for work, I felt totally devoid of taste. I travelled in a tram that was crowded, hot and unpleasantly sweaty, my journey made all the more uncomfortable by the fact that I could not obtain a seat. Eventually I alighted at Gorringe's.

'You're late,' snapped a thin, balding man with sandy hair. I glanced at the clock. It was 7:01 a.m. Fortunately, Martha had informed me that this was Mr Jarvis of whom I had often complained to her.

'I'm sorry,' I said. 'There were unexpected delays owing to the heavy traffic.'

'I think you have forgotten something, Johnson.' What could I have forgotten apart from my memory? Ah! It had to be in that book of business etiquette which I had studied yesterday.

'I really do apologize, *sir*,' I said.

'That's better, Johnson. And take an earlier tram in the future. We don't want this sort of thing to happen again. Pity about your accident. We've had to give your desk to Mr Birkin but I think you will find everything else as it was. Mr Gorringe requires all the figures by Friday.' He waved me away through a door that led to a dusty room where three thin men with pinched, drawn faces, all wearing spectacles, were hunched over ledgers and busy at their work. My place was now at a small desk, away from the window. It was piled with ledgers and the chair was uniquely uncomfortable.

I found no difficulty in executing this mechanical, repetitive job other than the torturing tedium. Nobody spoke in the morning. At 1:00 p.m. we were allowed our lunch break in the staff canteen. You *had* to have lunch in the staff canteen and it was bad beyond belief, though the price was docked from one's wages. As for my three colleagues, Mr Birkin said nothing, Mr Pemberton had nothing to say and Mr Wilshire had nothing to say and said it.

'I say,' he shovelled mouthfuls of atrocious cottage pie into his mouth and chewed thoughtfully. 'Delicious! Gorringe's certainly knows how to look after us! Well, we're not exactly eating with the plebs, are we?' This was true. The manual workers ate here between 12:30 p.m. and 1:00 p.m. Management did not have to eat here at all. 'Had a wonderful weekend. Took the wife to see Oxford Street. We couldn't afford to buy anything *there*, of course, but she was absolutely thrilled to see it. My goodness, 1:29. Better get back to work.'

I worked until 6:00 p.m. and then went home to my wife.

2

This was my life for the rest of my life unless I secured promotion. Even then, it would be more of the same, only slightly better paid. For two weeks I endured this hell, still being incapable of recognizing any of it within my memory. Then I began to dream and all my dreams possessed a disturbing coherence and consistency.

In every dream, my name was Peter More and I lived

in a Georgian house in Richmond Avenue, Barnsbury. There were two sphinxes outside that house, and there were sphinxes sculpted in stone outside the neighbouring houses. As Peter More, surgeon, I led the life of a gentleman, enjoying my pleasures without a care in the World. To me these dreams were vastly more than mere dreams: they were the veritable stuff of *memory*.

On Saturday night of my third week, I informed Martha that I was going for a stroll after work and she acquiesced in the tone of a wife who is bored by her husband. She did not appear to care when I might be back as long as I did not spend too much money. I took a series of trams, omnibuses and the Underground railway until I arrived at the Caledonian Road in all its crude, rude and lewd vulgarity, then entered that haven of tranquillity that is Barnsbury via Richmond Avenue. As I saw the sphinxes, I recalled how, in some other life as Peter More, I had made enquiries and discovered that these came from Ancient Egypt, had been looted by Napoleon, that Wellington's Army had taken them from the French Emperor and that they had somehow arrived here in 1849. Other than that, nobody could tell me anything further at all.

There was a gilded coach and six horses standing outside the house of Peter More. Suddenly, and to my complete stupefaction, the front door with a chunky lion as its brass knocker proceeded to open and out stepped an exquisitely dressed man with an extraordinarily beautiful woman. He was laughing gently and she was laughing throatily as he escorted her to the gilded carriage and they were ushered within by a coachman who was rather better dressed than I was. Yes, I felt envious but there was rather more to it than that. *The elegant man was the very spitting image of me.*

3

It was over the ensuing weeks and partly through dreams that I managed to reconstruct the fragments of my memory. I confided in no one, least of all Martha, who appeared to have no interest in conversation whatsoever other than to ask what I might want for dinner. I could occasionally afford to go to a public house and much of my thinking was done over cheap beer.

Gradually, I became convinced that *I* was Peter More, a *brain* surgeon, living pleasantly in Richmond Avenue, a man who relished both his work and his pleasures. My mother had died in childbirth though a pair of twins had survived, Peter and Jeremy, virtually identical in every physical aspect. Identical twins are supposed to love one another but from the start we *hated* each other. Our father was a somewhat remote individual, though not unkind in his personal dealings with his twin sons. We looked so alike that we were often mistaken physically for one another. There the resemblance ended. I hate to say this of my own twin brother but he was foul.

Even though Jeremy and I hated one another most of the time and fought each other bitterly, there were moments when we became close, as though the 'More and More' twins were in fact one brain functioning in two bodies. Even so, there were astonishing differences of behaviour. Jeremy was stealing from shops by the age of twelve. At the age of sixteen, he managed to rape a young factory girl, and there were other disgraceful incidents too numerous to mention. Our father finally threw up his hands in despair, had Jeremy confined to an asylum under the name of 'Derek Johnson' so as not to bring disgrace upon the family name and wrote him out of his will.

I was the blue-eyed boy and after a dazzling school career,

I studied Mathematics at Peterhouse College, Cambridge, gaining a First Class degree with Distinction before I proceeded to the study of Medicine and became a brain surgeon. From time to time, I thought of Jeremy and particularly of the moment when we had been together at the bottom of the garden, both of us aged eight. Certainly what lay there was curious, consisting as it did of mossy stone masonry. To the right, there was a plaque stating simply S.P.Q.R. To the left there had been fashioned the profile of a face and, underneath, the letters FAVSTVS. The alcove in between was blank but before it there was a statuette so blunted by the wind and the rain that it was now of no recognizable shape at all, merely twisting and writhing to no purpose.

It was there that my twin brother Jeremy took a knife he had stolen from father's kitchen and slit his forearm so deeply that the blood began to run.

'You must do that too and in front of the Gods,' he said, 'or else you are a coward.' I am no coward so I did that too. 'Now we shall mingle our blood,' he said. We did. 'This makes us not only twins but also blood brothers forever. Say: "*If I am killed, you will be too.*"'

'*If I am killed, you will be too.*' The blood of our arms mixed and mingled before the queer, misshapen deity without a face and I did not really understand the nature of the oath I swore.

4

Time passed and father passed away, leaving his money and his property to me, without one penny to Jeremy. I found myself lacking in the slightest desire to see him, though as I pursued my highly successful career as a brain surgeon I did employ a private detective to keep track of my twin. I learned that Jeremy had been released from the asylum and under the name father had given him, Derek Johnson, had married Martha, a former prostitute, and was working as a clerk at Gorringe's, Streatham. Occasionally I received a card from Jeremy asking for a meeting but I always ignored the matter. I gave strict instructions to my manservant Arthur to turn him away from the door should he choose to call. I wanted absolutely nothing to do with him. Apparently he had called in person on a number of occasions and Arthur had always obeyed my instructions.

That much was in the light yet there was still the darkness to explore. I could recall little other than a stroll by the Embankment one humid July evening and a sudden blow to my skull. I had awoken to find myself dispossessed from my life and shunted into the exceptionally unpleasant life of Derek Johnson as Jeremy More usurped my own life. How had he done so?

I was determined to confront him. On the following Sunday afternoon, I stormed up to Richmond Avenue, at least insofar as one can 'storm' by tram and bus and Underground railway, and hammered on the big brass knocker. The gilded coach, I noticed, was standing outside. It was the manservant Arthur who opened the door but his face fell as he saw me.

'Good day, Arthur!' I exclaimed cheerily. His expression froze.

'I am sorry, sir. Mr More has instructed me to state that you are not to be admitted.'

'Oh, for heaven's sake, I *am* Mr More!'

'Yes, sir. But I am sorry to say that Mr *Peter* More has given me my instructions.'

'I *am* Peter More!' I shouted. 'Arthur, don't you recognize me?'

He looked at my clothes with the utmost disdain.

'No, sir, I am afraid that I do not.'
He slammed my own front door flat into my face.

5

The plan I devised was relatively simple. The first part involved observation of the house with the sphinxes in Richmond Avenue. I discerned that my twin brother usually left the place in the evening wearing evening dress. I had sufficient savings to hire evening dress for a night; and, if necessary, to hire a series of hansom cabs.

There was a sublime irony in me, Peter More, tracking down myself, the man regarded as being Peter More, in order to regain my lost inheritance and to escape from the hell to which he had consigned me.

There was just enough money left to rent for one week a bedsit in Battersea and to obtain the requisite equipment.

As it happened, he made the matter relatively easy for me by going for a solitary stroll along the Embankment, rather as though he was musing upon some particular event that had taken place there previously. Somehow I knew exactly what he was going to do for it was as though one brain had synchronized the two of us. No one was looking as I coshed him, then emptied brandy over his clothes. To the cabman, it must have looked as though I was helping a friend who had had too much to drink, since I had pulled Jeremy's hat down so as to obscure his facial features. We went to the bedsit I had rented in Battersea and there I used chloroform and extracted from my bag certain tools of the surgeon. They were crude compared to the instruments with which I had once worked and with which I would work again but now I knew precisely how my evil twin had performed his feat.

It took me some time to perform the operation, which

involved the severing of nerve endings so as to impose a state of amnesia. As I did so, I recalled how Jeremy had been so fascinated by my obsessive study of brain surgery during my adolescent years that he had initially resolved to take it up for himself, and for a time had studied the subject assiduously. Clearly, he had continued with his studies in later life, since this was what he must have done to me, though not quite effectively enough.

I kept him under continued sedation and was aided in my task by knowing that his habits were virtually identical to mine. I had often dismissed my carriage in order to stroll and I had frequently been absent from my home for the night, choosing instead to sleep either at my club or in the bed of some charming young lady. It was necessary, however, while my patient slumbered in his coma, to visit my home, which he had usurped. I also had to return the evening dress which I had hired for the night.

It took me several hours for the exchange of identities to be accomplished. Eventually, as dawn came, there was Jeremy lying naked upon the bed, covered by sheets and blankets. I now wore *his* evening dress, which included his wallet containing proof of identity and a hundred pounds in addition to his purse, which contained forty-seven guineas in gold sovereigns. I then sent a telegram to my manservant Arthur, asking him to ensure that my coach was present outside my club at 11:30 a.m.

My club, of course, found nothing unusual in my wandering in at 11:00 a.m. for a spot of mid-morning refreshment while still wearing evening dress from the night before. Walters, my coachman, appeared punctually and I think he saw nothing untoward in the Gladstone bag I was carrying. This contained my hired evening dress. On my return to my home in Richmond Avenue, Arthur greeted me with his customary courtesy and deference.

Everything within was virtually as I had left it, apart from one or two matters I discovered in my study. The desk was stacked with books on brain surgery and I gathered from my leather-bound book of appointments that Jeremy as Peter had taken four weeks of leave. There was also an assignation with one Camilla Partride at her home in Mayfair this coming evening at 8:00 p.m. for dinner.

I changed into a plain frock coat with narrow velvet trousers, then, informing Arthur that I would probably be away for the weekend and did not require the services of Walters, I returned my hired evening dress and paid for keeping it longer than the terms of our agreement. The next step was to visit the hospital where I worked and where I was told that they would be very pleased to see me operating this coming Monday. Here I also obtained some drugs and syringes without the slightest difficulty. I now bought some horrible cheap clothes at a street market and returned to the bedsit in Battersea.

Jeremy was still in a coma. It took me several sweaty hours to dress him in the clothes I had bought. When he started to stir, I gave him a shot of morphine that made his limbs rather more relaxed and easier to manipulate. When night fell, I poured beer all over him, then 'helped' him out into the street where I hailed a cab, asking to be dropped off by Cleopatra's Needle.

That is where I left him. No one saw me cosh him again so as to disguise my brain surgery. What would happen to him was a foregone conclusion. The police would eventually find a drunken, comatose man who had been coshed and whose wallet showed his identity as Derek Johnson of Clapham. He would be taken to a public hospital where the doctors were far too busy to raise any questions. His wife Martha would be traced and he would probably awaken to see her by his bedside: they were welcome to one another.

It remained for me to throw the Gladstone bag into the Thames. This contained the blood-stained and brain-bespattered rubber sheet upon which he had lain as I had performed my operation, also the tools I had used. Father Thames was at high tide and in no time at all these goods would be swirled into the docks at Wapping.

I proceeded to dinner with Camilla whom I had not seen in a couple of months, though evidently my twin brother had, and found her to be as beautiful and charming as ever. Clearly, though, she had not been able to tell the difference between Jeremy and myself when he had made love to her, nor did she notice anything different now; or any*one*, I might add.

Oh! It was such a pleasure to saunter on the streets of Mayfair that sunny Sunday morning! I kept twirling my ebony walking cane with the sheer delight of the matter. I had recovered my inheritance, I would be delighting in more of Camilla's company, I would be returning to a home I adored and, on Monday, to work I loved. I derived an especial sadistic pleasure from contemplating the fate of my loathsome twin, returned to Clapham and Martha and Gorringe's if lucky, a fate he so richly deserved. I felt no guilt at all. Had he not endeavoured by foul means to consign me to the fate he had chosen for himself?

Some might state that I was too merciful, that I should simply have killed him and employed my ingenuity to rid myself of the body. I could not have done so since I knew the oath between twins that was sealed in blood:

'*If I am killed, you will be too.*'

6

I returned to the life I had enjoyed so much, feeling as though I had escaped from Hell via Purgatory into

Heaven. Unfortunately, there remained one nagging fear
and it was that if *I* had managed to recover my memory
despite Jeremy's operation on my brain, then despite his
incompetence and my vastly superior skills, was it not
possible that, via dreaming, he might do so also?

My worst fears were confirmed one evening when I was
relaxing in my library and reading a Sherlock Holmes
story in *The Strand* magazine while sipping a glass of dry
sherry and intermittently reflecting on the joys of Camilla
on the preceding night. Arthur knocked and entered,
wearing a grave expression upon his lean, cadaverous
features.

'I am very sorry to trouble you, sir, but there is, I think,
a matter I should draw to your attention.'

'Oh? What?'

'Your brother, sir.'

'What of him?'

'He appeared on the doorstep today, sir, just as he did
several weeks ago.' I recalled that on that previous occasion,
the disreputable and impoverished brother had in fact been
me. 'I trust I acted properly, sir, in obeying your instructions
and turning him away.'

'Yes, yes, of course, Arthur.'

'It is just that he left me with this envelope, sir.'

'Ah, thank you, Arthur.' My flesh prickled, my hand
shook and my intestines acquired a dreadful chill as I
accepted the proffered hand-delivered envelope. 'That
will be all.'

'Very good, sir.'

I ripped it open to discover the following message,
scrawled in pencil upon cheap, yellow paper.

'I KNOW WHERE YOU LIVE. YOU KNOW WHERE
I LIVE. LET US MAKE PEACE NOW. GIVE ME HALF
OF EVERYTHING YOU HAVE SO I CAN HAVE AT

LEAST HALF OF MY RIGHTFUL INHERITANCE. OTHERWISE YOU WILL DIE. REMEMBER: *IF I AM KILLED, YOU WILL BE TOO.*'

I decided to hire a bodyguard.

'That was the document,' said the celebrated retired Inspector, Robert Cutforth of the Yard. 'I know it may sound completely mad to you. It certainly sounded so to me. The fact is that Peter More, brain surgeon of Richmond Avenue, leading exactly the life he describes here, was found dead in his study forty-eight hours later. True to his word, he had hired a bodyguard, who was sitting outside the study and who swears that he saw nobody and heard nothing. The testimony of Arthur the manservant and Walters the coachman, who were having tea together in the kitchen downstairs, is the same.

'Obviously we checked out the bodyguard. He had no criminal past and nor did either Arthur or Walters. As I've said, within the room of the deceased, there were no signs of entry and the windows had recently been locked from the inside. Dr Peter More had been shot through the heart, yet there wasn't a gun to be found. The whole matter was absolutely impossible. There was only the document I have shown you, which was lying neatly on his desk.

'Obviously I was completely bewildered; and then a bright colleague of mine alerted me to another case which, on the face of it, had no conceivable connection at all. A man living in a basement flat in Clapham had shot himself while his wife Martha was out shopping. He had left a suicide note behind. Here it is:

THE SUICIDE NOTE OF JEREMY MORE

Since I am going to end my life with a revolver bullet to my heart as soon as I have finished the writing of this letter to myself and to the World in general, I would like any interested parties to know why.

As a child, I was very close to my twin brother Peter, so much so that it was hard for anyone to tell the physical or mental difference between us, though I was always his leader in those days. Of course, I shall never forget the moment when we swore an Oath of Blood before a misshapen stone deity and pledged that *If I am killed, you will be too*.

Time passed and we grew to hate one another and our father grew to hate me. For a time I emulated Peter in endeavouring to learn all I could about brain surgery and though for a time I abandoned that study I eventually returned to it.

Yes, I opted for the unusual and I was rejected by my father and by my own twin brother. Disowned and disinherited, I drifted into work as a clerk at Gorringe's as a preferable alternative to starvation, with a wife whom I neither loved nor liked yet who gave me comfort in bed at night. Gradually, increasing rage grew within me and I became determined to revenge myself and reclaim my inheritance.

The plan I devised was relatively simple. The first part involved observation of the house with the sphinxes in Richmond Avenue. I discerned that my twin brother usually left the place in the evening wearing evening dress. I had sufficient savings to hire evening dress for a night and, if necessary, to hire a series of hansom cabs.

There was just enough money left to rent for one week a bedsit in Battersea and to obtain the requisite equipment.

As it happened, he made the matter relatively easy for me by going for a solitary stroll along the Embankment, rather as though he was musing upon some particular event that had taken place there previously. Somehow I knew exactly what he was going to do for it was as though one brain had synchronized the two of us. No one was looking as I coshed him, then emptied brandy over his clothes. To the cabman, it must have looked as though I was helping a friend who had had too much to drink, since I had pulled Peter's hat down so as to obscure his facial features. We went to the bedsit I had rented in Battersea and there I used chloroform and extracted from my bag certain tools of the surgeon.

There is no need to go into the details of how I stole his identity. The fact remains that a poor man was found coshed and taken to a hospital for the indigent, where not many questions were asked. I had been studying various books relevant to my new identity and it gave me great pleasure to step into the shoes of Peter More. I do not suppose that anyone ever suspected the transposition for a moment; certainly not his beautiful but utterly stupid lady friend, Camilla. The one difficulty was the matter of reporting for work as a brain surgeon but I felt that, given four weeks of leave and study, I would be no worse than any other.

I had, unfortunately, reckoned without the extraordinary recuperative powers of my twin. Within a few weeks, he had taken his revenge, doing to me exactly what I had done to him. I woke up in hospital with no idea who I was and with

THE LABYRINTH OF SATAN

Martha sitting by my bedside. On the following Monday morning I entered Gorringe's to be informed that having been demoted from Clerk to Junior Clerk, I had now been demoted again to Deputy Junior Clerk.

My hateful twin, however, had not bargained for my own formidable powers of recuperation. For two weeks I endured this hell into which I had once more been consigned in a state of blurred confusion. Then the memory of this miserable state came back to me and slowly I began to realize who I was once more. Strange dreams also brought back the memory of the delectable though brief time when I had taken the life of my twin, Peter More, and sent him to the hell that was now once again mine.

The hatred between us really is remarkably intense. I endeavoured to confront my twin at his home but Arthur slammed the door flat in my face; he had been so deferential to me during the days when he fancied that I was Peter. I left an envelope with him, reminding Peter of the Oath we once swore. At that time I was surreptitiously reading books in our father's library and some were to do with Voodoo, Obeah and Black Magic.

I was hoping that Peter might respond so that we could have a peaceful meeting: perhaps he could give me my share and I would then go away and not trouble him any longer. But he has ignored me once more. I have ploughed my last savings into the only other possible alternative, since I cannot face undertaking my previous operation again. I have no future and so I shall shoot myself and, in so doing, I shall shoot the swine too.

I have never had love in my life ever since the swearing of our Oath. He has broken that Oath. Goodbye, Peter. Once upon a time, I loved you.

'**O**ne problem,' said Cutforth of the Yard, 'is that this man claiming to be Jeremy More who had shot himself through the heart had earlier poured sulphuric acid on his face and hands, rendering him virtually impossible to identify. His wife Martha swore that she had been married not to Jeremy More but to Derek Johnson for the past seven years. She had noticed no change at all in the behaviour of her husband during the period when he might have been Peter More.

'Moreover,' he continued, 'the birth certificates state that there *were* twins, Peter and Jeremy More. Jeremy More *did* change his name to Derek Johnson by deed poll prior to his marriage to Martha Coughlin. Perhaps he did that out of self-hatred, a fact backed up by the use of sulphuric acid to make positive identification impossible.'

'Sorry?' I interposed. 'Not quite with you there.'

'I've *seen* the birth certificate of the Derek Johnson who kept on getting demoted at Gorringe's. Unfortunately, both his parents are dead and he seems to have no surviving relatives. Don't you see my point? The dead man found with a bullet in his heart might have been either Derek Johnson or Jeremy More. No documents can prove it one way or another. But let us suppose, for the sake of argument, and however unlikely it may be, that Jeremy More shot himself in the heart with a silver bullet. How can it be possible, as determined by our forensic experts, that at precisely the same time Peter More died with a silver bullet through his heart?'

'*If I am killed, you will be too*,' I said. 'That is the trouble with twins.'

'This tortures my rationality. *It's not possible!*'

'Everything in this universe is possible, Inspector,' I replied.

'What a bizarre tale, Septimus!' I exclaimed.

'I trust that you enjoyed it, Venetia.'

'But . . . but did any of this actually *happen?*'

'If you don't believe me,' he replied, 'don't. Alternatively, invite Cutforth of the Yard to dinner. You have already confirmed his existence.'

'Have you confessed to Cutforth that you are Jack the Ripper?'

'Of course I have,' this impudent imp replied. 'He did not believe me for a moment. Cutforth is an exceedingly clever man but I wonder if he is anything more. He will not believe anything unless it is supported by documentary evidence or else he sees the matter actually taking place before him. I have tried confessing to him until I am virtually blue in the face and he has responded with severe interrogation, proving triumphantly that, in the context of the stratagems I have described, I could not possibly have committed these murders. He admits that he does not know who did but he is certain that it was not me.'

'I don't suppose that it was,' I commented.

'Poor Inspector Cutforth,' Septimus replied. 'He is one of those highly intelligent men who finds it impossible to believe the improbable.'

'This – um – Septimus Keen,' I said to Venetia, 'really does seem to be as you have described; indeed, a wild and dangerous young man.' My head was spinning not only on account of the champagne, brandy, opium and hashish I had imbibed but also on account of the astonishing tales I had heard. I no longer knew what was real and what was not. For all I knew at that moment, Venetia Fielding might rip off her petticoats and reveal herself to be Septimus Keen . . . no, that could not be possible. 'Surely,' I heard myself say, 'the thing to do would be to alert the police to your suspicions before more women are horribly butchered.'

'I have,' Venetia replied, 'and I was treated as if I were a harmless, well-intentioned lunatic.'

'That is how I am feeling here and now,' I responded. I felt that if I did not go now, the walls would collapse all around me. 'Venetia, your hospitality has been so delightful and this Club is simply divine. I would be most interested in the possibility of joining were that to be a possibility. However . . .'

'. . . you discern that the time is getting on and you have just remembered an appointment elsewhere.'

'Well – um – yes, actually.'

'Are you sure,' she smiled like a lazy cat, 'that you would not like to get to know some of our members . . . better?'

'Very kind, Venetia. Perhaps another time.' I would have felt more comfortable had she not repeated my every word in chorus with me and then followed her mimicry with a most infuriating smirk.

I managed to take my leave, noticing that, as I passed through the various rooms, the ladies were looking at me with what struck me as being an interest that verged upon the positively lascivious. It was a relief to bid farewell to Venetia and clamber dizzily into my gig. Once inside, I very nearly fainted.

What a relief it is to be home! That is to say in our town house. It is so good to be alone sometimes. There is a room at the top of this house, an attic room, that has a simple desk and a chair and that is where I am writing this. I wonder if at one time some poet may have lived here. There is an astonishing view before me from my window here. If I look up, I see the stars and wonder whether there are, spinning around them, other planets such as ours.

I look upon the rooftops of London and see smoking chimneys. I wonder about the mystery of London, a city in which so many diversities occur that not even the most intrepid explorer could ever comprehend the matter in its entirety. Across the street from me, I see a respectable middle-class dinner party in progress and the cups are filled and emptied in tedious moderation. These kindly, decent (no doubt) people do not begin to imagine what could be going on all around them. There is what looks like a garret in the next house and I am not quite sure what is transpiring there. There are Chinese blinds, so I can only see shadows in the lamplight. Insofar as I can tell, a man is performing some curious and possibly obscene rite that causes him to hold some sort of doll in his hand. That is all that I can tell amongst the shadow-play. Down in the street, I see that it is raining and people are scurrying about their various purposes as if they were insects.

Enough! Amelia, we really must get together with Sir Percy to discuss the perplexing matter of Septimus Keen.

With love,
Barbara

EDITOR'S NOTE

Despite the bewilderment of Barbara Crockford, Venetia Fielding was in fact speaking of hypotheses concerning Jack the Ripper that have since been seriously advanced.

Inspector Abberline did indeed investigate the Jack the Ripper murders as a deputy to Detective Chief Inspector Swanson, and the former retired from the police force on 7th February 1892. It is curious that within the preceding four weeks, there was the official announcement regarding the death of the Duke of Clarence; (14th January); the death of his Cambridge tutor, J.K. Stephen (3rd February); and the death of Sir William Gull's coachman, John Netley, who had allegedly tried to run down Alice Crook, illegitimate daughter of Annie Crook and the Duke of Clarence (6th February).

The alleged diaries of Inspector Abberline are in the possession of Joseph Sickert, who claims to be the illegitimate son of the artist Walter Sickert and Alice Crook. The matter may be studied with advantage in *The Ripper & The Royals* by Melvyn Fairclough (Duckworth, London, 1991).

The diaries of Inspector Abberline apparently contain the following entry:

'Saturday March 20th.
    I marched with the National Guard then Buckingham Palace

Garden & was seen by the King and Queen. Very disappointed
I could not go and see him'.

Fairclough argues that this refers to an event recorded
by the Court Circular in *The Times*, for on Saturday,
20th March 1915, King George V commanded the City
of London National Guard Volunteer Corps, under G.T.B.
Cobbet, to march past him and Queen Mary in the Palace
garden on that afternoon.

Fairclough further argues that the Duke of Clarence
was still alive. Having been confined to an asylum for
setting off a Sandringham fire deliberately on 1st November
1891, he had subsequently been removed to Glamis Castle,
and apparently he died there in 1933. Fairclough has a
photograph obtained from Joseph Sickert that is printed in
Fairclough's book, appearing to show the Duke of Clarence
painting at Glamis in 1910, one purporting to have been
taken by his mother, Queen Alexandra.

According to Fairclough, the 'him' that Abberline was
wanting to see was the Duke of Clarence, still alive
and well.

The 1988 TV series in which Michael Caine starred as
Abberline further validated the story that this ex-Inspector
had access to the truth.

Sir William Gull, the Royal Physician, has been accused of
being Jack the Ripper in *Jack the Ripper: The Final Solution*
(Harrap, London, 1976). By contrast, Fairclough sees him as
being part of a high-level Freemasonic conspiracy, the head
of which was the syphilitic Lord Randolph Churchill.

In endeavouring to negotiate one's way through this maze
of mingled fact, legend and myth, there are at least a few
facts. Annie Elizabeth Crook, mistress of the future heir
to the throne, the Duke of Clarence, and mother of his
child, though this has been doubted, was born in 1864 and

died on 3rd February 1920. Her daughter Alice Margaret Crook was born on 15th April 1885 and died in 1950, having married one William Gorman on 14th July 1918. Joseph Sickert was born on 22nd October 1925 and at the time of this writing is still in being. He claims to be the illegitimate son of Alice Margaret Crook and Walter Sickert (1860–1942) with whom he has enjoyed intimate conversations containing revelations.

One of these revelations is that Netley, who allegedly died by drowning in the Thames in 1892, apparently faked his own death after failing to run down Alice Crook. It seems that he finally died in 1903. On 26th September that year, it was reported in both the *West London Gazette* and the *Marylebone Mercury* that John Netley, aged 43, had been thrown from his seat as he drove his coach down Park Road and that a kick from one of his horses had fractured his skull and killed him. At the inquest, the Jury returned a verdict of accidental death.

There are curious entries in the Abberline diaries held by Joseph Sickert. One reads:

'John Netley 1903
drown
believe to have drowned.'

The entry dated 12 November 1903 reads:

'J.C. Netley murdered under his own coach. Payment for Alice?'

Peculiarly enough, the death occurred at *Clarence* Gate.

The theory advanced by Venetia Fielding to Barbara Crockford regarding William Henry Bury as Jack the

Ripper is best pursued by William Beadle in *Jack the Ripper: Anatomy of a Myth* (Wat Tyler Books, Essex 1995).

There is an intriguing Jack the Ripper tour at the London Dungeon, in which the case for and against several leading suspects is presented with commendable clarity after some well-executed drama. This is recommended.

In *Masterpieces of Murder* (1992), the crime historian Jonathan Goodman revealed that he had strongly argued the case for Jack the Ripper being one Peter J. Harpick, which had brought him a deluge of letters. Peter J. Harpick is, of course, an anagram for Jack the Ripper, a spoof; yet Goodman's case is more convincing than many others.

(A.S.)

CHAPTER ELEVEN

FROM THE DIARY
OF SEPTIMUS KEEN

(THE HANGMAN'S TALE)

> 'O what a tangled web we weave;
> When first we practise to deceive!'

As I eat my toast and marmalade, I wonder who I am today and who I shall be. Maintaining three identities was difficult enough but, thanks to Doctor Lipsius, I now have a fourth physical presence. I really must endeavour to avoid careless errors that mar the conviction of the roles I play. Smoking a panatella as Sir Richard Knight would when I was being Bob Brown and conversing with Sir Percy Sulgrave really was a rather ghastly error.

Lipsius was delighted with my report, however, and I thoroughly enjoyed the new slant I gave to the matter by a mock impersonation of all of my colleagues. As Bob Brown, I had initially found Sir Percy Sulgrave to be a complete ass, though subsequent developments showed that I had underestimated him. As Sir Richard Knight, I found Lady Amelia Stanhope to be beautiful and charming and it is my intention to seduce her. As Sir Richard I have already seduced the voluptuous Barbara Crockford and so I enjoyed conversing with her as Venetia Fielding. Were it not for the exigencies of the plot whereby the strategy is produced by Lipsius and the tactics directed by Davies, I would relish the prospect of sapphically seducing her in the Athena Club and of hearing her gasp of amazement as I lifted up my petticoats to reveal . . .

GERALD SUSTER

Sir Percy's perspicacity has caused me to spend some time in the rearrangement of matters. I felt that he might alert the police to Bob Brown and Marcia Road so I installed a drunken tramp who was mentally defective and gave him the name of Mick Jones. The police now think that Sir Percy is an idiot. Since my Bill Smith/Bob Brown persona is one that satisfies me and an aspect of my personality that I find necessary to enact, I have had to concoct another identity. My Bill Smith/Bob Brown persona now lives in a bedsit in Neasden. Neasden has to be one of the most hideous districts in London. Just beyond it, there are the beauties of the countryside but the place itself is full of red, raw villas and there is a strong sense of evil. Even so, it is the tasteless sort of place where Fred Robinson might choose to live for sometimes that is who I am now.

Many people assume false identities for all manner of reasons. The two rather large men I had employed to intimidate Sir Percy, one of whom resembles a bear and the other a gorilla, have been employed by me before and seem to change their names with every job they do. I am not the only Protean one. The trouble is that it can become quite complicated, trying to keep track of all one's various identities.

There is also the matter of my tendency to steer into the eye of the hurricane. Perhaps it was what Poe called 'The Imp of the Perverse' that made me give the card of Bob Brown to Sir Percy; that made me take Lady Amelia Stanhope back to my home as Sir Richard Knight; that led me to dilly-dally with Barbara Crockford as Venetia Fielding; that inspired me to blame all the Jack the Ripper murders upon Septimus Keen . . .?

'Septimus Keen' was originally just a pseudonym I used for my tales. When Lipsius and his colleagues realized that I was leading a triple life and Lipsius started to call me Septimus, it gradually became obvious to me that I had to establish a fourth identity. Obviously this could not be under the name of Septimus Keen, since under three guises I had told three people that he was Jack the Ripper under three guises; but I wanted somewhere quiet where I could *be* Septimus Keen.

As Lucien Stuart, unpublished writer with a slender private income, I have taken a flat in Maida Vale from where I can see the house of Sir Percy Sulgrave, just across the Grand Union Canal. The furniture as supplied by the landlady is absolutely hideous, consisting as it does of chintzy and cluttered ornamentation which Mrs Pemberton thought 'might be inspiring for a literary gentleman'. I want to smash every fucking vase in the room, I want to wreck every item of the ugly Holloway Road furniture, I want to tear the sentimental realist paintings from the walls and piss on them . . . but then the question comes: what does Septimus Keen really want?

I don't want to set up yet another persona as Lucien Stuart, which is simply a name of convenience so that I can be myself. I already have three parts to play and I want to relax when I am off stage, so to speak. I don't just *act* the parts of Sir Richard Knight, Venetia Fielding and now Fred Robinson, I *become* each one of them. Yes, I do not allow a thought that arises in one to arise in another. Venetia Fielding adores Oscar Wilde, for instance, whilst Fred Robinson thinks him detestable and Sir Richard Knight thinks that he is an excellent dramatist whose personal life is open to question. At least they all eat toast and marmalade.

Now, here I am, eating toast and marmalade and wondering: who on Earth *is* Septimus Keen? I have spent so much time in erasing my former identity and in being others that I fear I no longer know.

What clothes does he wear? The silken dressing gown in sapphire blue that presently adorns my body is all very well

319

here and now. But what is suitable here and now when I go out? The clothes in which I arrived as Lucien Stuart? Well, I suppose that a grey frock coat with narrow grey striped trousers, a white silk shirt and a floppy bow tie in deep blue satin might be appropriate, yes, and I could wear faded hand-made shoes of black leather so as to give the impression of a literary gentleman who is not concerned with appearance. I will obviously have to do something about the dreadful decor here since I simply do not like it. Yet further questions remain and, fortunately, money is hardly a problem.

What does Septimus Keen eat? What does he drink? What are his daily habits? I have told so many different stories about him that I no longer know what it is that I really want for myself. What does he think? What do I think? What *is* the 'I' that does the thinking? What is 'I', anyway? Merely a set of ideas and impressions.

This grouping of ideas and impressions that now assembles itself within my – or is it 'my'? – mind, reminds me that it is Septimus Keen, presently living under the name of Lucien Stuart, whom I want to be like me.

I know. I shall do whatever my instincts prompt me to do. I have installed a telescope so that I may stare at the stars. I shall also use it to discern the movements of Sir Percy Sulgrave. I suddenly realize that it does not matter how my flat is furnished. If I want elegance, Sir Richard Knight or Venetia Fielding can supply that. If I want utterly abominable taste, I can become Fred Robinson. As Septimus Keen, I don't need to give a flying fuck about my furniture. I shan't be having any guests. My personae have friends but I do not need them. It is good to have a place where I can live alone.

But what shall I eat tonight?

* * *

Later.

My earlier resolutions have worked out well for me. It is two in the morning and I delight in writing this as I watch the sluggish waters of the canal. Pipes of opium and hashish have done me a great deal of good and I have certainly enjoyed a most interesting evening.

I decided that I would simply follow the movements of Sir Percy Sulgrave in the guise of Lucien Stuart and study him as one would a rare and endangered species. There was one precaution that I had to take, though. I could disguise myself in many ways but my blue eyes would be remembered. This matter, however, could be resolved by the wearing of darkly tinted spectacles. As for the hair, it was just so easy to reach for another wig. Lucien Stuart would look rather fetching in a piled-up, slicked-back pompadour, I felt, and a razored blond moustache, just above the upper lip, would complement the get-up perfectly.

The final move was to hire a gig for the day, since an advantage of my residence was that there was a stable one could rent. The pony was presently plunging her head into a nosebag of hay as I watched the movements of Sir Percy. In fact, there were no movements until midday. Perhaps Sir Percy was also eating toast and marmalade. Finally he emerged from his house and waved for his phaeton which his coachman promptly brought to him. Sir Percy sprang with alacrity into his open carriage just as I sprang into mine. It was easy to follow him through St John's Wood and via Baker Street, Oxford Street and Regent Street to the Café Royal. There are stables behind it so I simply followed the coachman.

Leaving my gig, I reflected on how I really liked the Café Royal. On the ground floor, one could have a first-class meal accompanied by the finest wines of the rarest vintage. One could also sit there with a cheap beer, a fact that attracted the custom of so many writers and artists. I entered to see that Sir Percy had taken a table for four. I managed to secure a table for one next to his and ordered the same drink as he did, an amontillado. Sir Percy lit a cigarette: Virginia, judging by the aroma. I decided that I would do the same. After a few minutes I was very pleased to see that my expedition had hardly been in vain. He was joined at his table by Lady Amelia Stanhope and Mrs Barbara Crockford, which could not have suited my purposes better. Sir Percy ordered a bottle of Krug champagne and so did I.

I regarded the room. Frank Harris was holding court, his voice booming at the centre table as he harangued his guests. One of these was Oscar Wilde, whose personal life was a matter of much rumour. It was said that his relationship with Lord Alfred 'Bosie' Douglas had aroused the enmity of the latter's father, the Marquess of Queensberry, who had publicly insulted Wilde and that Wilde was now suing Queensberry for criminal libel. That extraordinary socialist agitator and superb critic of music George Bernard Shaw was there, as was the exquisite artist Aubrey Beardsley. Whistler and Degas were sitting at another table with a man I did not know, some sycophantic nonentity or other: though as Richard Knight or Venetia Fielding I would have greeted the Duke of Devonshire.

As I sat at my marble table, I caught sight of my reflection in the gilded looking-glass and saw a strange dandy. Really, who was I? The assumption of multiple identities continued to confuse me. Sir Percy was busy ordering food. What sort of food would Septimus Keen order from the Menu? What would Lucien Stuart order? What did *I* really want, God damn it? I decided that I wasn't hungry and continued to drink champagne, while listening keenly, if the pun may be pardoned, to the conversation at the table of Sir Percy.

'Oh, Thomas is well, thank you,' the voluptuous Barbara Crockford was saying. 'He sends you his best wishes. Presently he is visiting America and there he will make more money. The Americans are apparently ahead of us in the use of machinery and engineering. It means, I understand from Thomas, that they can manufacture products rather more cheaply than we can and export them profitably into England. Thomas intends to find out about their methods of engineering so as to establish them, perhaps, and use them here. He also intends to buy goods cheaply there and sell them expensively over here. He is a very clever man.' Prawns in a sauce of cream and brandy were served to them. They looked and smelled so enticing that I decided to order a dish for myself.

'Mmm, good prawns!' Sir Percy exclaimed as he chewed them thoughtfully. 'Although we haven't exactly come here to discuss prawns, have we? The three of us have really been through a rather extraordinary period, I feel. We have all seen the correspondence between us. The fact is that in our separate ways, we have met three separate individuals all of whom claim to know the identity of Jack the Ripper. Bob Brown claimed that he was Robert Stephenson to me; Sir Richard Knight claimed that he was J.K. Stephen to you, Amelia; and Venetia Fielding claimed that the Ripper was William Bury to you, Barbara. Moreover, each individual mentioned claimed that these were merely pseudonyms of one Septimus Keen who writes extraordinary and outlandish tales. Septimus Keen obviously cannot be three separate individuals with differing histories.' He quaffed his glass of champagne and poured more for the ladies and himself. 'I detect the hand of Doctor Lipsius,' he added darkly.

'Percy, how can that be?' Amelia demanded. 'I know

that you are obsessed with him yet I have always found him charming. Are you about to inform us that this is all part of his infernal cunning?'

'Yes,' said Sir Percy.

'Then why don't you go to the appropriate authorities?' Barbara demanded.

'I might as well go to the appropriate authorities and ask them to arrest the Home Secretary,' Sir Percy retorted. 'One requires proof and in the case of a man such as Lipsius, proof is virtually impossible to find.' He sighed wearily. 'Oh, Lipsius makes sure of that.'

'If you have no proof,' Amelia observed with cutting asperity, 'how can you make these allegations against Doctor Lipsius?'

'I know, I know . . .' Sir Percy sighed again. 'Let's go on to the turtle soup, shall we? What would go well with it? Hm, perhaps a white Bordeaux . . . yes, since we'll be having white Burgundy with the next course. Did you know that the turtle is the only sea reptile, unless you count the salt-water crocodile, and that it has no predators other than Man? Anyway, dear ladies, I would like you to help me, since you have been so kind as to attend this little luncheon. You see, what has happened to us is *so* much in the style of Lipsius. My proposal, therefore, is that you, Amelia, keep an eye on Sir Richard Knight and that you, Barbara, keep an eye on Venetia Fielding. Ah! here comes the soup!'

'Percy,' said Amelia as she picked up her spoon with the utmost delicacy, 'are you seriously suggesting that I should sit in my carriage outside his house? That would be so . . .' she blushed as she searched for words, 'so *vulgar.*'

'Oh, no, nothing as vulgar as that, Amelia,' he responded.

'No, no, my dear Duke!' the voice of Frank Harris boomed and echoed throughout the room. 'I know nothing of the joys of homosexuality. You must ask my friend Oscar here about *that*. But if *Shakespeare* had asked me, I would have felt compelled to submit.'

'Frank, you find life crude and leave it raw,' said Oscar Wilde.

'A poor thing, Oscar,' Whistler shot at him from the adjacent table, 'but for once, your own.'

'With you, James,' Oscar retorted, 'vulgarity begins at home and should be allowed to stay there.'

'And from whom did you steal that one, Oscar?' Whistler snapped back. 'You're always picking the plums from my puddings to peddle in the provinces.'

'You float like a butterfly, James,' Oscar said, a reference to the butterfly signature Whistler had adopted, 'but you fail to sting like a bee.'

'I like Oscar Wilde,' Sir Percy murmured, 'though I cannot bear his friend, Lord Alfred 'Bosie' Douglas. The latter's father has set out to ruin Wilde, y'know. I hope to high heaven that it never goes to court: Wilde would be a fool to bring an action. All those grooms and stable lads are a pretty grisly set of oicks. But let us go on to the next course. Sole Capri!'

From my vantage point, I saw them being served with a grilled Dover sole, smothered in bananas and mango chutney. It looked so enchanting that I decided to order one too, though I differed on the choice of wine. Whereas Sir Percy took a Pouilly Fuissé from Burgundy, I chose a Pouilly Fumé from the Loire.

'With all possible respect,' Sir Percy was saying, 'I don't think that you two intelligent ladies quite appreciate my strategy. Both Sir Richard Knight and Miss Venetia Fielding claim to know the identity of Jack the Ripper. I am asking you to visit both individuals *simultaneously.*'

'Oh, Sir Percy!' Barbara hooted with laughter. 'You

can't possibly be suggesting that they are one and the same, can you?'

'I claim simply that it would be an interesting experiment,' he responded. Clearly the man was not quite as much of a fool as he appeared to be.

'In the exceptionally unlikely event that they were,' Amelia pointed out sharply, 'I cannot see how much this exercise would achieve. Sir Richard Knight would be At Home at one time and Venetia Fielding would be At Home at another.'

'Percy, it is just not possible,' Barbara insisted, 'that Sir Richard Knight and Venetia Fielding could be the same individual.'

'Consider the experiment shown by Knight to Amelia here,' he retorted smartly. 'Does that not show you that *anything* is possible?'

'Don't you think,' Barbara suggested cautiously, 'that your pursuit of Jack the Ripper is in danger of becoming a trifle obsessive?'

'Not at all, my dear,' Sir Percy returned coolly. '*Five women died*! And in the most horrible manner . . . how can you possibly criticize me for wanting to bring the fiend who was responsible to justice in the Courts of Law?'

'I applaud your genuine zeal, Percy,' Amelia responded as she ate her sole with every sign of evident enjoyment. Mine had now arrived and it was excellent. 'But is conversation about the Ripper really a suitable topic at luncheon?'

'No,' said Sir Percy, 'it is not. And you might think that my idea is mad. But will you help me with it?'

'Yes,' said Amelia.

'Yes,' said Barbara, adding: 'Gosh! It does sound ever so frightfully exciting!'

'Jolly good,' said Sir Percy, 'so let's dig in.'

I felt mildly uneasy as they did so, since I did not want

Sir Richard Knight and Venetia Fielding to be under observation. What would happen when one visited the other to *become* the other? There was, of course the possibility of using Fred Robinson.

After the Sole, they enjoyed rare roast rib of beef that was positively swimming in blood, accompanied by a fine red Burgundy, a Nuits St Georges. I decided to have that wine with my next dish, a small, rare and thick fillet steak, also swimming in blood, and accompanied by a portion of buttered spinach.

Their conversation turned to matters of inconsequential gossip and social trivialities. I concentrated upon the enjoyment of my meal, hoping that the obsession of Sir Percy would eventually compel him to return to the original topic. Here I was not disappointed. After the plates were cleared away, Sir Percy ordered Crêpes Suzette and a bottle of Chateau D'Yquem. I ordered coffee and armagnac. I do not have a sweet tooth.

'I *know* you're thinking that I'm being a bit of a bore,' Sir Percy was saying, 'but the facts are undeniable. I have spoken to Sister Mary, a nun, and to Mrs Elgar, a cleaning lady. Both were present at a clandestine marriage at St Saviour's Chapel, Maple Street and it was a Roman Catholic marriage between the Duke of Clarence and Annie Elizabeth Crook. But Sister Mary was subsequently transferred to another convent and Mrs Elgar was sacked on the following day.

'I have spoken with that excellent artist Walter Sickert,' Sir Percy continued. 'Late in 1885 and shortly after the birth of the illegitimate royal daughter Alice Margaret Crook, Walter Sickert was walking towards his studio at 15 Cleveland Street. There was a brawl in the street, which was unusual for the area, but it distracted attention from 6 Cleveland Street, where Annie Crook had a basement flat. Walter Sickert informs me that he saw two men emerging with Annie Crook, whom they bundled into a coach. Sickert remains convinced that Sir William Gull, Royal Physician, slit nerve endings so as to render Annie Crook an amnesiacal semi-imbecile.'

I watched with fascination as the waiter fried the thin pancakes and added Grand Marnier, lemon juice and orange juice, with a pinch of scattered cinnamon.

'I see the sinister hand of Doctor Lipsius in all of this,' Sir Percy pronounced with an air of definitive finality, 'and that means we are going to have to find his minion Septimus Keen, whom we three have all encountered by proxy. At that instant, the waiter tossed the cognac into the pan, struck a match and the dish then flashed with flames of blue and yellow. In the course of this delightful eruption of fire, I could not resist the temptation of turning to the table and saying:

'Excuse me, I am terribly sorry to trouble you, yet I could not help but overhear mention of my name just now.'

All three gaped at me with astonishment as the waiter gave them their pudding. I suppose I should have pretended to be Lucien Stuart but I could not resist the next move:

'Good day to you. My name is Septimus Keen.'

'Then why don't you come over and join us?' Sir Percy requested with commendable calm. 'A plate and a pancake for my guest here,' he added offhandedly to the waiter. 'Oh, and bring glasses. Mr – ah – Keen would probably like a glass of the Chateau D'Yquem. A pleasure to meet you, Mr Keen.' He performed the introductions and the women stared at me with growing fascination. 'You don't by any chance write stories, do you?'

'Yes, I do, Sir Percy.' From behind my darkly tinted lenses, I stared into his cold azure eyes.

'I may have read some of your stuff, possibly,' he

commented as he ate his Crêpes Suzette. It was clear that, physically, he was a strong man. '*Whodunnit*?'

'Yes, I wrote that.'

'*The Lost Love*?'

'Yes, I wrote that.'

'And *More and More*, by any chance?'

'Yes, I wrote that. Sir Percy, you astonish me. I had no idea that my tales had entered into so distinguished a circulation.'

'Do you mind my asking you these questions?'

'No, not at all. Ask me anything you like.'

'Do you know Sir Richard Knight?'

'No.'

'Bob Brown?'

'No.'

'Venetia Fielding?'

'No. Who *are* these people?'

'Well,' Sir Percy scoffed the last of his crêpes, 'don't you think that it is odd that your tales, which you state that you wrote, ended up in the hands of the individuals I mentioned, with whom you state you have no acquaintanceship?' Amelia and Barbara were regarding me eagerly, almost hungrily.

'No, not especially,' I replied. 'Sir Percy, you must understand my position.'

'Oh, I'd be only too delighted to do so. I trust that you will be joining us for coffee and brandy?'

'Yes, certainly and with utmost pleasure. I suspect that I am even more puzzled than you and it is very kind of you to offer. Please continue with your questions since it appears that it is possible that you may suspect me of something that I have not done. This is not the first time that this misfortune has befallen me. Allow me to explain myself.'

'A man,' said Amelia 'can explain his views, thoughts and opinions. He might even be able occasionally to explain his feelings. But *himself* . . .?'

'That is a first-class question, Madam,' I replied; and I was sincere. I also wished that I were Sir Richard Knight entertaining this slim and elegant bitch to a spot of supper. 'No, I cannot explain *myself* . . .' *How true*, I thought. 'But I can explain what I do. I am in the fortunate position of having a private income that makes of me a gentleman of leisure. Now, do you see George Bernard Shaw over there?'

'The socialist agitator,' Sir Percy commented disapprovingly.

'The superlative critic of Music,' Amelia observed admiringly.

'Do you mean the red-bearded man in that horrible Jaeger woollen suit?' Barbara asked. 'I think these notions of "rational dress" are dreadful.'

'There is truth in all your statements,' I responded as the coffee and cognac came. 'It was Shaw, however, who said: "A permanent holiday is a good working definition of hell." And I agree with him. I apply myself to the writing of tales, some of which are based upon events in my life and some of which are not. I don't need any more money and I am utterly indifferent to fame. Why, therefore, should I have any dealings with a publisher? I admit that I do employ a typist to make a number of copies of my works. These I distribute freely to persons whom I might meet in public places and I must say that it gives me pleasure to hear that these copies are being passed from hand to hand and repose with people far removed from my acquaintanceship.'

'Do you know Doctor Lipsius?' Sir Percy enquired gently.

'No; who is he?'

'A courageous and magnanimous patron of the Arts,' Amelia informed me. 'Perhaps you should meet him.'

'Perhaps I should, Lady Amelia. But I lead a somewhat reclusive and sheltered life on the whole, far removed from the mainstream of events.'

'Have you followed the Jack the Ripper case at all?' Sir Percy enquired as he selected a Corona from the cigar box proffered to him.

'To a limited extent. That was – what? – about six years ago, wasn't it?'

'Roughly, yes.' He flicked a finger to indicate that the waiter should offer cigars to me and I was in the mood for a big, long and fat Corona. 'Perhaps you can help us.'

'I'll see what I can do.'

'Why would Bob Brown of the East End, Sir Richard Knight of Great Russell Street and Venetia Fielding of Cheyne Walk all attribute the Ripper murders to Septimus Keen?'

'I have absolutely no idea,' I answered. 'Possibly my stories disturbed them and, since one of my themes is Death, they thought that someone who writes about murder is capable of committing it.'

'Why should three people whom you do not know alight upon the same name?' Sir Percy demanded.

'Your guess is as good as mine,' I replied evenly as I blew out three perfect smoke rings in succession. 'I must admit that I find this whole matter to be baffling in the extreme and also most deeply disturbing. I would like to meet these peculiar people who have been accusing me of these horrific crimes. How may I get in touch with them?'

'Are you *really* Septimus Keen?' Barbara Crockford abruptly intruded upon the conversation, giving every sign of mild drunkenness. 'For all we know, you might have overheard our conversation and you are simply pretending

to be him. You might just be making fun of ush . . .' She
was slurring her words now. 'Can you prove to me that
you are Septimus Keen?

'Barbara!' Amelia squealed.

'I can,' I said, 'tell you a story in the style of Septimus
Keen that will establish the matter of my identity beyond
all reasonable doubt.' For me, this was a new phenom-
enon. I could in a trice, in other guises, establish my
identity as Fred Robinson, Sir Richard Knight and/or
Venetia Fielding. Presently I could establish my identity
as Lucien Stuart. I carried no documents that confirmed
me as Septimus Keen.

'Why do you wear those strange dark glasses?' Amelia
asked.

'Doctor's orders.'

'Not those of Doctor Lipsius, I trust?' Sir Percy smiled.

'Sorry, who?' My expression was blank.

'I'm awfully curious about your eyes,' said Barbara. 'Can
I take your glasses orf?' I had fucked this bitch as Sir Richard
Knight.

'No,' I returned. 'the light would harm my pupils.' I sipped
my coffee. Across the room, an acquaintance of Venetia
Fielding, that young rake Lord Horby, had just entered
and was joining the table of Frank Harris. 'I do write tales
about death,' I said. 'Why is it sometimes legal to commit
murder? Actually, I was simply sitting here and thinking
about the matter when I heard my name mentioned. I was
composing another of my tales. This one is based upon what
a hangman told me in a Stoke Newington public house.'

'Once upon a time, they lived happily ever after,' Barbara
murmured as she sloshed back more brandy.

'Tell us the tale,' Sir Percy requested.

'Certainly,' I responded, 'and I shall tell it to you from
the hangman's point of view.'

THE HANGMAN'S TALE

by

Septimus Keen

F irst of all, and before anything else, allow me to state that I am innocent. Totally and utterly innocent.

I have never done any harm to any other human being with malice aforethought, as they say in court. I have just done my job and an honourable occupation it is, too. How many people would be brave and bold enough to do it? There's also a great deal of technical skill that's required.

I am completely normal. Even when I was quite busy at my work, I led a regular family life and so on. I am a useful member of society, a product of that society and I cannot see anything wrong with what I have done. You might do the same. *I am innocent*.

Ever since I was a nipper, I've wanted to be a hangman. What made me go that way is a matter of which I am not really quite sure. I reckon that it was probably something to do with the fact that roundabouts where I was brought up, I was totally unimportant. I'm talking about Clapton, East London, where my dad worked at a brick factory and me mum took in washing. I was one of ten children and I went to the Board School where I learned nothing. All they ever did there was shout at you and hit you. They made out like you was never going to be nothing.

There was this pub that my dad used to go to, the Rose and Crown. Sometimes me mum went there with him, too, though only occasionally. It was that sort of area. My dad came home from the pub one day and over tea, bread and dripping, he said, in a tone of awe:

'Guess who's running the Rose and Crown now, Doris. It's John bloody Buchan!' My mum shivered slightly.

'Who's he, dad?' I asked. Since I was the eldest, it was my turn to speak ahead of the others.

'What, you don't know about John Buchan?' my dad roared. I did not. 'He's only the Queen's hangman, just retired.'

'What's a hangman do, dad?'

'He *hangs* people, you stupid git! Murderers, robbers, people worse than that. He strings them up. And good for him is what I say. We're better off without them. Hats off to Johnny Buchan is what I say. He's rid us of many a bad man.'

All my friends with whom I played in the street were as fascinated as I was by John Buchan. He was a tall, thin man with sandy hair and a wispy moustache, quite well dressed in conservative clothes and he did not look threatening at all. Yet strong men used to get out of his way and he was regarded with a respect tinged with fear. It was said that among others he had hanged Charlie Jones, who had raped and killed three women; Bill Paynton, who had murdered two men; and Michael Peters, the Peckham Terror.

'Oh, he's a good bloke, John,' my dad used to say about him. 'And you should see the trade in the Rose and Crown. *Everybody's* going there nowadays.' I felt so powerless in those days that I wanted to be like John Buchan who had hanged so many famous people and who was so revered. I left school as soon as I could and followed my dad into the local brick factory. I was very proud when he took me down the pub and introduced me to my hero, John Buchan, who had hanged so many murderers. I wanted to be like him.

My dad died of asbestos poisoning or something like that.

Anyway, it clogged up his lungs and he was spitting blood by the end. I carried on working at the brick factory and going to the Rose and Crown. After a time I met Jackie, whom I married, and she has been and is a lovely wife to me; and I'm very proud of our two children, Don, named after my dad, and Janice, named after my mum. Meanwhile I kept going to the pub and I got to talk to John Buchan, though everybody else wanted to do that too. For some reason, he took a shine to me and introduced me to his wife Edna and his son Andy and his daughter Carol.

One night I was thrilled when he invited me to tea and showed me a toy he had made. Out of wax, yes, it was made out of wax. There was a gallows and, hanging from it, a puppet. He would strike a match and light the rope, which was made out of wax, and as he did that, he would pull out his stopwatch. The hanging figure's rope would melt and he would drop.

'Twelve seconds, Pete,' John Buchan would say. 'That's all it takes. Just twelve seconds. Better make some more waxen rope now.'

'I want to be like you,' I said, thinking of the sheer power it would give me over another human being and the local respect it would win me.

'You could be,' he said and I felt thrilled to bits. It was the greatest day of my life when I went for an interview at the Home Office, on the recommendation of John Buchan, to seek a job as a hangman. I passed all the tests and was appointed as an assistant after some months of training. It isn't a full-time job, in fact, but the money was a useful bonus on top of the wages I was by now receiving for my work at the brick factory. There is also the matter of respect tinged with awe.

The job is no different, really, from being a soldier and killing people in defence of Queen and Country. Well,

I suppose you could say that enemy soldiers would be fighting back and trying to kill *you*; but what I'm saying is that the men and women *I* hanged deserved to die because they had killed other people. I am a firm believer in capital punishment. Of course, some bloody feeble liberals say that it should be abolished and replaced with life imprisonment but, to my way of thinking, putting a human being in a cage for life is much more cruel. I think that it is best to put them out of their misery and remove a danger to society here and now. After all, what do you do with a mad dog?

Hanging was cruel in the old days. Why, they used to hang a bloke in public via slow strangulation and his eyeballs virtually popped out of his head as the crowd jeered: and then, when he was only half-dead, the executioner would rip open his intestines, dangling them in the air in front of everybody. Then they'd cut the culprit up into four pieces. Now, I will have nothing to do with that sort of thing, though I do believe that if it were done for the worst crimes, it might make people think twice before they committed them.

The way hanging is done these days is civilized and humane. You're welcomed to the gaol by the prison governor and told all about the man you have to hang. Then you are put in a room with your colleague and given a meal and a large jug of good beer. Meals vary from prison to prison, though Reading Gaol is noted for its hospitality. On the night when my story really begins, we had *double* pie and mash with peas followed by suet pudding with *extra* custard.

You chat with your colleague and sometimes a warden comes round to tell you about the criminal and how he is behaving and also to take you on a tour of inspection of the gallows, which latter is mandatory, and I am glad of that since I have an abounding pride in my craft. Up until a certain point, I had never hanged a man who came back to have the job done again. There were no ghosts hanging around my gallows. I had a sure touch and as soon as I secured promotion, I ensured that we had the best rope that money could buy. This is Kentucky hemp and it needs to be oiled and stretched with sandbags so you can thin it down to make a sturdy inch all around. That way it makes a nice knot.

Whatever my faults, I am a meticulous man and I suppose I am also a bit of a stickler for discipline, order and neatness. I liked to keep the scaffold as clean as I liked my wife to keep the house. I used to clamber up the twelve steps time and again, since the trapdoor ran along the twenty-foot platform and the hinges needed careful checking. I used to put my own weight against the supports to test the great oaken crossbeam, there to hold my noose. Finally I would jerk the trigger arm and let a 200-pound sandbag drop and then I would know that the gallows were in proper working order.

It was business as usual, that night in Reading Gaol, and Paul Simpson and I, who had worked together before, were tucking in to a good, hearty meal. This time they had allowed me to inspect everything earlier. Bill Clifton, one of the two wardens appointed to watch over the condemned man and make sure that he didn't kill himself before the Law did, dropped by for a beer and a chat.

'This could be difficult,' he said.

'How so?' I replied. 'The men *I* hang, they never even twitch.'

'He objects to it.'

'Who wouldn't?' Paul said. 'They all do.'

'He says he will not hang.'

'Then he's in for a surprise, isn't he?'

'Pete,' Bill said to me, 'I've been with many condemned men. This one is somehow – um – different.'

'There's nowt so queer as folk,' said Paul.

'He says,' Bill told us, 'that he is a victim of society.'

'We all are,' I said. 'What did he do?'

'He killed his wife and children and tried and failed to kill himself.'

'Hang the bastard,' I said.

'He says that they were all starving to death and that it was more merciful to end it quickly rather than slowly.'

'So it sometimes is,' said Paul. 'As he'll be finding out.'

'Normally they go quietly,' said Bill, who had been with HM Prison Service for thirty years. 'They are resigned to their fate. They know that it is inevitable. But not this one.'

'What's his name?' Paul asked. I think I'd asked originally but I had forgotten.

'Alan Priestley. Claims to be the seventh son of a seventh son. Claims that gives him supernatural powers. Claims that he won't be executed by hook or by crook. Also claims that if he is, through our breaking of the Law, he will come back to haunt and destroy his executioners.'

'Claims rather a lot, really, doesn't he?' Paul commented. 'Given the fact that we'll be hanging him tomorrow.'

'He'll be resisting all the way,' Bill told us.

'Oh, yeah?' Paul raised an eyebrow and smiled.

'Yeah,' Bill continued, 'he's been reading that Doctor Johnson geezer. You know. That Boswell who recorded all his sayings. Alan Priestley keeps looking at me in that strange way of his and quoting Doctor Johnson: "*Sir, when a man knows he is to be hanged, it concentrates his mind wonderfully.*"'

'I'm sure it does,' Paul said. 'You'd think it might.'

'The point is,' said Bill, 'that, like I've told you, he's going to put up a fight. He's already told me that he'll be going *screaming* to the gallows. Not very sporting of him, is it?'

'Damn' bad form, sir,' Paul remarked.

'Mr Simpson,' I told him in mock protest, 'do I detect a slight trace of sarcasm in your attitude?'

In fact, this was a serious matter. The execution would be attended by men selected by the Home Office. Normally, it is a very simple matter. The pair of hangmen enter the cell and bind the prisoner who is then marched to the gallows. That takes about eleven seconds. One quick pull of the trigger release and the man drops into eight feet of air. The neck breaks and death is instantaneous. I can't think of a more merciful method for the life of me.

The difficulty occurs if the condemned man resists. Home office Rules and Regulations prohibit any unseemly scuffling on the scaffold.

'Have you given him the usual?' Paul asked thoughtfully.

'No good at all,' Bill returned. 'Me and Ken, we put it in his tea and he just threw it at us.'

'Well, I suppose it'll have to be Plan C, then,' I said. This was C for Clubs . . . the condemned man was clubbed into a state of semi-consciousness shortly before the hanging. After all, we couldn't have the delicate sensibilities of Home Office bigwigs upset by the sight of a man screaming not to be hanged. Although it was illegal, sometimes there was no other way to get the job done.

Bill had to go back on duty. Paul and I finished our beer and decided to make an early night of it. As I lay in my bed, I wondered what I'd do with the money and decided that the wife would really like a day out in Brighton.

On the following morning, we had breakfast and, like I said, they really treat you well when you're doing a hanging in Reading Gaol. There were *three* eggs with *three* strips of bacon, a gigantic pot a tea and mounds of toast with *fresh* butter. We really were treated proud and they gave us a choice of strawberry jam or marmalade too.

As agreed under Home Office Rules and Regulations, we then did our duty and marched to the condemned cell. Bill and Ken had obviously done their bit since the place stank of blood, piss and shit and they'd clearly been cleaning up for quite a while. Alan Priestley must have had a very strong mind because, as we grabbed him, he somehow managed momentarily to tear away our masks and see our faces before Bill clubbed him round the back of the neck. We tied him up tight and we virtually had to carry him to the gallows though, in front of those bigwigs, we had to make it look as though he was fully conscious and accepting his just punishment. The rope went around and I sprang the trap. End of story.

But it wasn't. The first inkling I had that something was wrong was when I looked at the body dangling on the end of the rope. He did not have an erection.

Most men, when they're hanged, get a right bloody boner on them, but don't ask me why since I'm not an anatomist. I held my breath as the doctor examined him. The bastard was still alive. This was all highly embarrassing and severely impugned my professional skills.

There was nothing for it but to cut him down and to sever the rope around his neck, which I had fancied to be a perfect noose. Nobody seemed to know quite what we should do now. Should we hang him again now or do it later? I am just a minion so that was hardly my decision. While everyone was messing about, the condemned man did something quite astonishing. By all rights, his neck should have been broken but he somehow managed to wiggle it and his mask slipped off.

I never see the faces of the men and women I hang. The mask is slipped on as their backs are turned to me. I will never forget the waggling of his head as his arms writhed behind his back within their thongs of leather.

'God damn you!' he gasped and spat out blood. 'I will – ugh! – damn you all . . .'

The face was pinched, pallid and pale, as though he had not eaten for a month, and I learned later that he had been on hunger strike. I was hit by the gaze of his soulful dark eyes. They blazed with an insane hatred as the doctor ran forward. And then the man closed his eyes and died. The doctor muttered something about a heart attack within my earshot though the Press later announced just another routine hanging.

For me and for Paul, who had some office job with a coal mining firm up in Yorkshire, the consequences were unfortunate. I went back to the brick factory after a most enjoyable day out with the wife at Brighton, though we both thought that some of the immorality on display there was a complete disgrace. A letter from the Home Office then informed me that my services as a hangman were no longer required. Shortly afterwards I heard from Paul that the same thing had happened to him. I suppose there must be quite a number of people applying to be a hangman and who are ready to die for that job.

The next few months were very distressing and I am not just talking about the loss of extra income. I could salvage my social reputation in the pub by saying that I'd received promotion and was only called in on special cases. In time, I'd say that I'd retired and that sixty people swinging around on the end of a rope was enough for anybody. No, what I really missed was the satisfaction of the job. I thought of moving to France where they have regular executions and the brick factories are presently booming, I'm told. But I can't speak French and give me hanging to the guillotine any day of the week. At least the heads don't mouth things after they've been cut off.

Except for Alan Priestley. Time and time again his pinched, pallid, half-starved face with his burning, vengeful gaze came back to haunt my nightmares. The accusatory gaze of those soulful dark eyes told me that I was a murderer. He had killed his starving wife and children to spare them further torture and he had tried to kill himself, only for the Law to intervene with myself as its instrument in an endeavour to kill him. I would wake up screaming from the sight of his face.

After a time, I began to get rope burns on my neck. There was no accounting for them. I just had these painful purple bruises and grazes. My favourite parlour game, which I had learned from John Buchan – who had ended up in debt and hanging himself, incidentally – was the hanging of wax figurines. But, increasingly for me, it lost its savour.

It was the words, too. All the time in my nightmares, I kept hearing the hoarse voice of Alan Priestley gasping:

'You have hanged an innocent man.'

But he wasn't innocent at all, was he? I mean, he *did* kill his wife and children. It's hardly my fault if he only had one leg and his wife was blind and the pair of them couldn't get any work.

Then maybe the figure of Alan Priestley in my dreams wasn't referring to himself at all. Maybe he was referring to George Freeman whom I hanged for his slaying of a policeman. Some writer later dug into the case, spent his own money in the Courts of Law and managed to prove convincingly that George Freeman could not possibly have committed the murder. He was hanged all the same, though. You can't exactly say 'Sorry' afterwards.

It came to the point where I used to dread going to sleep. If I couldn't hang anyone by day, I was hanging them a-plenty by night. Time and time again in my nightmares, I hanged Alan Priestley and each time his face remained alive to state:

'You have hanged an innocent man.'

I ended up throwing my wax hanging toy into the fire, much to the disappointment of Don and Janice, my two kids, and even Jackie, my wife, was sorry to see it go since she said that it livened up cold winter's evenings at home. I suppose that what made me do that was the news that my old mate, Paul Simpson, had hanged himself. Bill and Ken were the next to go. Both men were separately 'Murdered by Person or Persons Unknown', that was the Coroner's verdict, and in each case, though Bill lived in Acton and Ken in Hendon, the murders were accomplished via strangulation with a rope. The killer was eventually caught and it seemed that he had killed a number of men in this way for no particular reason other than the satisfaction that it gave him. He was, of course, sentenced to be hanged.

Then my nightmares took on an even more disturbing hue. As I lay abed at night next to the wife and shortly before I fell asleep, there would be this sensation as if a pair of giant tweezers was squeezing on my temples. I'd fall asleep eventually, dreading that event, and then I'd have the nightmare.

I would be in the condemned cell, screaming out my rage. Then there would be the tramp of boots and I would be beaten with truncheons into a soggy insensibility. Next two men would come and bind me, march me out to the scaffold, one of them would spring the trap and the worst horror of the matter was that I would still be alive, dangling on the end of a string like a mutilated puppet.

I have had two years of these nightmares and it has affected my behaviour profoundly. I have lost my job at the brick factory and have been unable to find another.

My wife recently had an accident with some ammonia she was handling and she has gone blind. Our fate is slowly to starve to death since I am no longer the celebrity in the locality that I once was. Word has got around that I am no longer a hangman.

They must be joking! My wife and children are hanging from the beams in this house, having died quickly and peacefully. They never even twitched. I used the best well-oiled Kentucky rope, of course. I might as well die the way I lived, I reflect, as I tie the noose around my own neck and stand on a chair.

In front of me I see the pallid face and burning eyes of Alan Priestley and he is laughing 'Ha ha ha' as he licks his lips over the prospect of hanging an innocent man.

L ight shimmered on the crystal glasses as I finished my tale.

'How grisly,' Lady Amelia commented.

'That is possibly the *ghastliest* tale I have ever heard!' Barbara Crockford squealed, although it was obvious that she had enjoyed some sort of vicarious thrill.

'I found it rather interesting, myself,' Sir Percy pronounced with an air of decisive finality. 'Tell me, Mr Keen, may I by any chance have your card?'

'By all means.' I passed him a card which read simply: Septimus Keen: Man of Letters.

'Where can I get in touch with you so that we can discuss certain matters in the privacy they may require?'

I gave the man a false address in Camden Town since I did not wish to see him again in my role as Septimus Keen. Then I took my leave of Sir Percy, thanking him for his hospitality and expressing my wish to see him again at some future date that would be mutually convenient, kissed the hands of the ladies and, waving gaily to the company, made my excuses and left.

I knew that Sir Percy was hooked now. But dangers remained and I did not relish the role of the biter bit.

CHAPTER TWELVE

FROM THE DIARY
OF SEPTIMUS KEEN

(ALL IN A DAY'S WORK)

'At eight o'clock in the morning of a sweltering summer in July, Mr Richmond took his customary hearty breakfast of porridge with brown demerara sugar and cream, followed by four fried eggs with four strips of unsmoked back bacon, a pork sausage, fried kidneys and tomatoes, and fried bread. With his repast he drank strong Assam tea, with milk and three spoonfuls of white sugar, that he poured from a brown farmhouse teapot containing sufficient liquid to sustain him for half a dozen cups as he then ate his way through a dozen slices of hot buttered toast with marmalade. He did not trust people who failed to eat a proper breakfast when there was serious work to be undertaken.'

I look at what I have just written and marvel at the distinctions between fact and fiction. I am endeavouring to compose a new tale as I sip green chartreuse by candlelight and gaze occasionally at the moonlight glimmering on the water of the canal. Yesterday I dined with Doctor Lipsius, Richmond, Davies and Helen. The menu was astounding.

Tortue Liée
Consommé de Bœuf froid
Whitebait à la Diable et au Naturel
Pain de Saumon à la Riche
Sauces Genovoise et Hollandaise
Cailles Braisées Printanières Demi-Glace

Cotelettes d'Agneau Rachel
Canetons à la Voison au Coulis d'Ananas
Salade des Gobelins
Hanche de Venaison à l'Anglaise
Sauces Porto et Cumberland
Granitésau Champagne
Poulardes roties flanquée d'Ortolans
Asperges d'Argenteuil sauce Mousseline
Oeufs de Faisan Parmentier
Croutes à l'Ananas
Coupes Petit-Duc
Petites Friandises
Fondants au Chester
Petites Glaces au café et Pain bis Vanillees
Petites Gaufrettes

It is hard to recall the number of wines we enjoyed with this splendid feast. Doctor Lipsius is very fond of sherry and so we partook of fino, manzanilla and amontillado before going in to dine. Champagne was served, then the white Bordeaux of Sancerre, then Gewürtztraminer from Alsace, a Chateau Mouton Rothschild from Bordeaux, arguably the finest claret I have ever savoured, Chambertin from Burgundy, Chateau d'Yquem from the same region, oloroso sherry, vintage port, madeira, cognac and armagnac. Cigars from Cuba and Jamaica and the Dutch East Indies were offered, also cigarettes from Virginia, Russia, Turkey, Egypt and Havana. If one chose to smoke a pipe, one could make one's own mixture from pots of Virginia, Burley, Cavendish, Yenidje, Latakia and Perique; and opium and hashish were freely available in three hookahs, two separate and one mixed.

Doctor Lipsius was hosting the dinner for a number of reasons, both material and spiritual. In the course of his researches in the British Museum, he had discovered the following:

Fragment of a Graeco-Egyptian Work upon Magic, from a Papyrus in the British Museum, edited for the Cambridge Antiquarian Society, with a Translation by Charles Wycliffe Goodwin, 1852.

Goodwin's Translation

An address to the god drawn upon the letter.

I call thee, the headless one, that didst create earth and heaven, that didst create night and day, thee the creator of light and darkness. Thou art Osoronnophris, whom no man hath seen at any time; thou art labas, thou art lapōs, thou hast distinguished the just and the unjust, thou didst make female and male, thou didst produce seeds and fruits, thou didst make men to love one another and to hate one another. I am Moses thy prophet, to whom thou didst commit thy mysteries, the ceremonies of Israel; thou didst produce the moist and the dry and all manner of food. Listen to me: I am an angel of Phapro, Osoronnophris; this is thy true name, handed down to the prophets of Israel. Listen to me, ... hear me and drive away this spirit.

I call thee the terrible and invisible god residing in the empty wind, ... thou headless one, deliver such an one from the spirit that possesses him. . . . . strong one, headless one, deliver such an one from the spirit that possesses him . . . . deliver such an one . . . . This is the lord of the gods, this is the lord of the world, this is he whom the winds fear, this is he who made voice by his commandment, lord of all things, king, ruler, helper, save this soul . . . . angel of God . . . . I am the headless spirit, having sight in my feet, strong, the immortal fire; I am the truth; I am he that hateth that ill-deeds should be done in the world; I am he that lighteneth and thundereth; I am he whose sweat is the shower that falleth upon the earth that it may teem; I am he whose mouth ever burneth; I am the begetter and the bringer forth (?); I am the Grace of the World; my name is the heart girt with a serpent. Come forth and follow. – The celebration of the preceding ceremony. – Write the names upon a piece of new paper, and having extended it over your forehead from one temple to the other, address yourself turning towards the north to the six names, saying: Make all the spirits subject to me, so that every spirit of heaven and of the air, upon the earth and under the earth, on dry land and in the water, and every spell and scourge of God, may be obedient to me. – And all the spirits shall be obedient to you . . .

'Capital! Eh? Hm?' Lipsius beamed benevolently upon us as he inhaled from the hookah of hashish. 'That is what we shall be using at the next *esbat*,' he passed around our copies, 'which will be in exactly one month from this day. Now, I have pencils here since I wish you to make certain alterations. Change the words "Moses" and "Israel" to "Lucifer" and "Albion". Change "God" to "Satan".'

'Presumably there will be a sacrifice?' Helen asked.

'Naturally, my dear,' Lipsius returned gravely and she purred with satisfaction. 'I have never understood any objection to the matter. After all, heaven knows how many turkeys are sacrificed every Christmas. Can the slaughterhouse really claim any moral superiority over a Temple? As for child sacrifice, I am simply putting the poor creatures out of the misery of a lifetime of penal servitude followed by death in a workhouse. I am on occasion a most merciful man. However, at our next magical meeting, there will, one trusts, be big game.'

'Yes, doctor,' I said; and I proceeded to describe my adventures as Sir Richard Knight, Bob Brown and Venetia Fielding, including also my encounter with Sir Percy, Lady Amelia and Barbara seven days before.

'Septimus,' Helen interposed, 'do I detect an impish desire to parody our activities?'

'Helen,' I returned, 'do I detect by any chance a slight trace of sarcasm in your attitude?' She laughed maniacally.

'All rather splendid work, really.' The teeth of Doctor Lipsius gleamed in the light of the ornately wrought golden lamps that burned only the most pristine oil of the olive.

Richmond, Davies and Helen then proceeded to inform Lipsius of various other matters that did not directly concern me but that gave me ideas for further stories. It was altogether an exquisitely enjoyable evening.

And so now I am sitting here as I try to pen another tale. It is fortunate that I have overheard the talk of Sir Percy, Lady Amelia and Barbara and I am not in the least disturbed by the plans of Sir Percy to undertake experiments in surveillance. My three personae will simply not be At Home for a time, at least not until the matter suits me as comfortably as a well-worn glove. I essay another paragraph in my tale, which is provisionally entitled: *All In A Day's Work*.

'Richmond regarded his house with pride as he seized his bowler hat and baggy morning coat. He felt that beige really rather suited him, and so did his home, a large and ugly red-brick villa by Putney Hill, which he had furnished lavishly and in execrable taste. 'Lavish' and 'execrable' were also words that could be used to describe his ginger moustache, which merged into a pair of bulbous chin-whiskers, and his charmless face, with its muddy and reptilian eyes set in pale waxy skin.'

I recalled the 'Wanted' poster printed in Phoenix, Arizona that Doctor Lipsius had shown me one evening. The reward had been ten thousand dollars and the crimes were all Murder. Yesterday, at the house of Lipsius, I had heard the tale of Richmond from the man's own lips yet now I puzzled in perplexity over my paragraphs. I knew that he had a red-brick villa by Putney Hill since he had told me so and the others had confirmed the matter. I knew also from personal contact with him that the man was usually expensively but badly dressed in clothes that bore the embarrassing bloom of newness. It was a marvel to witness the way in which his massive fist would grip a small crystal sherry glass as if intent upon crushing it and he drank aged amontillado as though it was beer.

Much else was mere supposition. I had no idea what the man usually had for breakfast. For all I knew, the interior of his villa by Putney Hill was furnished in exquisite taste, and by describing it as 'lavish' and 'execrable', I had done my estimable colleague a grave injustice. He had told me that he amused himself with amateur boxing, drinking, eating and visiting popular theatres, the music halls, public houses and Mayfair's finest brothels, though it was possible that he was lying to me. His political views, resolutely Conservative and invariably uninformed, might be a blind, too. In fact, I knew very little of him and my description of Richmond was a union of what he had told me and the use of my own imagination.

There is a gap, therefore, though one trusts not a chasm, between what Richmond thought, felt and did in *reality* on the morning I intend to describe, and the words I use to describe the events, relying at moments not only on the words he spoke to me but also upon my own *imagination*.

Imagination must be sharply distinguished from Fantasy. It would be Fantasy if, in my story, I had Richmond sprouting wings and flying across the River Thames. Fantasy is what cannot happen and Imagination encapsulates what can. One of my favourite poets, Samuel Taylor Coleridge, has written wonderfully well upon the distinction though in his personal life, perhaps owing to his addiction to opium, he was on occasion liable to confuse the matter.

Charles Lamb, that charming essayist and friend of Coleridge, relates the tale of their intended visit to the Lamb and Flag, Covent Garden, for the expressed purpose of enjoying good beer. Just outside the public house, Coleridge seized Lamb by the buttonhole of his coat and began to lecture him on Metaphysics. Lamb would have been quite happy to listen to Coleridge's learned disquisition on Metaphysics over a pint or several since he was aching for beer but, to his grief, he saw that the eyes of Coleridge had closed and the Master was in full flow. Lamb knew as well as all the other friends of Coleridge that if one asked the poet a question in the morning, he would still be answering it without interruption in the evening. Lamb therefore produced a penknife from his pocket and sliced away the thread holding the button to his coat. Leaving Coleridge lecturing the button, he vanished inside the public house and reappeared two hours and four pints later, to find Coleridge still lecturing his button.

Lord Macauley was a learned man who dismissed Fantasy as a tiresome and irrelevant distraction and who thought that Imagination had to serve a visibly productive purpose.

This conviction was sometimes not quite so apparent in his personal life. A friend described a railway journey from London to Manchester with Macauley. There was a third man in the compartment whom Macauley engaged in conversation, if it can be called that, since, for the hours that the journey took, our determined rationalist spoke and no one else did. Macauley shook his fellow-passenger's hand warmly at the journey's end. 'There goes,' he said to his friend, 'the most interesting man that I have ever met.'

My description of Richmond's morning will not partake of Fantasy. I shall write down what he told me yesterday evening, his Reality, and where appropriate, embroider it with my own Imagination.

ALL IN A DAY'S WORK

by

Septimus Keen

1

On a sweltering July morning, Harry Connell is feeling proud, pleased and prosperous. He has every reason to feel so since his business affairs are flourishing. Harry keeps the Hat and Feathers, Stratford and it is doing a roaring trade. Harry is proud of his East End origins and sometimes astonishes his friends by quoting Chaucer and mentioning 'Stratford atte Bowe'. He likes to read in his leisure time and has no difficulty in reading Chaucer at all since the words are crystal-clear to anyone who uses Cockney pronunciation. Harry is always insisting, quite rightly, that the Cockneys are the true and original Londoners.

It is unfortunate indeed that his wife Ethel died in the cholera epidemic five years before and this caused him much grief at the time but he is over it now. His son Sid runs certain sections of the family business and his daughter Myrtle is married to Steve, a decent sort, who does his job of minding the pub quite capably. There isn't only the pub to be minded, since Harry has many other interests. There are the gambling dens, the opium dens, the tarts on the street, the fencing of stolen goods, the companies that mend carriages and supply horses, and the shopkeepers and those who have eating houses who pay this benevolent man money to ensure that their windows are not smashed and their business premises, customers and employees come to no harm. Fat Harry, a stocky, balding man of late middle age, is well liked in the locality and feels that, whilst it is hardly his ambition to be King of England, he is at least the king of Stratford atte Bowe.

Naturally, there have been revolts and endeavours to take away his kingdom from time to time. The rebels have invariably ended their days in the Thames, near Wapping, with bricks stuffed into their clothing. The latest threats, from a man called Wilson, worry him no more than any he has experienced previously. He will deal with them in his usual manner since he is the guv'nor of his manor. He has ten hard men working for him and he can and does have a tart any time that he chooses to do so. He can tell Mr Wilson, who wants a share of his active profits, to bugger off.

He lives quite well in a flat above his pub. Access to it is through a door marked PRIVATE, outside which loiter two strong men in his employment, and then it is up a flight of stairs down which many a strong man has been thrown. Fat Harry is certainly not expecting the sudden heavy tramp of boots up the stairs and the entry of Mr Wilson, he of the ginger moustache which merges into a pair of bulbous chin whiskers. This can only mean that Wilson has arrived with some powerful friends, enabling him to immobilize the guards downstairs. Fat Harry does not know that Wilson, whom he thinks to be from South London, is also known as Richmond.

It is fortunate, Fat Harry thinks, that he is seated at his desk since he keeps a revolver in the right-hand top drawer. It is unfortunate, he thinks, that Wilson already has his own shooter out and is shoving it deep into his belly. There is not much Harry can do other than raise his hands. Richmond pulls two pairs of handcuffs from the pocket of his baggy morning coat and with his right hand still jamming his gun into the fat of Harry uses his left to secure the wrists of Harry to the arms of the chair he has called 'the stoutest in all of East London'.

'What is it, Mr Wilson?' Fat Harry is frightened now and fighting to stay calm. 'This has to be some sort of misunderstanding.'

'You could call it that, Harry,' Richmond leers at him, 'you could call it that.' Richmond cracks the barrel of his Webley across the bridge of Harry's nose. Two jets of blood spurt out of it and there is a muffled moan from the figure chained to the chair. 'Don't scream, Harry. It'll simply make me want to press the trigger.'

'Let's talk about it . . .' Harry sobs.

'Too late for that, Harry. I only wish that you had been reasonable. For Christ's sake, I sent three men to see you, to reason with you, and what happened? One of them got a broken arm, one of them received a broken leg and the third had two legs broken. Open wide, Harry.' Harry refuses so Richmond smashes the barrel of his gun through Harry's teeth and as the man's jaw sags open and bone and blood spill out, he stuffs a ball-gag into his mouth and then ties a cloth around the jawbone, knotting it at the back of the neck. 'Scream all you want, Harry, there's certain matters to be discussed. First there is the matter of revenge. Tit for tat, ennit? No hard feelings.' Richmond places his boot on Harry's right elbow and pulls with both arms, breaking it as though he were snapping a matchstick. 'Nothing personal. Just business,' he tells the chained figure who emits a muffled moan. Richmond does the same with the left elbow. On each occasion, the snap of the bone has sounded like a firecracker.

The eyes of Harry are wide and distorted with terror as Richmond produces a hammer from his pocket and with two blows proceeds to smash the knees of Harry, who faints from the pain. As he waits for his victim to recover consciousness, Richmond helps himself from a cabinet containing drinks, pouring a large scotch whisky, which he drinks with evident enjoyment, reflecting upon the satisfying nature of the sound when bones are crunched. He then passes time by extracting a blindfold and a vial of prussic acid from his pockets, which he places upon the desk directly in front of Fat Harry. Slowly and methodically, he also searches the drawers of Harry's desk, pocketing not only his revolver but also any possible item of interest. These go into Richmond's right-hand pocket, though from his left he extracts another document that appears to be legal in nature and again places it on the desk by the blindfold and the vial of prussic acid. Since Fat Harry seems to be taking his time in recovering from his stupor, Richmond has another whisky, then thoughtfully extracts a steel box from his pocket and places that upon the desk. Helen is always criticizing him for his lack of style and he fears that Doctor Lipsius may also be of the same opinion but he is determined to remedy the situation.

'Now, Harry,' he says when the man at last shows signs of life, 'don't take it too hard. You haven't had a bad innings but now it's outings. We're generous people. You can keep all the cash you've got piled away for your retirement and we'll never trouble you again.' Richmond bares his large, discoloured teeth in an unpleasant grin. 'All you have to do is sign all your present business interests over to us as listed in this document here and we won't be bothering you again. This is,' he tapped the paper on the desk, 'a *legal* document. It is a contract. And since a contract requires Offer, Acceptance, Intention to Create Legal Relations and Consideration, since my associates and I consider your business interests to be worth something, we will give you

Consideration.' He flips a penny coin onto the desk, which lands head down.

There is silence as a pair of anguished and terrified eyes regard the document upon the desk.

'Blind or something?' Richmond demands. 'You see, if you're going to be that way and not sign this very reasonable contract, I might have to make you see sense. You could be more blind than ever, of course. I can put prussic acid on this blindfold here and tie it around your eyes and then you'd see nothing ever again. Also I'm told it's quite painful. Danny Miller, he wasn't reasonable. Lost his sight. Now in a home and walks with a cane. Crying shame.'

Fat Harry's trembling hand reaches forward for the pen Richmond has thoughtfully extended for him. He is so terrified of the consequences of not signing that he manages to move his arm despite the dreadful pain of his broken elbow. The chain on the handcuff gives him just enough slack to let him sign shakily.

'Thank you. Highly sensible.' Richmond pockets the contract. 'That is the official business concluded. Now we come to the unofficial business, everything that is not in the contract. Well, it all goes to me and my associates, obviously. *Everything* you have in Stratford. If you want to start up another business somewhere else, of course that's up to you, and the best of British luck! If you agree, nod once. Otherwise I'll have to make you see my point, or else you won't be seeing anything at all.'

The chained, gagged figure nods once as blood runs down his face from his nose and his mouth and is soaked up by his gag. His helpless broken limbs remind Richmond of a straw doll destroyed by a child in a tantrum. Richmond knocks once from within upon the door to the study of Fat Harry and then opens it.

In the hallway there are two of Fat Harry's men upon their

GERALD SUSTER

hands and knees. Behind them there are two of Richmond's
men who have placed revolvers to the napes of their necks.
These are the men hired by Bob Brown on the occasion
that he met Sir Percy. They must now crawl towards their
former boss, the broken and disfigured Fat Harry.

'What are you doing here, then?' Richmond demands.
'Straying a bit. What are you doing on my manor? Didn't
you realize that it's all under new management?' A tall,
strong, clean-shaven young man enters the room. 'Turn
your stupid heads around.' They obey. 'That's Alan. From
now on, he's in charge here. And don't think, Harry,' he
added over his shoulder to the sweating, sobbing figure, 'that
your son Sid and your son-in-law Steve will be coming back.'
Suddenly Richmond opens the casket of steel upon the desk
to reveal four severed thumbs, snaps it shut and replaces it
within his coat pocket as Fat Harry faints again and his
men squeal in horror at the revolting obscenity of the thing.
'Count yourself lucky that it didn't happen to you, lads,'
Richmond chuckles, then he unlocks the handcuffs binding
Harry, which is of no use to the latter's useless limbs, and
slips them in his pocket. 'I never wish to see your faces
round these parts again.'

'Thank you, Mr Wilson, sir.'

'Thank you, Mr Wilson, sir.'

'Go!'

Fat Harry's men, formerly feared, run as swiftly as mice
who have scented a cat.

'All right, now move it!' Richmond shouts and his bear
and gorilla slip an oilskin over the chair of Fat Harry and
then take it out of the room and down the stairs with the
casual attitude of removal men. It will be noticed in the
pub that the chair of Fat Harry, 'the stoutest of all in East
London', is being taken away for repairs.

'All yours, Alan,' Richmond tells the strong young man

who beams with pride and pleasure. 'I'll be by once a week to see the accounts.'

'Lovely, guv'nor,' Alan replies. 'Don't reckon Fat Harry will be back.'

'Nah!' Richmond laughs. 'What's he going to do? Call the police?'

2

On a sweltering July afternoon, Roger Melrose MP is feeling proud, pleased and prosperous. He has every reason to feel so since all his affairs are flourishing. At the age of forty-five, he is a Junior Minister well positioned for a future seat in the Cabinet and a bright future is forecast for him by the Whips' Office. He has a seat so safe in the South-East of England that the electors would vote for a pig if it were the Tory candidate.

Roger Melrose MP is only too well aware that in the South-West of England, the electors would vote for a pig if it were the Liberal candidate. Had he been born in the South-West, he would be a Liberal. He has no political principles whatsoever although *The Times* has recently commended his speech on the theme: 'Tory Democracy Means Fair Shares for All.' Roger Melrose is rather proud of the vote-winning potential of this meaningless slogan. He has arisen at ten o'clock in the morning today to prepare another sensational speech that he hopes will receive favourable notice in *The Times* and its theme is: 'The Vital Importance of Christian Family Values'. Roger is fully qualified to speak on that theme since he has a wife and two children; and one can see his face in the church of his constituency every Sunday.

His face is rather like an overripe beetroot, with hairs sprouting from his ears and nose and over his upper lip.

Upon the scalp of his skull, his dark brown hair is receding and a few greasy strands cover his scabby flesh before the crown. His features may appear to be unprepossessing but he can console himself by his knowledge of the fact that he can buy for an hour of pleasure an endless variety of thirteen-year-old girls, which happens to be his particular pleasure. Money has never been a problem for Roger Melrose.

His father was a railway magnate and later a Member of Parliament. The son is still Chairman of the Board of Directors of the company that his father founded. His positions as a Member of Parliament and as a Junior Minister have also secured him a dozen non-executive directorships in the City and half a dozen 'consultancies' to various firms up and down the country for companies that are delighted with the advice he gives and express appreciation in terms of remuneration for his invaluable services. Roger Melrose, all admit, is a master of bringing together men who proceed to discover a mutual interest that is financially profitable.

He expects today to be as pleasant as every day has been for as long as he can remember. It might even be *particularly* pleasant. He is going to lunch with the beautiful Arabella Symington, a wealthy widow and also a clever woman of business, whom he thinks he can out-clever any day of the week and, if necessary, twice on Sundays. It is not that she is unintelligent; far from it. But she is a woman and Roger Melrose intends to seduce her.

Arabella Symington offers a unique service, though her business card states, somewhat blandly, that she is a 'Financial Consultant'. Certainly she has a high head for calculations and gives wise advice concerning the behaviour of the Stock Exchange; she also knows an astonishing variety of influential people. In common with

Roger Melrose, she likes to introduce one man to another for a business proposition in exchange for a percentage of the profits from both sides should any worthwhile business be done.

Roger Melrose meets Arabella at Mangan's in The Strand at one o'clock p.m. It is his favourite restaurant and he is punctual, securing his favourite table and ordering malt whisky and water. As expected, Arabella appears ten minutes later, looking delectable in a tight mauve suit of brushed silk. She asks for a dry vermouth, then, whisking her petticoats in a manner calculated to arouse the blood pressure of Roger Melrose, she asks if she may peruse the menu.

Roger has no doubt whatsoever concerning his own choice of fare since he will order his favourite foods. This will consist of turtle soup followed by a dozen raw oysters. Mrs Symington surprises Mr Melrose by declaring that she will join him. He is not used to women who love oysters as much as he does. Then he will have his favourite dish, the speciality of the house, which is steak and kidney pudding. Arabella decides to have a fillet steak and wants it 'just waved over a candle'. Vegetables are chosen and various fine vintages selected, there is engagement in idle chit-chat and Roger Melrose is infatuated by the beauty of this young woman, who has a face that is quaint and piquant with eyes of shining hazel. He has no idea that she leads another life as Helen.

'Congratulations, Mr Melrose,' she remarks over the turtle soup.

'Oh, the speech, ah, yes. One of my better ones, I thought. Seems to have captured much attention, even if I say so myself, Mrs Symington.'

'Oh, I wasn't referring to your speech, Mr Melrose,

undeniably edifying though it was. I was referring to your promotion.'

'Ah, yes,' he smiled. 'Most unexpected. I never fancied that Robinson & Ward would want me on the Board but there we are.'

'Not Robinson & Ward, Mr Melrose. I refer to your appointment as a non-executive Director at UK Steel.'

He wonders what on earth he can possibly say without appearing to be ignorant. He is vaguely aware that there *is* a company called UK Steel which has put in a tender to manufacture railway lines and rolling stock but he has paid the matter little attention since he is already a director of Grimstone Steel; and he will be exercising every ounce of his influence to ensure that that latter company gets the contract.

'How did this honoured yet highly unexpected elevation come about, Mrs Symington?' he enquires as he slurps his turtle soup.

'It comes about in six weeks,' Helen replies brightly, 'when the contract with UK Steel is signed.'

'On . . .?'

'I think you know.'

'I'm sorry but that is impossible,' he returns as the oysters arrive. 'You must be aware of my loyalty to Grimstone.'

'Ah! Loyalty! How I admire it!' Helen chortles as she squeezes fresh lemon upon her oysters and regards the tremulous flinch of these still-living beings. 'But now your loyalty will be to UK Steel. On the same terms, of course.'

'That is not possible.'

'Everything is possible, Mr Melrose.' She devours her first oyster and drinks the juices greedily. 'Mmm. Heavenly. I absolutely adore the thought that they are alive when we are eating them. Which way do you find gives you the most enjoyment: the straight swallow? The bite through the centre? The long chew? The last is alleged to have the qualities of an aphrodisiac. *Of course* you will be joining the board of UK Steel and pursuing its interests, Mr Melrose. It is greatly to your advantage.'

'Possibly so, Mrs Symington, but,' he shifts uneasily upon his broad and flabby buttocks, 'it is going to be Grimstone.'

'No, it is not.' Helen seizes some buttered brown bread, bites at it daintily and chews thoughtfully. 'Have you ever heard,' she enquires gently, 'of Julia Flack?' She places a drop of hot pepper sauce upon her next oyster and it flinches. So does Melrose.

'No.'

'Lizzie Skate?'

'No.'

'Donna Carling.'

'No!'

'Bessie Wyatt?'

'NO!' Melrose is now anointing his oysters with the sweat that is dripping from his brow. 'What *is* this?'

'How funny you look when you change colour!' Helen giggles and sips some champagne. 'Although I'm not really sure if puce suits you so well. Yet isn't it even funnier,' she adds gaily, 'when all the prepubescent girls that I have named are intimately familiar with *you*?'

'There is no truth in this disgusting libel whatsoever!' he blusters. 'To whom *have* you been listening?'

To the young girls themselves,' she responds sweetly and laughs. 'Oh, Mr Melrose, I had no idea that you are like that! Not that it worries me in the slightest. Nor should it worry you as long,' her hazel eyes harden, 'as you agree to behave yourself and to be a good boy in the future.'

'This is all a pack of lies!' he expostulates as spittle and sweat fly all over the table.

'Ann Shanklin, Carol Hirst, Frieda Watkins, Emma Birt, Myrtle Peters . . . do you want me to go on?' She regards him as though she is a hawk who has a lamb within her claws. 'Just sign the contract I have in my bag and do your job, will you?' She smirks at his discomfiture. 'That way we shall all be happy and no one need ever hear of the names I mentioned . . . unless, of course, you misbehave. Naturally I shall also be requiring your future Parliamentary services. Obviously you will be in receipt of appropriate remuneration.'

'I will sign later, if I may,' he answers, his voice choked as if he is in the midst of strangulation.

'No, Mr Melrose. Now.'

'No.'

'Very well. The *Pall Mall Gazette* will no doubt be intrigued by the unusual nature of your leisure activities.'

He signs.

'I must go,' he declares.

'Oh, but dear, sweet, charming Mr Melrose, great benefactor of the British Public, why? You still have half a dozen oysters to eat, and then it is your favourite beefsteak-and-kidney pudding; oh, and given the fortunate nature of our agreement, no doubt you will relish the thought of *extra* cream with your treacle sponge.' She titters and he does not. He knows that he cannot commit an act of gross bad manners. He knows that *she* knows his shameful secret, though how she came by that knowledge, he cannot fathom. He is forced to eat his formerly beloved oysters. He has to run to the lavatory where he vomits and there follows a violent bodily eruption of winds and waters. Returning to the table he *has* to have his steak-and-kidney pudding; and she has ordered extra vegetables in the form of carrots, peas, cabbage and boiled potatoes.

She cuts into her rare fillet steak and watches the resulting squirt of blood with satisfaction. With it, she takes a few peas and a small green salad, also one boiled new potato. She praises the latter and urges him to eat more. As he visibly sickens, she watches the sight with undisguised glee. She absolutely *insists* that he *must* have his treacle sponge with *extra* cream and keeps pressing wine upon him. His visits to the lavatory are blithely excused.

When the meal is over, he pays the bill and is as relieved at its end as a prisoner in the dungeon of Torquemada at the conclusion of his interrogation. He knows that her information, however she has received it, gives her the power to ruin him utterly and so now she virtually owns him, lock, stock and barrel.

He escorts her to her carriage, an open Victoria. As a final insult, disdainful in her departure, she publicly places a peck upon his right cheek.

3

On a sweltering July night, Fanny Isaacs is feeling proud, pleased and prosperous. She has every reason to feel that way since it has been a good year for business and she is expecting her partner to join her for some champagne at her house in Mayfair. There are one or two matters to discuss after which they will both go on to separate dinners. In Fanny's case, she will be seeing her lover, one Sarah Coombs, who works for her. Despite her intimate knowledge of human nature in all its manifold forms, she is still unclear regarding the pleasures of the Mr Ralph Hayes whom she is expecting. Perhaps he is among that rare breed of men who are asexual.

Fanny Isaacs has every reason to be glad of having Mr Hayes as her business partner. Five years ago he advanced her the capital that has enabled her to fulfil her vision and to lead the life of luxury she has always desired. Fanny had begun her working life as a match girl in an East End factory. That had meant a bleak future of fourteen hours a day for a pittance with the probability of death from consumption by the age of thirty. It made no sense if one could earn as much in five hours by means of prostitution. It also made no sense to prostitute oneself to drunken sailors for pennies in the East End when one could do the same for rather more with drunken toffs in the West End.

Fanny has gradually learned that people have different tastes. There are many men who have plenty of money and who are willing and eager to pay large sums to be spanked, caned, lashed, birched and whipped. Others wish to be bound or dressed in ladies' clothing. These strange gentlemen are invariably harmless and the only violence they wish done is to themselves. Fanny has found that, with many, she treats them as if she were tucking them into bed like babies: they usually return for more. Having built up a small but flourishing trade in Soho and having minded her savings, she thinks fondly still of her first venture as an employer, a modest brothel of flagellation in St John's Wood.

'It's the fact that one of my clients was a Cabinet Minister that drew me to the attention of Mr Hayes,' she tells her lover Sarah as they caress one another between the sheets. Even after five years of their business partnership, she calls him 'Mr Hayes' and he calls her 'Miss Isaacs' and they always treat one another with the utmost courtesy. 'His proposition to me was simple,' she has told Sarah; 'he puts up the money, I do the business, he looks after any problems and he takes fifty per cent of the profits and one hundred per cent of the information.'

Fanny Isaacs is forty now, though she looks ten years older. Her face is pudgy, though one can see that once upon a time it might have been beautiful; even now, it is not unattractive. She has a voluptuous figure and wears the finest of silken gowns. Her rich black hair still retains its gloss and she can afford to go to the finest beauty parlours and drink the most exquisite of wines. Gone are the days when she was merely a prostitute: she directs Trend Entertainments Ltd, a flourishing and profitable company with many West End interests, including control of every notable brothel of flagellation in London.

She no longer has to work at anything other than accountancy, recruitment and the collection of information. She fully intends that her daughter Henrietta will in due course go to London University. Anyone who knows her from the old days would be delighted by her success were it not for one worrying factor. In the East End of her youth, she was celebrated as 'the girl with the golden eyes'. She still has golden eyes but their sparkle has been dulled during the interceding years by over-indulgence in alcohol, opium and even morphine. In her more reflective moments, she tells herself that she needs it to take away the pain for, in her heart of hearts, she knows just how many young lives she is destroying.

In her somewhat garish living room, where the floor is littered with the skins of the tiger, the leopard and even the Brazilian jaguar, and the walls are littered with dreadful paintings deemed to be fashionable, she smokes another pipe of opium and pours herself another glass of brandy. She has resolved not to take another shot of morphine until midnight. She hopes that Mr Hayes will not be in the mood he is possessed of sometimes, which leads him to go through the accounts with a scrupulous attention that might make any sane woman scream from tedium. Presently the accounts are in something of a mess, if the truth be told. Fanny's obsessive betting on the horses is partly to blame and here her business skills have deserted her entirely. She has lost a lot of company money on the matter but there is no need to worry since she will pay it back.

Yes, she is looking forward to seeing Mr Hayes tonight. This mysterious man is such an excellent partner, cynical bounder that he is. He has squared both the police and every endeavour to move in upon this operation.

'Don't worry about it, Miss Isaacs,' this smooth, smiling, clean-shaven man always says. 'Just leave it to me.' There has never been a problem that Mr Hayes has not solved and she is aware that he has done so with methods that are swift, ruthless and deadly. Sometimes, she reflects with a smile, there is a certain acid wit about them. Who can forget the Metropolitan Police Inspector who was silenced by the knowledge that occasionally he liked to prance around wearing the ball gown of an aristocratic lady?

A further virtue of Mr Hayes, Fanny reflects, is that he has a wide and deep knowledge of perfectly legal substances that have a wonderful effect upon the brain and body. He has introduced her to morphine, far more striking and immediate in its effect than opium which cannot be injected; and on his last visit, he introduced her to a substance finer still: heroin. Fanny hopes that Mr Hayes might bring her more of that tonight.

She is delighted when, on the dot of eight o'clock, the smooth, smiling, clean-shaven gentleman arrives, punctual to the minute, as always, and, as usual, quite immaculately dressed in severe and sober fashion. Mr Hayes is unquestionably a *gentleman*. She offers him Pol Roget champagne from an ice bucket especially prepared or else

Courvoisier cognac. He smiles and accepts both. For a time they chatter pleasantly about inconsequentialities. Then his face becomes serious.

'Miss Isaacs,' he tells her, 'there is a matter that worries me gravely.'

'And what is that, Mr Hayes?'

'Have you ever heard,' he sighs heavily, 'of a Mr Wilson?'

'Oh, my God! Yes, I have.'

'One gathers that he he has expanded the range of his business interests in the East End. Stratford, notably.'

'I have heard that, Mr Hayes.' Fanny Isaacs has a lively and alert intelligence service. 'I gather that Fat Harry Connell has retired from business owing to ill health.'

'Precisely.' Davies extracts a silver cigarette case which he proffers to Fanny. Both take Turkish cigarettes. 'It is none of my business what Wilson chooses to do in the East End. It becomes my concern if he chooses to invade the West End.' Fanny has no idea that Hayes is Davies nor that Wilson is his partner, Richmond. She merely notes a tremble of his hand as he strikes a match and lights both their cigarettes. There are ashtrays before both of them, fashioned out of ivory. 'I have received threats of death.'

Initially, the statement does not register with Fanny, since she has imbibed much alcohol and opium throughout the day.

'But he is no match for your ingenuity, surely?' she states eventually.

'I trust not. But Wilson is the most formidable opponent I have been up against in quite some while. The man will stop at nothing. I intend to see this through but I am concerned about your own position. In the admittedly unlikely event of anything happening to me, I would not want there to be any misunderstanding concerning our business relationship. In short, Miss Isaacs, if the worse comes to the worst, I want the business to go one hundred per cent to you. I have signed a document to that effect.' He produces it. 'Would you care to sign it also?'

Naturally she reads it, while feeling a profound sense of gratitude for his concern in the matter of her welfare.

'Wilson hates women, unfortunately,' he continues. 'I shall arrange for you to have bodyguards. But in the highly unlikely event of some mishap occurring to you in what could be a war, I trust that you will do the same as I have done.' Fanny signs instantly and Davies takes the document. 'Of course,' he smiles, 'I shall stop Wilson before he stops us but you really must be careful, Miss Isaacs. One cannot be too careful these days. Oh, you don't have the accounts, do you? Tedious, I know, but it needs to be done. Ah, thank you. I'll take these with me for a couple of days and return them to you as I usually do.' She nods. 'How's the morphine going down with the girls?'

'A treat, Mr Hayes, a treat. They just keep coming back for more. You'll probably see from the Accounts that I have opened lines of credit . . .'

'What a benevolent idea!' Davies chuckles sardonically. 'There is no problem about supply for any good girl. And now, my dear, I have an especial treat for you. Here is a syringe. And here is a solution of heroin. It is the finest cure for morphine addiction that is known to modern medicine. I have tried it myself and derived great profit and enjoyment thereby. Take it after I have gone, my dear, and you will enjoy a wonderful evening.' The talk returns to trivialities as Fanny regards Davies gratefully. Five minutes later, the man bows himself gracefully out of the room, leaving Fanny smiling like an idiot.

Davies has left Fanny with a shot of heroin sufficient to kill a whole room packed with people. She is no longer efficient and he has found someone else to run the business.

He has thought of blending the solution of heroin with nitric acid since that would make the blood boil in her veins, but there is no point in doing that unless he can be present to view the matter.

4

Just before midnight on a sweltering July night, Doctor Lipsius is feeling proud, pleased and prosperous. The news has reached him that the missions of Richmond, Helen and Davies have all been successfully accomplished. There is now the matter of Gregory Naylor, a thorough nuisance, to which he must attend.

Gregory Naylor is a Brother of the Light, a man pledged to do battle with the Lords of Darkness. His activities have on occasion caused Lipsius acute inconvenience. Presently he has gone into hiding and thinks himself to be in a stronghold that is impregnable. The tongue of Lipsius flicks out to moisten his thin lips as his yellow, beady eyes regard the clay image he has fashioned. It is in the likeness of Gregory Naylor. It also contains hairs and nail clippings of Gregory Naylor, thoughtfully retrieved by a cleaning lady in the pay of Lipsius.

Presently, Gregory Naylor, fully aware of the dark designs of Lipsius and of the demons that drive his demented brain, is living in a room without windows, the door of which only he can open. Two armed guards patrol the household. In consequence, Lipsius has sought for the method he deems to be most immediately expedient.

Lipsius knows, of course, that the secret of Sorcery is Imagination powered by a one-pointed Will and that physical images are employed to give the matter focus. He utters one word as he hammers a nail through the heart of the clay image he has taken so many pains to shape:

PAZUZU: and anyone who might hear it could think this word to be either an obscene expletive or else the name of a demon.

Lipsius then takes an armagnac and retires to bed, safe in the knowledge that the death of his enemy will duly be reported in the Press as due to a fatal heart attack. Of course, no one will ever connect him with this death since he is miles away at the time.

Do I honestly believe that Lipsius killed an enemy at a distance? I know only what he has told me; and certainly the death by heart failure of Gregory Naylor MP *was* reported in *The Times*.

I cannot vouch for every word of the conversations earlier in my tale but I built upon everything that Richmond, Helen and Davies had told me.

Now I prepare to write my masterpiece: Sir Percy Sulgrave.

Here my every word will be transmuted into action.

CHAPTER THIRTEEN

FROM THE JOURNALS
OF SIR PERCY SULGRAVE

Monday

Yoicks! Tally ho! There is nothing like the thrill of the chase to make a man relish the joys of life. Since neither Barbara Crockford nor Amelia Stanhope are ready and willing to assist today my quest for Justice in the apprehension and arrest of Jack the Ripper, I am required to employ hired help.

I remain convinced that the nefarious Doctor Lipsius is behind it all. Somehow his infernally ingenious mind has contrived a plot whereby the key figure is one Septimus Keen, whom I met the other day and did not trust. I had him followed to his home in Maida Vale, just across the Grand Union Canal from my own.

I am fully prepared to spend my money upon the arts of detection and my agents have elicited the following facts:

1: This small flat is rented from a Mrs Pemberton by a Mr Lucien Stuart although Mr Septimus Keen appears to live there.

2: The address given to me by Septimus Keen is bogus.

3: Sir Richard Knight has 'gone to the Continent' and no one knows when he will return. There *is* a Sir Richard Knight listed in *Burke's Guide to the Landed Gentry* but the address given is in Hampshire, not London. The Club is Boodles.

4: Venetia Fielding of Chelsea has apparently decided to take a sea voyage to America, there to visit relatives.

5: Mick Jones of Marcia Road is a drunken, half-witted imbecile who knows nothing of the whereabouts of Bob Brown.

6: Doctor Lipsius continues to lead the life of a wealthy scholar and charitable gentleman.

I shall take my telescope, the most powerful that money can buy, watch Septimus Keen and follow him.

Tuesday

Damn! What an unsatisfactory day I had on Monday! Septimus Keen did not move from the flat of Lucien Stuart. What did he do all day and all evening? Read books? What did I do all day? Looked through a telescope and paid someone else to look as well and also to make enquiries.

At least there has been one breakthrough. Monies paid to Mrs Pemberton have elicited the information that her tenant, Lucien Stuart, writer, answers to the physical description of Septimus Keen. I hope that he emerges from his lair. It is essential for me to learn his habits.

I am slightly out of temper since the shares I bought in Grimstone Steel have tumbled on the Stock Exchange since the rail contract has gone to UK Steel. Apparently, my contacts tell me, a decisive voice in that matter was that of my acquaintance, Roger Melrose MP. I am really rather astonished. I had always thought that, since he is a longstanding friend of Grimstone Steel, one could count on him. What can have happened?

Wednesday

At last things are moving, though in which direction it is presently impossible to tell.

According to Sir John Knight of Hampshire, his father Sir Richard Knight died two years ago and Sir John is now a member of Boodles. This information has been confirmed by Boodles. That means that whoever is posing as Sir Richard Knight is bogus. Could this be another alias of Septimus Keen?

Moreover, my prey has finally emerged from his flat though his initial appearance was disappointing. He bought a pint of milk from the milkman, then vanished indoors.

He emerged at twilight. I followed him to the Rose and Crown where he had a pint of India Pale Ale and spoke to no one. Nor did he recognize me since I was wearing a false beard and moustache along with a battered bowler hat and a loud Norfolk jacket with knickerbockers, something I would never normally wear. It was easy to shadow him to the Four Sisters, where he had a pint of four ale and spoke to no one, though he did make some notes on the back of an envelope with a pencil. At the Duke's Head, he had a pint of porter and was drawn into a cordial argument about Socialism, which he appeared to advocate. At the Nag's Head, he had a pint of best bitter and was drawn into a somewhat acrimonious argument about Socialism, which he now appeared to oppose. Thence he returned home.

I cannot quite understand this man.

Thursday

At last! I watched Keen step out into the street and hail a passing hansom. It was time for the cabman I was keeping to follow him. We journeyed through St John's Wood to Regent's Park and, as he alighted, I noticed that Septimus Keen was carrying a brown paper bag. I followed at a distance in order to discern the vile purpose for which he might be having it in his possession and took up my vantage point about a hundred yards away. He stood by the pond and extracted crumbs of bread from his bag, which he proceeded to feed to the ducks and geese.

I was distracted from following this apparently innocent activity by a sound of sobbing. I turned to discern a young lady wearing a frilly white blouse and a black, bell-shaped skirt who appeared to be possessed by the most abject misery. She was crying into her faded gloves and I distinctly heard the words:

'Oh, no! Please! Please, not him again!'

'Madam,' I said, since we Sulgraves pride ourselves upon always assisting a damsel in distress, 'you seem to be a little afflicted. Can I perhaps help you in any way?'

'Who could help me against this *fiend*!' she wailed.

'Possibly I can,' I replied. 'I will in any event gladly listen to anything you might wish to tell me.'

'Thank you, sir,' she replied and turned towards me a face that was quaint and piquant, rather than beautiful, with eyes of hazel that shone with her tears. 'I thank you for your kind consideration and concern but I fear that you will not believe me.'

'I find these days so strange, Madam,' I responded, 'that I am virtually ready to believe anything, or at least to listen.'

'Sir, you are too kind. Yet I suspected that you are a chivalrous gentleman the instant I set eyes upon you,' she replied in a high, lilting voice. 'Allow me to unburden myself. Do you see that gentleman there?' Her eyes flickered to indicate Septimus Keen; I sat up with doubly renewed interest as I nodded. 'It looks as though he is engaged in the perfectly innocent operation of feeding the ducks, does it not? Believe me, sir, something more sinister is afoot.'

'Who is he?' I asked innocently.

'I do not know,' she replied. 'I do not know anything about him whatsoever save for the fact that he follows me, which makes me feel quite acutely uncomfortable.'

'Understandably so,' I agreed indignantly. 'It is an outrage.'

'It is *horrible* to be followed, do you not think?'

'Frightful,' I agreed. 'Allow me to introduce myself. Sulgrave is the name, Sir Percy Sulgrave, at your service.'

'My name is Patricia Ward. I give music lessons. The generosity of deceased relatives provides for my modest home yet it is essential for me to supplement my slender income. I have no doubts concerning my skills nor of my ability to impart them, and it is a pleasure so to do to a younger generation, though I also tutor adults. My piano is perfectly adequate but,' she added with a casual toss of her long, wavy auburn hair, 'some wish to be taught upon their own premises since the family has purchased, say, a French Concert Grand. In consequence it is necessary for me to travel, and I do not object to this since it is fascinating to step inside the homes of other people. I enjoy my work, especially when I am teaching Chopin, but I do not enjoy receiving communications such as *this*!' With a trembling hand, Patricia Ward extracted a piece of cheap paper from her bag and passed it to me. I looked and saw that it read:

I WANT YOUR PIANO LESSONS. MIDDAY SATURDAY COMING. I WANT YOU. MEET ME AT THE FOOT OF NELSON'S COLUMN. JACK.

It had been done upon a typewriter.

'How intensely distressing,' I commented.

'I was petrified.'

'Who would not be?'

'Naturally I did not meet this "Jack" at Nelson's Column.'

'When was this?'

'Four weeks ago. And it has all become worse and worse. Three weeks ago, *this* was thrust through my letter-box.' Miss Ward dug within her bag and her gloved fingers extracted a blood-stained and short, sharp knife, which she passed to me. I fingered it gingerly.

'I presume that you have been to the police . . .?'

'Of course, Sir Percy, but it is of no use at all. They inform me that they can do nothing unless someone does something, by which time it may be too late.'

I thought of Jack the Ripper and reflected that it would be. Even so, the Ripper murders were connected with Whitechapel, certainly not with the pastoral surroundings of Regent's Park. I essayed another question.

'What makes you connect these highly disturbing events with the man a hundred yards away who is feeding the ducks, Miss Ward?'

'He has been following me. I am sure that he has been spying on me. I never know just when he will be there but at least three times in a week, yes, he is following me. If I take the Underground railway, he is there. If I take a tram or a horse-bus, he is there. If I take a hansom cab and dismount, I alight to see another hansom cab and *he* is dismounting. If I go to the National Gallery to admire Vermeer, *he* is there to admire Rembrandt. I cried just now because I came here to Regent's Park so that I could enjoy some peace and quiet. And there *he* is!' She broke down into a renewed fit of sobbing.

Suddenly, Septimus Keen turned to face us and ran towards us, waving his arms madly in the air. I stood up to defend Miss Ward with the knife she had passed to me. As he came close, I saw his hideously malefic expression, his teeth bared, and I heard the scream of Patricia Ward. Behind me I heard a masculine roar. My head flicked back to see a policeman. But I was not expecting him to cosh me.

THE CONFESSION OF
SIR PERCY SULGRAVE

I awaken in a prison cell and I try to remember. I see bare stone walls, a plank bed and a bucket for urination and defecation. This can be seen from the spyhole. There is also a pencil and a pile of cheap paper. I have used the hours by writing the preceding passages.

I am sweating with terror and so I have endeavoured to keep my sanity by writing an account of the previous four days, or at least I think it was four days. How long have I been here? I no longer know nor do I care as I endeavour to recover my memory. How long ago was it since I wrote 'Thursday' and was coshed by a police constable as I endeavoured to defend Patricia Ward from Septimus Keen? That is my memory of the matter.

They tell me that I had a short, sharp, bloodstained knife in my hand and that I was endeavouring to rip the features of Patricia Ward as a Mr Lucien Stuart rushed to her assistance and that I was apprehended in the threatened act by PC Dawkins, already having slashed the lady once, the blood being found upon the knife I held. I have no memory of the trial. The verdict was 'Guilty' and I am sentenced to be taken to a certain private place, there to be hanged by the neck until I am dead.

Since there is nothing that I can do about that, it is my last chance to tell the truth, the whole truth and nothing but the truth. We all have a dark side to our nature and sometimes we transfer it onto others, hence my obsession with Doctor Lipsius. All the deeds I did by dark I blamed upon him since *I* am Jack the Ripper.

That is why I have followed in the Ripper's footsteps, investigating my own crimes. Yes, I slaughtered that foul group of blackmailing prostitutes, Mary Anne Nicholls, Annie Chapman, Elizabeth Stride, Catherine Eddowes and Mary Kelly. I admit that it was an error to kill Elizabeth Stride, thinking that she was Mary Kelly. Later that night, I killed Catherine Eddowes thinking that she was Mary Kelly. Still later, roughly six weeks later, I killed the *real* Mary Kelly.

Why? One motive was simply my loyalty to the Royal Family. A second is that I *hate* women. My mother endeavoured to emasculate me and ever since I left her smothering caresses, I have wanted to have nothing to do with women. I am homosexual and a further reason for hating women is that they take my lovers away from me. Women are foul and unclean, they smell and give one diseases, yet I have to admit that on occasion I have been unable to resist the stinking loins of a cheap prostitute and I despise myself as much for that fact as I despise them.

Sexual murder is like rape done with a knife, yet unless it is done with artistry it possesses all the savour of boiled cod. This was in fact a rite of Black Magic of the deepest dye, done to free myself forever from the pernicious influence of Woman.

All human beings seek some form of immortality and I do not believe in a heaven or a hell. My existence will terminate as I mount the gallows. I am a homicidal maniac and I wish to die this way, having founded a legend of infamy without parallel.

Sir Percy Sulgrave (Bart)

EDITOR'S NOTE

Regarding *The Confession of Sir Percy Sulgrave*, it must be stated that he is not the only author who has written of the difficulties in identifying Mary Jane Kelly.

According to Melvyn Fairclough in *The Ripper & The Royals* (Duckworth, London, 1991), the woman horribly slaughtered in Miller's Court was not Mary Kelly but her friend, Winifred May Collins; Mary Kelly, it seems, fled from Royal vengeance and escaped to Canada, assisted by Walter Sickert.

(A.S.)

CHAPTER FOURTEEN

FROM THE DIARY
OF SEPTIMUS KEEN

I think I shall treasure the memory of the events that transpired today for the rest of my life.

I picture a cellar that has been transformed into a Temple. In the East there is a High Altar, covered with a crimson cloth upon which has been embroidered in gold the figure of the Goat of Mendes. Behind it there is a black trapezoid, fashioned out of a meteorite that has fallen upon Earth, and upon it stands a writhing octopus that has been crafted out of silver. Tall black candles inserted in twisting silver serpents illuminate the Temple with an eerie glimmer. In front of the altar, there is a black coffin made of ebony and before that, incongruous for the occasion, a wooden soapbox, yet above this, a noose hangs from an iron hook implanted in the ceiling. Five antique chairs from the eighteenth century have been placed around the Altar so as to form an Inverse Pentagram, the Star of Satan. Lipsius and Helen sit at the top two angles. The next two seats are currently unoccupied. I sit at the bottom angle and all of us are wearing robes of soft black silk.

Yes, that is how it was when Lipsius rang a bell. This *cling* was followed by a *clang* as the basement door opened and two hooded men marched through escorting another hooded man whom they stood upon the soapbox, tying the noose around his neck. The executioners, or so they purported to be, also wore black silken robes and now removed their hoods to reveal themselves as Davies and Richmond, a fact that I had known all along.

The victim's wrists had been bound tightly behind his back with thongs of leather and were he to step off the soap-box he would strangle to death very slowly. He could not see through his hood but holes had been cut around the ears so that he could certainly hear.

I had to admire the ingenuity of Lipsius, and that of Davies, too, whose idea it had been to have our victim, Sir Percy Sulgrave, coshed by Richmond disguised as a policeman when the noble baronet, no less, endeavoured gallantly to defend Helen from the seemingly murderous assault of Septimus Keen. Until today, moreover, I had had no idea that Lipsius was in possession of a decaying property in Harlesden. I have only ever visited Harlesden once before in my life and that was to ascertain whether or not it is quite as evil as Arthur Machen alleges in his excellent tale 'The Inmost Light'. Here beautiful countryside, trees and meadows and streams, merge into red, raw villas and upon the streets of this apparently innocuous suburb there is a prevailing atmosphere of menace. I now saw my intuition amply justified by the actions here tonight of Lipsius.

As the figure before us twitched with apprehension, standing so unsteadily upon the undignified scaffold, Lipsius arose and we did so too.

'UNTU LA LA ULULA UMUNA TOFA LAMA LE LI NA AHR IMA TAHARA ELULA ETFOMA UNUNA ARPETI ULU ULU ULU MARABAN ULULU MAHATA ULU ULU LAMASTANA . . .' he intoned. 'That is the Lunar language, the language of the Moon, most appropriate since tonight is the night of the full Moon. But does anyone know what it means?'

'Yes,' said Helen in her high, clear voice. 'It means: "Ye hounds! Ho! Ho! Tally-ho! Scent the poison of the path.

Here! There! Bark! Sweep around! There goes the quarry down the glade of mossy rock. The foremost has caught him! Tally-ho! Tally-ho! The hunt is ended." Does that ring a bell, Sir Percy?' she said sweetly, then added a yelp of 'Yoicks!'

'The signature.' Lipsius glanced at Richmond, who strode forward purposefully with a document and a pen, which latter he thrust into the unwilling fingers of our captive. He then endeavoured to manipulate the prisoner's fingers so as to scrawl a signature upon the document.

'Resistance,' he muttered.

'A clean break,' said Lipsius.

There was a *snap!* and a scream as Richmond broke the little finger of Sir Percy's right hand.

'Bit silly of you, Sir Percy,' he said. 'I only wish you'd cooperate with us and then it will all be over soon enough. Of course, I could break all your fingers one by one, or kick away the scaffold and let you strangle for a bit but since we intend in the end to let you go free, there's not much point in your resisting us now, is there?' There was a low moan and then our victim managed to scrawl a signature on the document that, at a nod from Lipsius, Richmond passed over to me.

'Read out what Sir Percy has signed,' Lipsius ordered.

I read our captive *The Statement of Sir Percy Sulgrave* and *The Confession of Sir Percy Sulgrave*, both of which I had written.

'So you see, Sir Percy,' I admonished the sad figure on the makeshift scaffold, 'whilst you were thinking that *you* were following *me*, *I* was following *you*. How I enjoyed leading you into such a merry dance! It must have been quite a shock to be transported abruptly from a bench in Regent's Park to a condemned cell. Of course, I know that you did not write what I have read, but I can get inside

403

your head and, if you have been keeping a diary over the
past few days, my wager is that it is not so very different
from the one I have composed for you. Let us look at the
entries. Yes, on Monday I was in bed all day, which is why
you did not see me venture forth into the streets. Why was
I in bed all day? I am lazy. On Tuesday it was a joy to lead
you through a labyrinth of pubs in a quest that proved
to be utterly pointless. Naturally, when writing as you, I
threw in all sorts of details that I expected you to discover.
The climax was the scene in Regent's Park when I just *knew*
you would endeavour to rescue a damsel in distress.'

'You think that you are so clever, Sir Percy,' Davies
interposed, 'but you are not. Every man is a condemned
criminal, only he does not know the date of his execution.
You came in here thinking that you had been framed for
murder since the blood kindly donated by "Miss Ward"
was upon the knife she passed to you in the Park. We
had staged the condemned cell so well that doubtless you
thought that you were being led to a formal execution for a
crime you did not commit – as happens usually once a week
under Her Majesty's Government. As a matter of cold fact,
you are standing upon a soapbox with a rope around your
neck because you have blundered into the hands of Doctor
Lipsius, the man you have sought to destroy.'

'It is not enough for me,' Lipsius remarked sardonically,
'to destroy the body of a man. First I wish to destroy his
mind. I wish to wreck his every sense of reality.'

'You have now confessed, Sir Percy,' Helen came in, 'to
being Jack the Ripper. Many will believe that confession.'

'As a matter of fact,' Lipsius stared directly at me, 'I
have a confession to make, Septimus.' The body of Sir Percy
twitched at the mention of the name. 'I and my associates
had absolutely nothing whatsoever to do with the Jack the
Ripper murders, I am sorry to say. We only told you those

tales because we wanted to observe your reaction, to discern if you were fit to be one of us, which you obviously are and I forecast a bright future for you. The *real* Ripper, of course, was no more any of us than it was Septimus Keen, who framed himself, or Sir Percy Sulgrave standing here in this undignified fashion and whom we have framed. The real culprit committed suicide ages ago by flinging himself into the Thames, though some allege that he was thrown there. I refer to Montague Druitt.'

'No,' said Davies, 'it was Robert Stephenson.'

'No,' said Helen, 'it was J.K. Stephen.'

'No,' said Richmond, 'it was Sir William Gull.'

'One can make out a moderately convincing case for at least thirty-one more,' Lipsius returned genially, 'including the Duke of Clarence, who is proclaimed dead but may be alive. All this, Sir Percy, was good bait to lure you into my web. As you stand there on your soapbox, for you lack even the dignity of a decent scaffold, you cannot imagine, my dear sir, just how much I despise you. You think you are so rational and yet you have failed to comprehend just how multidimensional is that fiction that you have the temerity to call reality. You do not understand that everything in this Universe depends upon the position of the observer. Nothing is true. Everything is permitted. Within a century, the evil that I do will be called good by some. In fact . . .'

Here, the mocking monologue of Lipsius was abruptly cut short by a banging and a crashing that came from above. The doctor's visage registered momentary alarm, then he said, quietly and calmly:

'The proceedings of this evening are now terminated. Come with me.' As the sounds of banging and crashing increased in volume, I now understood why Lipsius had insisted earlier that we placed our clothes in bags within a chest in the corner of the Temple prior to changing into our robes. As we seized these, Lipsius ripped away a curtain to disclose a heavy steel door and ushered us through into a passageway. Moving surprisingly swiftly for so portly a man, he seized his own bag and quietly addressed his departing words to Sir Percy.

'As promised, I shall let you go free now.' He kicked away the soapbox.

The passage led to an adjacent house, back to back, that was also owned by Lipsius. We changed our clothes quickly and departed on our separate ways.

My experiences have convinced me that there are indeed demons in the midst of Mankind and that I am now one of them.

CHAPTER FIFTEEN

FROM THE LETTERS
OF AMELIA STANHOPE

D ear Barbara,

   Thank *heavens* we were keeping track of Sir Percy, though my heart nearly failed when one of my agents saw him being dragged away from Regent's Park by a uniformed police constable and I made, as you know, quite frantic enquiries.

Well, it has all been hushed up now and I am ever so frightfully grateful for your help. The fact that the police had no record of arresting Sir Percy is a significant fact in a case is quite exceptionally puzzling.

Percy was only saved in the nick of time. The police burst into an empty, decaying house in Harlesden and I still can't get over what they found when they burst into the basement: a Satanic temple with Percy hanging from a hook in the ceiling. *Ghastly*, isn't it? Some time in Guy's Hospital has cured him of his physical injuries, including severe rope burns around his neck, though his hair has turned quite white. The mental damage is rather more severe and he is presently recuperating at a private hospital in the country. I do not know for how long he may be there for, in common with the doctors, I find it very hard to make sense of his apparent ravings.

Did Doctor Lipsius and his associates *really* kidnap him for a Satanic sacrifice? It does sound highly unlikely, especially in view of the fact that the title deeds of this derelict house are in the name of Sir Percy Sulgrave. Yes, there is a secret passage from its basement into the house that backs upon it, but this residence is equally derelict and the title deeds are apparently (once more) in the name of Sir Percy Sulgrave.

There is also the matter of the typed confession, which Percy did definitely sign, stating that *he* was Jack the Ripper. I can barely bring myself to believe *that*, though I always found his obsession with the matter to be somewhat unhealthy and unwholesome, and one has to look askance at a man who is found hanging in the basement of a house he owns and that has been furnished as a Satanic temple, with a confession to being Jack the Ripper in front of him.

Fortunately he is under the care of the noted psychiatrist Dr Wildman, who is perturbed by the high dosage of a drug called *heroin* which Percy had apparently been taking.

Anyway, Babs, I shall keep you informed of all future developments.

I had dinner with Sir Richard Knight last night and he asked me to send you his very best regards. He has been abroad and tells me he feels much better for the fact. I am starting to take him seriously and am looking forward to dining with him again on Saturday.

I rather appreciate his cynical wit. Let us face it, my dear, we both of us live in an utterly immoral society and, since we are its beneficiaries, neither one of us has the slightest desire to improve it. All the best to Thomas.

Love and kisses,

Amelia